TRANSFERENCE

10.23.08.12.98

14.36.11.06.98

BLACK MASK

TRANSFERENCE

Created by **MICHAEL MORECI** and **RON SALAS**

Written by **MICHAEL MORECI**

Issues #1-3, Art by **RON SALAS**

Issue #4, Art by **TONI FEJZULA**

Issue #5, Art by **CHRIS PETERSON**

Issues #1-4, Colors by **TAMRA BONVILLAIN**

Issue #5, Colors by **MARISSA LOUISE**

Lettered by **JIM CAMPBELL**

Covers by **RON SALAS**

Produced by **MATT PIZZOLO**

Book Design, Production and Layout **PHIL SMITH**

BLACK MASK

Published By Black Mask Studios LLC

TRANSFERENCE trade paperback volume 1. First Printing. February 2020. Copyright © 2020 Michael Moreci and Ron Salas.
All rights reserved. Published by Black Mask Studios, LLC. Office of publication: 2798 Sunset Boulevard LA CA 90026.
Originally published in single issue form as TRANSFERENCE #1-5 by Black Mask Studios. No part of this publication may
be reproduced or transmitted, in any form or by any means (except for short excerpts for journalistic or review purposes)
without the express written permission of Michael Moreci, Ron Salas or Black Mask Studios, LLC. All names, characters,
events, and locales in this publication are entirely fictional. Any resemblances to actual persons (living or dead), events,
or places, without satiric intent, is coincidental. Printed in Korea.

For licensing information, contact: licensing@blackmaskstudios.com

TABLE OF CONTENTS

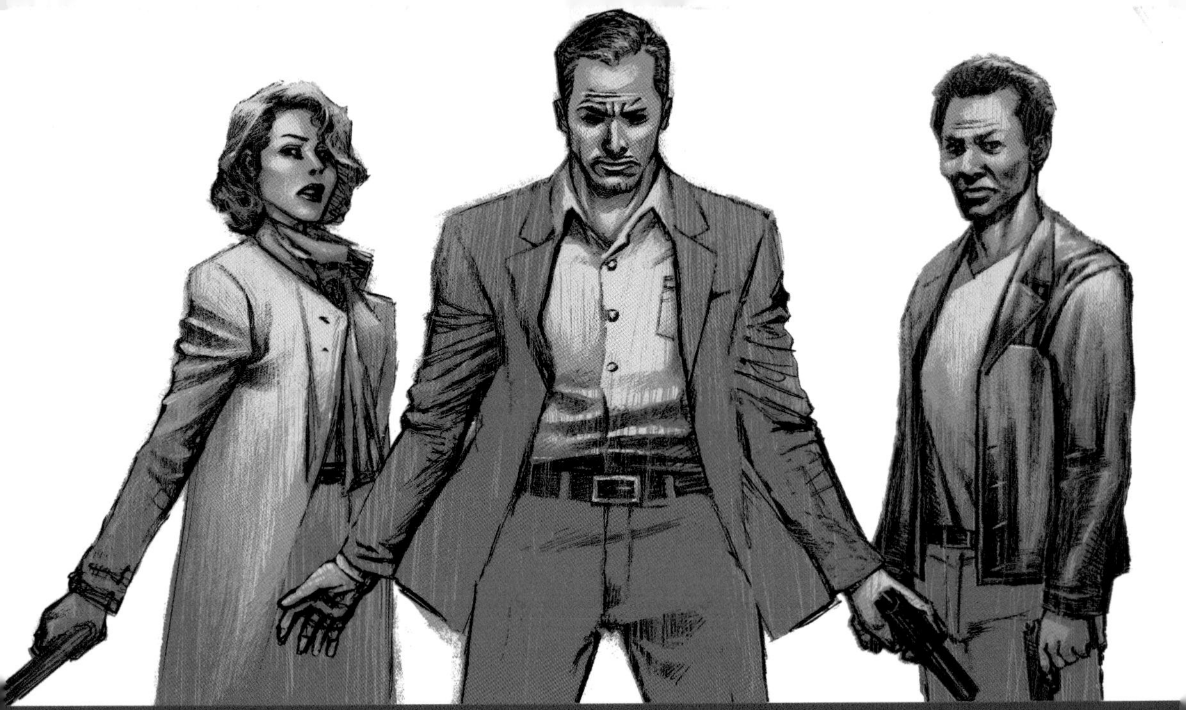

ISSUE 1

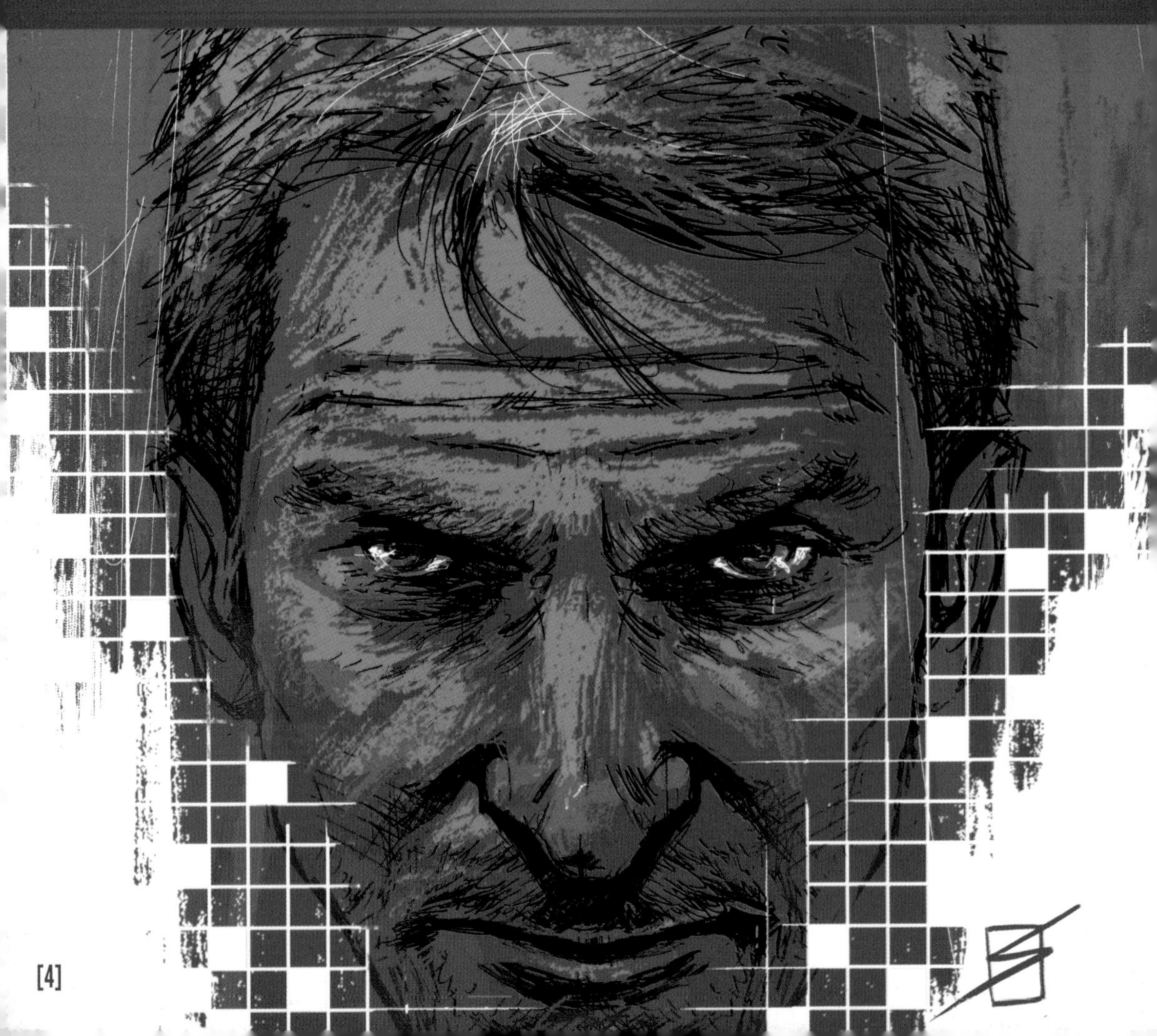

OUTSIDE PARIS.
Eight months ago.

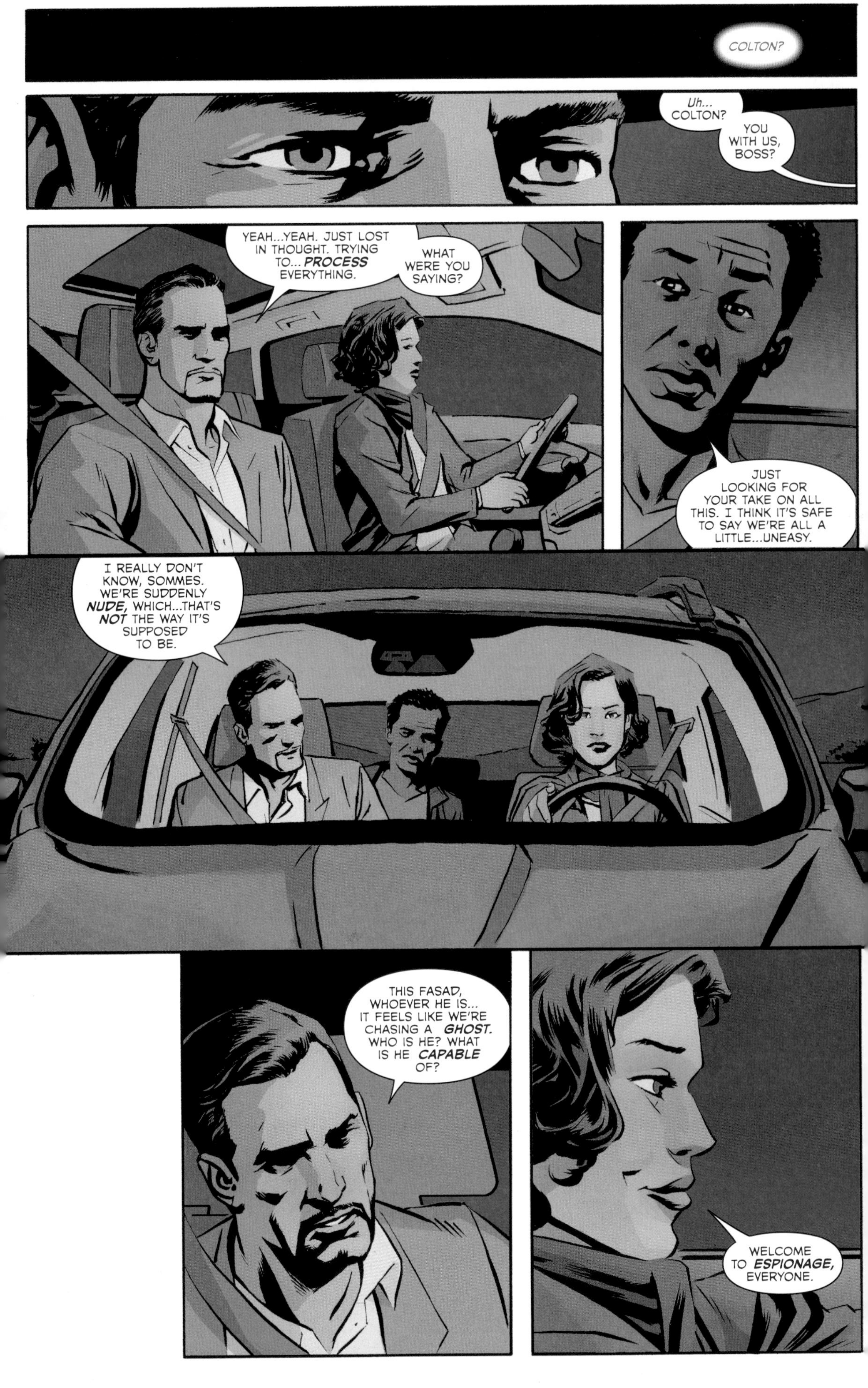
COLTON?
Uh... COLTON?
YOU WITH US, BOSS?
YEAH...YEAH. JUST LOST IN THOUGHT. TRYING TO... PROCESS EVERYTHING.
WHAT WERE YOU SAYING?
JUST LOOKING FOR YOUR TAKE ON ALL THIS. I THINK IT'S SAFE TO SAY WE'RE ALL A LITTLE...UNEASY.
I REALLY DON'T KNOW, SOMMES. WE'RE SUDDENLY NUDE, WHICH...THAT'S NOT THE WAY IT'S SUPPOSED TO BE.
THIS FASAD, WHOEVER HE IS... IT FEELS LIKE WE'RE CHASING A GHOST. WHO IS HE? WHAT IS HE CAPABLE OF?
WELCOME TO ESPIONAGE, EVERYONE.

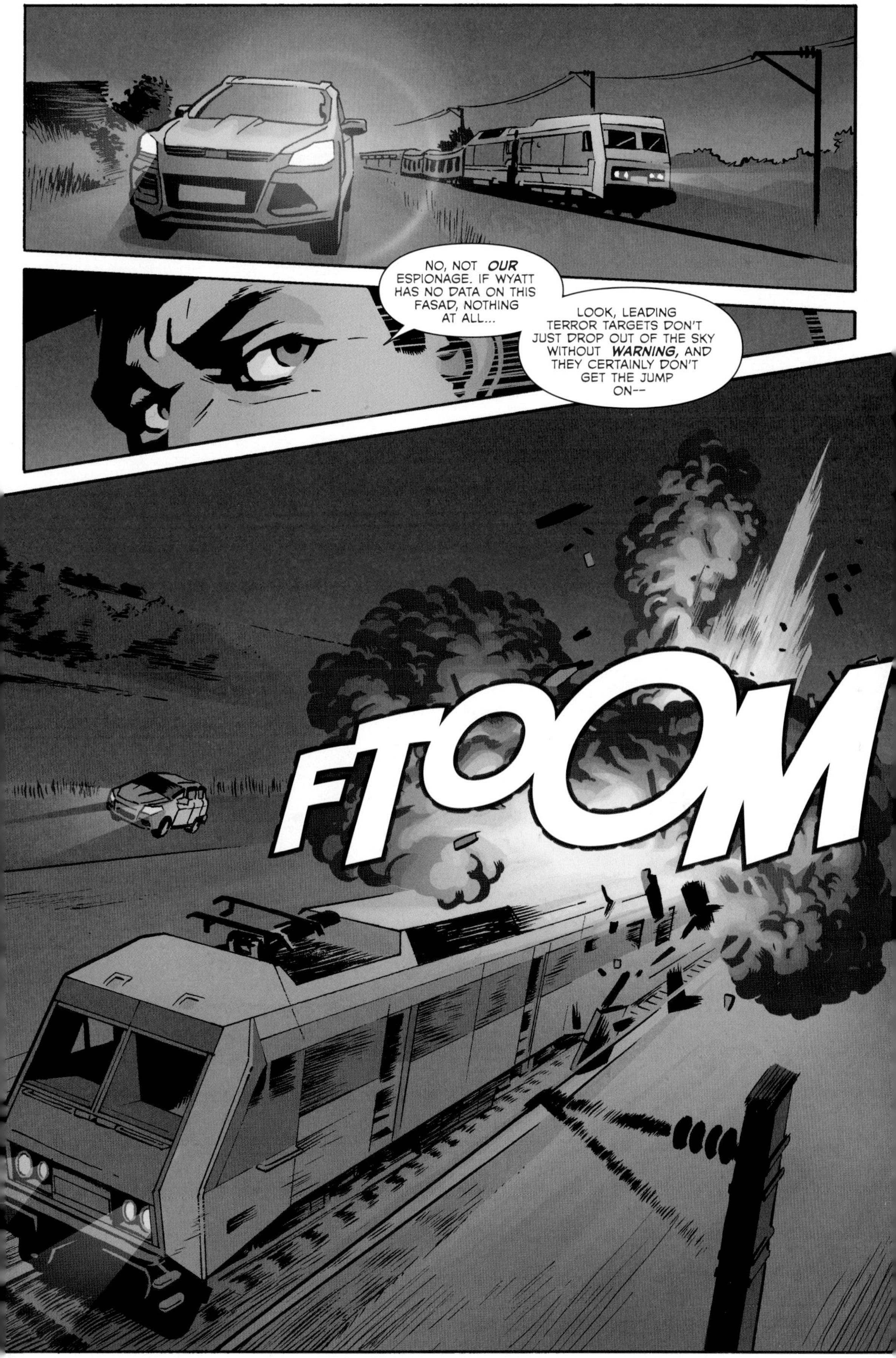
NO, NOT *OUR* ESPIONAGE. IF WYATT HAS NO DATA ON THIS FASAD, NOTHING AT ALL...
LOOK, LEADING TERROR TARGETS DON'T JUST DROP OUT OF THE SKY WITHOUT *WARNING,* AND THEY CERTAINLY DON'T GET THE JUMP ON--
FTOOM

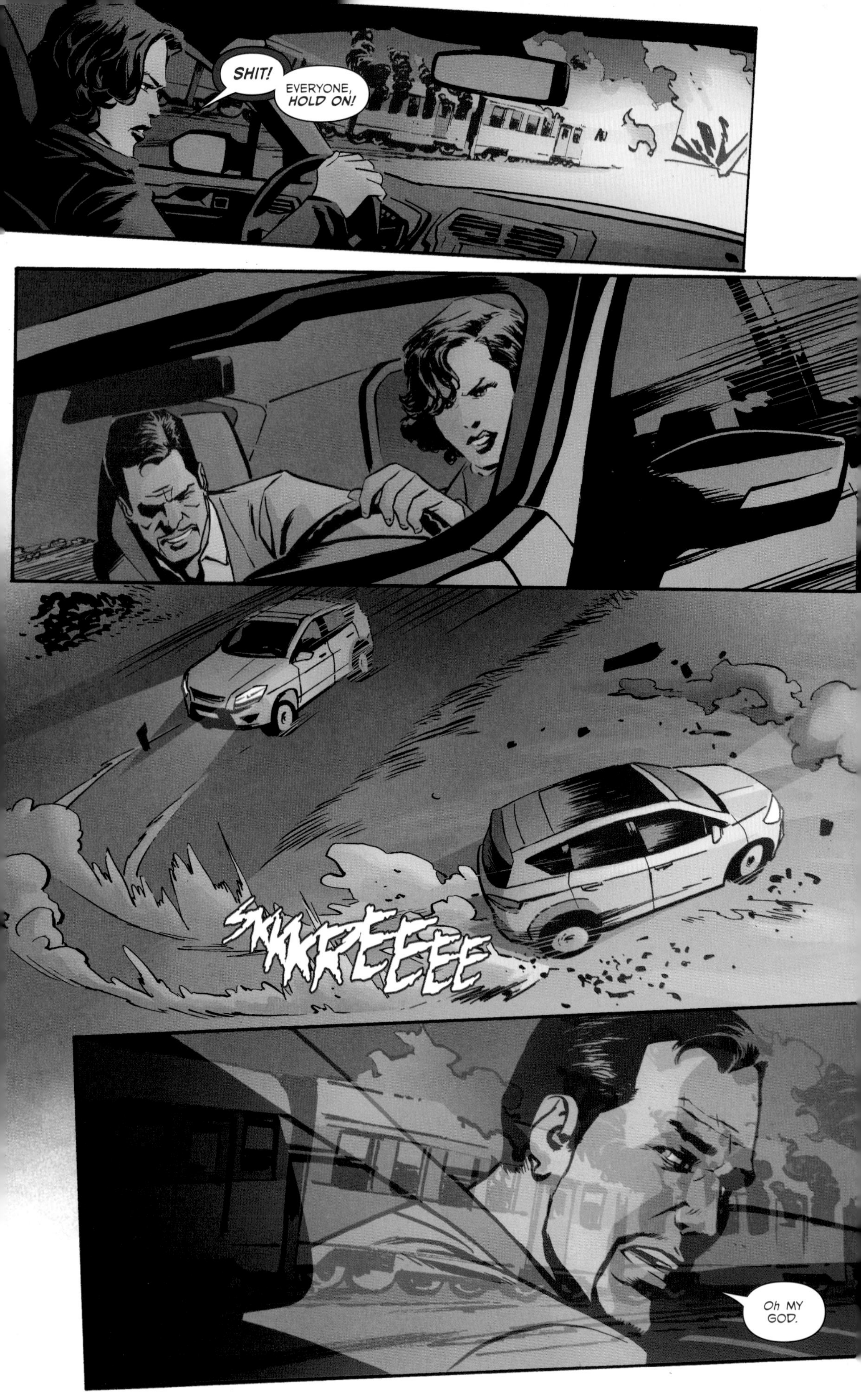
SHIT!
EVERYONE, HOLD ON!
SKKKREEEEE
Oh MY GOD.

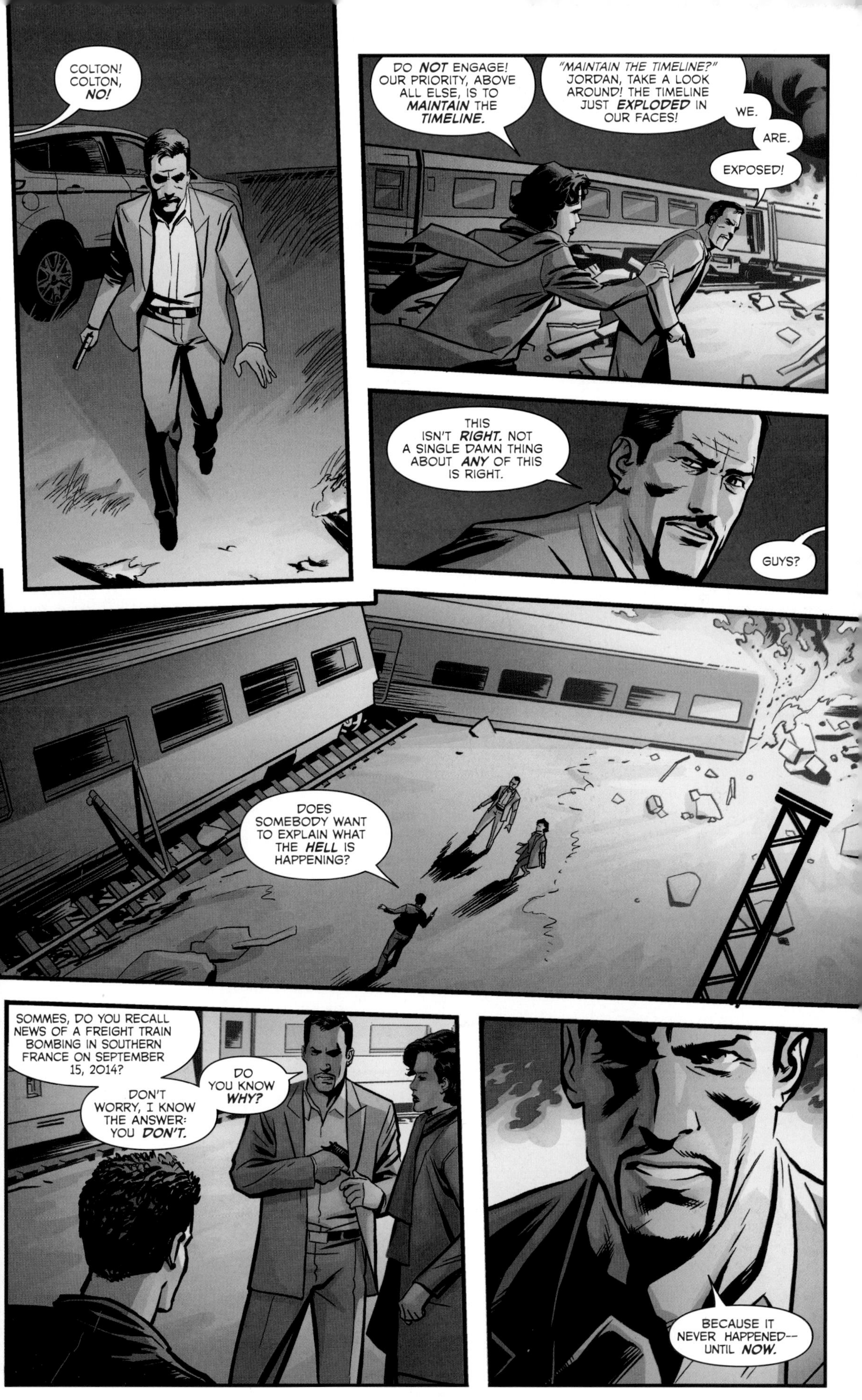
COLTON! COLTON, NO!
DO NOT ENGAGE! OUR PRIORITY, ABOVE ALL ELSE, IS TO MAINTAIN THE TIMELINE.
"MAINTAIN THE TIMELINE?" JORDAN, TAKE A LOOK AROUND! THE TIMELINE JUST EXPLODED IN OUR FACES!
WE.
ARE.
EXPOSED!
THIS ISN'T RIGHT. NOT A SINGLE DAMN THING ABOUT ANY OF THIS IS RIGHT.
GUYS?
DOES SOMEBODY WANT TO EXPLAIN WHAT THE HELL IS HAPPENING?
SOMMES, DO YOU RECALL NEWS OF A FREIGHT TRAIN BOMBING IN SOUTHERN FRANCE ON SEPTEMBER 15, 2014?
DON'T WORRY, I KNOW THE ANSWER: YOU DON'T.
DO YOU KNOW WHY?
BECAUSE IT NEVER HAPPENED-- UNTIL NOW.

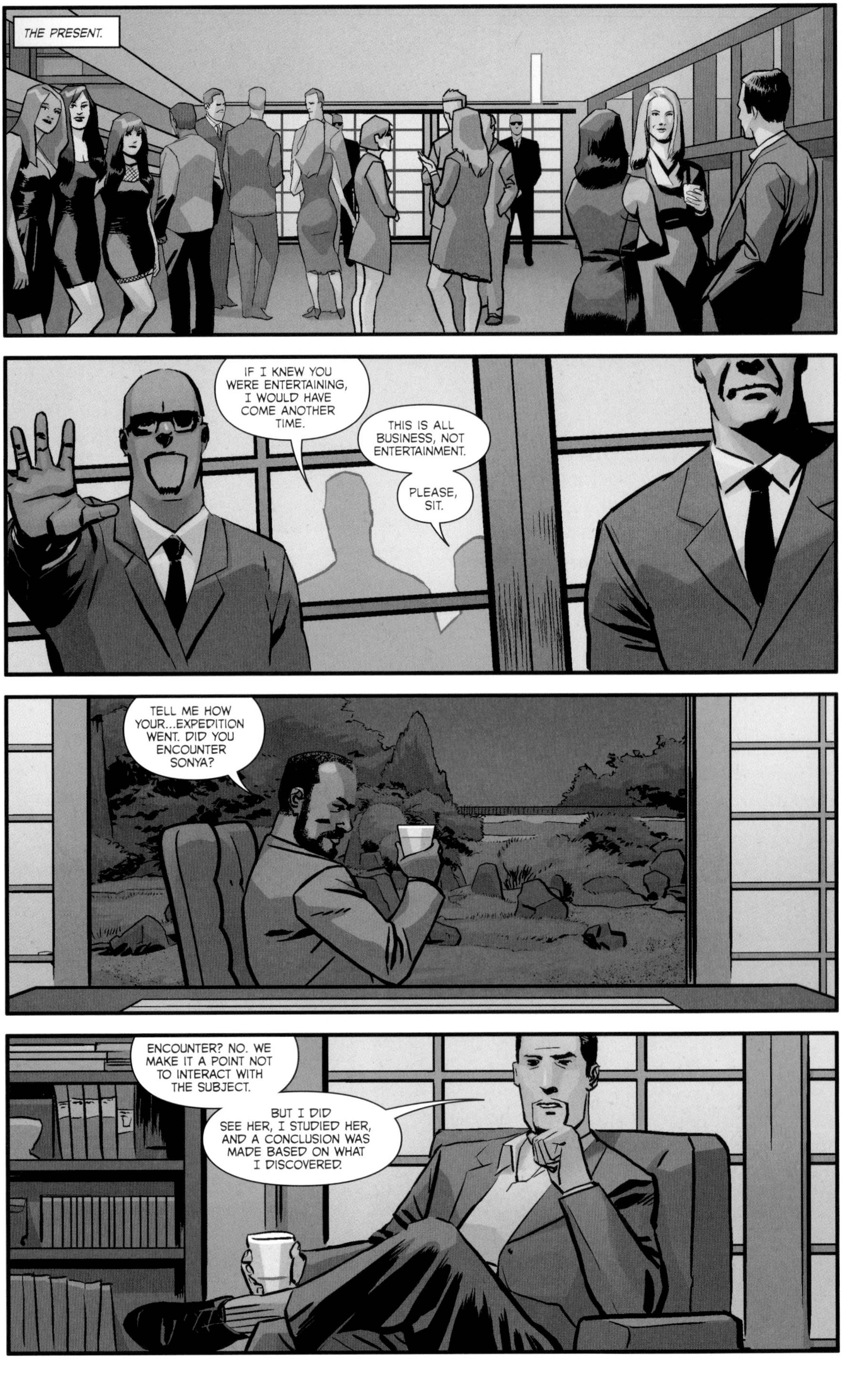
THE PRESENT.
IF I KNEW YOU WERE ENTERTAINING, I WOULD HAVE COME ANOTHER TIME.
THIS IS ALL BUSINESS, NOT ENTERTAINMENT.
PLEASE, SIT.
TELL ME HOW YOUR...EXPEDITION WENT. DID YOU ENCOUNTER SONYA?
ENCOUNTER? NO. WE MAKE IT A POINT NOT TO INTERACT WITH THE SUBJECT.
BUT I DID SEE HER, I STUDIED HER, AND A CONCLUSION WAS MADE BASED ON WHAT I DISCOVERED.

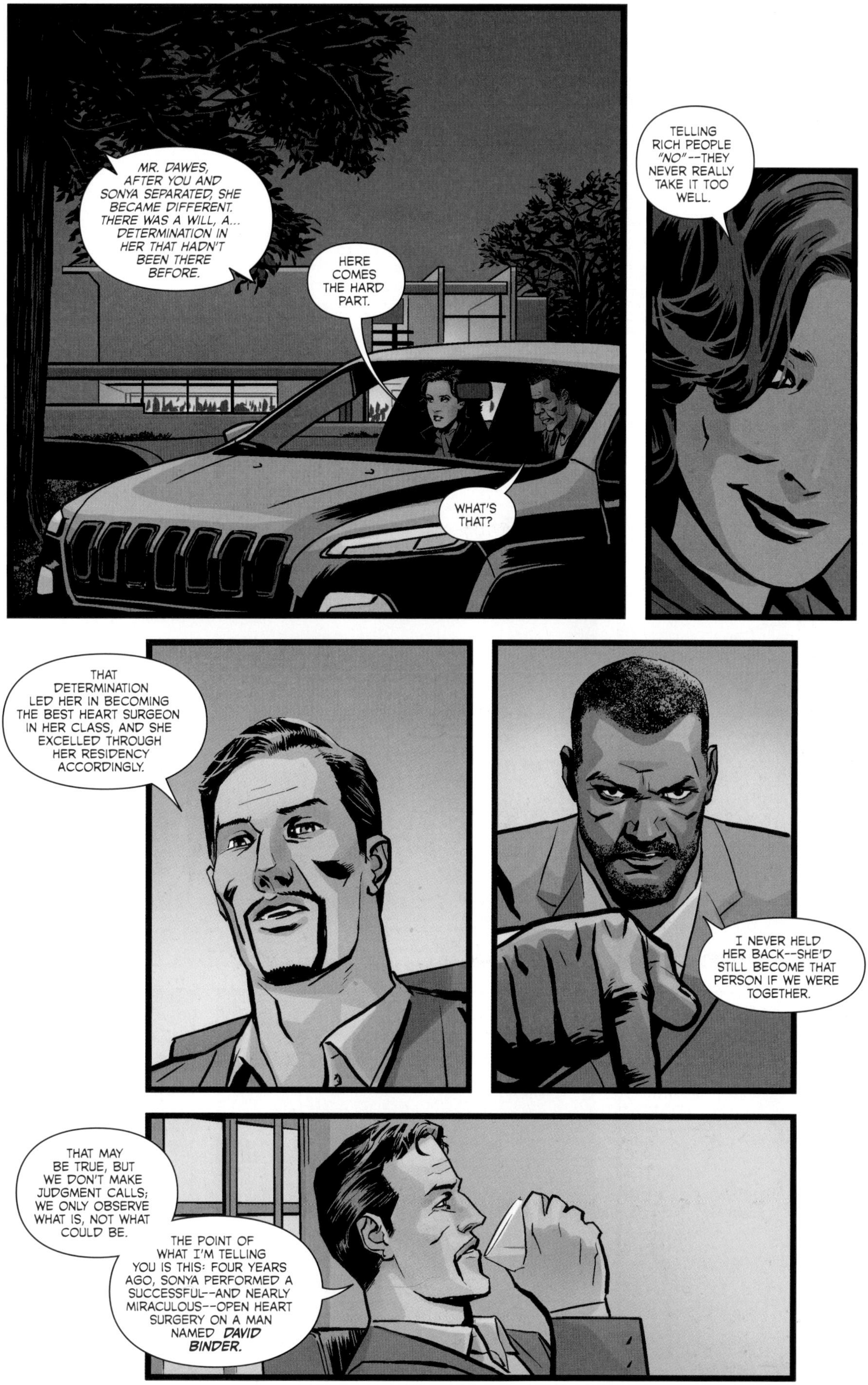
MR. DAWES, AFTER YOU AND SONYA SEPARATED, SHE BECAME DIFFERENT. THERE WAS A WILL, A... DETERMINATION IN HER THAT HADN'T BEEN THERE BEFORE.
HERE COMES THE HARD PART.
WHAT'S THAT?
TELLING RICH PEOPLE *"NO"*--THEY NEVER REALLY TAKE IT TOO WELL.
THAT DETERMINATION LED HER IN BECOMING THE BEST HEART SURGEON IN HER CLASS, AND SHE EXCELLED THROUGH HER RESIDENCY ACCORDINGLY.
I NEVER HELD HER BACK--SHE'D STILL BECOME THAT PERSON IF WE WERE TOGETHER.
THAT MAY BE TRUE, BUT WE DON'T MAKE JUDGMENT CALLS; WE ONLY OBSERVE WHAT IS, NOT WHAT COULD BE.
THE POINT OF WHAT I'M TELLING YOU IS THIS: FOUR YEARS AGO, SONYA PERFORMED A SUCCESSFUL--AND NEARLY MIRACULOUS--OPEN HEART SURGERY ON A MAN NAMED ***DAVID BINDER.***

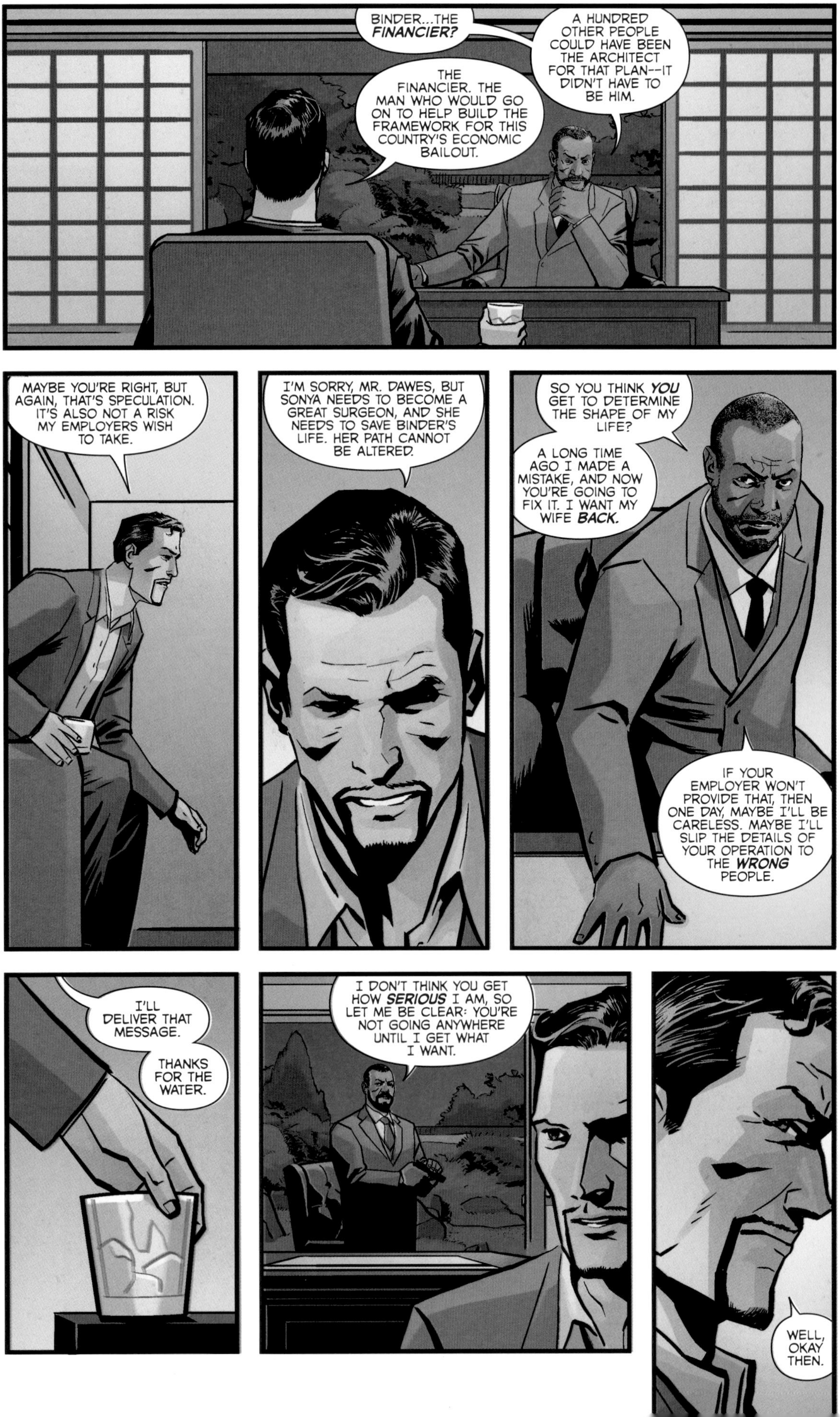

BINDER...THE *FINANCIER?*
THE FINANCIER. THE MAN WHO WOULD GO ON TO HELP BUILD THE FRAMEWORK FOR THIS COUNTRY'S ECONOMIC BAILOUT.
A HUNDRED OTHER PEOPLE COULD HAVE BEEN THE ARCHITECT FOR THAT PLAN--IT DIDN'T HAVE TO BE HIM.
MAYBE YOU'RE RIGHT, BUT AGAIN, THAT'S SPECULATION. IT'S ALSO NOT A RISK MY EMPLOYERS WISH TO TAKE.
I'M SORRY, MR. DAWES, BUT SONYA NEEDS TO BECOME A GREAT SURGEON, AND SHE NEEDS TO SAVE BINDER'S LIFE. HER PATH CANNOT BE ALTERED.
SO YOU THINK *YOU* GET TO DETERMINE THE SHAPE OF MY LIFE?
A LONG TIME AGO I MADE A MISTAKE, AND NOW YOU'RE GOING TO FIX IT. I WANT MY WIFE *BACK.*
IF YOUR EMPLOYER WON'T PROVIDE THAT, THEN ONE DAY, MAYBE I'LL BE CARELESS. MAYBE I'LL SLIP THE DETAILS OF YOUR OPERATION TO THE *WRONG* PEOPLE.
I'LL DELIVER THAT MESSAGE.
THANKS FOR THE WATER.
I DON'T THINK YOU GET HOW *SERIOUS* I AM, SO LET ME BE CLEAR: YOU'RE NOT GOING ANYWHERE UNTIL I GET WHAT I WANT.
WELL, OKAY THEN.

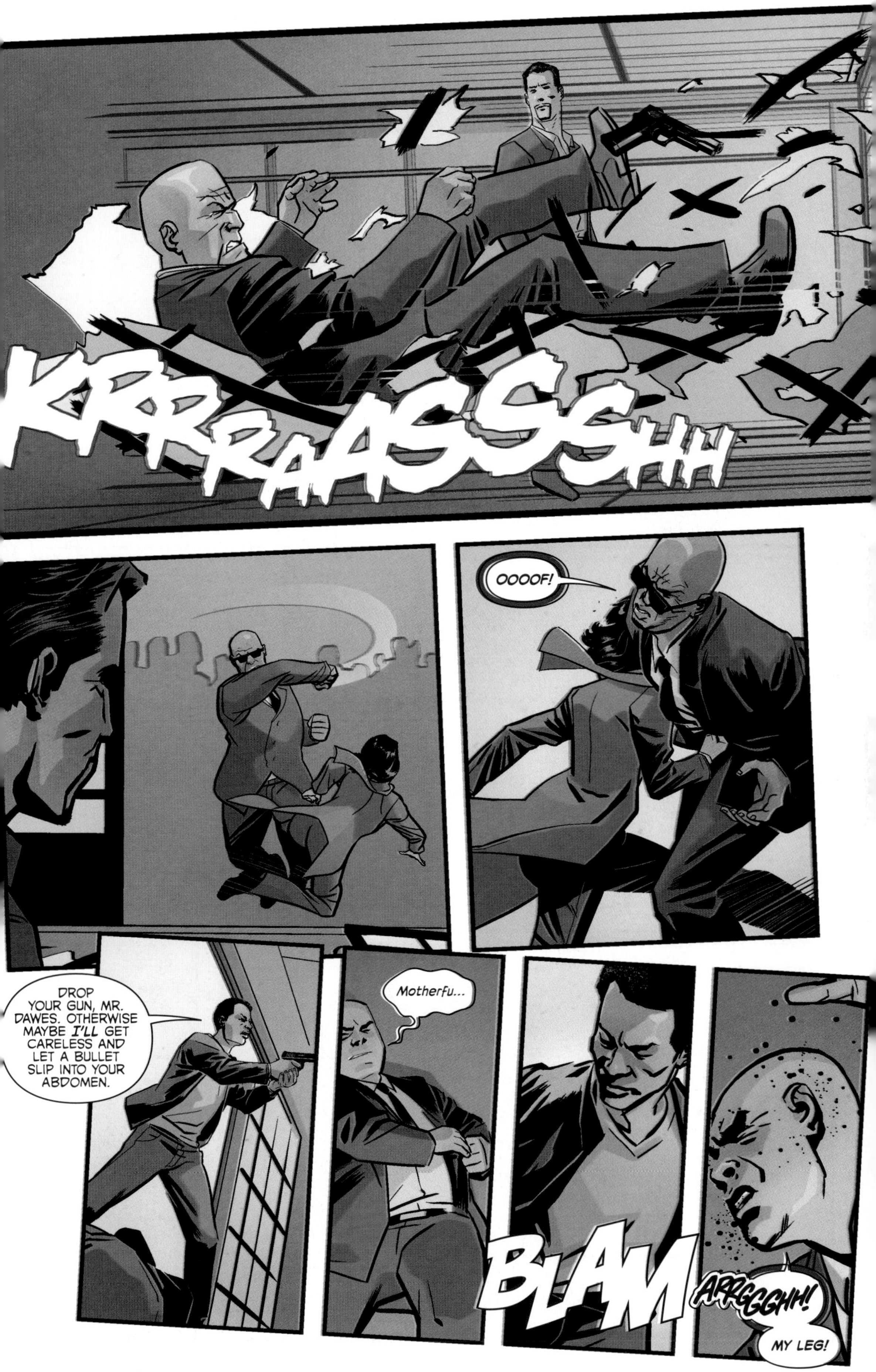
KRRRAASSSHH
OOOOF!
DROP YOUR GUN, MR. DAWES. OTHERWISE MAYBE I'LL GET CARELESS AND LET A BULLET SLIP INTO YOUR ABDOMEN.
Motherfu...
BLAM
ARRGGGHH!
MY LEG!

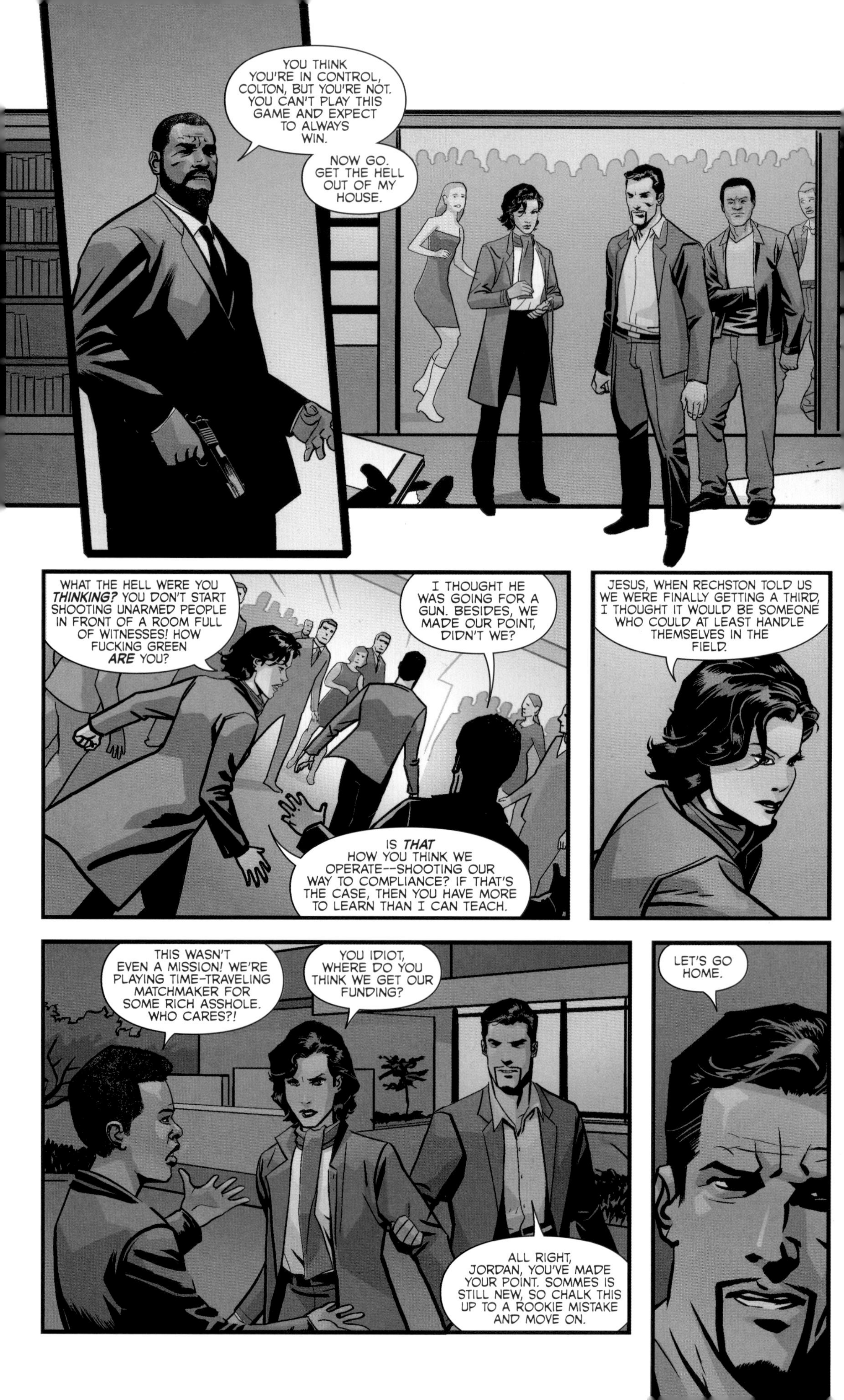
YOU THINK YOU'RE IN CONTROL, COLTON, BUT YOU'RE NOT. YOU CAN'T PLAY THIS GAME AND EXPECT TO ALWAYS WIN.
NOW GO. GET THE HELL OUT OF MY HOUSE.
WHAT THE HELL WERE YOU THINKING? YOU DON'T START SHOOTING UNARMED PEOPLE IN FRONT OF A ROOM FULL OF WITNESSES! HOW FUCKING GREEN ARE YOU?
I THOUGHT HE WAS GOING FOR A GUN. BESIDES, WE MADE OUR POINT, DIDN'T WE?
IS THAT HOW YOU THINK WE OPERATE--SHOOTING OUR WAY TO COMPLIANCE? IF THAT'S THE CASE, THEN YOU HAVE MORE TO LEARN THAN I CAN TEACH.
JESUS, WHEN RECHSTON TOLD US WE WERE FINALLY GETTING A THIRD, I THOUGHT IT WOULD BE SOMEONE WHO COULD AT LEAST HANDLE THEMSELVES IN THE FIELD.
THIS WASN'T EVEN A MISSION! WE'RE PLAYING TIME-TRAVELING MATCHMAKER FOR SOME RICH ASSHOLE. WHO CARES?!
YOU IDIOT, WHERE DO YOU THINK WE GET OUR FUNDING?
ALL RIGHT, JORDAN, YOU'VE MADE YOUR POINT. SOMMES IS STILL NEW, SO CHALK THIS UP TO A ROOKIE MISTAKE AND MOVE ON.
LET'S GO HOME.

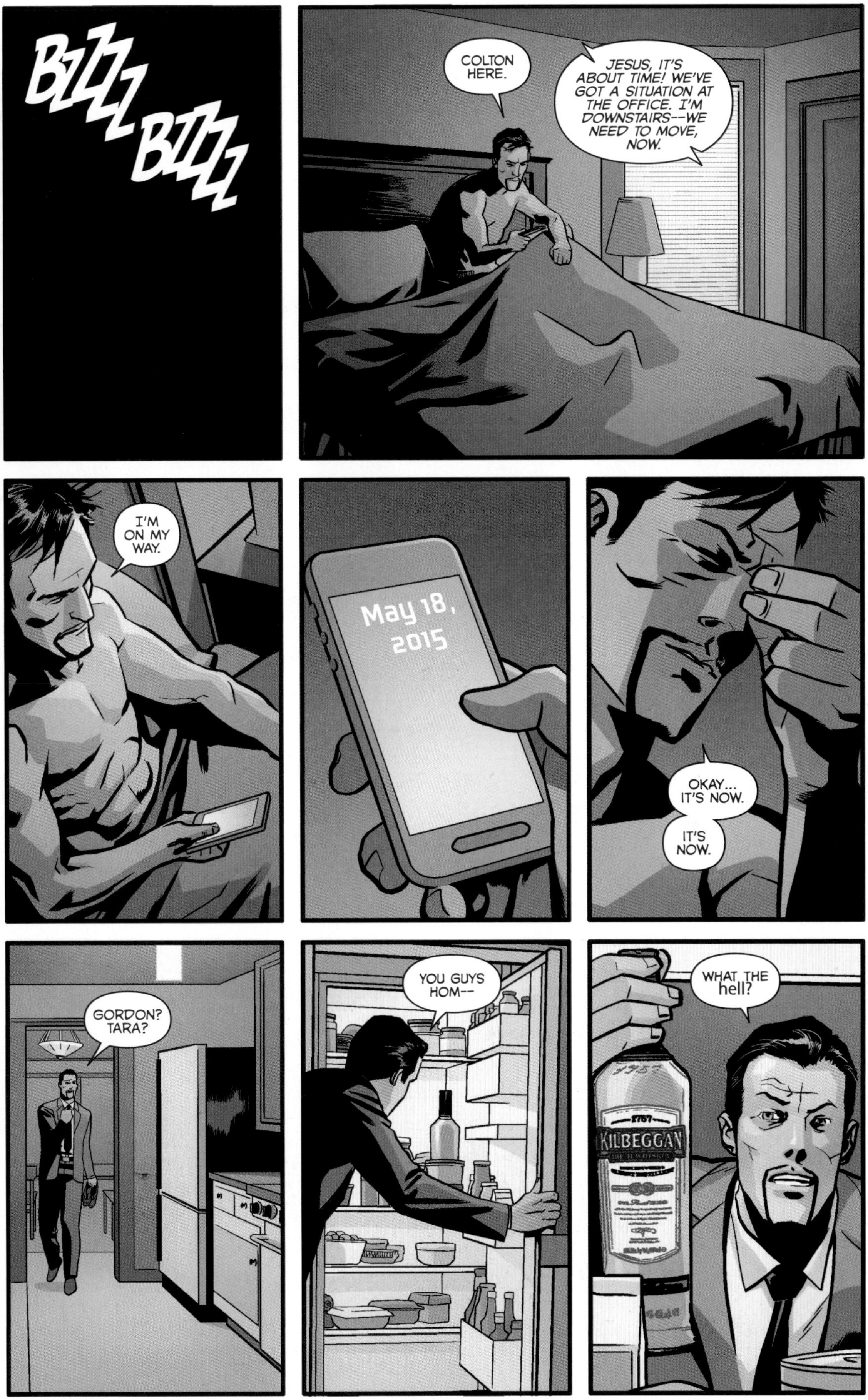
BZZZZ BZZZZ
COLTON HERE.
JESUS, IT'S ABOUT TIME! WE'VE GOT A SITUATION AT THE OFFICE. I'M DOWNSTAIRS--WE NEED TO MOVE, NOW.
I'M ON MY WAY.
May 18, 2015
OKAY... IT'S NOW.
IT'S NOW.
GORDON? TARA?
YOU GUYS HOM--
WHAT THE hell?
KILBEGGAN

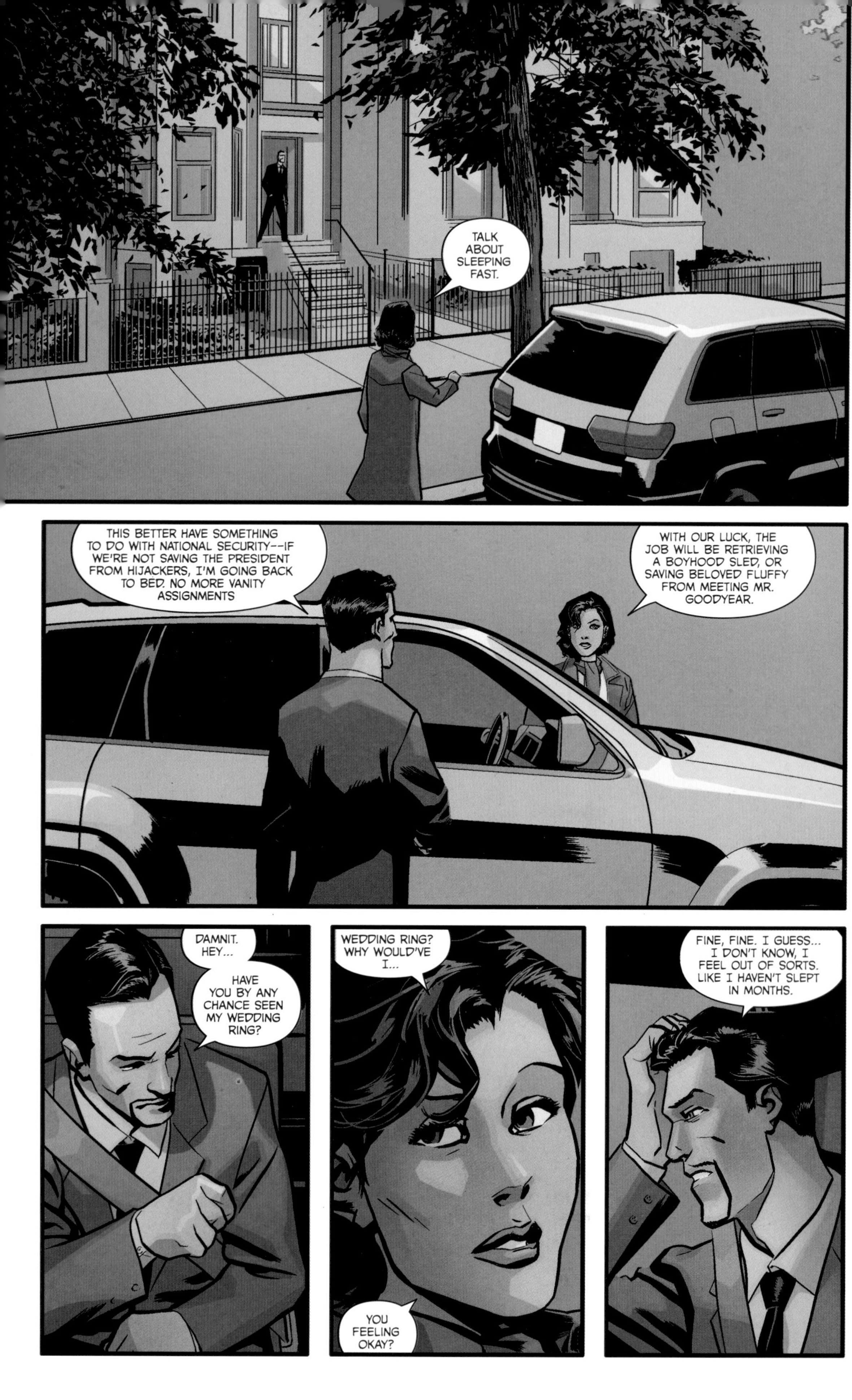
TALK ABOUT SLEEPING FAST.
THIS BETTER HAVE SOMETHING TO DO WITH NATIONAL SECURITY--IF WE'RE NOT SAVING THE PRESIDENT FROM HIJACKERS, I'M GOING BACK TO BED. NO MORE VANITY ASSIGNMENTS
WITH OUR LUCK, THE JOB WILL BE RETRIEVING A BOYHOOD SLED, OR SAVING BELOVED FLUFFY FROM MEETING MR. GOODYEAR.
DAMNIT. HEY...
HAVE YOU BY ANY CHANCE SEEN MY WEDDING RING?
WEDDING RING? WHY WOULD'VE I...
YOU FEELING OKAY?
FINE, FINE. I GUESS... I DON'T KNOW, I FEEL OUT OF SORTS. LIKE I HAVEN'T SLEPT IN MONTHS.

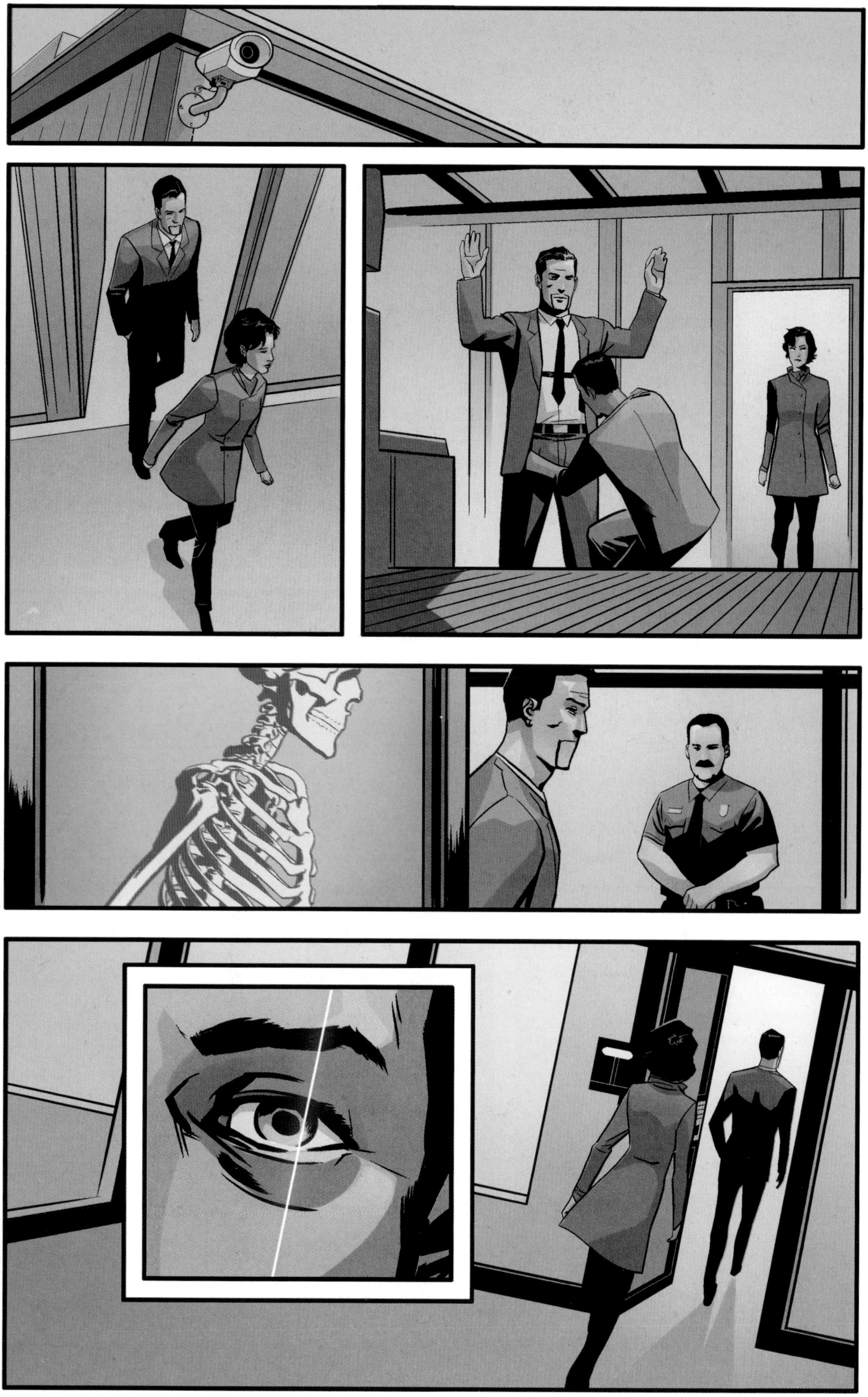

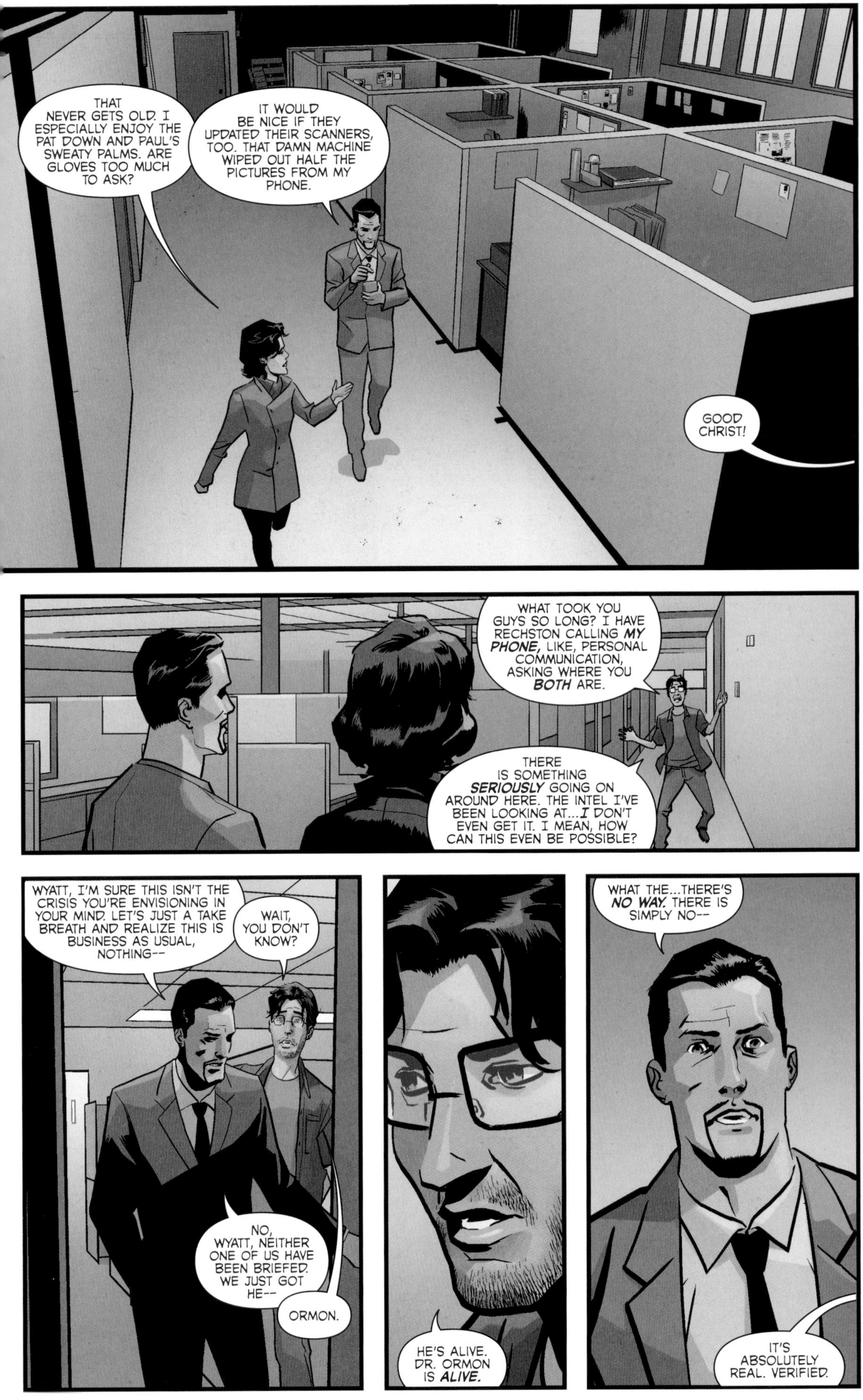
THAT NEVER GETS OLD. I ESPECIALLY ENJOY THE PAT DOWN AND PAUL'S SWEATY PALMS. ARE GLOVES TOO MUCH TO ASK?
IT WOULD BE NICE IF THEY UPDATED THEIR SCANNERS, TOO. THAT DAMN MACHINE WIPED OUT HALF THE PICTURES FROM MY PHONE.
GOOD CHRIST!
WHAT TOOK YOU GUYS SO LONG? I HAVE RECHSTON CALLING *MY PHONE,* LIKE, PERSONAL COMMUNICATION, ASKING WHERE YOU *BOTH* ARE.
THERE IS SOMETHING *SERIOUSLY* GOING ON AROUND HERE. THE INTEL I'VE BEEN LOOKING AT...*I* DON'T EVEN GET IT. I MEAN, HOW CAN THIS EVEN BE POSSIBLE?
WYATT, I'M SURE THIS ISN'T THE CRISIS YOU'RE ENVISIONING IN YOUR MIND. LET'S JUST A TAKE BREATH AND REALIZE THIS IS BUSINESS AS USUAL, NOTHING--
WAIT, YOU DON'T KNOW?
NO, WYATT, NEITHER ONE OF US HAVE BEEN BRIEFED. WE JUST GOT HE--
ORMON.
HE'S ALIVE. DR. ORMON IS *ALIVE.*
WHAT THE...THERE'S *NO WAY.* THERE IS SIMPLY NO--
IT'S ABSOLUTELY REAL. VERIFIED.

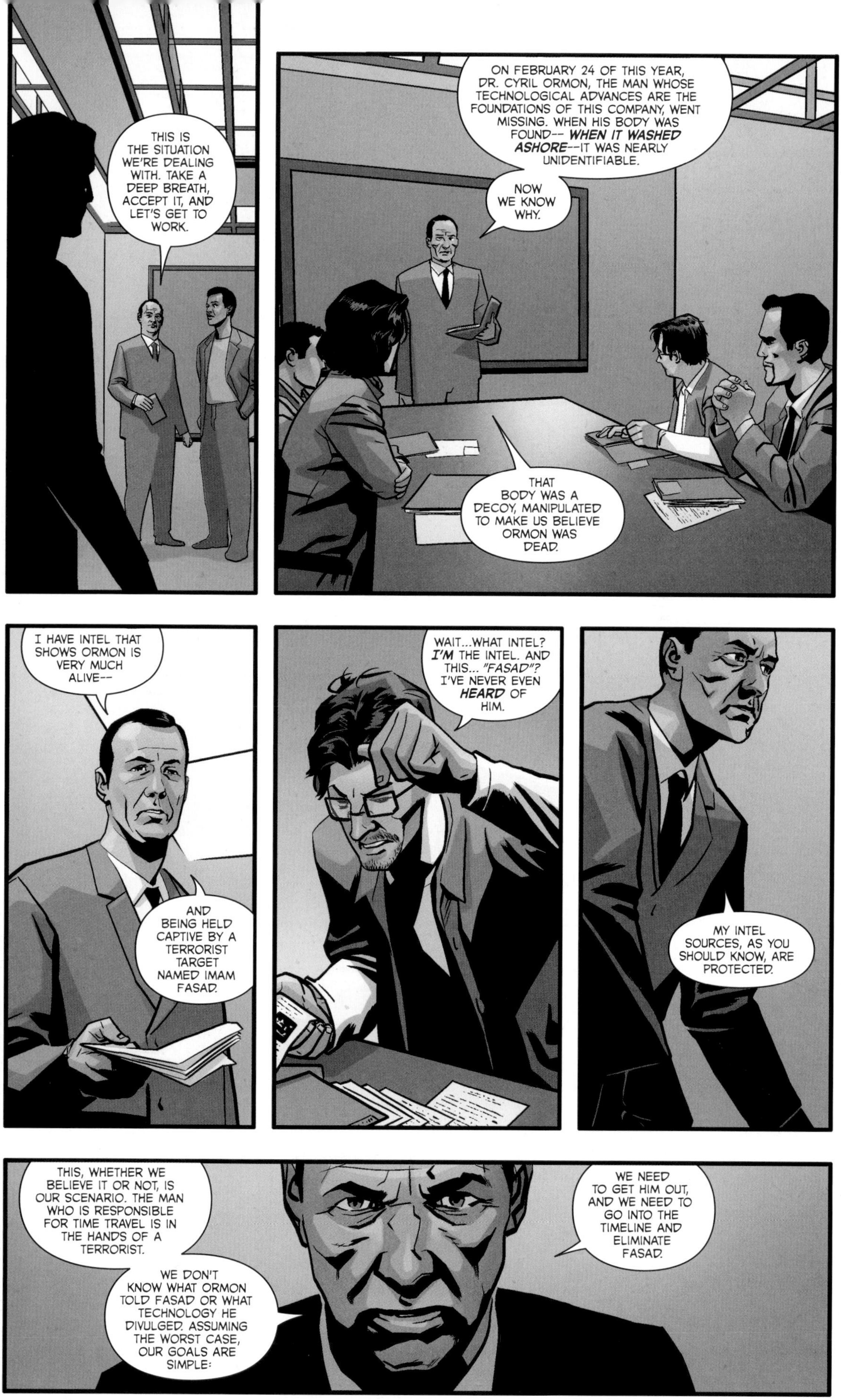
THIS IS THE SITUATION WE'RE DEALING WITH. TAKE A DEEP BREATH, ACCEPT IT, AND LET'S GET TO WORK.
ON FEBRUARY 24 OF THIS YEAR, DR. CYRIL ORMON, THE MAN WHOSE TECHNOLOGICAL ADVANCES ARE THE FOUNDATIONS OF THIS COMPANY, WENT MISSING. WHEN HIS BODY WAS FOUND-- WHEN IT WASHED ASHORE--IT WAS NEARLY UNIDENTIFIABLE.
NOW WE KNOW WHY.
THAT BODY WAS A DECOY, MANIPULATED TO MAKE US BELIEVE ORMON WAS DEAD.
I HAVE INTEL THAT SHOWS ORMON IS VERY MUCH ALIVE--
AND BEING HELD CAPTIVE BY A TERRORIST TARGET NAMED IMAM FASAD.
WAIT...WHAT INTEL? I'M THE INTEL. AND THIS... "FASAD"? I'VE NEVER EVEN HEARD OF HIM.
MY INTEL SOURCES, AS YOU SHOULD KNOW, ARE PROTECTED.
THIS, WHETHER WE BELIEVE IT OR NOT, IS OUR SCENARIO. THE MAN WHO IS RESPONSIBLE FOR TIME TRAVEL IS IN THE HANDS OF A TERRORIST.
WE DON'T KNOW WHAT ORMON TOLD FASAD OR WHAT TECHNOLOGY HE DIVULGED. ASSUMING THE WORST CASE, OUR GOALS ARE SIMPLE:
WE NEED TO GET HIM OUT, AND WE NEED TO GO INTO THE TIMELINE AND ELIMINATE FASAD.

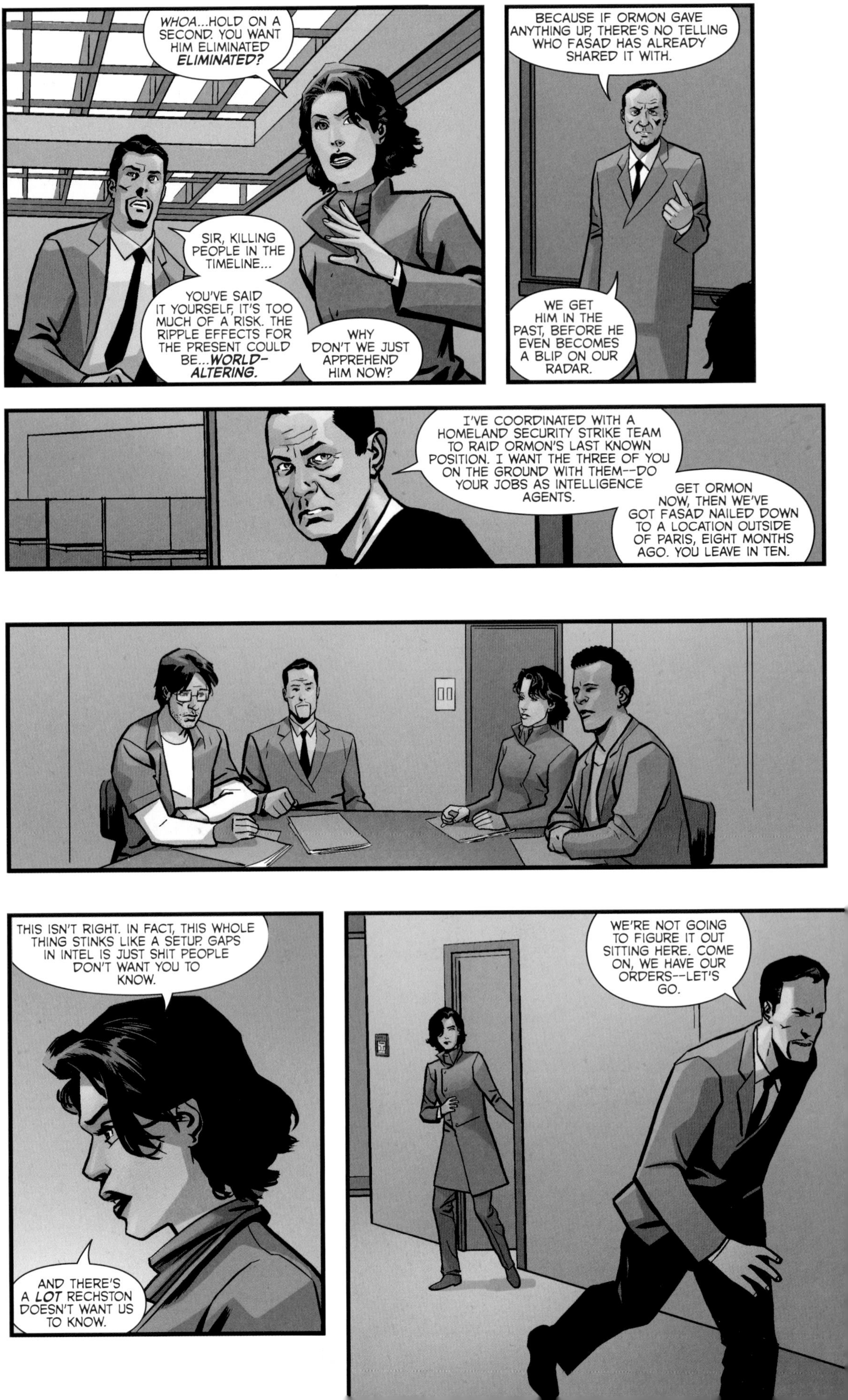
WHOA...HOLD ON A SECOND. YOU WANT HIM ELIMINATED ELIMINATED?
SIR, KILLING PEOPLE IN THE TIMELINE...
YOU'VE SAID IT YOURSELF, IT'S TOO MUCH OF A RISK. THE RIPPLE EFFECTS FOR THE PRESENT COULD BE...WORLD-ALTERING.
WHY DON'T WE JUST APPREHEND HIM NOW?
BECAUSE IF ORMON GAVE ANYTHING UP, THERE'S NO TELLING WHO FASAD HAS ALREADY SHARED IT WITH.
WE GET HIM IN THE PAST, BEFORE HE EVEN BECOMES A BLIP ON OUR RADAR.
I'VE COORDINATED WITH A HOMELAND SECURITY STRIKE TEAM TO RAID ORMON'S LAST KNOWN POSITION. I WANT THE THREE OF YOU ON THE GROUND WITH THEM--DO YOUR JOBS AS INTELLIGENCE AGENTS.
GET ORMON NOW, THEN WE'VE GOT FASAD NAILED DOWN TO A LOCATION OUTSIDE OF PARIS, EIGHT MONTHS AGO. YOU LEAVE IN TEN.
THIS ISN'T RIGHT. IN FACT, THIS WHOLE THING STINKS LIKE A SETUP. GAPS IN INTEL IS JUST SHIT PEOPLE DON'T WANT YOU TO KNOW.
AND THERE'S A LOT RECHSTON DOESN'T WANT US TO KNOW.
WE'RE NOT GOING TO FIGURE IT OUT SITTING HERE. COME ON, WE HAVE OUR ORDERS--LET'S GO.

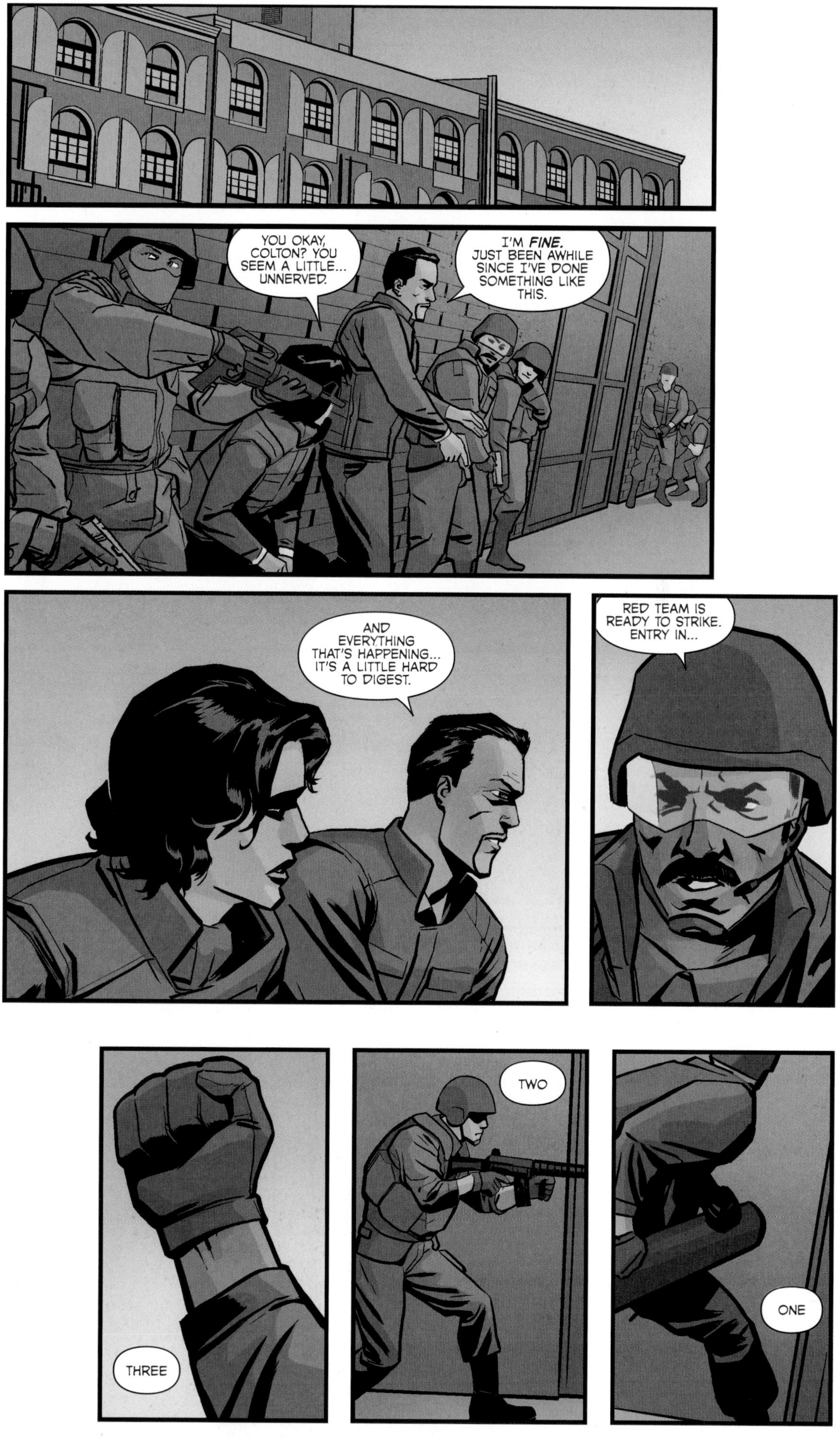
YOU OKAY, COLTON? YOU SEEM A LITTLE... UNNERVED.
I'M FINE. JUST BEEN AWHILE SINCE I'VE DONE SOMETHING LIKE THIS.
AND EVERYTHING THAT'S HAPPENING... IT'S A LITTLE HARD TO DIGEST.
RED TEAM IS READY TO STRIKE. ENTRY IN...
THREE
TWO
ONE

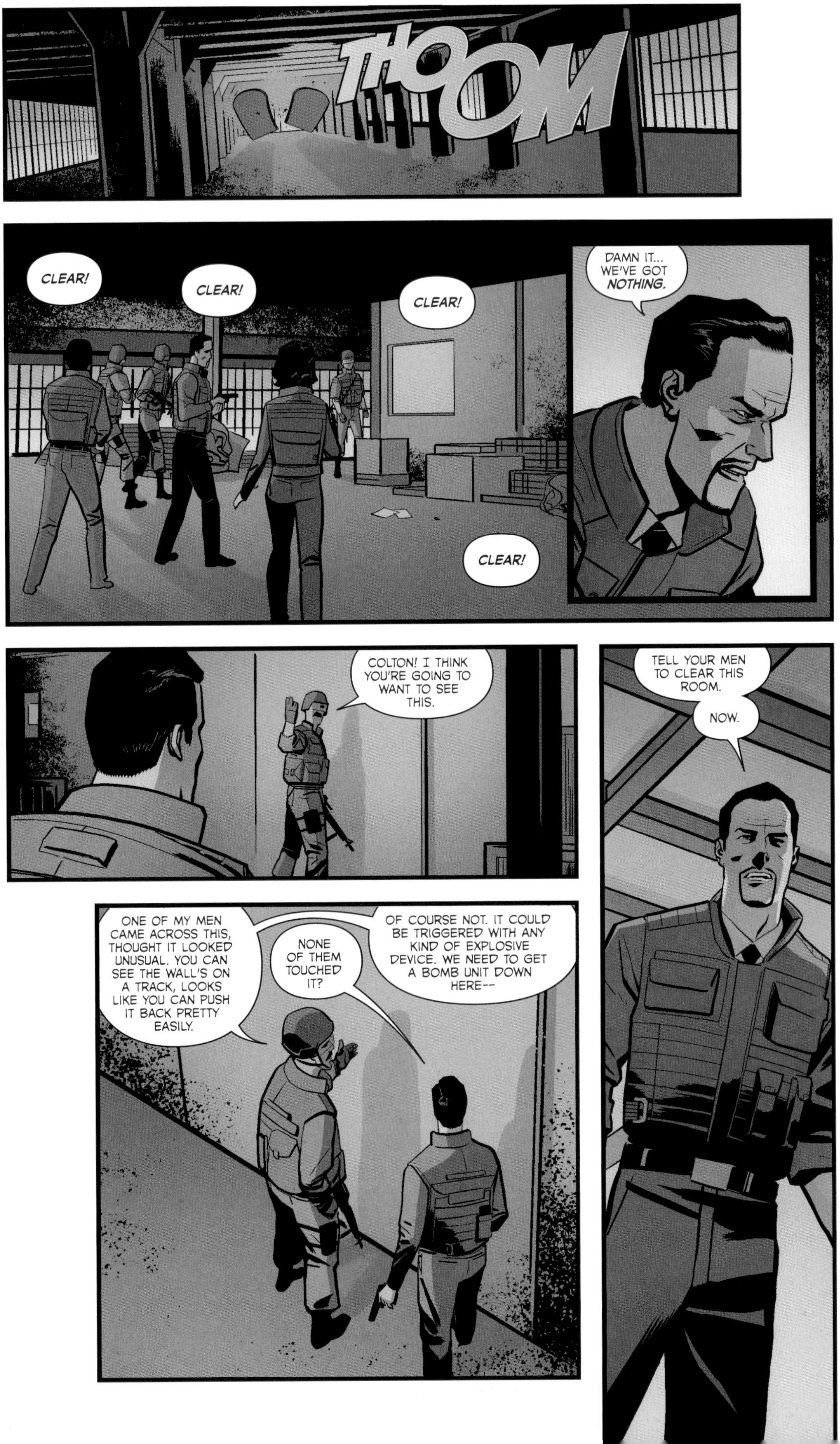
THOOM
CLEAR!
CLEAR!
CLEAR!
CLEAR!
DAMN IT... WE'VE GOT NOTHING.
COLTON! I THINK YOU'RE GOING TO WANT TO SEE THIS.
TELL YOUR MEN TO CLEAR THIS ROOM.
NOW.
ONE OF MY MEN CAME ACROSS THIS, THOUGHT IT LOOKED UNUSUAL. YOU CAN SEE THE WALL'S ON A TRACK, LOOKS LIKE YOU CAN PUSH IT BACK PRETTY EASILY.
NONE OF THEM TOUCHED IT?
OF COURSE NOT. IT COULD BE TRIGGERED WITH ANY KIND OF EXPLOSIVE DEVICE. WE NEED TO GET A BOMB UNIT DOWN HERE--

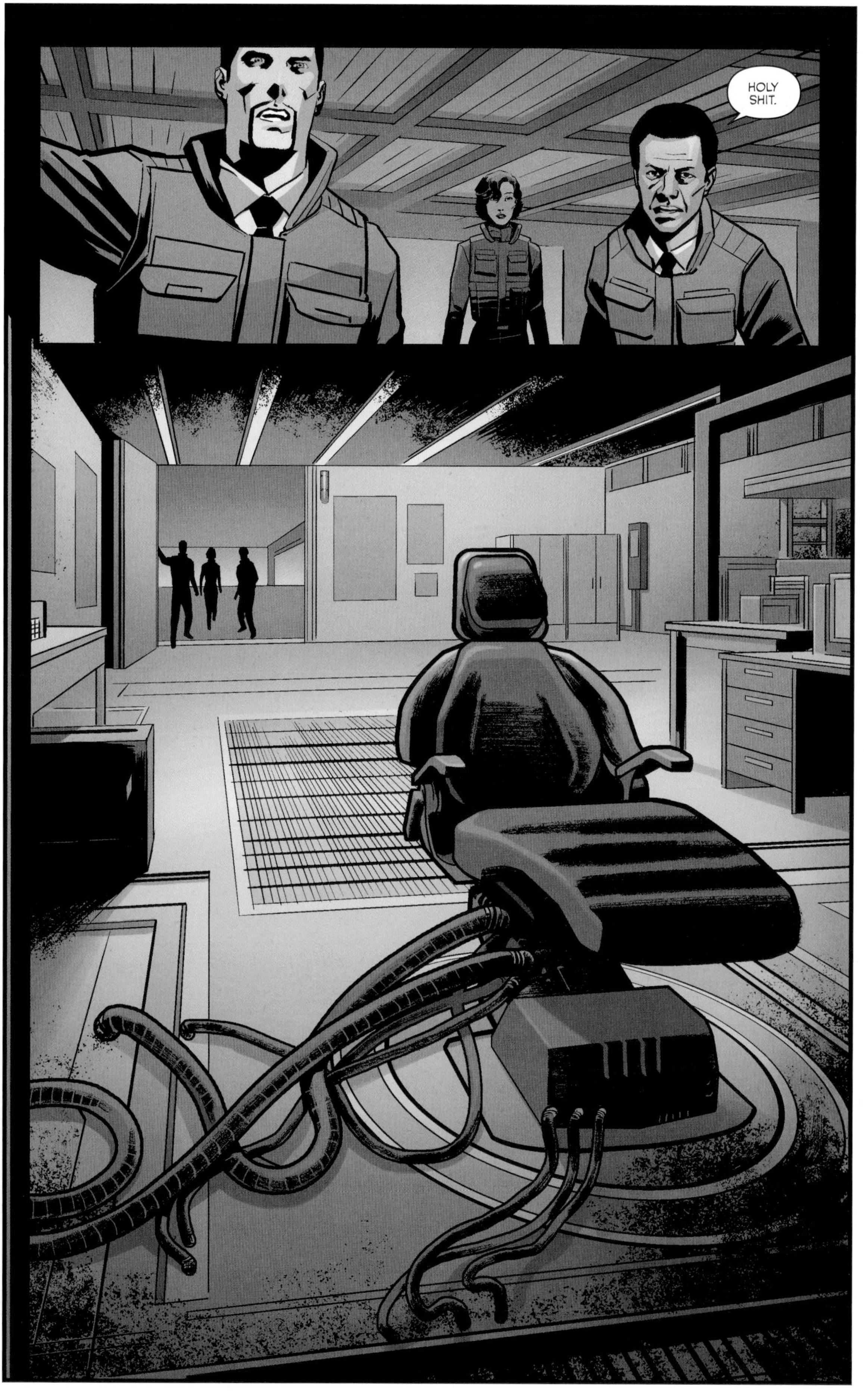
HOLY SHIT.

I GUESS THAT ANSWERS THE QUESTION AS TO WHETHER ORMON TURNED OVER THE TECH OR NOT.

HEY, GUYS...

WHAT DO YOU MAKE OF THIS?

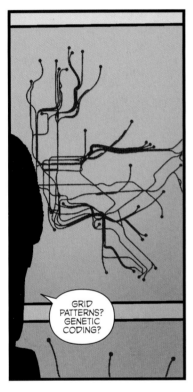

GRID PATTERNS? GENETIC CODING?

THEY LOOK FAMILIAR. COLTON, THESE PATTERNS MEAN ANYTHING TO YOU?

What the fuck?

1008 2001

1008 2001

COLTON, YOU THERE?

WHAT? NO, THAT'S NOT FAMILIAR TO ME. LET'S BAG IT, ALL OF IT.

GET RECHSTON TO SEND A TEAM DOWN HERE. WE NEED TO GET THE MACHINE TO WYATT AND KANNAN, SEE IF IT'S FUNCTIONAL.

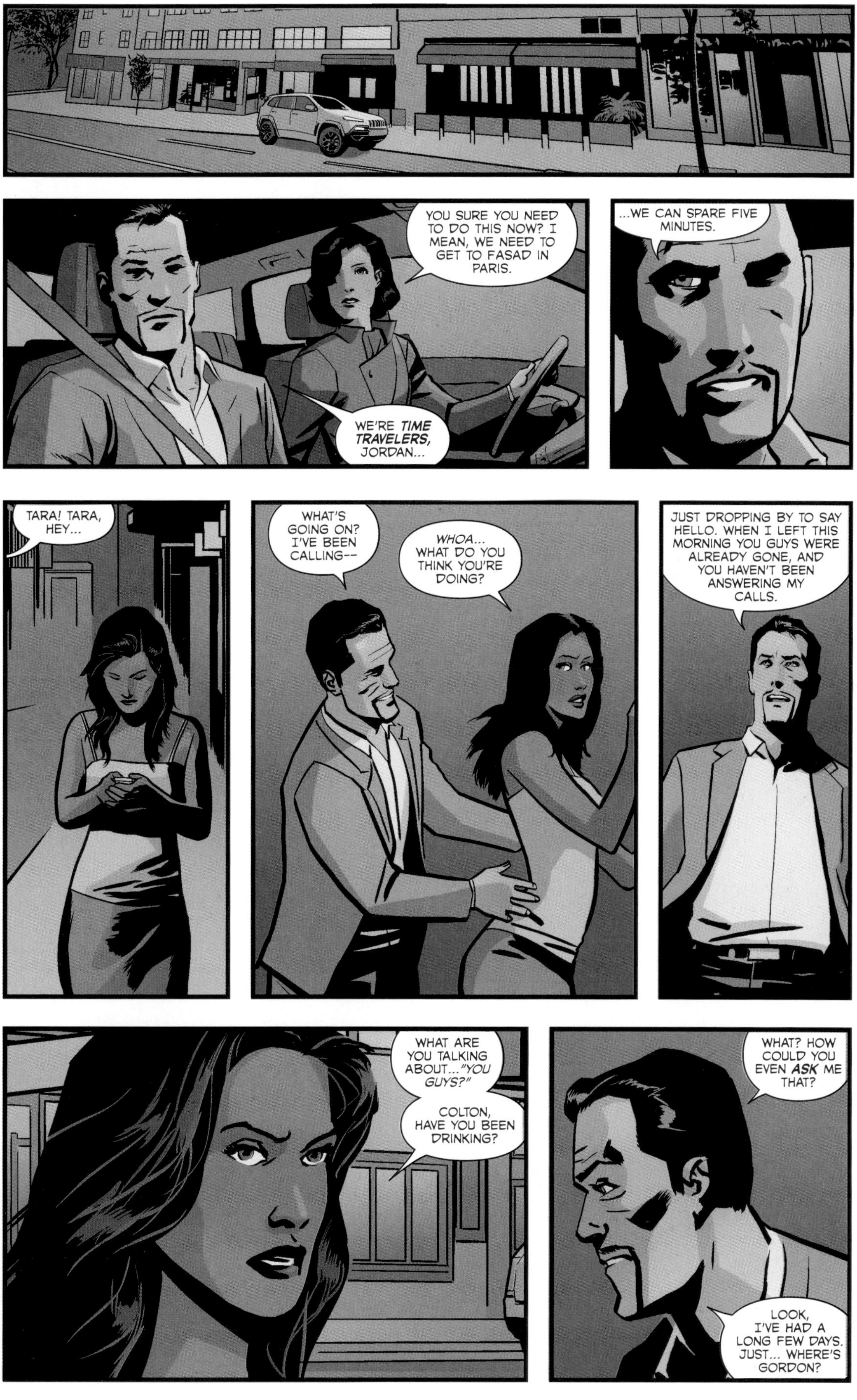
YOU SURE YOU NEED TO DO THIS NOW? I MEAN, WE NEED TO GET TO FASAD IN PARIS.
WE'RE *TIME TRAVELERS,* JORDAN...
...WE CAN SPARE FIVE MINUTES.
TARA! TARA, HEY...
WHAT'S GOING ON? I'VE BEEN CALLING--
WHOA... WHAT DO YOU THINK YOU'RE DOING?
JUST DROPPING BY TO SAY HELLO. WHEN I LEFT THIS MORNING YOU GUYS WERE ALREADY GONE, AND YOU HAVEN'T BEEN ANSWERING MY CALLS.
WHAT ARE YOU TALKING ABOUT... *"YOU GUYS?"*
COLTON, HAVE YOU BEEN DRINKING?
WHAT? HOW COULD YOU EVEN *ASK* ME THAT?
LOOK, I'VE HAD A LONG FEW DAYS. JUST... WHERE'S GORDON?

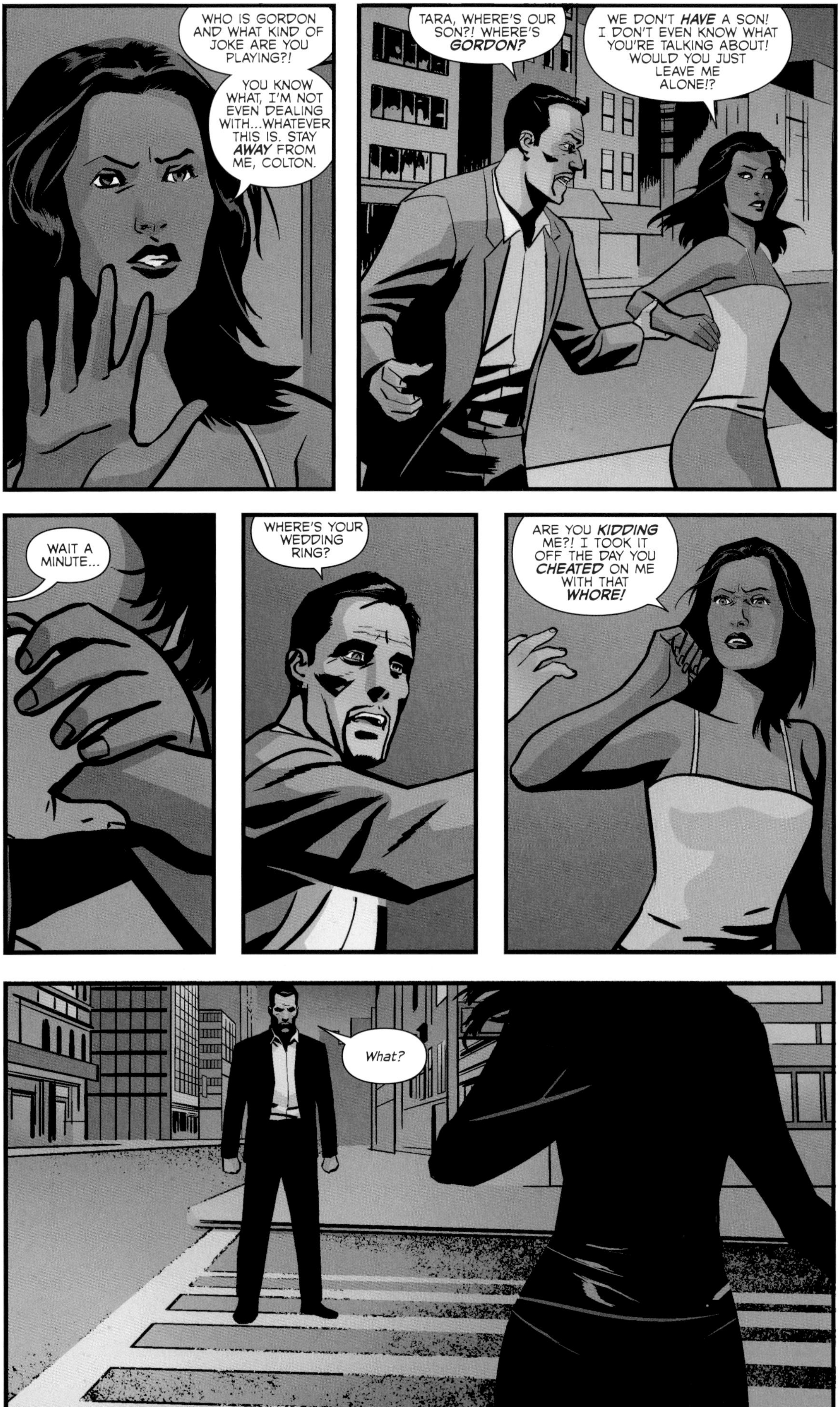
WHO IS GORDON AND WHAT KIND OF JOKE ARE YOU PLAYING?!
YOU KNOW WHAT, I'M NOT EVEN DEALING WITH...WHATEVER THIS IS. STAY AWAY FROM ME, COLTON.
TARA, WHERE'S OUR SON?! WHERE'S GORDON?
WE DON'T HAVE A SON! I DON'T EVEN KNOW WHAT YOU'RE TALKING ABOUT! WOULD YOU JUST LEAVE ME ALONE!?
WAIT A MINUTE...
WHERE'S YOUR WEDDING RING?
ARE YOU KIDDING ME?! I TOOK IT OFF THE DAY YOU CHEATED ON ME WITH THAT WHORE!
What?

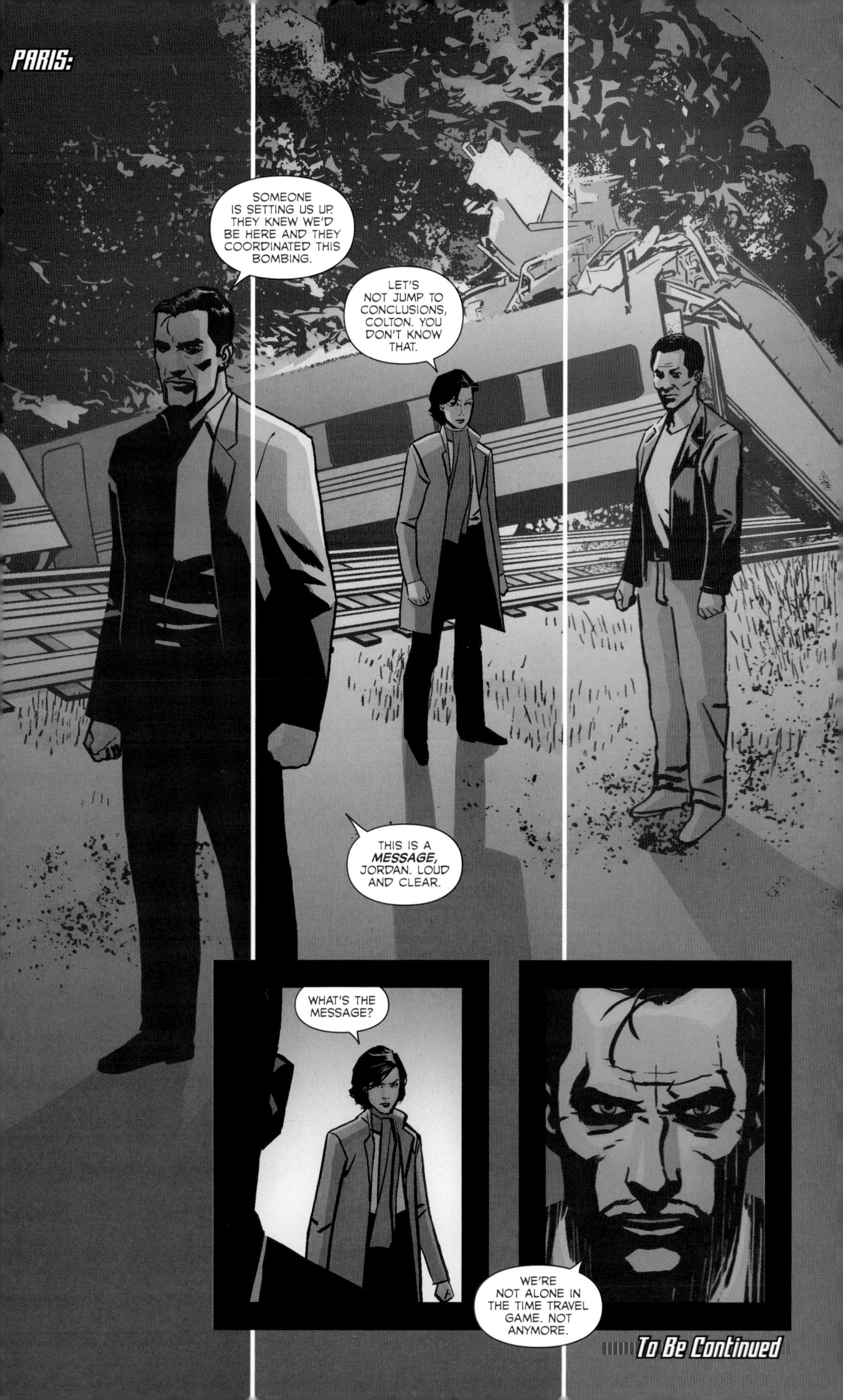
PARIS:
SOMEONE IS SETTING US UP. THEY KNEW WE'D BE HERE AND THEY COORDINATED THIS BOMBING.
LET'S NOT JUMP TO CONCLUSIONS, COLTON. YOU DON'T KNOW THAT.
THIS IS A *MESSAGE,* JORDAN. LOUD AND CLEAR.
WHAT'S THE MESSAGE?
WE'RE NOT ALONE IN THE TIME TRAVEL GAME. NOT ANYMORE.
To Be Continued

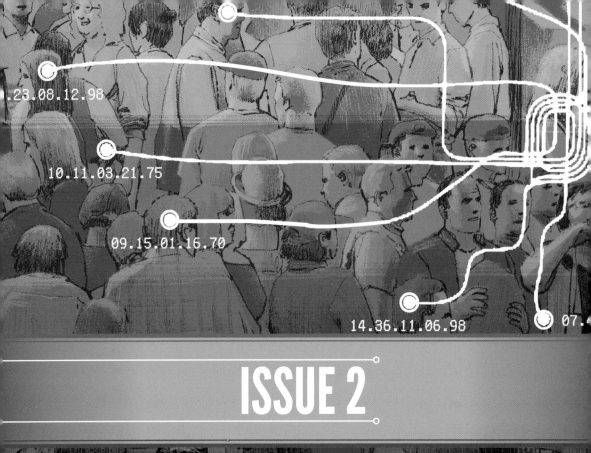

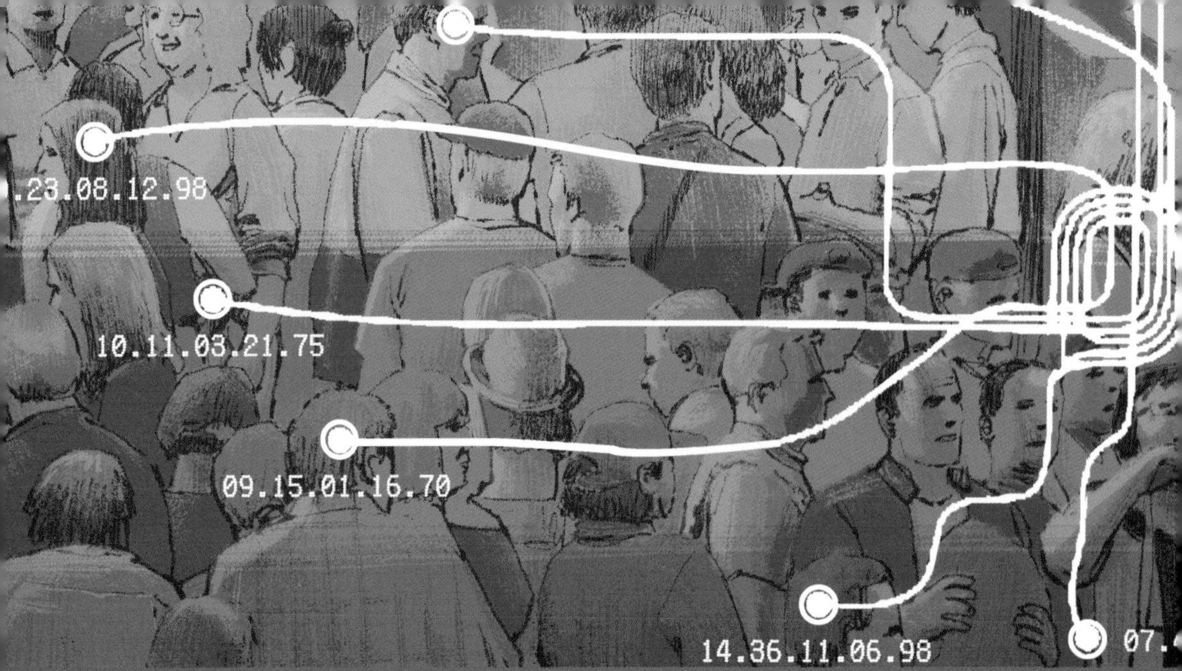
.23.08.12.98
10.11.03.21.75
09.15.01.16.70
14.36.11.06.98
07.

ISSUE 2

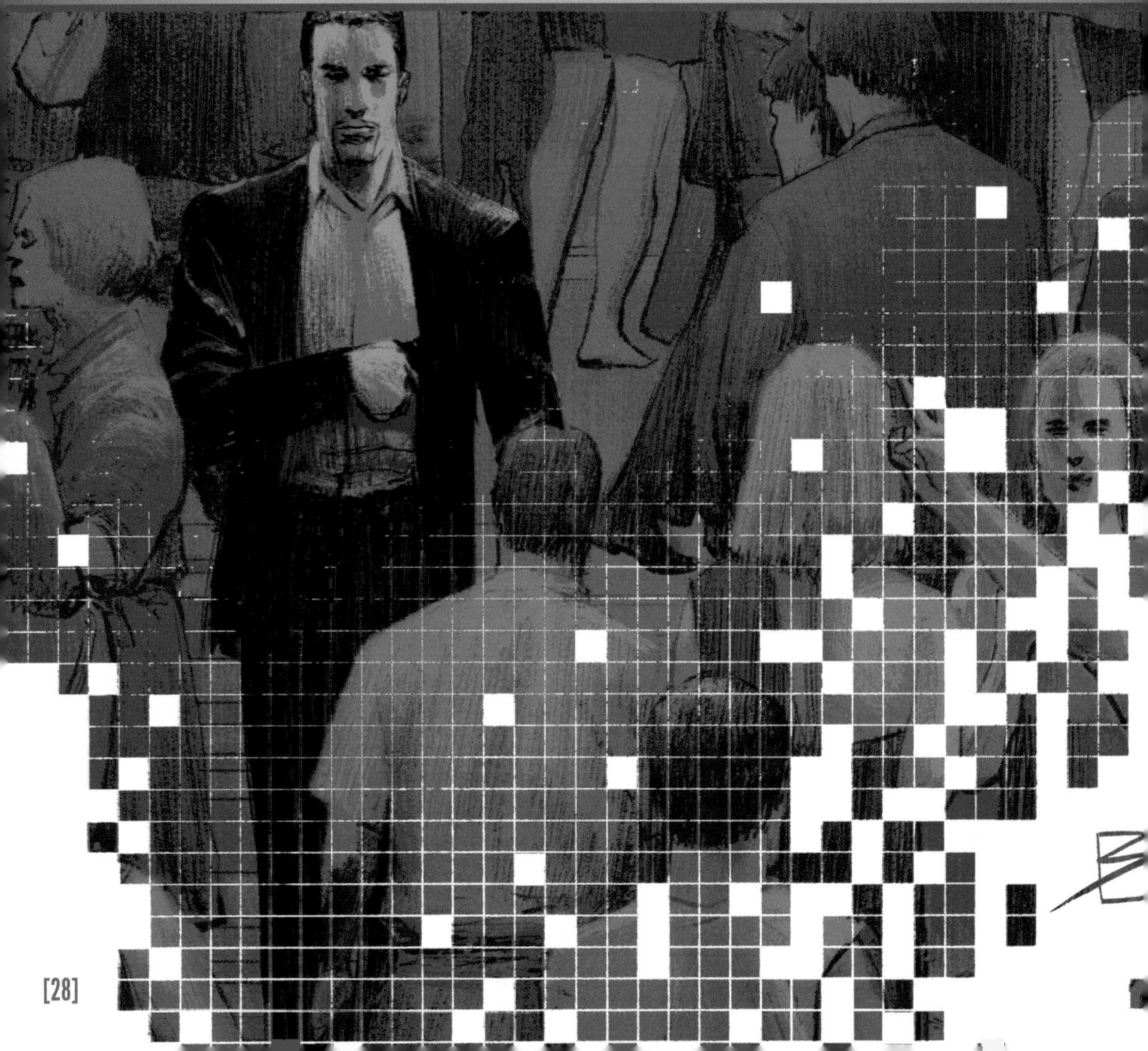

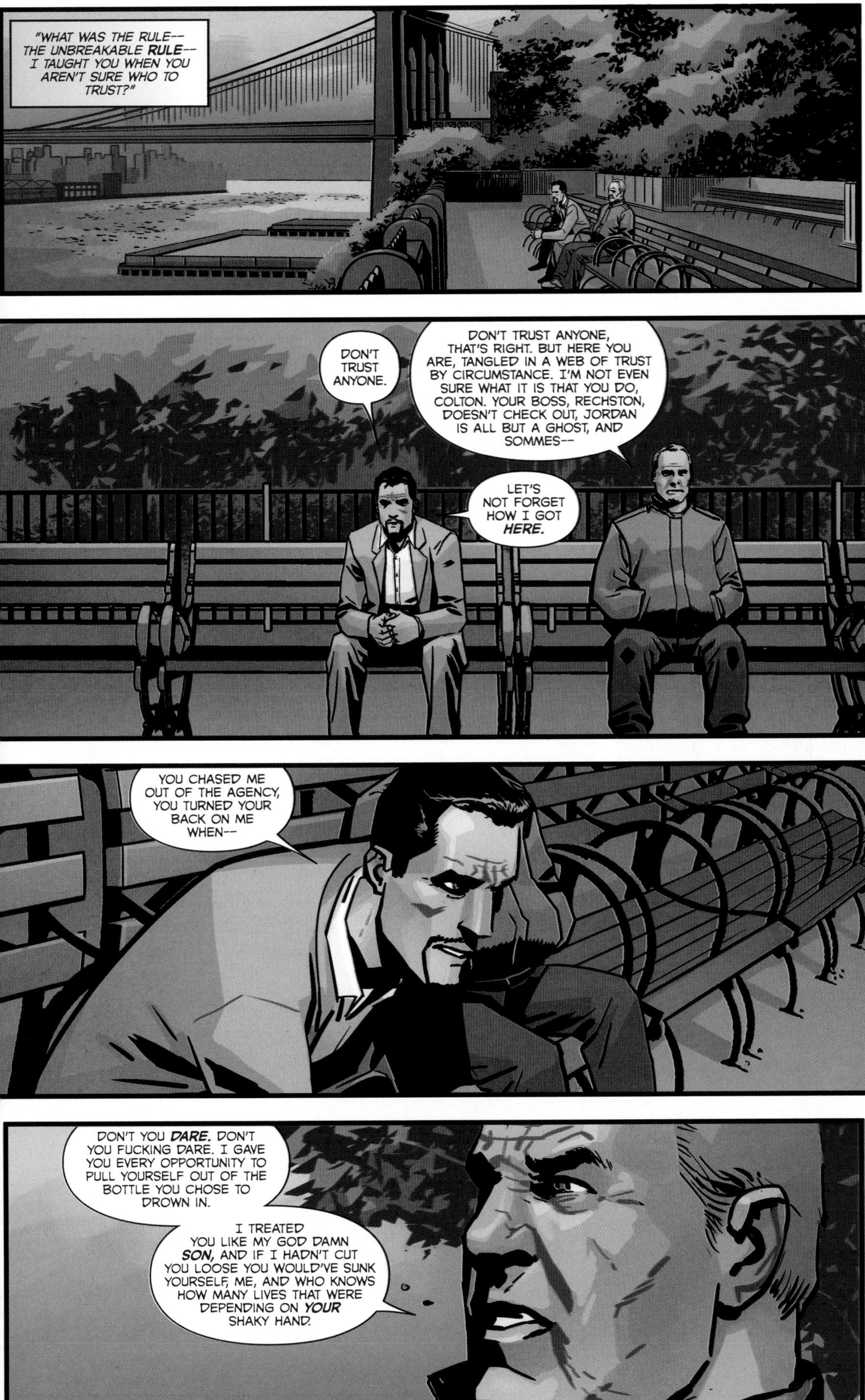
"WHAT WAS THE RULE-- THE UNBREAKABLE RULE-- I TAUGHT YOU WHEN YOU AREN'T SURE WHO TO TRUST?"
DON'T TRUST ANYONE.
DON'T TRUST ANYONE, THAT'S RIGHT. BUT HERE YOU ARE, TANGLED IN A WEB OF TRUST BY CIRCUMSTANCE. I'M NOT EVEN SURE WHAT IT IS THAT YOU DO, COLTON. YOUR BOSS, RECHSTON, DOESN'T CHECK OUT, JORDAN IS ALL BUT A GHOST, AND SOMMES--
LET'S NOT FORGET HOW I GOT HERE.
YOU CHASED ME OUT OF THE AGENCY, YOU TURNED YOUR BACK ON ME WHEN--
DON'T YOU DARE. DON'T YOU FUCKING DARE. I GAVE YOU EVERY OPPORTUNITY TO PULL YOURSELF OUT OF THE BOTTLE YOU CHOSE TO DROWN IN.
I TREATED YOU LIKE MY GOD DAMN SON, AND IF I HADN'T CUT YOU LOOSE YOU WOULD'VE SUNK YOURSELF, ME, AND WHO KNOWS HOW MANY LIVES THAT WERE DEPENDING ON YOUR SHAKY HAND.

YOU'RE RIGHT, OKAY? YOU'RE RIGHT. BUT I DIDN'T COME HERE TO FIGHT WITH YOU.

I NEED YOUR HELP.

WHAT I'M GOING TO TELL YOU...YOU'RE NOT GOING TO BELIEVE IT. NO MATTER HOW I FRAME IT, HOW I BRACE YOU, IT'S GOING TO COME OFF AS A JOKE AT BEST, AN INSANE FABRICATION AT WORST.

BUT IT'S THE TRUTH, AND I *NEED* YOU TO BELIEVE ME.

YOU WANT TO KNOW WHAT I DO?

I CONDUCT CORPORATE AND MILITARY ESPIONAGE THROUGH TIME TRAVEL.

... YOU KNOW, WHEN EVELYN LEFT ME, AS SHE WAS WALKING OUT THE DOOR--LITERALLY STEPPING OUT OF MY LIFE, SUITCASES IN HAND-- I HAD THE AUDACITY TO ASK HER WHAT I CAN DO TO MAKE HER STAY.

SHE STOPPED, LOOKED AT ME LIKE I WAS A WOUNDED ANIMAL, AND SAID... *"CHANGE."* NATURALLY, I ASKED HER WHAT I NEEDED TO CHANGE.

"EVERYTHING," SHE SAID.

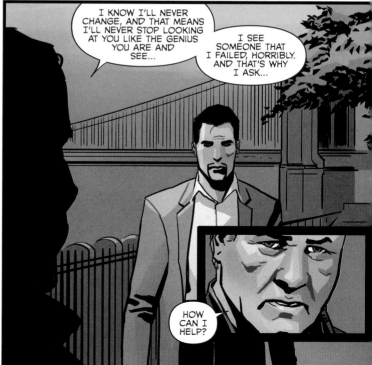

I KNOW I'LL NEVER CHANGE, AND THAT MEANS I'LL NEVER STOP LOOKING AT YOU LIKE THE GENIUS YOU ARE AND SEE...

I SEE SOMEONE THAT I FAILED, HORRIBLY. AND THAT'S WHY I ASK...

HOW CAN I HELP?

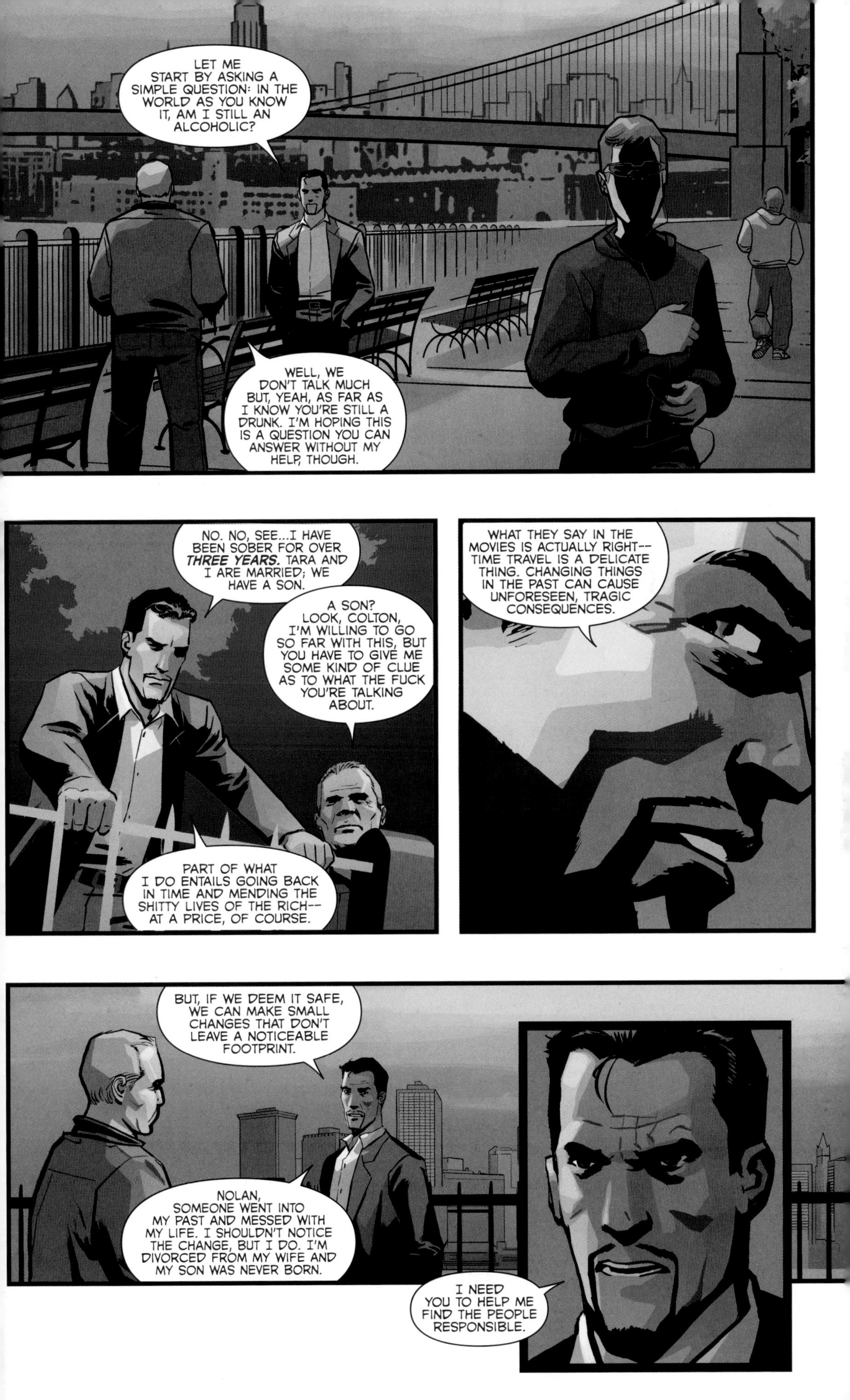
LET ME START BY ASKING A SIMPLE QUESTION: IN THE WORLD AS YOU KNOW IT, AM I STILL AN ALCOHOLIC?
WELL, WE DON'T TALK MUCH BUT, YEAH, AS FAR AS I KNOW YOU'RE STILL A DRUNK. I'M HOPING THIS IS A QUESTION YOU CAN ANSWER WITHOUT MY HELP, THOUGH.
NO. NO, SEE...I HAVE BEEN SOBER FOR OVER *THREE YEARS.* TARA AND I ARE MARRIED; WE HAVE A SON.
A SON? LOOK, COLTON, I'M WILLING TO GO SO FAR WITH THIS, BUT YOU HAVE TO GIVE ME SOME KIND OF CLUE AS TO WHAT THE FUCK YOU'RE TALKING ABOUT.
PART OF WHAT I DO ENTAILS GOING BACK IN TIME AND MENDING THE SHITTY LIVES OF THE RICH-- AT A PRICE, OF COURSE.
WHAT THEY SAY IN THE MOVIES IS ACTUALLY RIGHT-- TIME TRAVEL IS A DELICATE THING. CHANGING THINGS IN THE PAST CAN CAUSE UNFORESEEN, TRAGIC CONSEQUENCES.
BUT, IF WE DEEM IT SAFE, WE CAN MAKE SMALL CHANGES THAT DON'T LEAVE A NOTICEABLE FOOTPRINT.
NOLAN, SOMEONE WENT INTO MY PAST AND MESSED WITH MY LIFE. I SHOULDN'T NOTICE THE CHANGE, BUT I DO. I'M DIVORCED FROM MY WIFE AND MY SON WAS NEVER BORN.
I NEED YOU TO HELP ME FIND THE PEOPLE RESPONSIBLE.

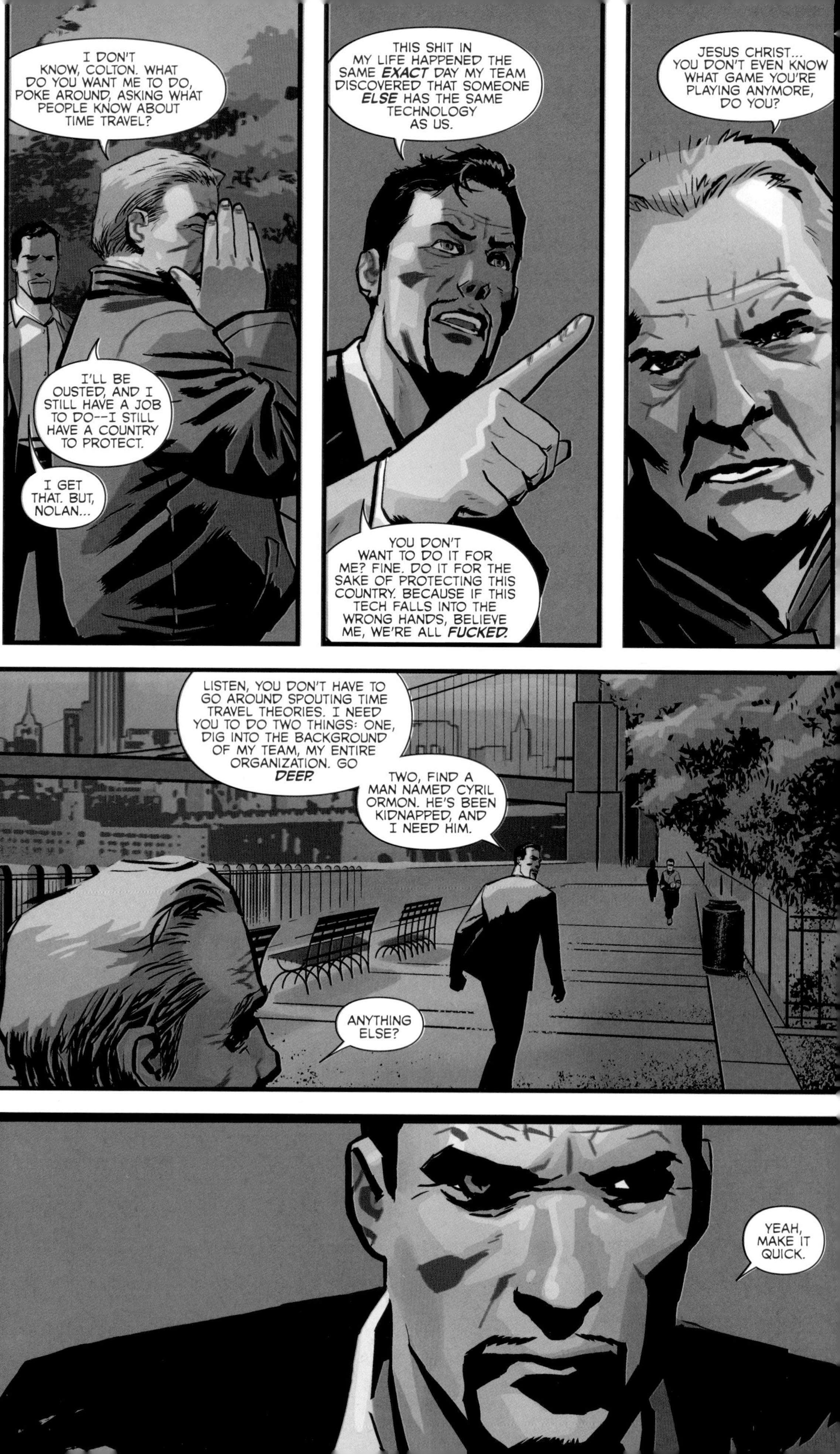

I DON'T KNOW, COLTON. WHAT DO YOU WANT ME TO DO, POKE AROUND, ASKING WHAT PEOPLE KNOW ABOUT TIME TRAVEL?
I'LL BE OUSTED, AND I STILL HAVE A JOB TO DO--I STILL HAVE A COUNTRY TO PROTECT.
I GET THAT. BUT, NOLAN...
THIS SHIT IN MY LIFE HAPPENED THE SAME EXACT DAY MY TEAM DISCOVERED THAT SOMEONE ELSE HAS THE SAME TECHNOLOGY AS US.
YOU DON'T WANT TO DO IT FOR ME? FINE. DO IT FOR THE SAKE OF PROTECTING THIS COUNTRY. BECAUSE IF THIS TECH FALLS INTO THE WRONG HANDS, BELIEVE ME, WE'RE ALL FUCKED.
JESUS CHRIST... YOU DON'T EVEN KNOW WHAT GAME YOU'RE PLAYING ANYMORE, DO YOU?
LISTEN, YOU DON'T HAVE TO GO AROUND SPOUTING TIME TRAVEL THEORIES. I NEED YOU TO DO TWO THINGS: ONE, DIG INTO THE BACKGROUND OF MY TEAM, MY ENTIRE ORGANIZATION. GO DEEP.
TWO, FIND A MAN NAMED CYRIL ORMON. HE'S BEEN KIDNAPPED, AND I NEED HIM.
ANYTHING ELSE?
YEAH, MAKE IT QUICK.

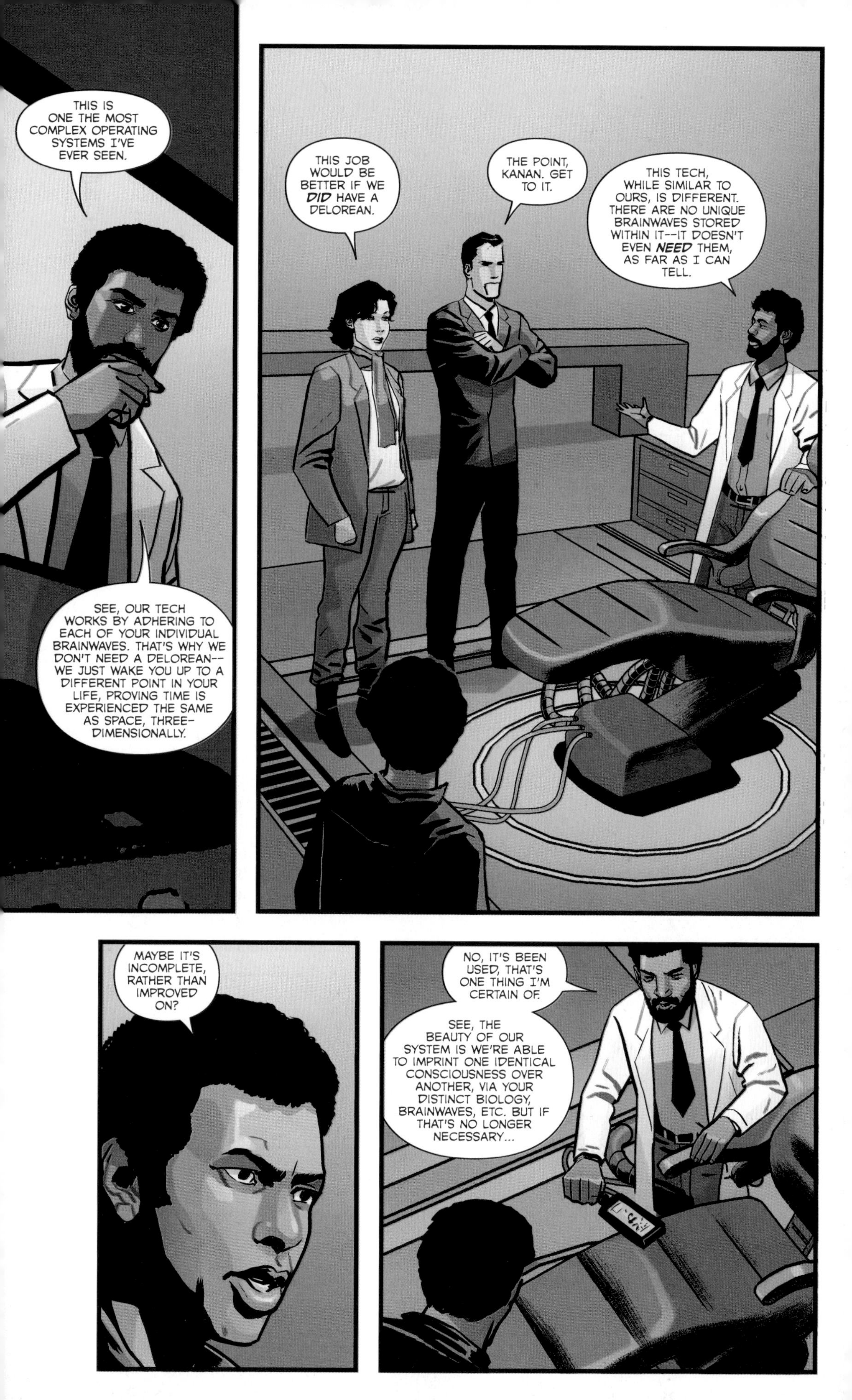

THIS IS ONE THE MOST COMPLEX OPERATING SYSTEMS I'VE EVER SEEN.
SEE, OUR TECH WORKS BY ADHERING TO EACH OF YOUR INDIVIDUAL BRAINWAVES. THAT'S WHY WE DON'T NEED A DELOREAN-- WE JUST WAKE YOU UP TO A DIFFERENT POINT IN YOUR LIFE, PROVING TIME IS EXPERIENCED THE SAME AS SPACE, THREE-DIMENSIONALLY.
THIS JOB WOULD BE BETTER IF WE *DID* HAVE A DELOREAN.
THE POINT, KANAN. GET TO IT.
THIS TECH, WHILE SIMILAR TO OURS, IS DIFFERENT. THERE ARE NO UNIQUE BRAINWAVES STORED WITHIN IT--IT DOESN'T EVEN ***NEED*** THEM, AS FAR AS I CAN TELL.
MAYBE IT'S INCOMPLETE, RATHER THAN IMPROVED ON?
NO, IT'S BEEN USED, THAT'S ONE THING I'M CERTAIN OF.
SEE, THE BEAUTY OF OUR SYSTEM IS WE'RE ABLE TO IMPRINT ONE IDENTICAL CONSCIOUSNESS OVER ANOTHER, VIA YOUR DISTINCT BIOLOGY, BRAINWAVES, ETC. BUT IF THAT'S NO LONGER NECESSARY...

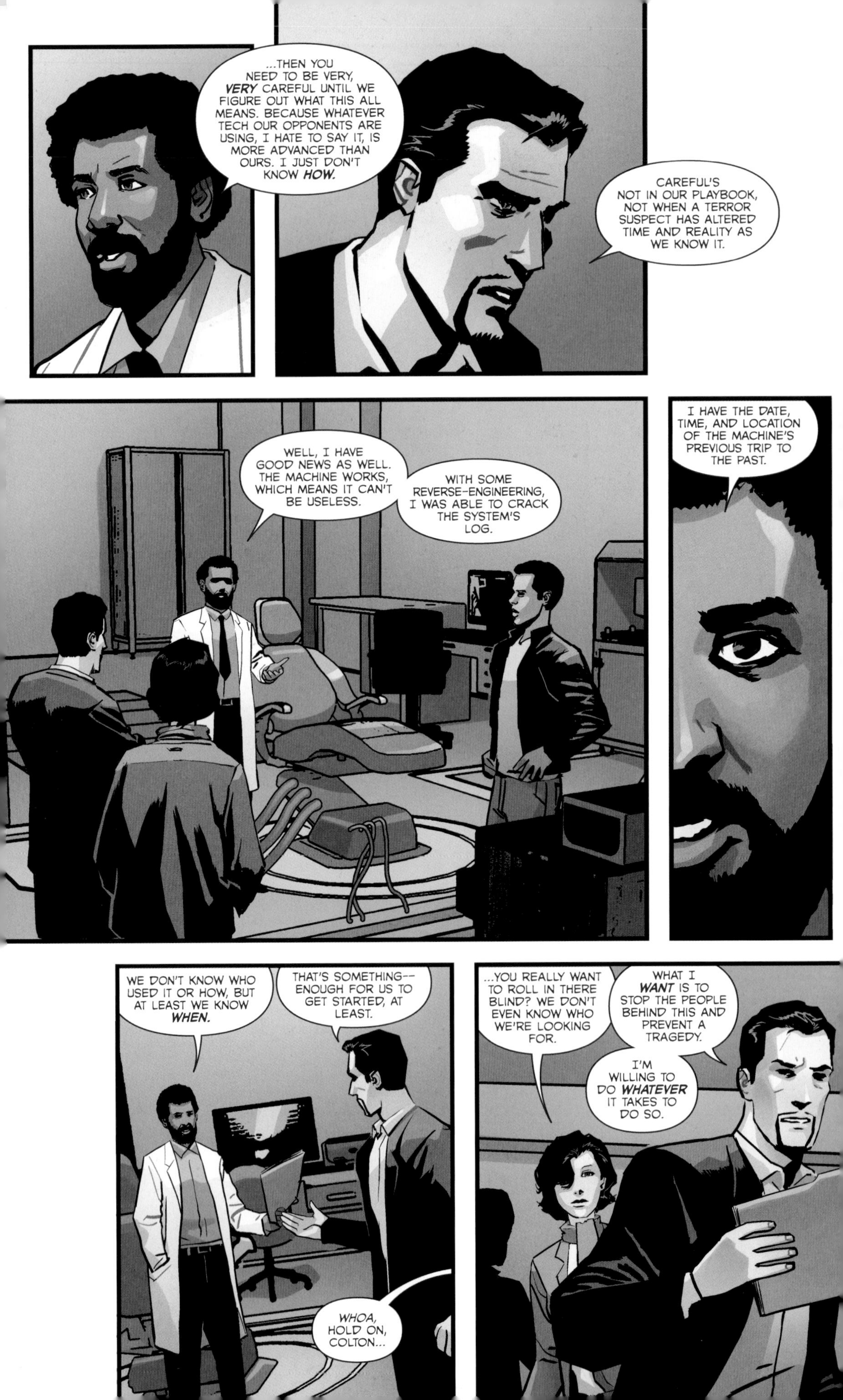
...THEN YOU NEED TO BE VERY, *VERY* CAREFUL UNTIL WE FIGURE OUT WHAT THIS ALL MEANS. BECAUSE WHATEVER TECH OUR OPPONENTS ARE USING, I HATE TO SAY IT, IS MORE ADVANCED THAN OURS. I JUST DON'T KNOW *HOW.*
CAREFUL'S NOT IN OUR PLAYBOOK, NOT WHEN A TERROR SUSPECT HAS ALTERED TIME AND REALITY AS WE KNOW IT.
WELL, I HAVE GOOD NEWS AS WELL. THE MACHINE WORKS, WHICH MEANS IT CAN'T BE USELESS.
WITH SOME REVERSE-ENGINEERING, I WAS ABLE TO CRACK THE SYSTEM'S LOG.
I HAVE THE DATE, TIME, AND LOCATION OF THE MACHINE'S PREVIOUS TRIP TO THE PAST.
WE DON'T KNOW WHO USED IT OR HOW, BUT AT LEAST WE KNOW *WHEN.*
THAT'S SOMETHING-- ENOUGH FOR US TO GET STARTED, AT LEAST.
WHOA, HOLD ON, COLTON...
...YOU REALLY WANT TO ROLL IN THERE BLIND? WE DON'T EVEN KNOW WHO WE'RE LOOKING FOR.
WHAT I *WANT* IS TO STOP THE PEOPLE BEHIND THIS AND PREVENT A TRAGEDY.
I'M WILLING TO DO *WHATEVER* IT TAKES TO DO SO.

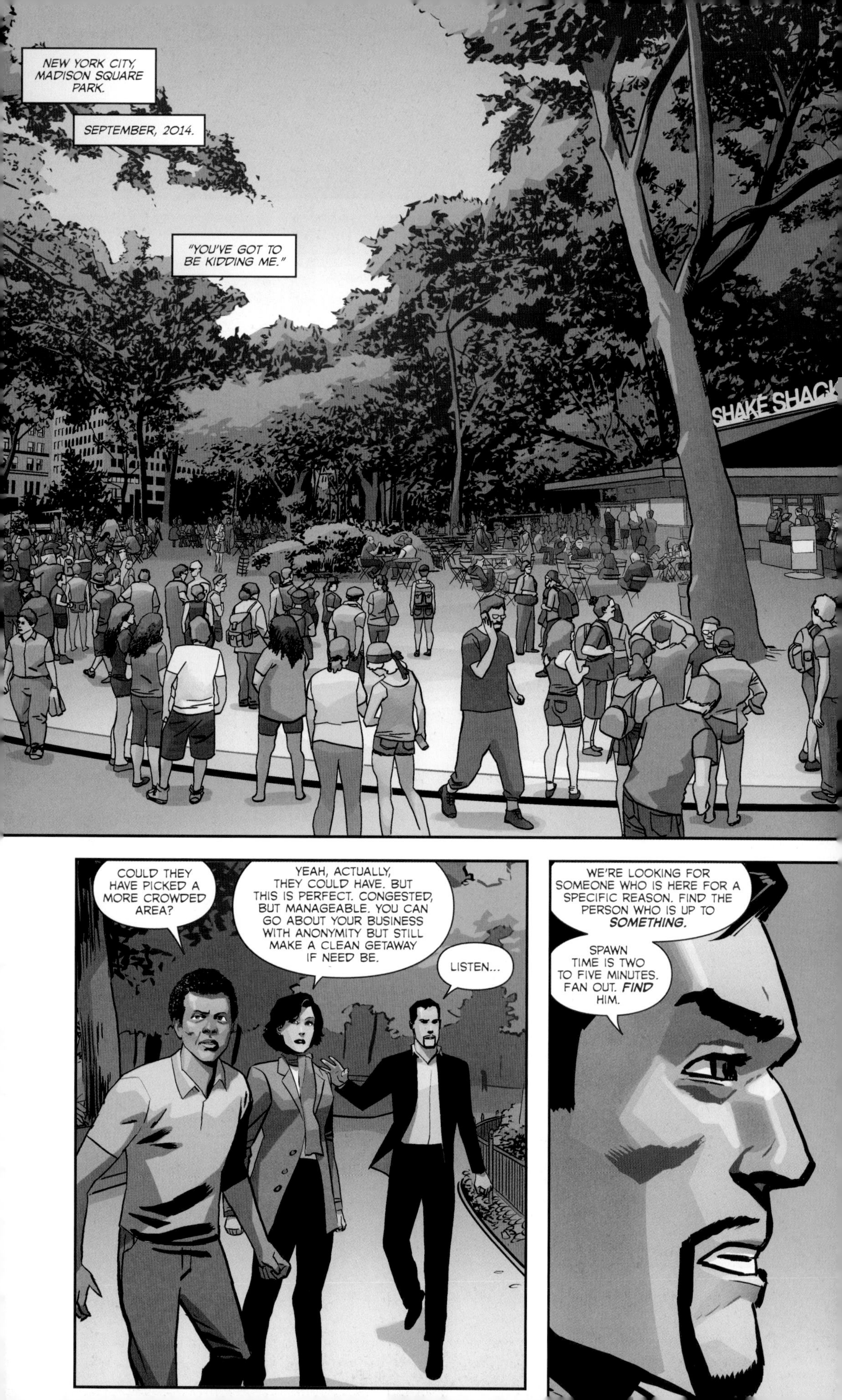
NEW YORK CITY, MADISON SQUARE PARK.
SEPTEMBER, 2014.
"YOU'VE GOT TO BE KIDDING ME."
SHAKE SHACK
COULD THEY HAVE PICKED A MORE CROWDED AREA?
YEAH, ACTUALLY, THEY COULD HAVE. BUT THIS IS PERFECT. CONGESTED, BUT MANAGEABLE. YOU CAN GO ABOUT YOUR BUSINESS WITH ANONYMITY BUT STILL MAKE A CLEAN GETAWAY IF NEED BE.
LISTEN...
WE'RE LOOKING FOR SOMEONE WHO IS HERE FOR A SPECIFIC REASON. FIND THE PERSON WHO IS UP TO ***SOMETHING.***
SPAWN TIME IS TWO TO FIVE MINUTES. FAN OUT. ***FIND*** HIM.

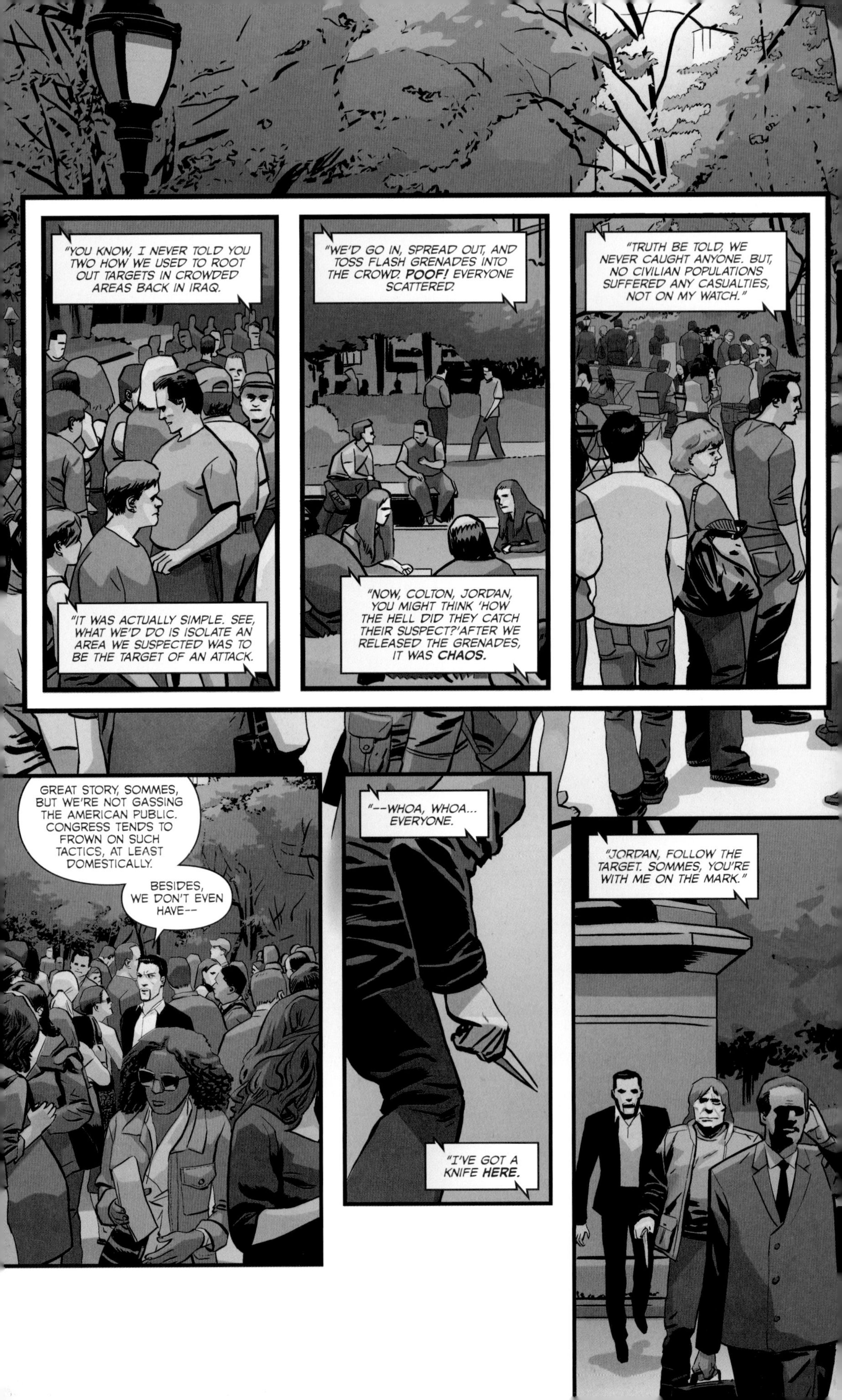
"YOU KNOW, I NEVER TOLD YOU TWO HOW WE USED TO ROOT OUT TARGETS IN CROWDED AREAS BACK IN IRAQ.
"IT WAS ACTUALLY SIMPLE. SEE, WHAT WE'D DO IS ISOLATE AN AREA WE SUSPECTED WAS TO BE THE TARGET OF AN ATTACK.
"WE'D GO IN, SPREAD OUT, AND TOSS FLASH GRENADES INTO THE CROWD. POOF! EVERYONE SCATTERED.
"NOW, COLTON, JORDAN, YOU MIGHT THINK 'HOW THE HELL DID THEY CATCH THEIR SUSPECT?' AFTER WE RELEASED THE GRENADES, IT WAS CHAOS.
"TRUTH BE TOLD, WE NEVER CAUGHT ANYONE. BUT, NO CIVILIAN POPULATIONS SUFFERED ANY CASUALTIES, NOT ON MY WATCH."
GREAT STORY, SOMMES, BUT WE'RE NOT GASSING THE AMERICAN PUBLIC. CONGRESS TENDS TO FROWN ON SUCH TACTICS, AT LEAST DOMESTICALLY.
BESIDES, WE DON'T EVEN HAVE--
"--WHOA, WHOA... EVERYONE.
"I'VE GOT A KNIFE HERE.
"JORDAN, FOLLOW THE TARGET. SOMMES, YOU'RE WITH ME ON THE MARK."

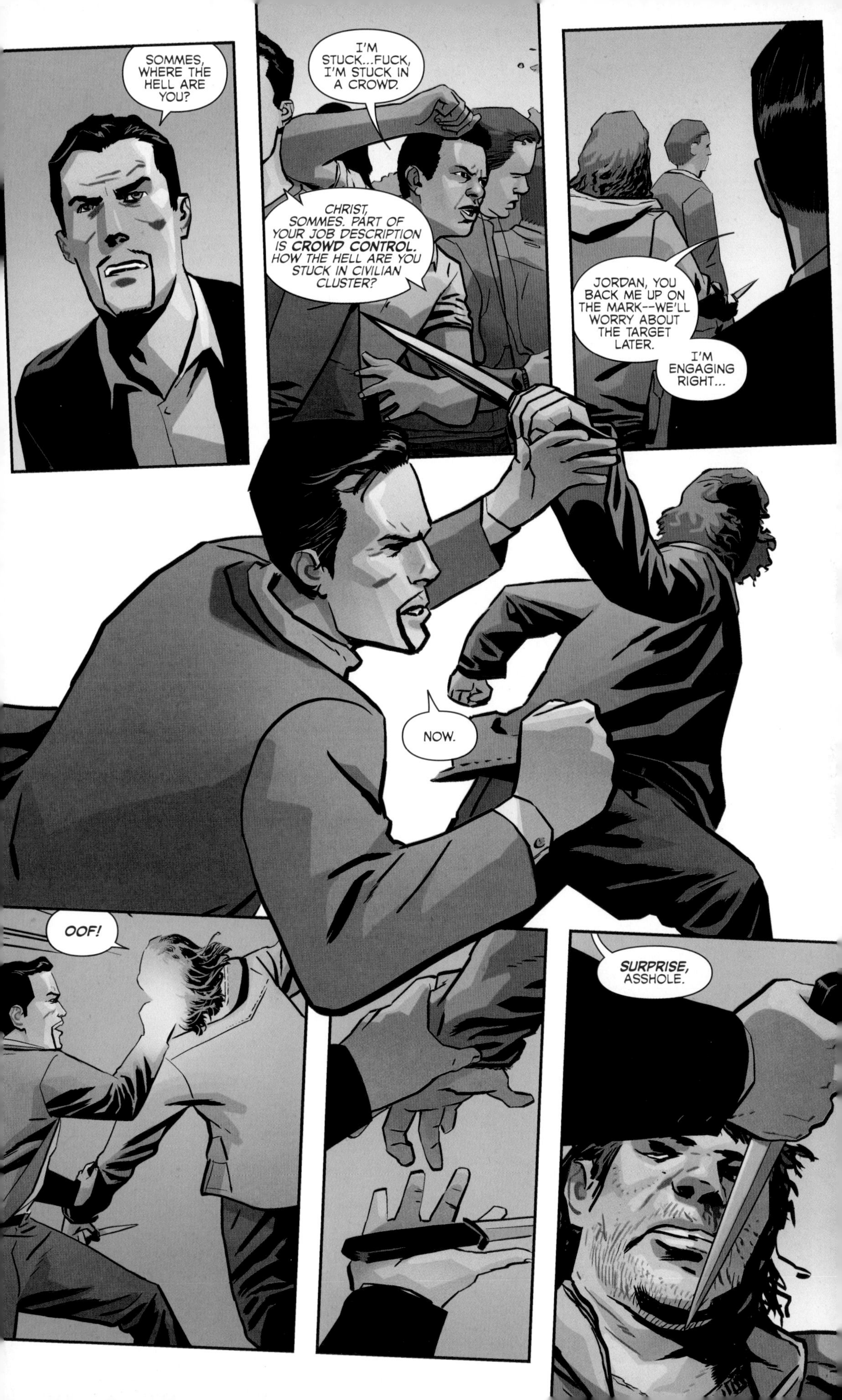
SOMMES, WHERE THE HELL ARE YOU?
I'M STUCK...FUCK, I'M STUCK IN A CROWD.
CHRIST, SOMMES. PART OF YOUR JOB DESCRIPTION IS **CROWD CONTROL.** HOW THE HELL ARE YOU STUCK IN CIVILIAN CLUSTER?
JORDAN, YOU BACK ME UP ON THE MARK--WE'LL WORRY ABOUT THE TARGET LATER.
I'M ENGAGING RIGHT...
NOW.
OOF!
SURPRISE, ASSHOLE.

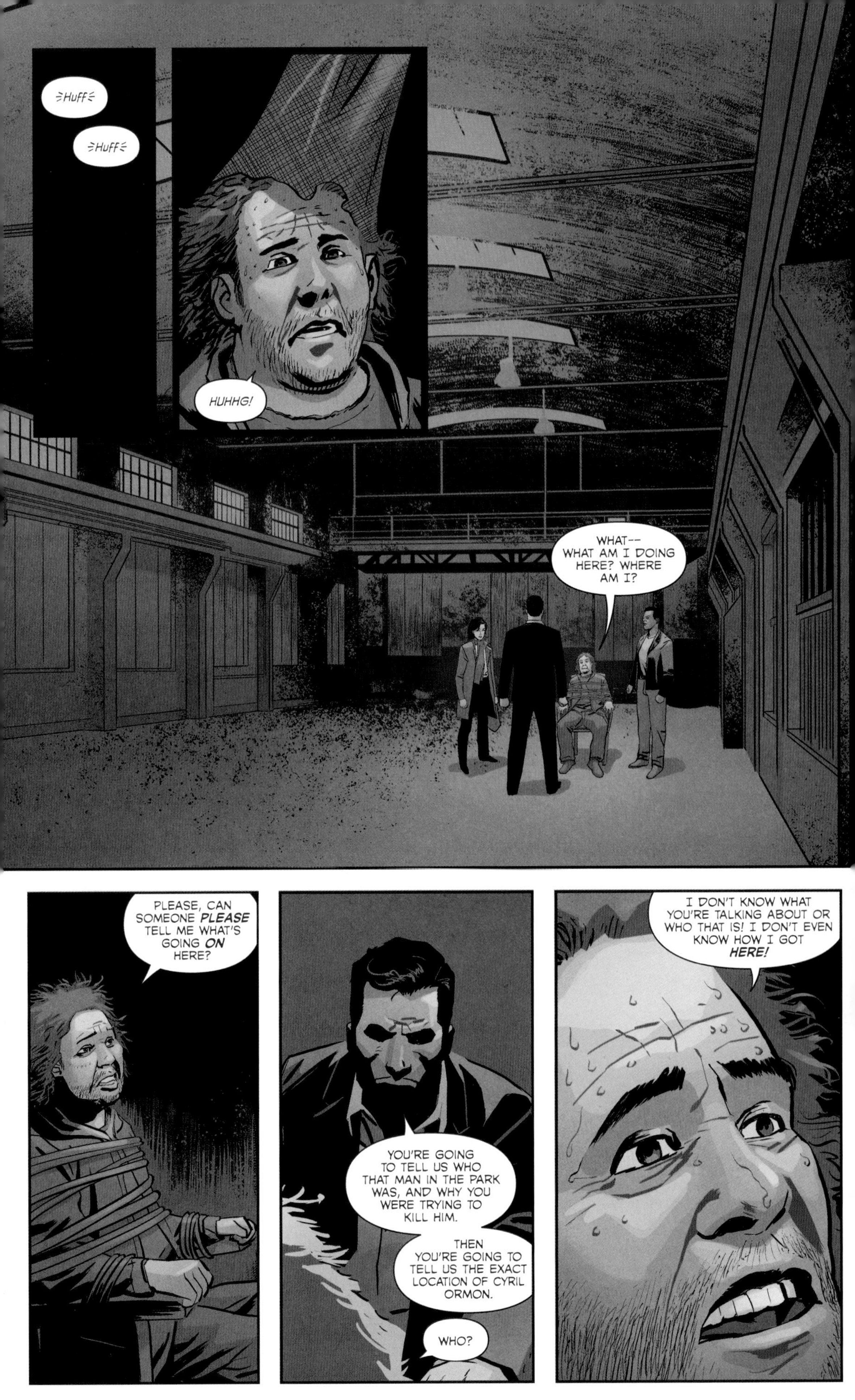
HUFF
HUFF
HUHHG!
WHAT-- WHAT AM I DOING HERE? WHERE AM I?
PLEASE, CAN SOMEONE *PLEASE* TELL ME WHAT'S GOING *ON* HERE?
YOU'RE GOING TO TELL US WHO THAT MAN IN THE PARK WAS, AND WHY YOU WERE TRYING TO KILL HIM.
THEN YOU'RE GOING TO TELL US THE EXACT LOCATION OF CYRIL ORMON.
WHO?
I DON'T KNOW WHAT YOU'RE TALKING ABOUT OR WHO THAT IS! I DON'T EVEN KNOW HOW I GOT *HERE!*

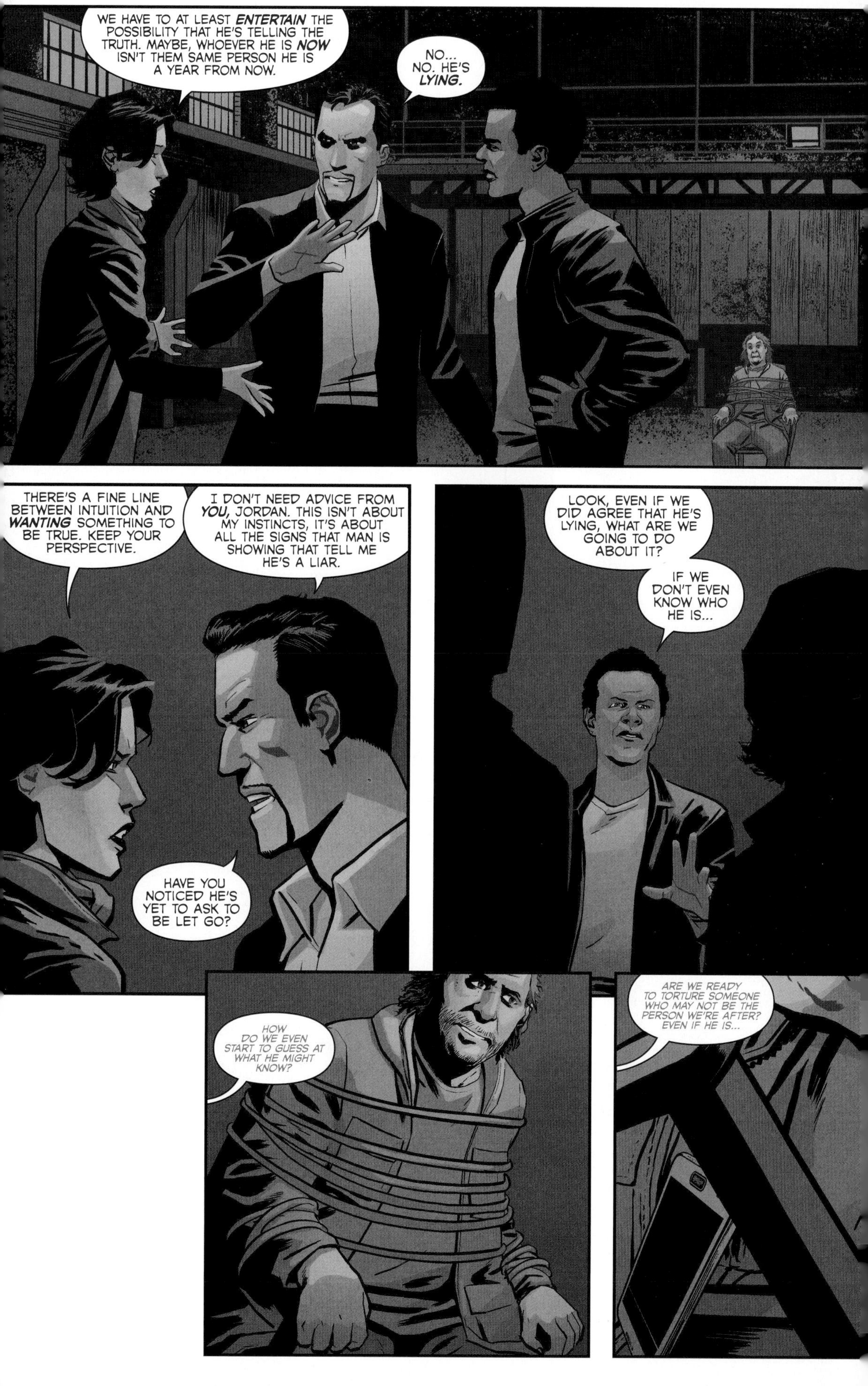

WE HAVE TO AT LEAST ENTERTAIN THE POSSIBILITY THAT HE'S TELLING THE TRUTH. MAYBE, WHOEVER HE IS NOW ISN'T THEM SAME PERSON HE IS A YEAR FROM NOW.
NO... NO. HE'S LYING.
THERE'S A FINE LINE BETWEEN INTUITION AND WANTING SOMETHING TO BE TRUE. KEEP YOUR PERSPECTIVE.
I DON'T NEED ADVICE FROM YOU, JORDAN. THIS ISN'T ABOUT MY INSTINCTS, IT'S ABOUT ALL THE SIGNS THAT MAN IS SHOWING THAT TELL ME HE'S A LIAR.
HAVE YOU NOTICED HE'S YET TO ASK TO BE LET GO?
LOOK, EVEN IF WE DID AGREE THAT HE'S LYING, WHAT ARE WE GOING TO DO ABOUT IT?
IF WE DON'T EVEN KNOW WHO HE IS...
HOW DO WE EVEN START TO GUESS AT WHAT HE MIGHT KNOW?
ARE WE READY TO TORTURE SOMEONE WHO MAY NOT BE THE PERSON WE'RE AFTER? EVEN IF HE IS...

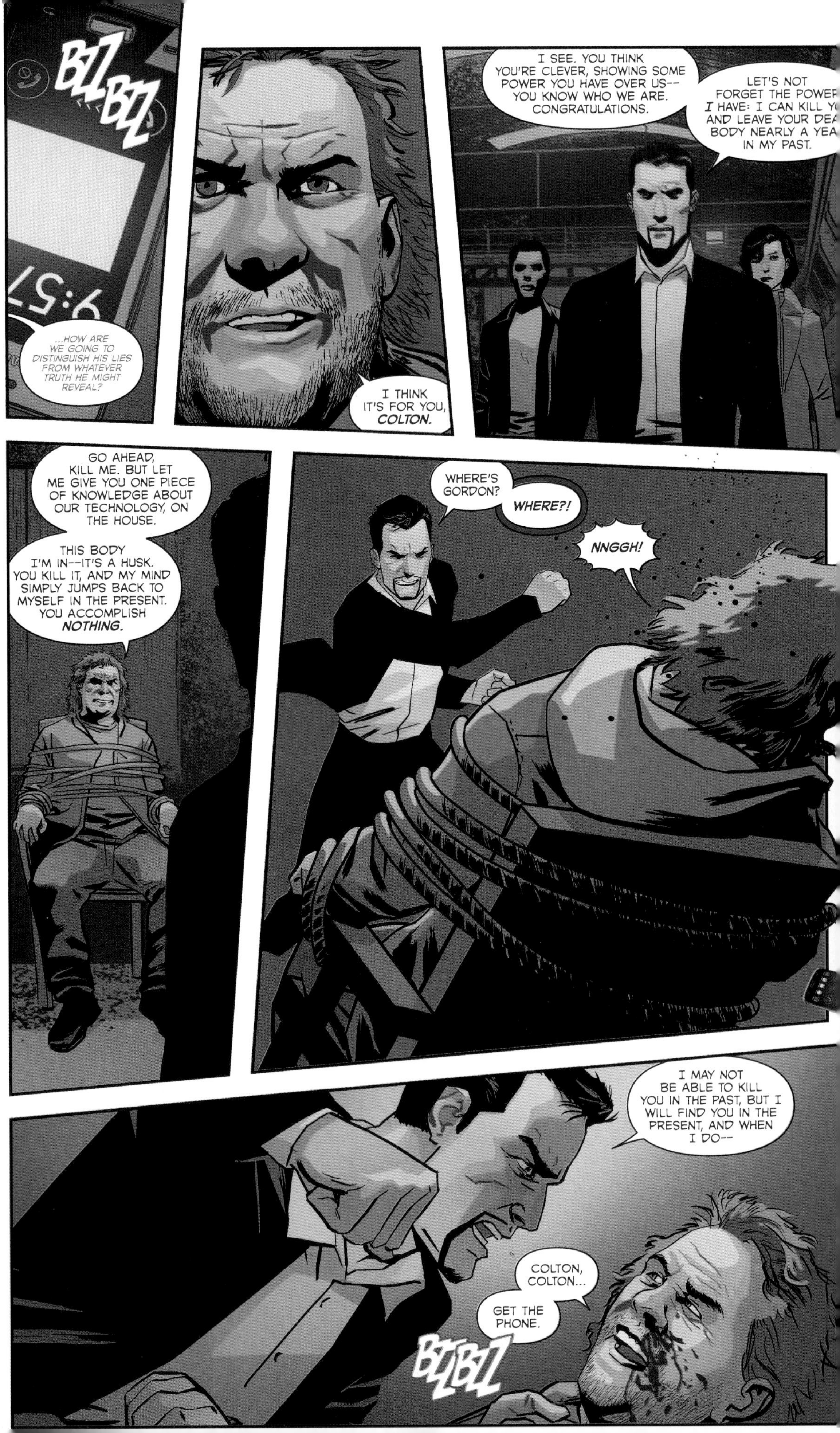
BZZ BZZ
9:57
...HOW ARE WE GOING TO DISTINGUISH HIS LIES FROM WHATEVER TRUTH HE MIGHT REVEAL?
I THINK IT'S FOR YOU, COLTON.
I SEE. YOU THINK YOU'RE CLEVER, SHOWING SOME POWER YOU HAVE OVER US-- YOU KNOW WHO WE ARE. CONGRATULATIONS.
LET'S NOT FORGET THE POWE I HAVE: I CAN KILL Y AND LEAVE YOUR DEA BODY NEARLY A YEA IN MY PAST.
GO AHEAD, KILL ME. BUT LET ME GIVE YOU ONE PIECE OF KNOWLEDGE ABOUT OUR TECHNOLOGY, ON THE HOUSE.
THIS BODY I'M IN--IT'S A HUSK. YOU KILL IT, AND MY MIND SIMPLY JUMPS BACK TO MYSELF IN THE PRESENT. YOU ACCOMPLISH NOTHING.
WHERE'S GORDON?
WHERE?!
NNGGH!
I MAY NOT BE ABLE TO KILL YOU IN THE PAST, BUT I WILL FIND YOU IN THE PRESENT, AND WHEN I DO--
COLTON, COLTON...
GET THE PHONE.
BZZBZZ

YOU MOTHER**FUCKER**.

THAT'S MY CUE, COLTON.

SAMSONG

THAT'S TIME'S UP. TIME'S UP.

HOW DID YOU GET THAT PHOTO? WHERE'S *GORDON*? WHERE *IS* HE?!

Nnngghhh... where...

GOD DAMN IT!

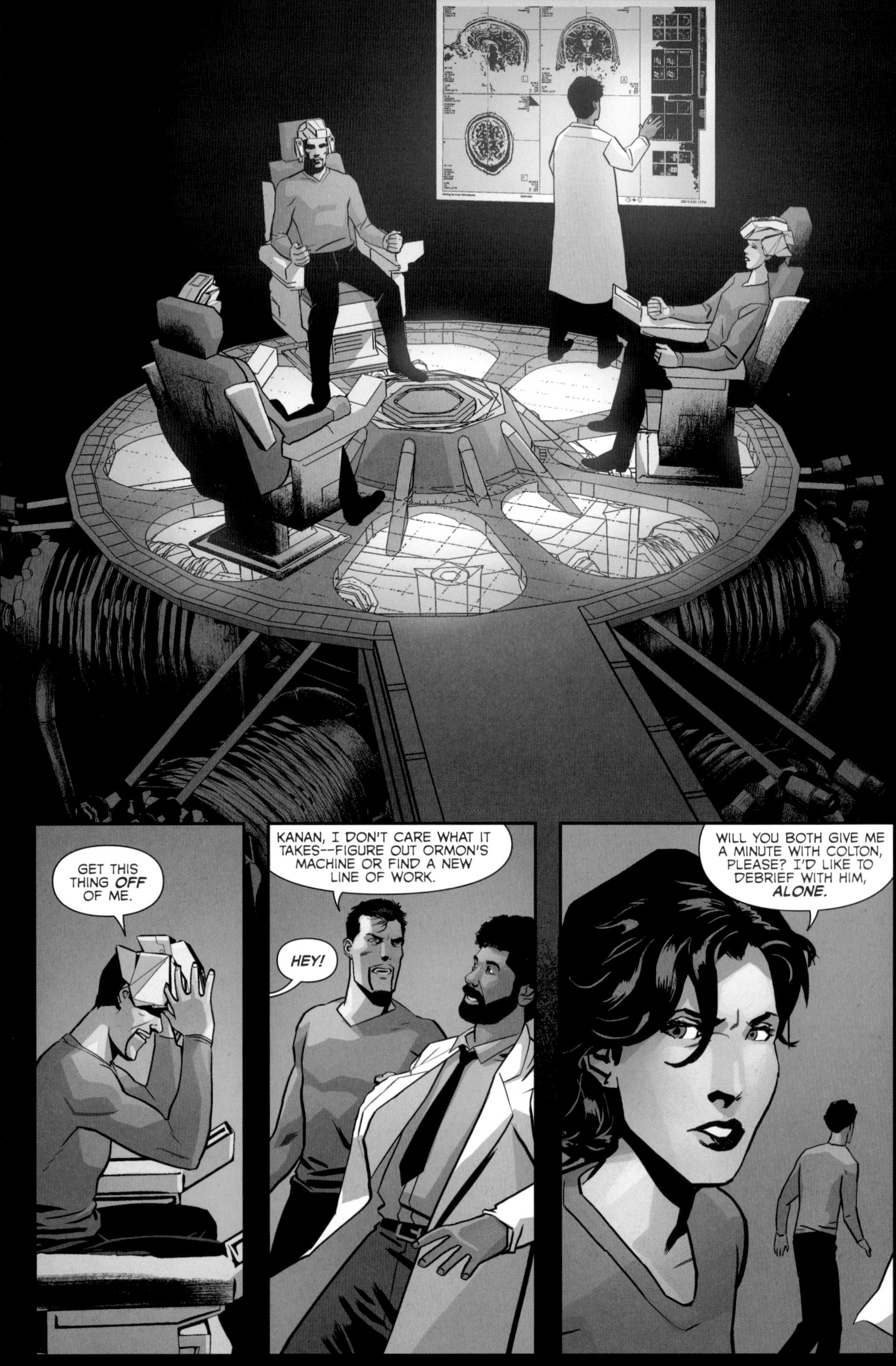
GET THIS THING *OFF* OF ME.
KANAN, I DON'T CARE WHAT IT TAKES--FIGURE OUT ORMON'S MACHINE OR FIND A NEW LINE OF WORK.
HEY!
WILL YOU BOTH GIVE ME A MINUTE WITH COLTON, PLEASE? I'D LIKE TO DEBRIEF WITH HIM, ***ALONE.***

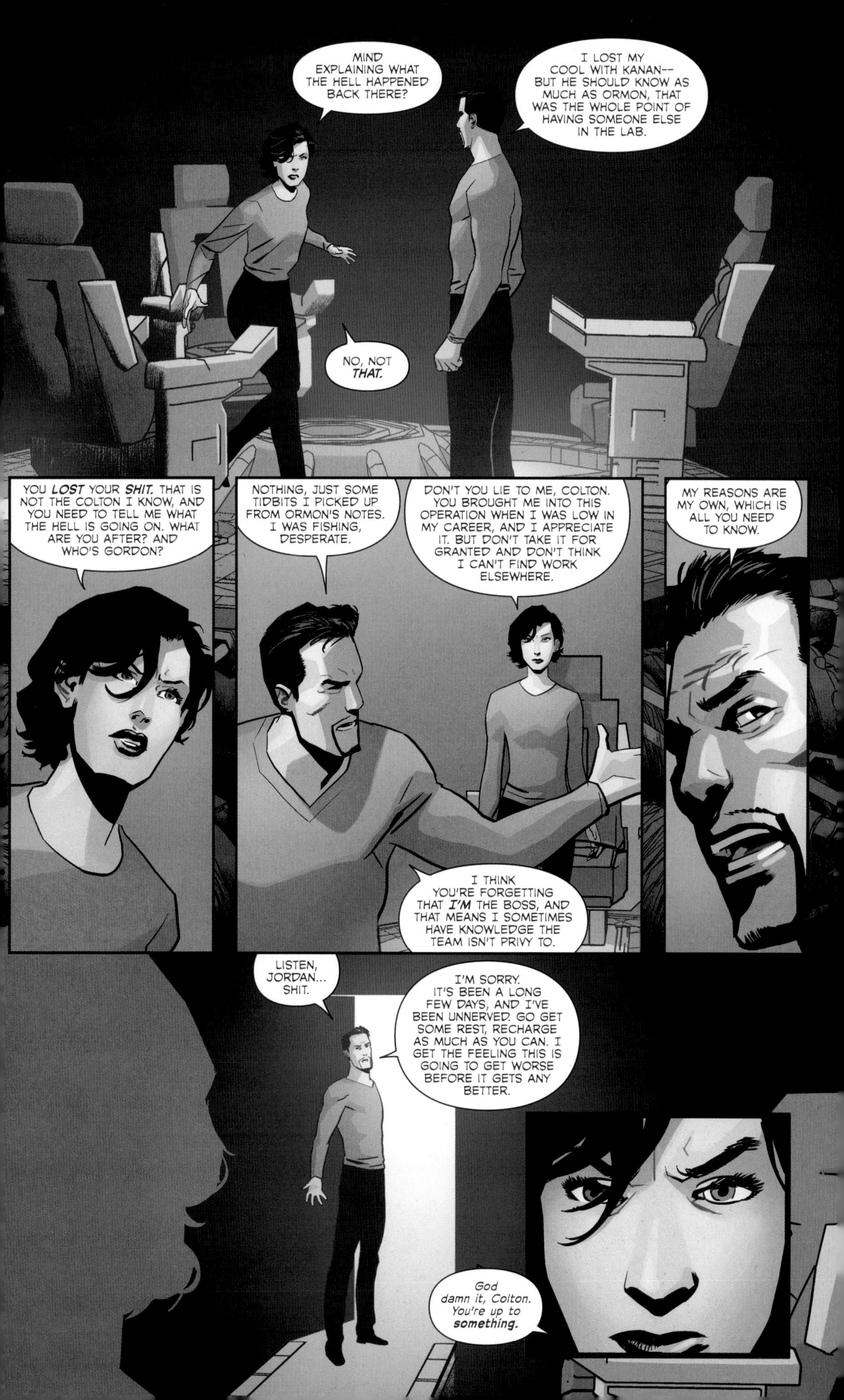

MIND EXPLAINING WHAT THE HELL HAPPENED BACK THERE?
I LOST MY COOL WITH KANAN-- BUT HE SHOULD KNOW AS MUCH AS ORMON, THAT WAS THE WHOLE POINT OF HAVING SOMEONE ELSE IN THE LAB.
NO, NOT ***THAT.***
YOU ***LOST*** YOUR ***SHIT.*** THAT IS NOT THE COLTON I KNOW, AND YOU NEED TO TELL ME WHAT THE HELL IS GOING ON. WHAT ARE YOU AFTER? AND WHO'S GORDON?
NOTHING, JUST SOME TIDBITS I PICKED UP FROM ORMON'S NOTES. I WAS FISHING, DESPERATE.
DON'T YOU LIE TO ME, COLTON. YOU BROUGHT ME INTO THIS OPERATION WHEN I WAS LOW IN MY CAREER, AND I APPRECIATE IT. BUT DON'T TAKE IT FOR GRANTED AND DON'T THINK I CAN'T FIND WORK ELSEWHERE.
I THINK YOU'RE FORGETTING THAT ***I'M*** THE BOSS, AND THAT MEANS I SOMETIMES HAVE KNOWLEDGE THE TEAM ISN'T PRIVY TO.
MY REASONS ARE MY OWN, WHICH IS ALL YOU NEED TO KNOW.
LISTEN, JORDAN... SHIT.
I'M SORRY. IT'S BEEN A LONG FEW DAYS, AND I'VE BEEN UNNERVED. GO GET SOME REST, RECHARGE AS MUCH AS YOU CAN. I GET THE FEELING THIS IS GOING TO GET WORSE BEFORE IT GETS ANY BETTER.
God damn it, Colton. You're up to ***something.***

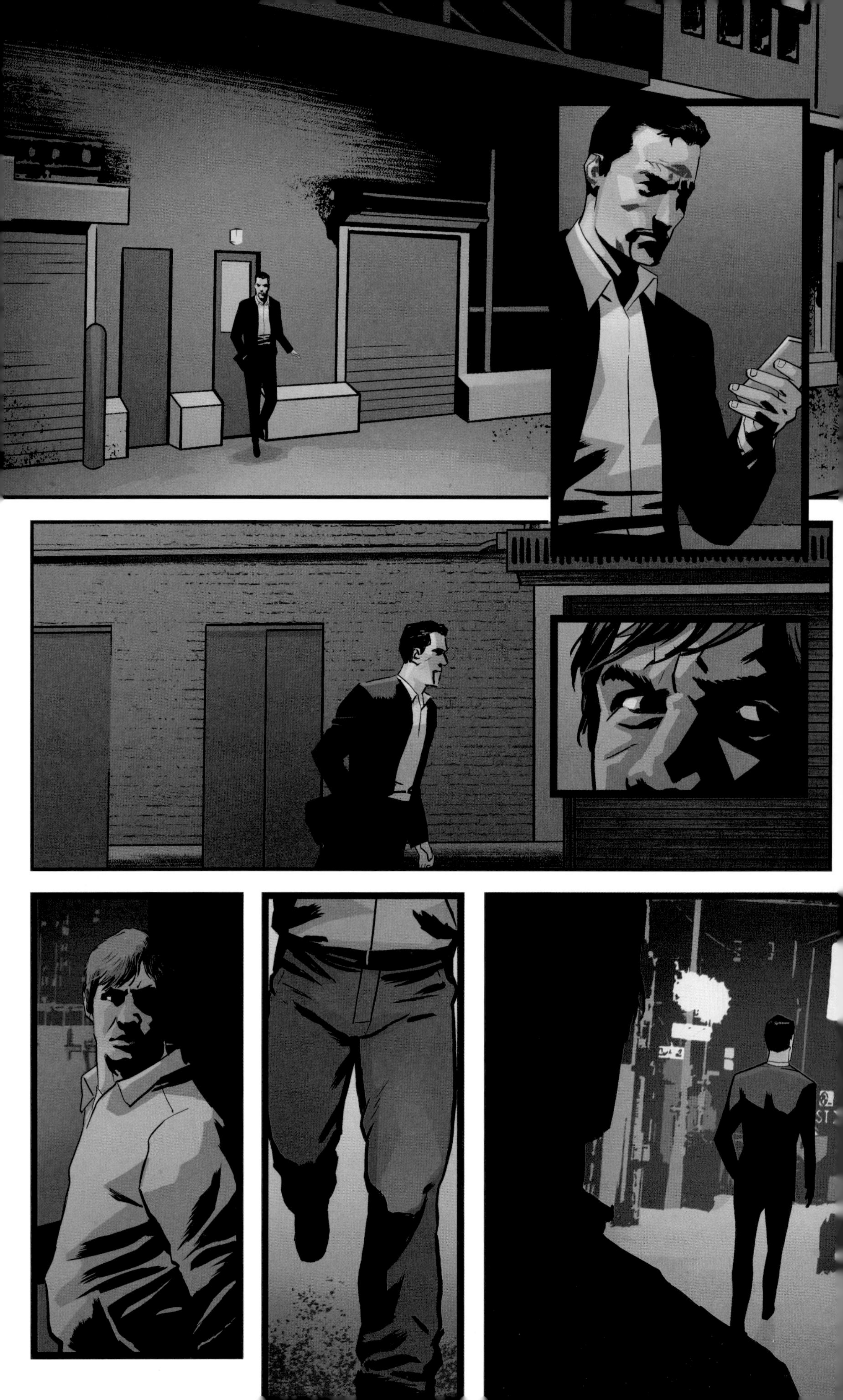

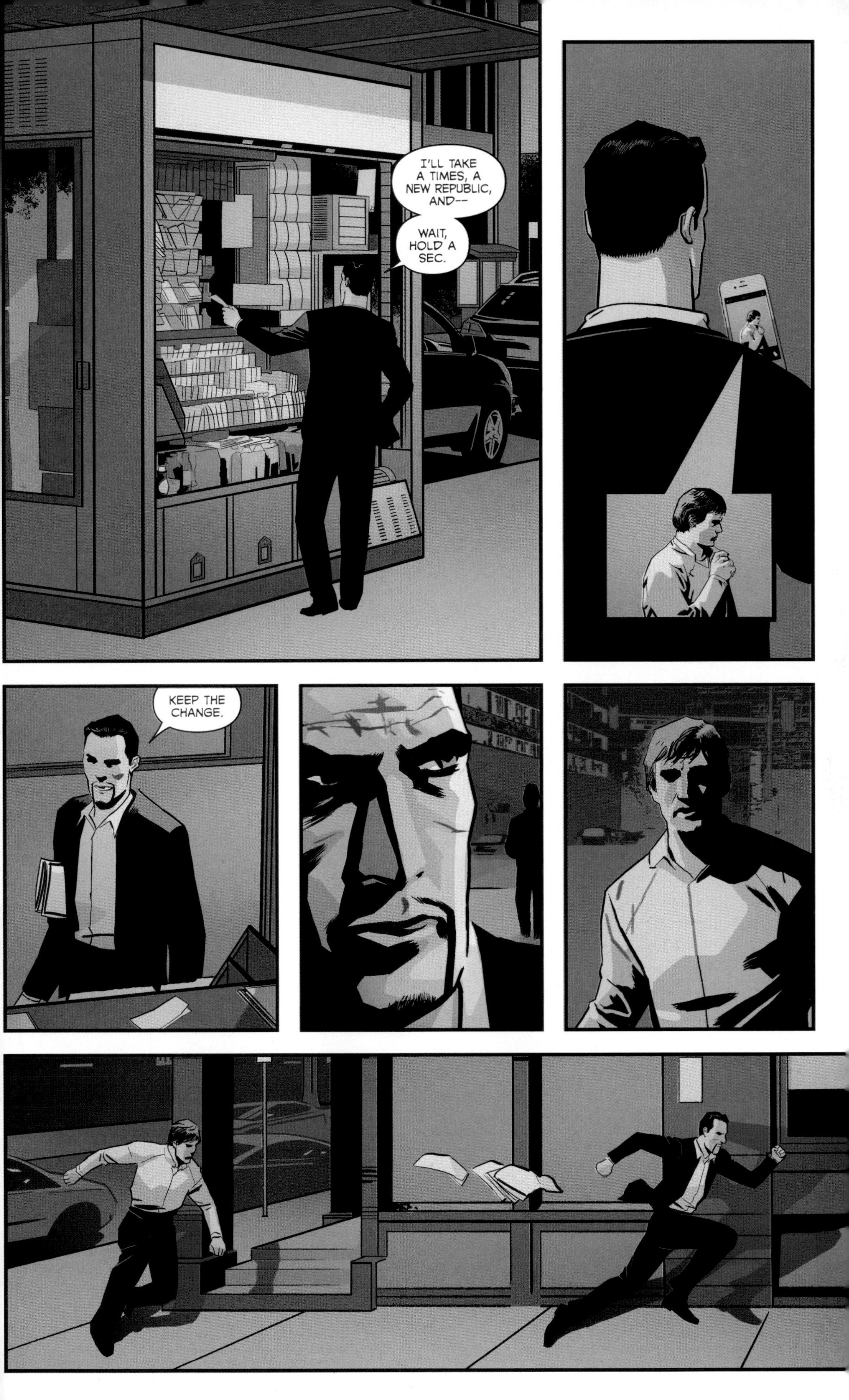
I'LL TAKE A TIMES, A NEW REPUBLIC, AND--
WAIT, HOLD A SEC.
KEEP THE CHANGE.

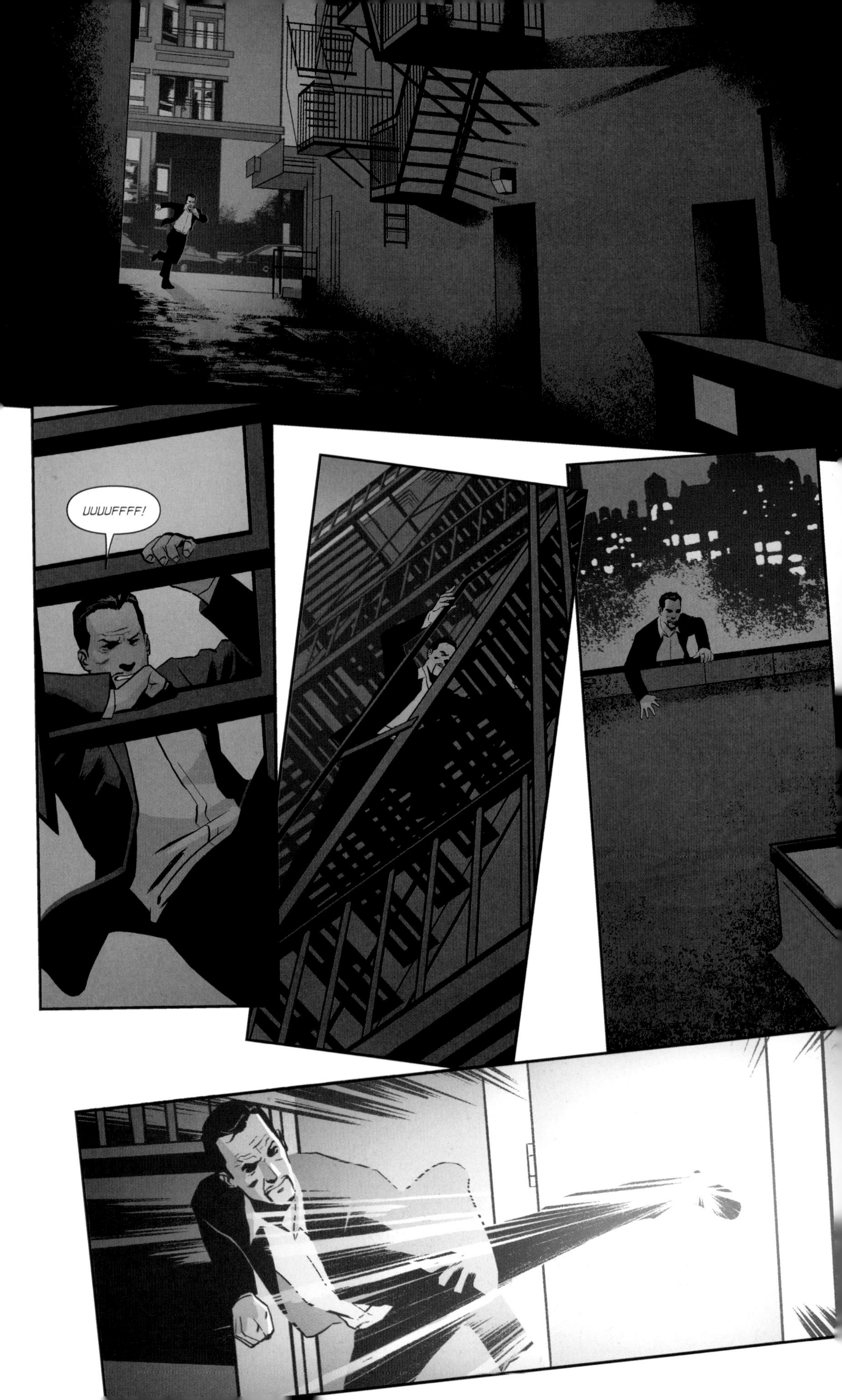
UUUUFFFF!

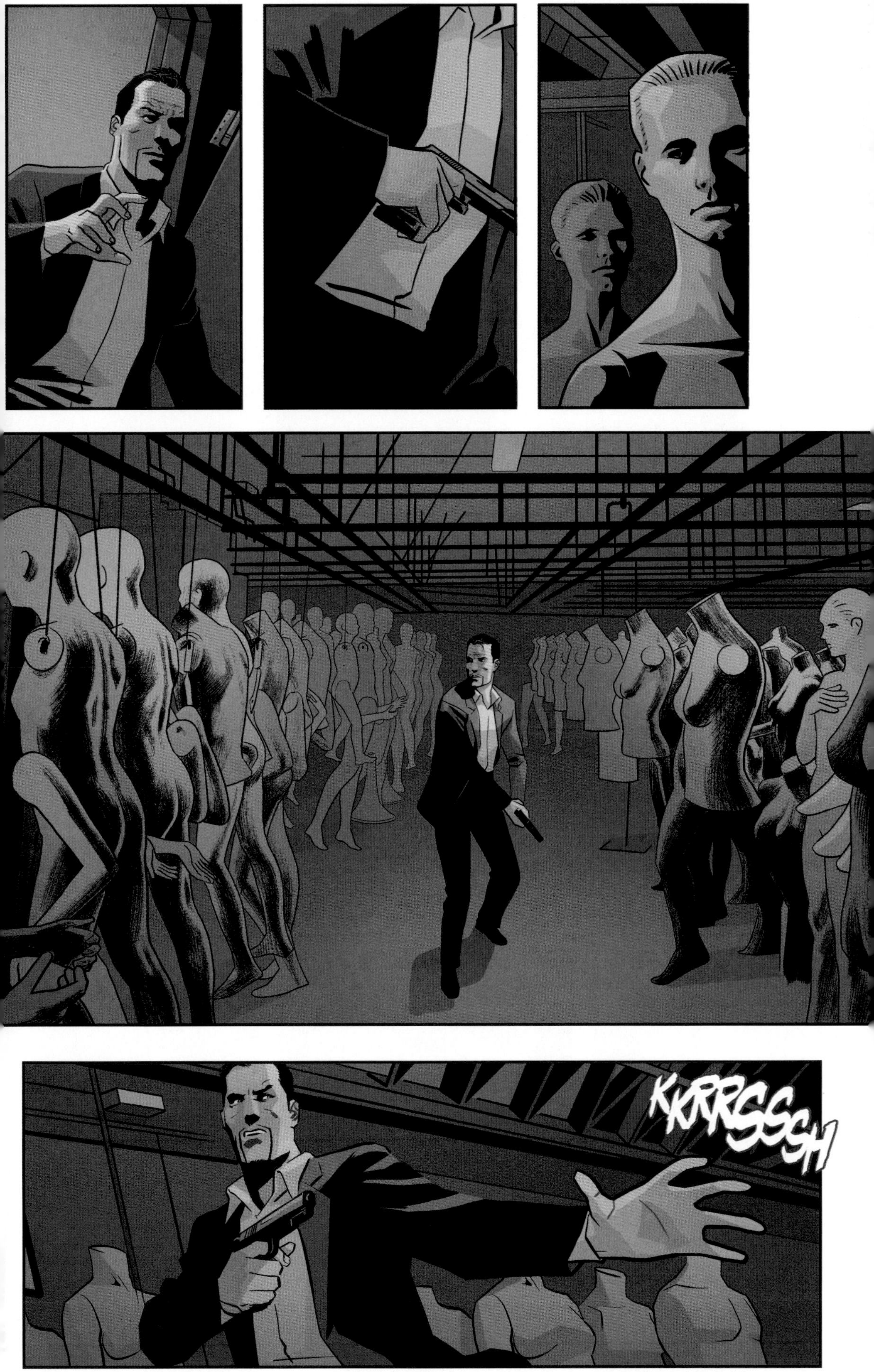
KKRRSSSH

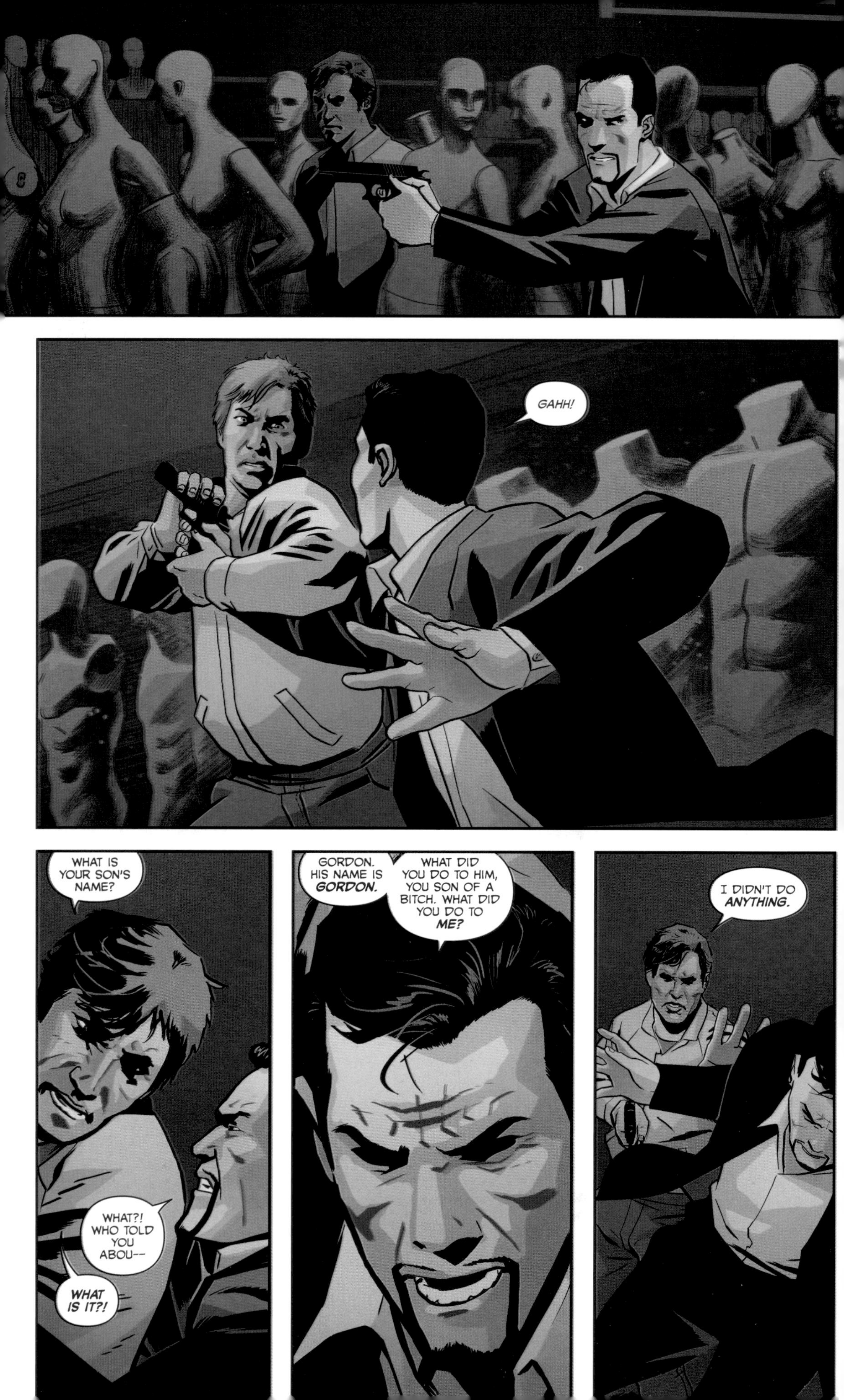
GAHH!
WHAT IS YOUR SON'S NAME?
WHAT?! WHO TOLD YOU ABOU--
WHAT IS IT?!
GORDON. HIS NAME IS GORDON.
WHAT DID YOU DO TO HIM, YOU SON OF A BITCH. WHAT DID YOU DO TO ME?
I DIDN'T DO ANYTHING.

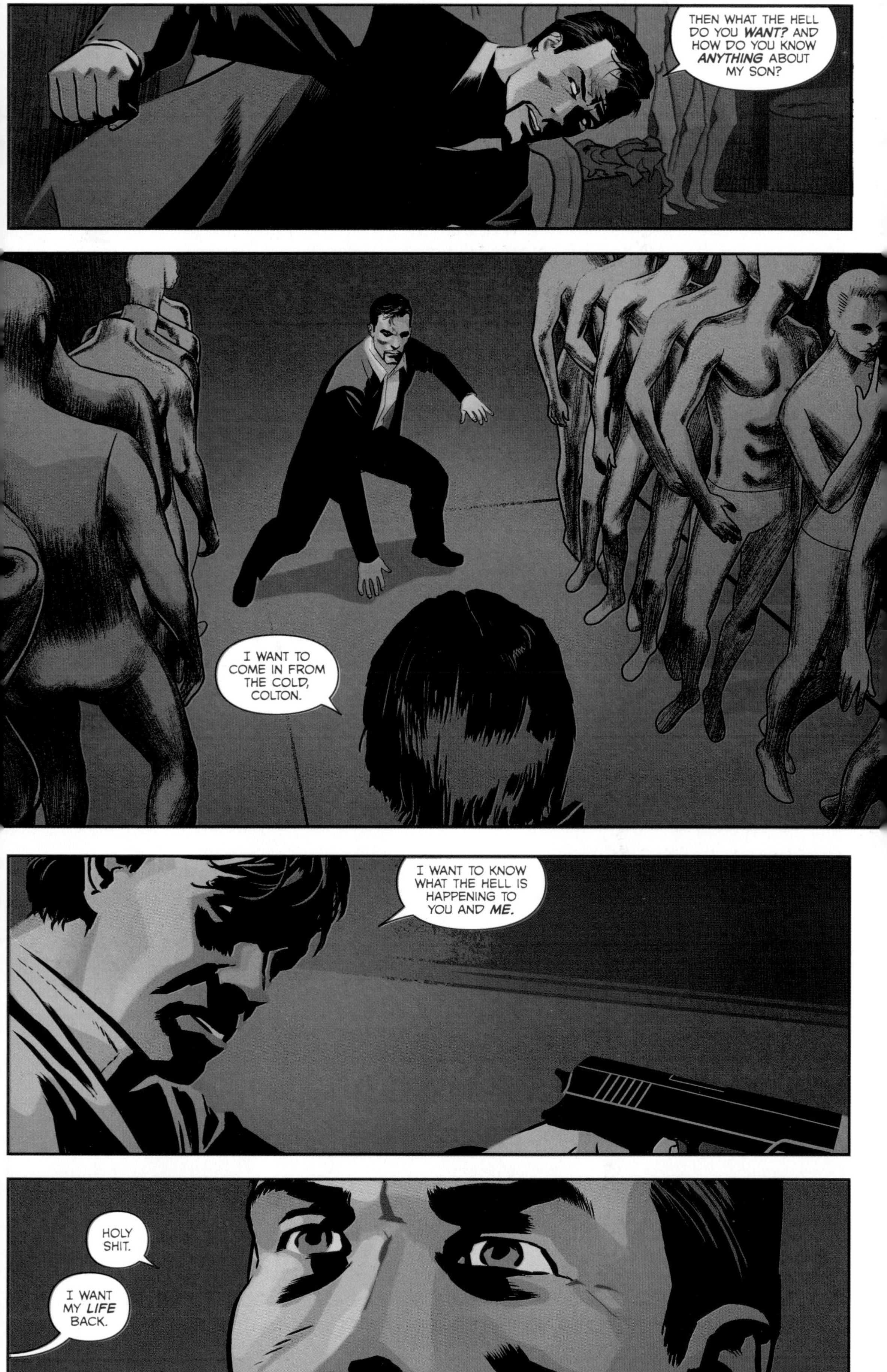
THEN WHAT THE HELL DO YOU WANT? AND HOW DO YOU KNOW ANYTHING ABOUT MY SON?
I WANT TO COME IN FROM THE COLD, COLTON.
I WANT TO KNOW WHAT THE HELL IS HAPPENING TO YOU AND ME.
HOLY SHIT.
I WANT MY LIFE BACK.

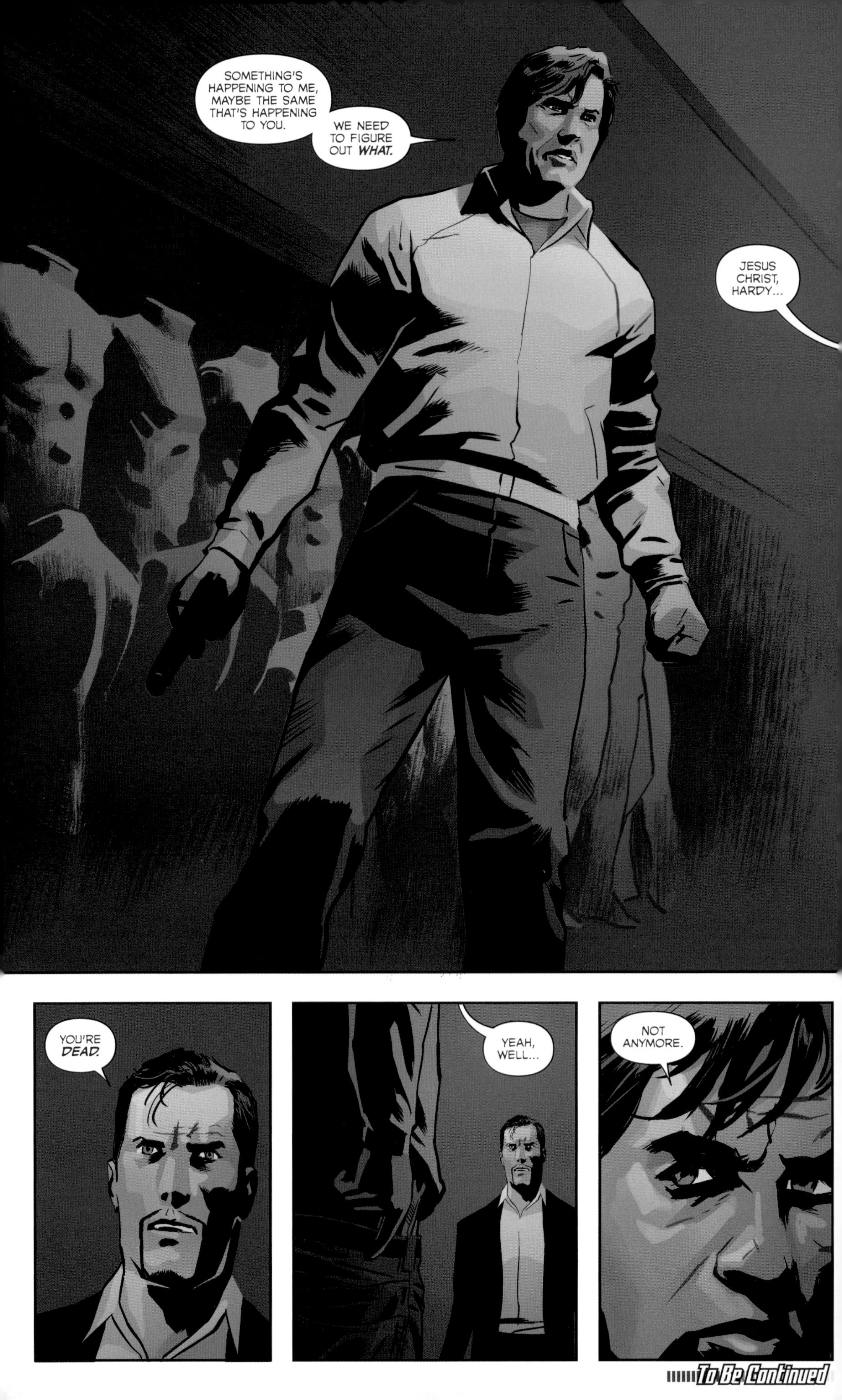
SOMETHING'S HAPPENING TO ME, MAYBE THE SAME THAT'S HAPPENING TO YOU.
WE NEED TO FIGURE OUT *WHAT.*
JESUS CHRIST, HARDY...
YOU'RE *DEAD.*
YEAH, WELL...
NOT ANYMORE.
To Be Continued

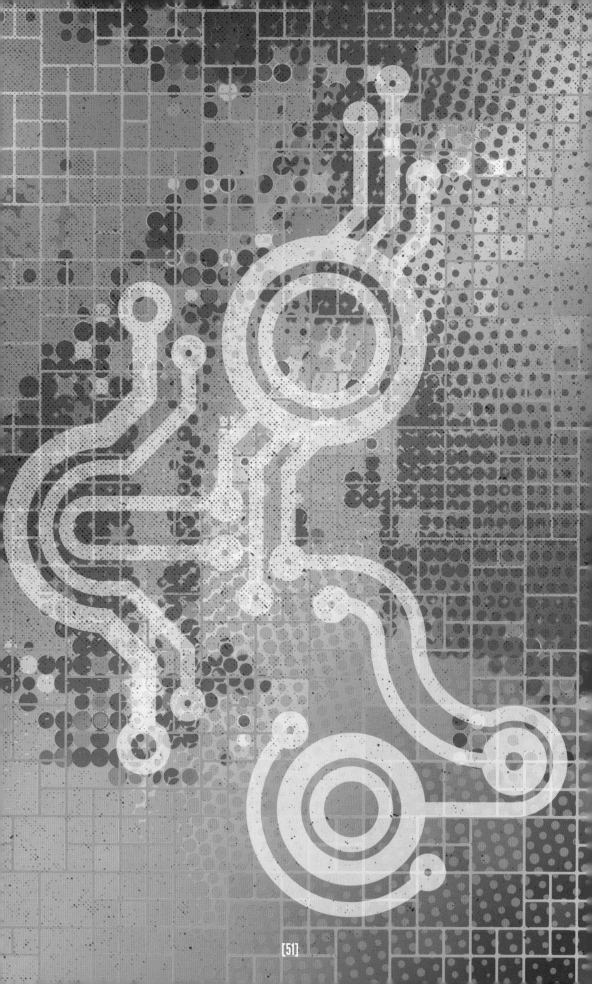

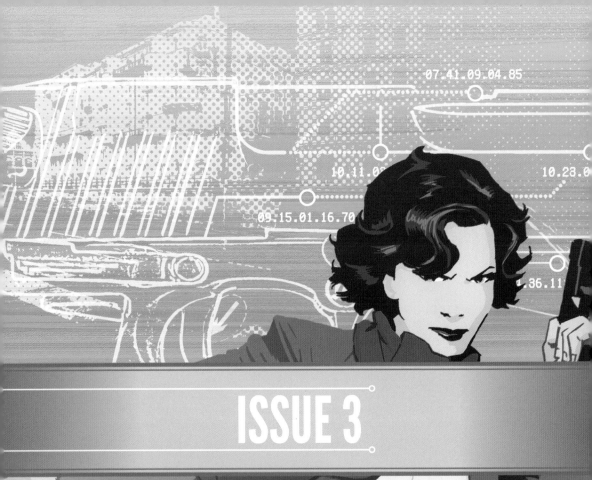

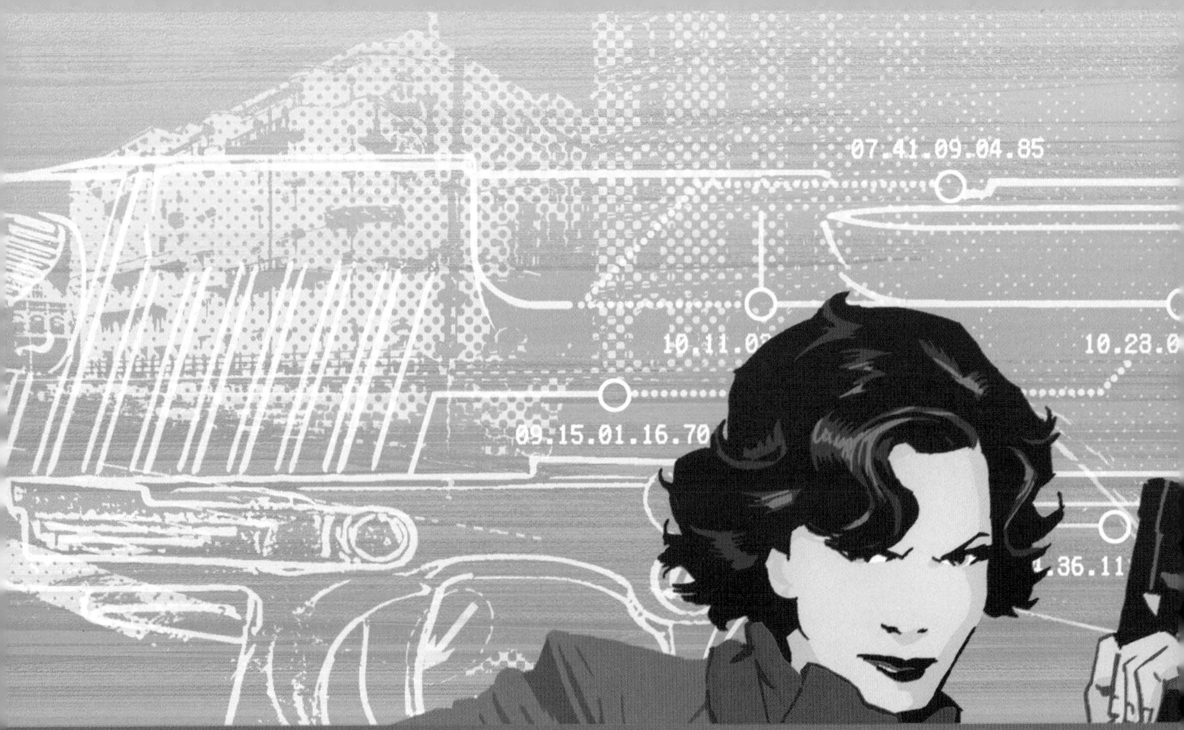
07.41.09.04.85
09.15.01.16.70

ISSUE 3

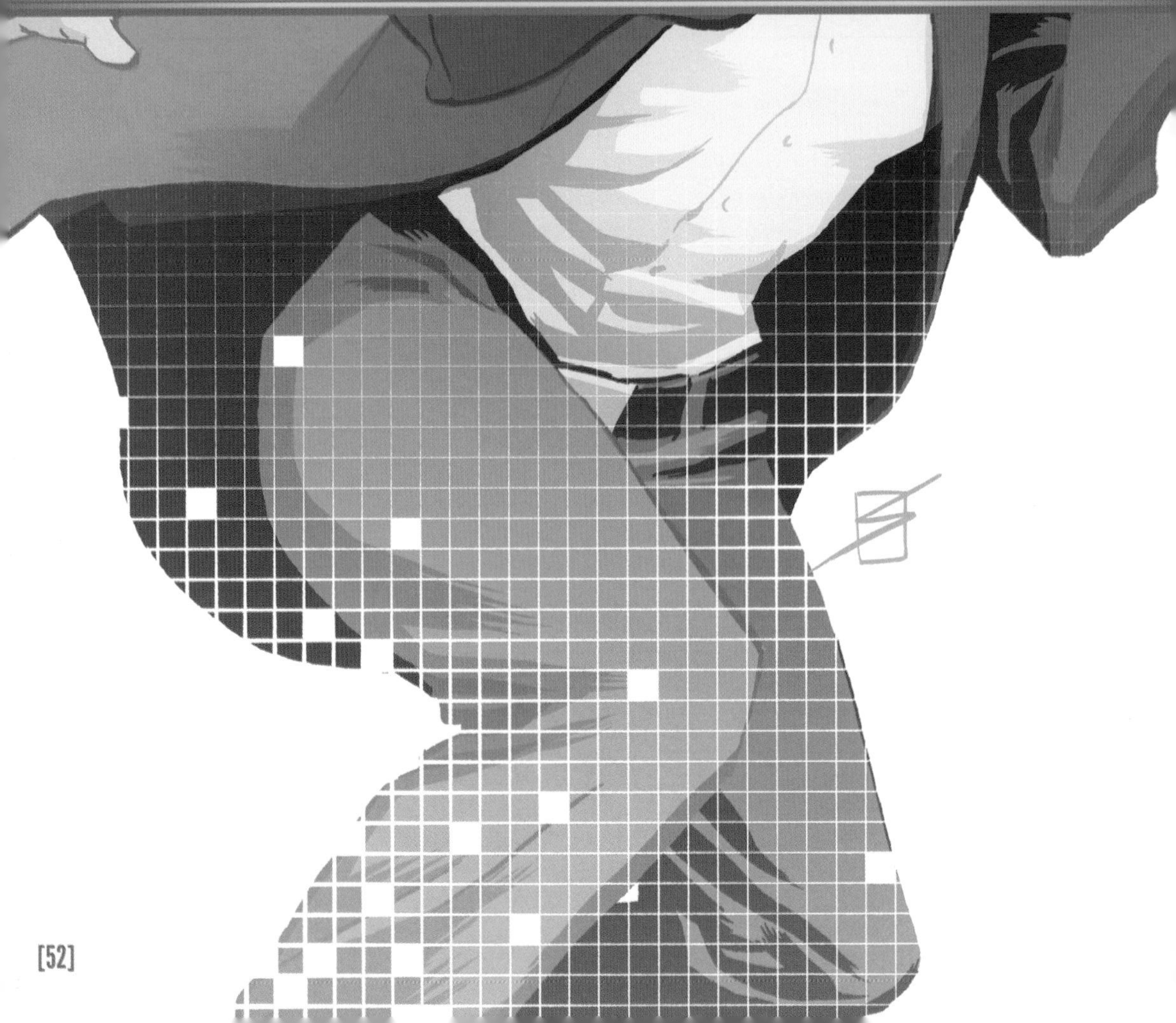

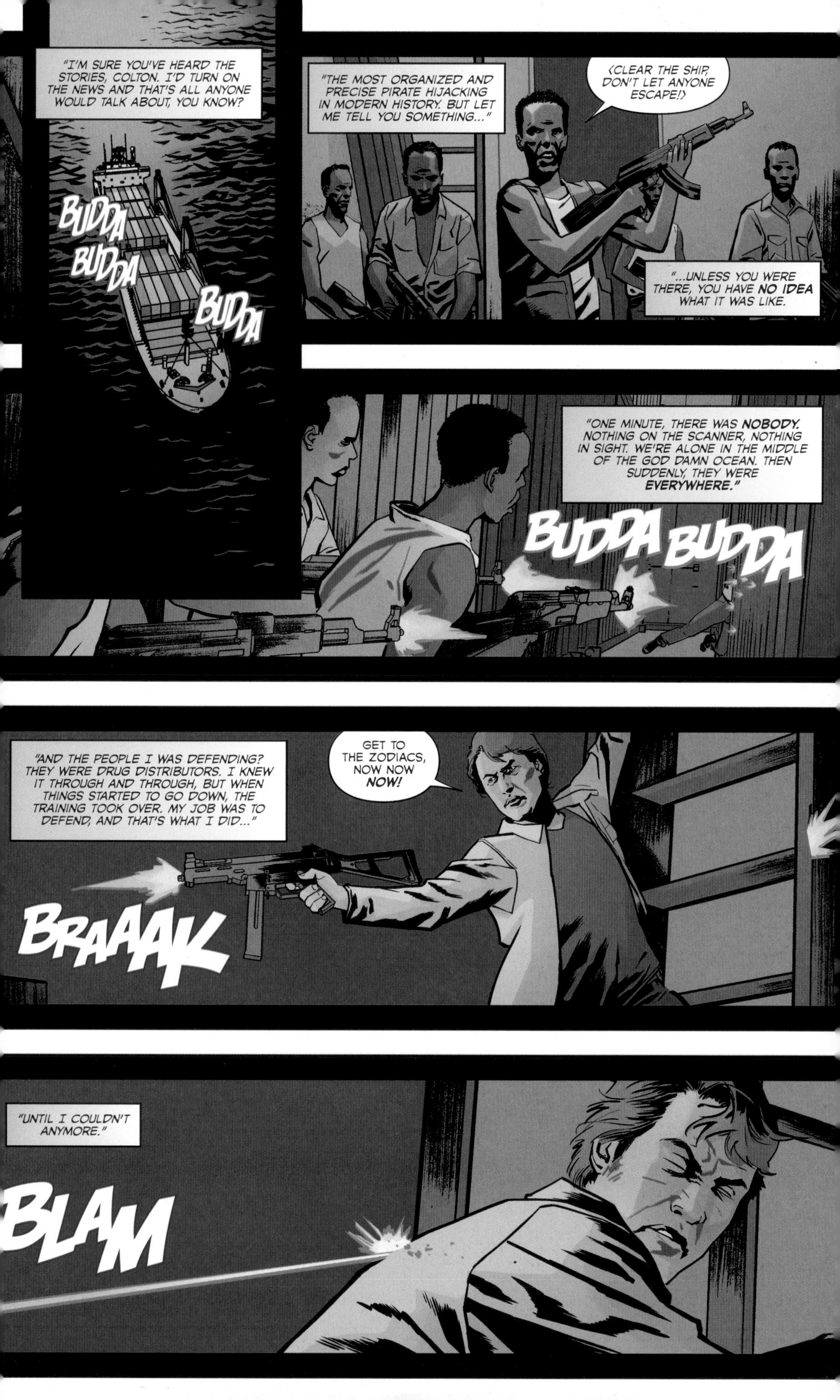
"I'M SURE YOU'VE HEARD THE STORIES, COLTON. I'D TURN ON THE NEWS AND THAT'S ALL ANYONE WOULD TALK ABOUT, YOU KNOW?
BUDDA
BUDDA
BUDDA
"THE MOST ORGANIZED AND PRECISE PIRATE HIJACKING IN MODERN HISTORY. BUT LET ME TELL YOU SOMETHING..."
‹CLEAR THE SHIP, DON'T LET ANYONE ESCAPE!›
"...UNLESS YOU WERE THERE, YOU HAVE NO IDEA WHAT IT WAS LIKE.
"ONE MINUTE, THERE WAS NOBODY. NOTHING ON THE SCANNER, NOTHING IN SIGHT. WE'RE ALONE IN THE MIDDLE OF THE GOD DAMN OCEAN. THEN SUDDENLY, THEY WERE EVERYWHERE."
BUDDA BUDDA
"AND THE PEOPLE I WAS DEFENDING? THEY WERE DRUG DISTRIBUTORS. I KNEW IT THROUGH AND THROUGH, BUT WHEN THINGS STARTED TO GO DOWN, THE TRAINING TOOK OVER. MY JOB WAS TO DEFEND, AND THAT'S WHAT I DID..."
GET TO THE ZODIACS, NOW NOW NOW!
BRAAAK
"UNTIL I COULDN'T ANYMORE."
BLAM

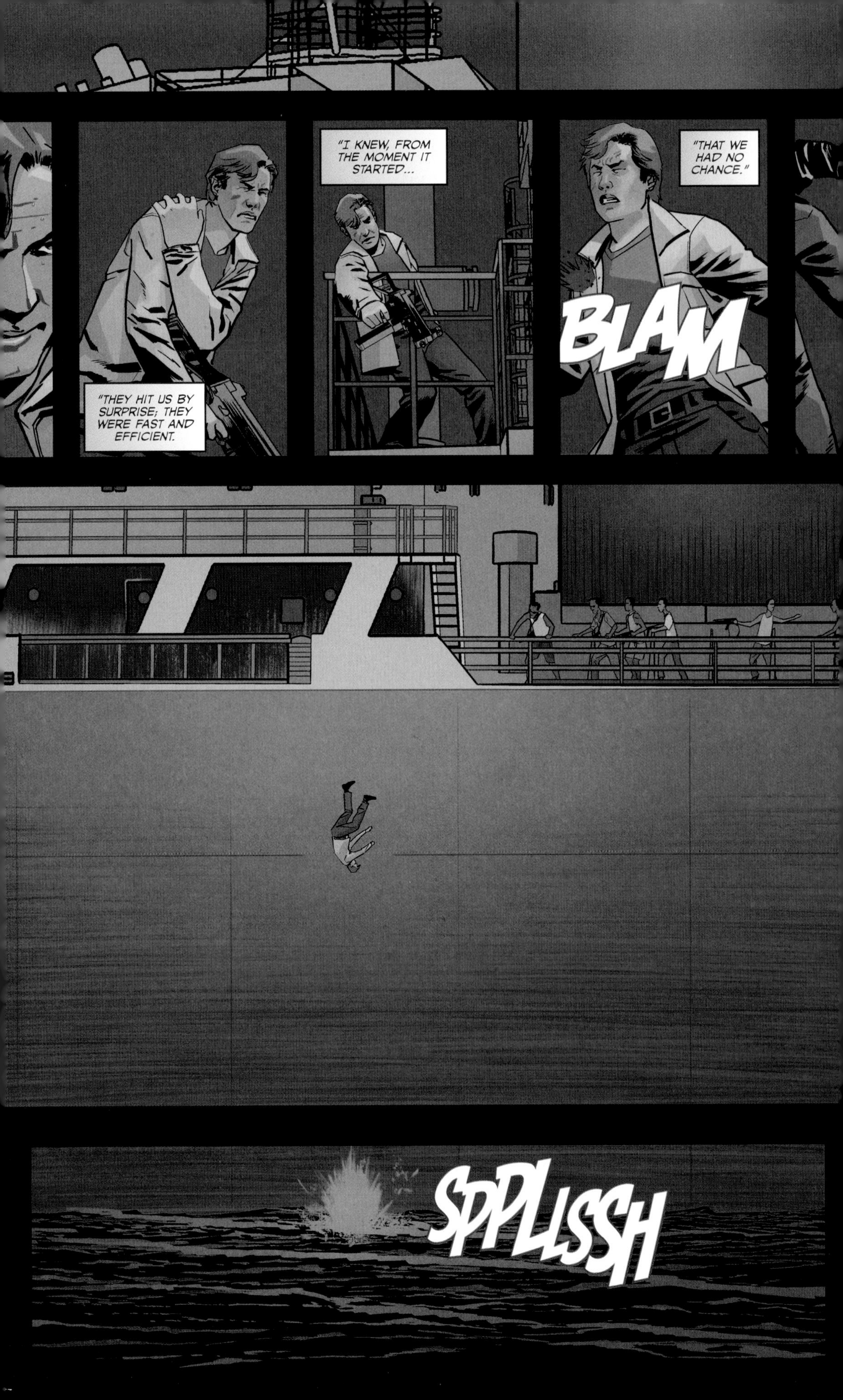
"THEY HIT US BY SURPRISE; THEY WERE FAST AND EFFICIENT.
"I KNEW, FROM THE MOMENT IT STARTED...
"THAT WE HAD NO CHANCE."
BLAM
SPPLSSH

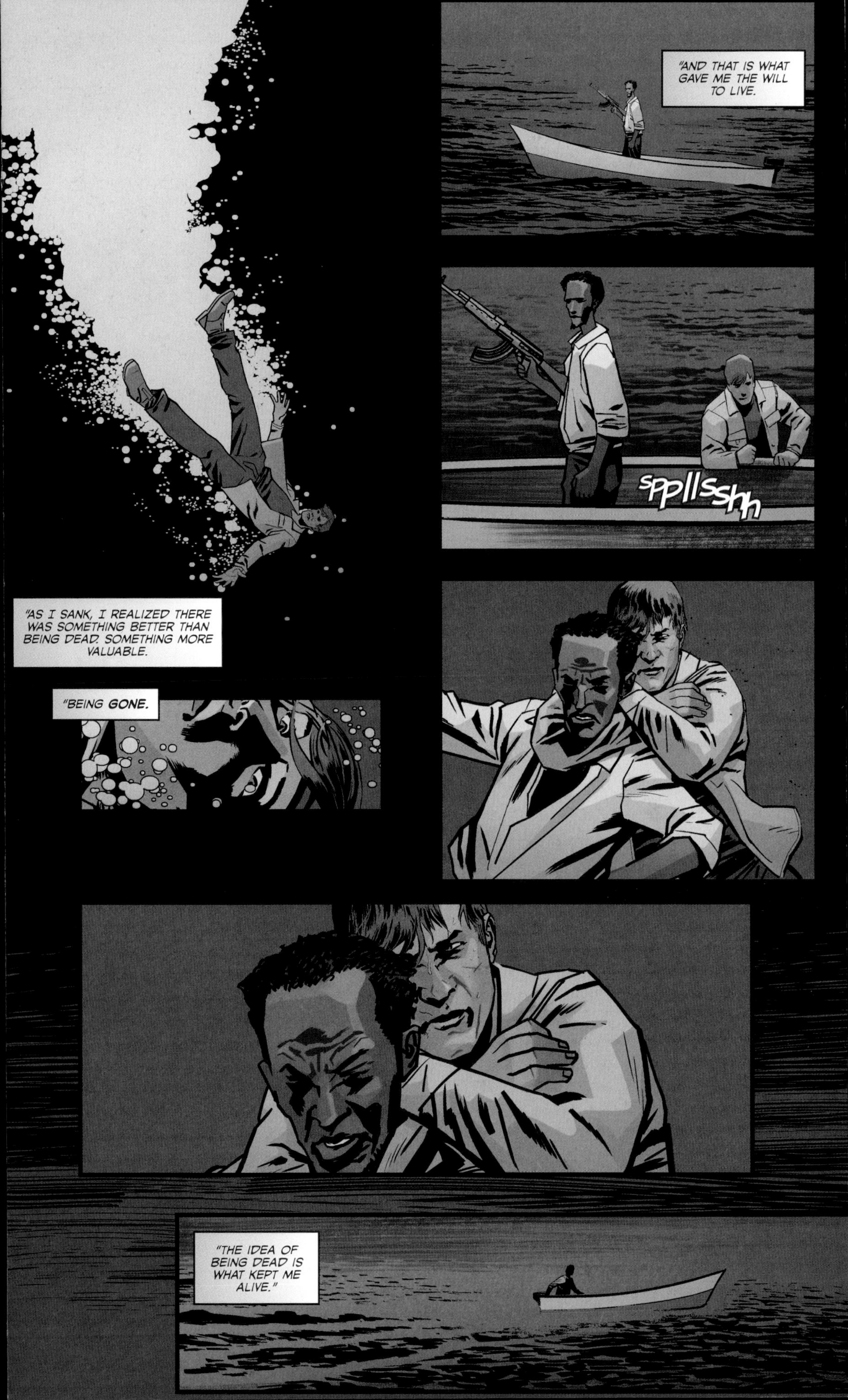
"AND THAT IS WHAT GAVE ME THE WILL TO LIVE.
SPPLLSSHH
"AS I SANK, I REALIZED THERE WAS SOMETHING BETTER THAN BEING DEAD. SOMETHING MORE VALUABLE.
"BEING GONE.
"THE IDEA OF BEING DEAD IS WHAT KEPT ME ALIVE."

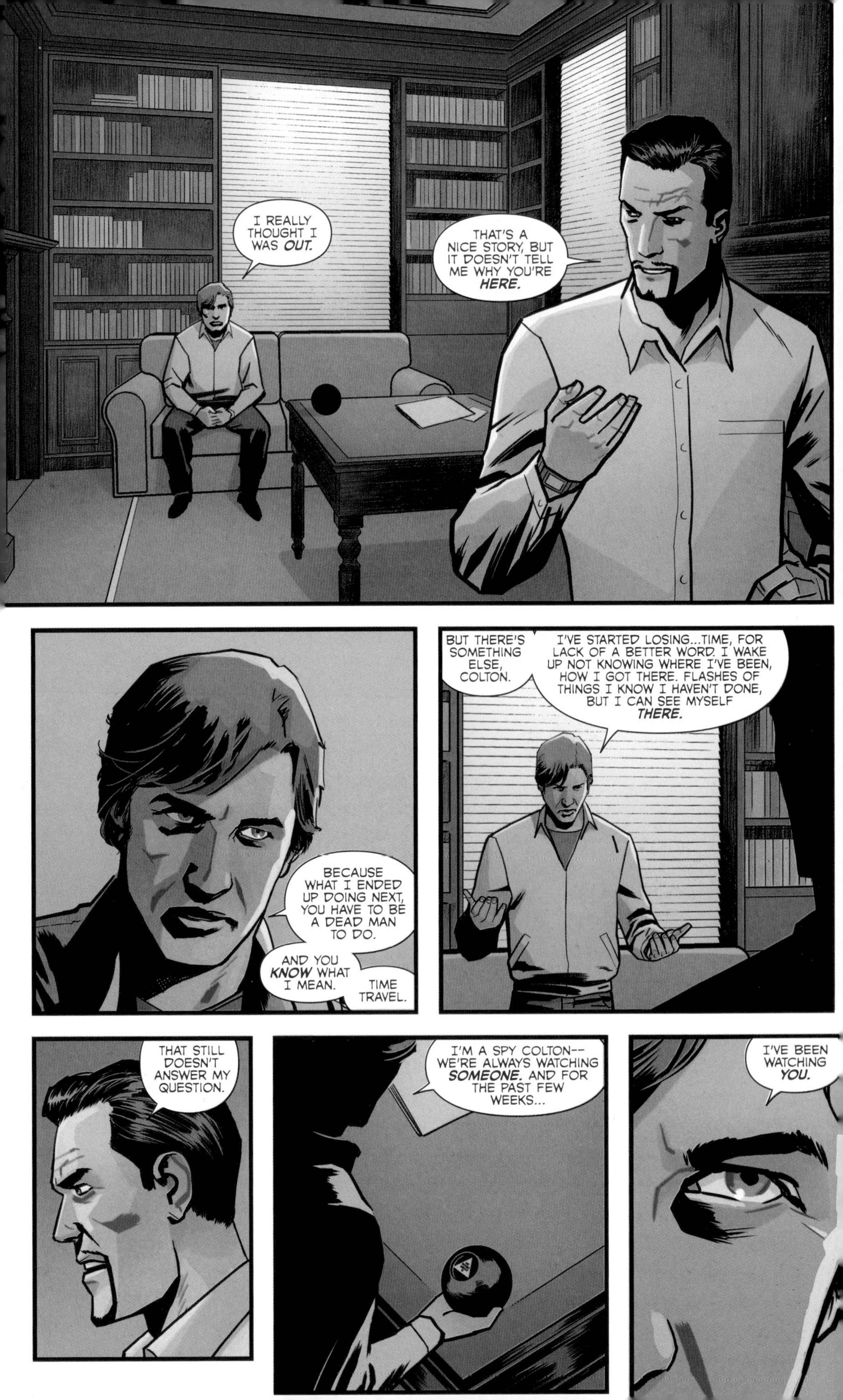
I REALLY THOUGHT I WAS OUT.
THAT'S A NICE STORY, BUT IT DOESN'T TELL ME WHY YOU'RE HERE.
BUT THERE'S SOMETHING ELSE, COLTON.
I'VE STARTED LOSING...TIME, FOR LACK OF A BETTER WORD. I WAKE UP NOT KNOWING WHERE I'VE BEEN, HOW I GOT THERE. FLASHES OF THINGS I KNOW I HAVEN'T DONE, BUT I CAN SEE MYSELF THERE.
BECAUSE WHAT I ENDED UP DOING NEXT, YOU HAVE TO BE A DEAD MAN TO DO.
AND YOU KNOW WHAT I MEAN.
TIME TRAVEL.
THAT STILL DOESN'T ANSWER MY QUESTION.
I'M A SPY COLTON-- WE'RE ALWAYS WATCHING SOMEONE. AND FOR THE PAST FEW WEEKS...
I'VE BEEN WATCHING YOU.

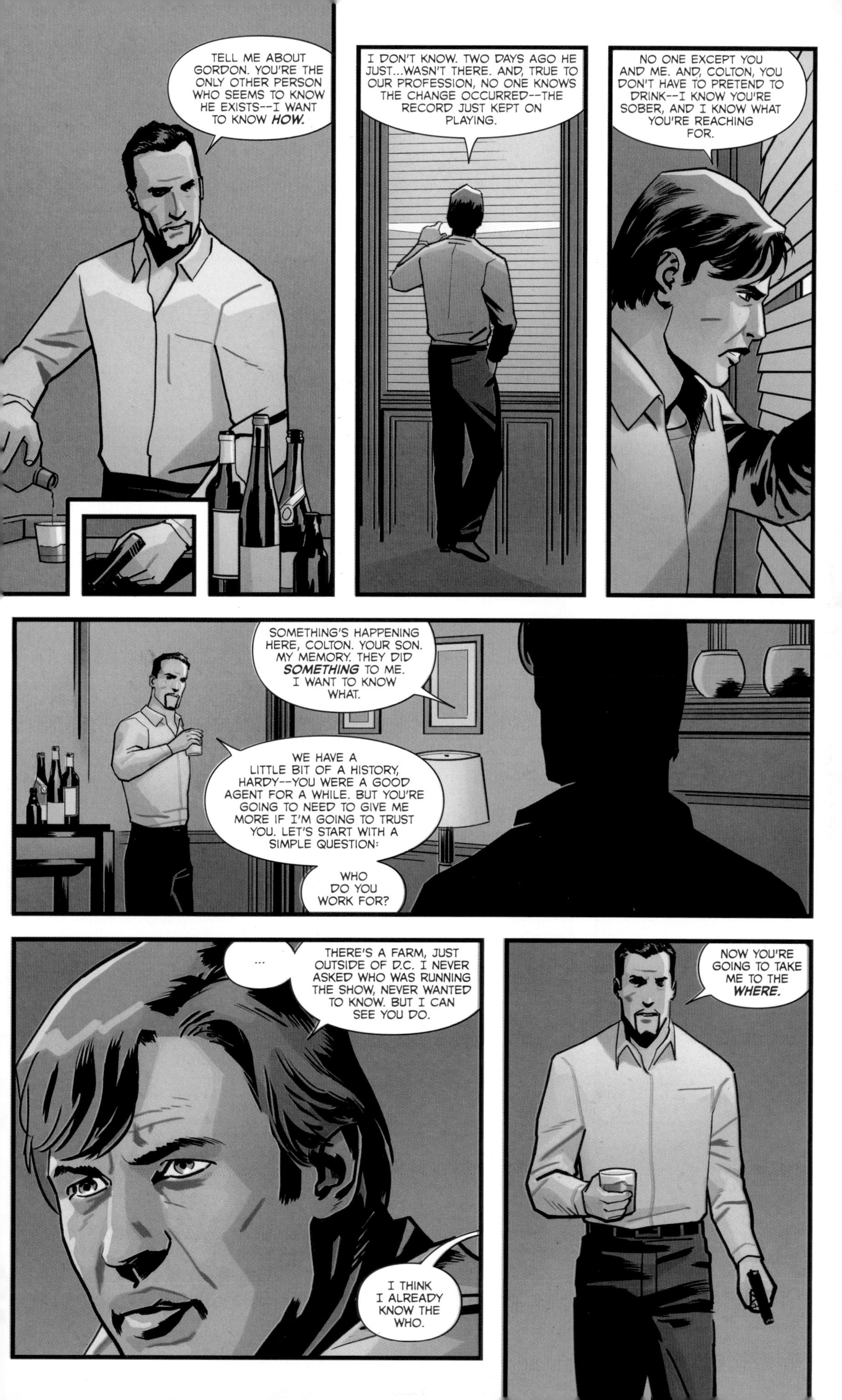
TELL ME ABOUT GORDON. YOU'RE THE ONLY OTHER PERSON WHO SEEMS TO KNOW HE EXISTS--I WANT TO KNOW HOW.
I DON'T KNOW. TWO DAYS AGO HE JUST...WASN'T THERE. AND, TRUE TO OUR PROFESSION, NO ONE KNOWS THE CHANGE OCCURRED--THE RECORD JUST KEPT ON PLAYING.
NO ONE EXCEPT YOU AND ME. AND, COLTON, YOU DON'T HAVE TO PRETEND TO DRINK--I KNOW YOU'RE SOBER, AND I KNOW WHAT YOU'RE REACHING FOR.
SOMETHING'S HAPPENING HERE, COLTON. YOUR SON. MY MEMORY. THEY DID SOMETHING TO ME. I WANT TO KNOW WHAT.
WE HAVE A LITTLE BIT OF A HISTORY, HARDY--YOU WERE A GOOD AGENT FOR A WHILE. BUT YOU'RE GOING TO NEED TO GIVE ME MORE IF I'M GOING TO TRUST YOU. LET'S START WITH A SIMPLE QUESTION:
WHO DO YOU WORK FOR?
...
THERE'S A FARM, JUST OUTSIDE OF D.C. I NEVER ASKED WHO WAS RUNNING THE SHOW, NEVER WANTED TO KNOW. BUT I CAN SEE YOU DO.
I THINK I ALREADY KNOW THE WHO.
NOW YOU'RE GOING TO TAKE ME TO THE WHERE.

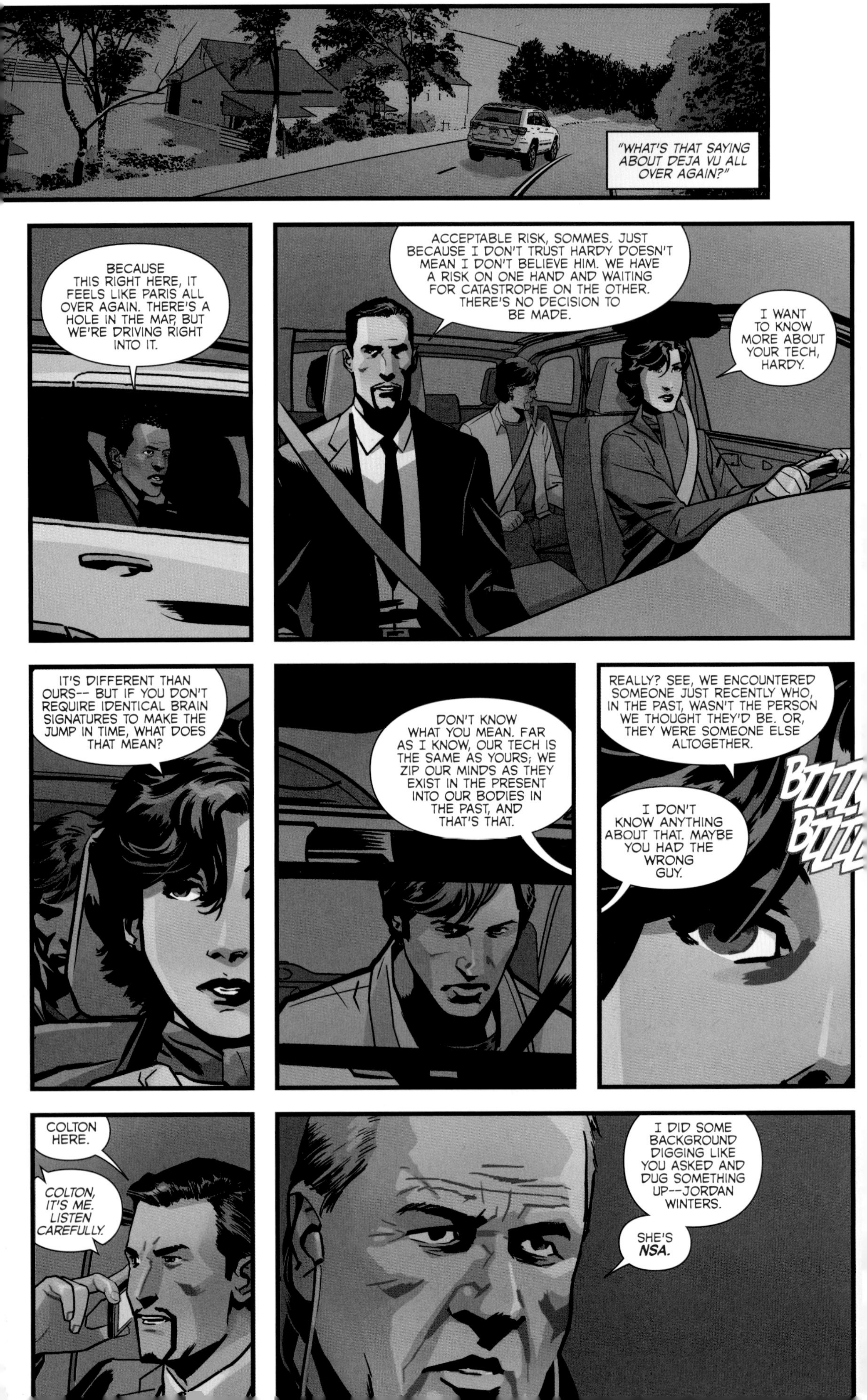
"WHAT'S THAT SAYING ABOUT DEJA VU ALL OVER AGAIN?"
BECAUSE THIS RIGHT HERE, IT FEELS LIKE PARIS ALL OVER AGAIN. THERE'S A HOLE IN THE MAP, BUT WE'RE DRIVING RIGHT INTO IT.
ACCEPTABLE RISK, SOMMES. JUST BECAUSE I DON'T TRUST HARDY DOESN'T MEAN I DON'T BELIEVE HIM. WE HAVE A RISK ON ONE HAND AND WAITING FOR CATASTROPHE ON THE OTHER. THERE'S NO DECISION TO BE MADE.
I WANT TO KNOW MORE ABOUT YOUR TECH, HARDY.
IT'S DIFFERENT THAN OURS-- BUT IF YOU DON'T REQUIRE IDENTICAL BRAIN SIGNATURES TO MAKE THE JUMP IN TIME, WHAT DOES THAT MEAN?
DON'T KNOW WHAT YOU MEAN. FAR AS I KNOW, OUR TECH IS THE SAME AS YOURS; WE ZIP OUR MINDS AS THEY EXIST IN THE PRESENT INTO OUR BODIES IN THE PAST, AND THAT'S THAT.
REALLY? SEE, WE ENCOUNTERED SOMEONE JUST RECENTLY WHO, IN THE PAST, WASN'T THE PERSON WE THOUGHT THEY'D BE. OR, THEY WERE SOMEONE ELSE ALTOGETHER.
I DON'T KNOW ANYTHING ABOUT THAT. MAYBE YOU HAD THE WRONG GUY.
COLTON HERE.
COLTON, IT'S ME. LISTEN CAREFULLY.
I DID SOME BACKGROUND DIGGING LIKE YOU ASKED AND DUG SOMETHING UP--JORDAN WINTERS.
SHE'S NSA.

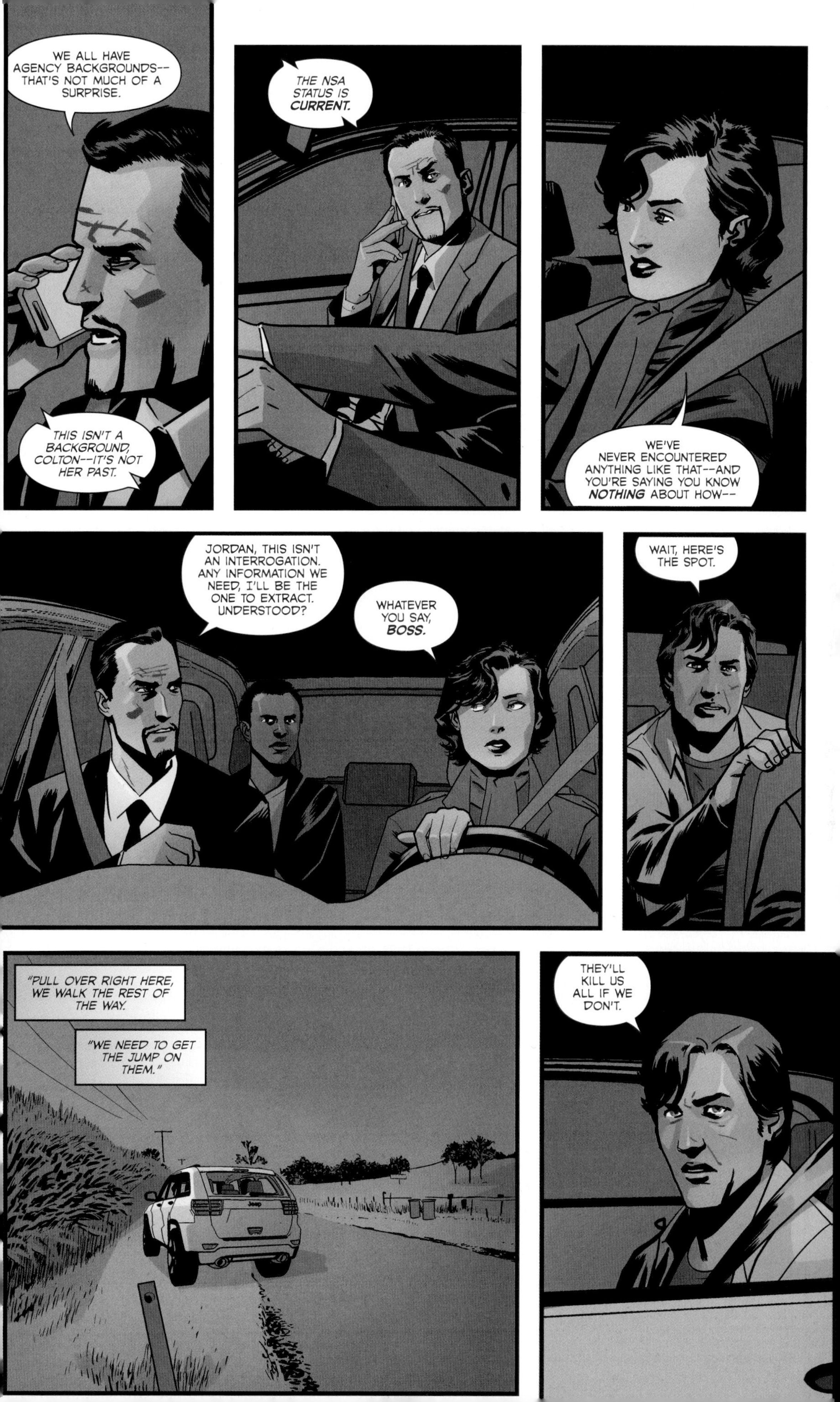
WE ALL HAVE AGENCY BACKGROUNDS-- THAT'S NOT MUCH OF A SURPRISE.
THIS ISN'T A BACKGROUND, COLTON--IT'S NOT HER PAST.
THE NSA STATUS IS CURRENT.
WE'VE NEVER ENCOUNTERED ANYTHING LIKE THAT--AND YOU'RE SAYING YOU KNOW NOTHING ABOUT HOW--
JORDAN, THIS ISN'T AN INTERROGATION. ANY INFORMATION WE NEED, I'LL BE THE ONE TO EXTRACT. UNDERSTOOD?
WHATEVER YOU SAY, BOSS.
WAIT, HERE'S THE SPOT.
"PULL OVER RIGHT HERE, WE WALK THE REST OF THE WAY.
"WE NEED TO GET THE JUMP ON THEM."
THEY'LL KILL US ALL IF WE DON'T.

DAMN IT, DAMN IT, DAMN IT.
WHAT WERE YOU DOING, ORMON? THERE'S NOT ONE CEREBRAL IDENTITY IN HERE--SO WHAT ARE YOU SENDING A CONSCIOUSNESS BACK TO? THAT'S HOW THIS WORKS, ONE MIND BACK TO ITS OWN--
WAIT.
TO SEND A MIND BACK IN TIME IT NEEDS AN ANCHOR, SOMETHING TO GRAFT ITSELF ONTO. BUT YOU FOUND SOMETHING, DIDN'T YOU? YOU DIDN'T NEED AN IDENTICAL MIND...
WE JUST NEEDED SHARED KNOWLEDGE.
SOMETHING LIKE, LET'S SAY...

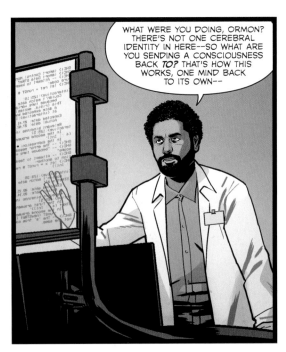

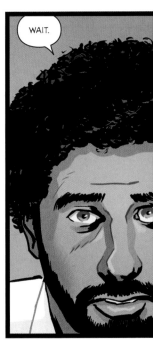

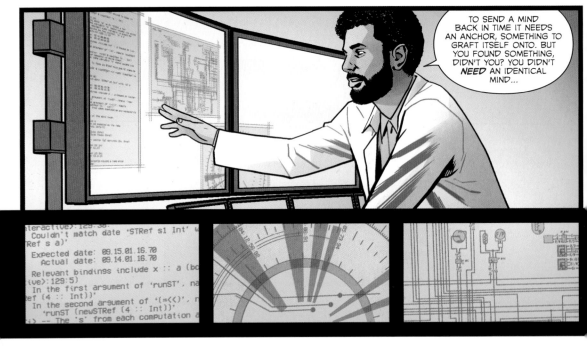

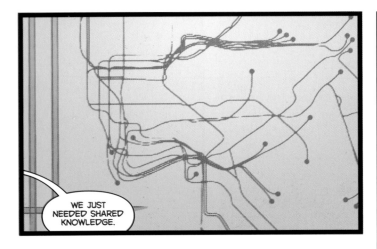

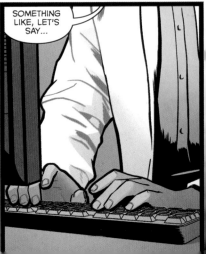

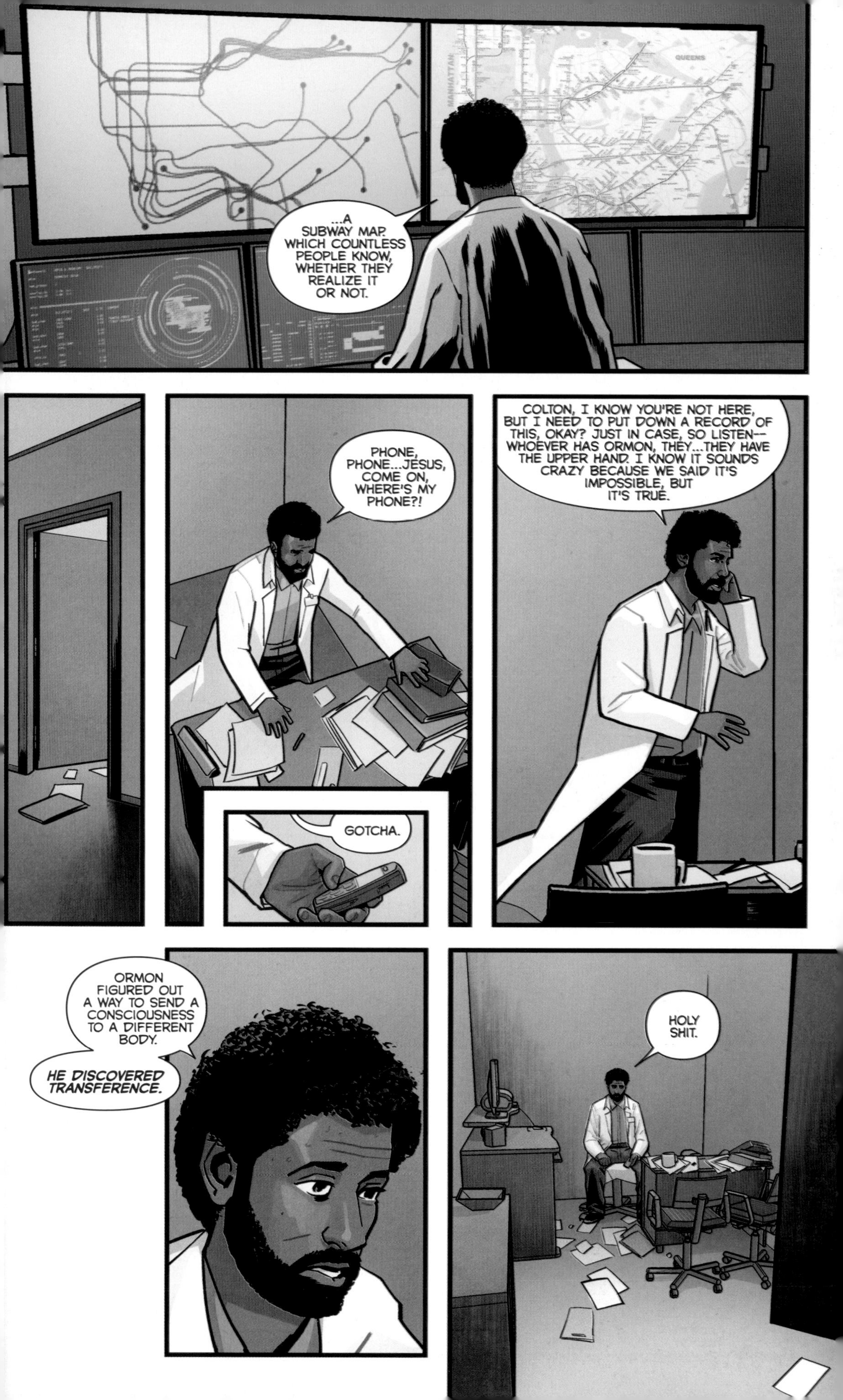

...A SUBWAY MAP. WHICH COUNTLESS PEOPLE KNOW, WHETHER THEY REALIZE IT OR NOT.
PHONE, PHONE...JESUS, COME ON, WHERE'S MY PHONE?!
GOTCHA.
COLTON, I KNOW YOU'RE NOT HERE, BUT I NEED TO PUT DOWN A RECORD OF THIS, OKAY? JUST IN CASE, SO LISTEN-- WHOEVER HAS ORMON, THEY...THEY HAVE THE UPPER HAND. I KNOW IT SOUNDS CRAZY BECAUSE WE SAID IT'S IMPOSSIBLE, BUT IT'S TRUE.
ORMON FIGURED OUT A WAY TO SEND A CONSCIOUSNESS TO A DIFFERENT BODY.
HE DISCOVERED TRANSFERENCE.
HOLY SHIT.

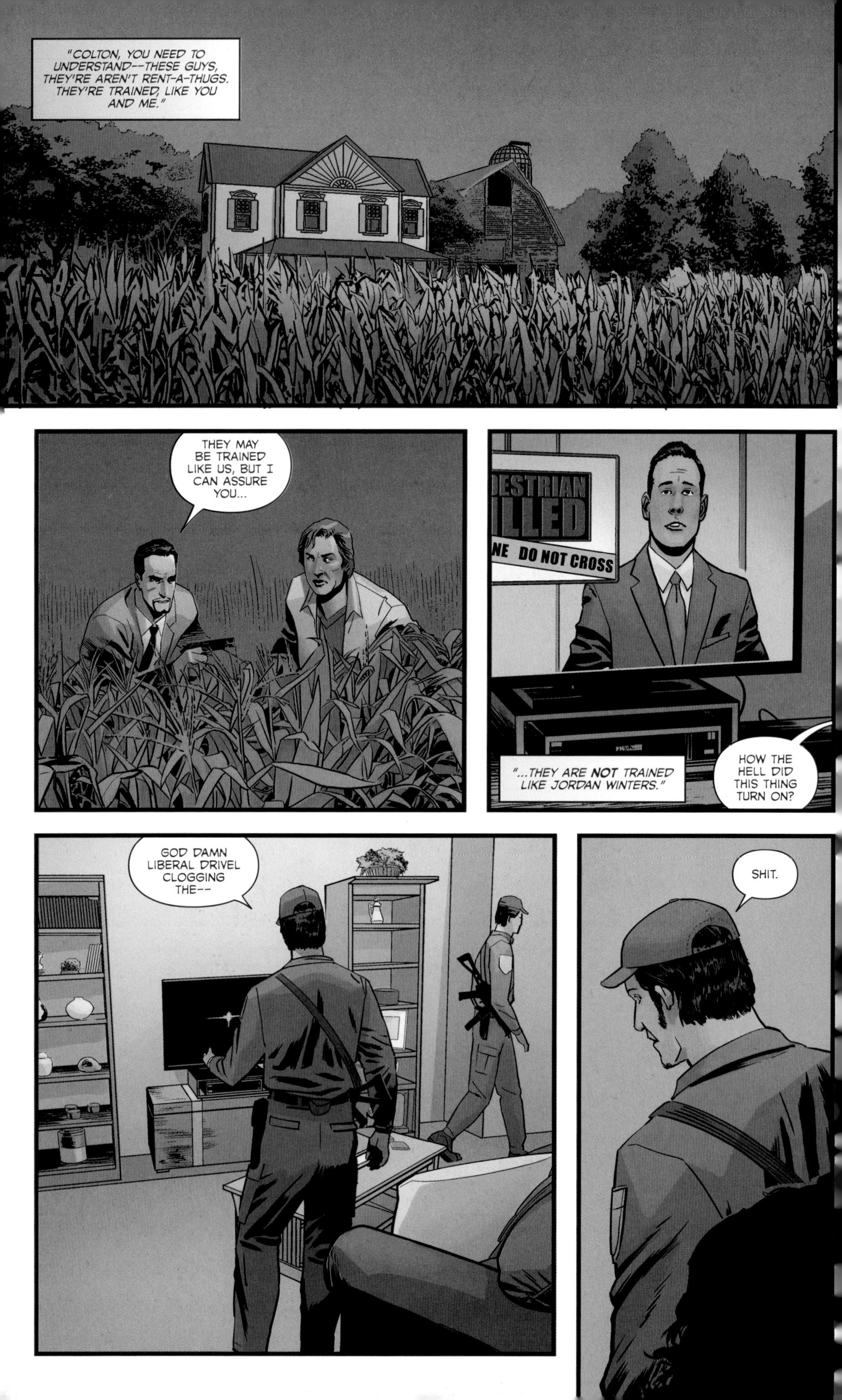
"COLTON, YOU NEED TO UNDERSTAND--THESE GUYS, THEY'RE AREN'T RENT-A-THUGS. THEY'RE TRAINED, LIKE YOU AND ME."
THEY MAY BE TRAINED LIKE US, BUT I CAN ASSURE YOU...
DESTRIAN
ILLED
NE DO NOT CROSS
"...THEY ARE NOT TRAINED LIKE JORDAN WINTERS."
HOW THE HELL DID THIS THING TURN ON?
GOD DAMN LIBERAL DRIVEL CLOGGING THE--
SHIT.

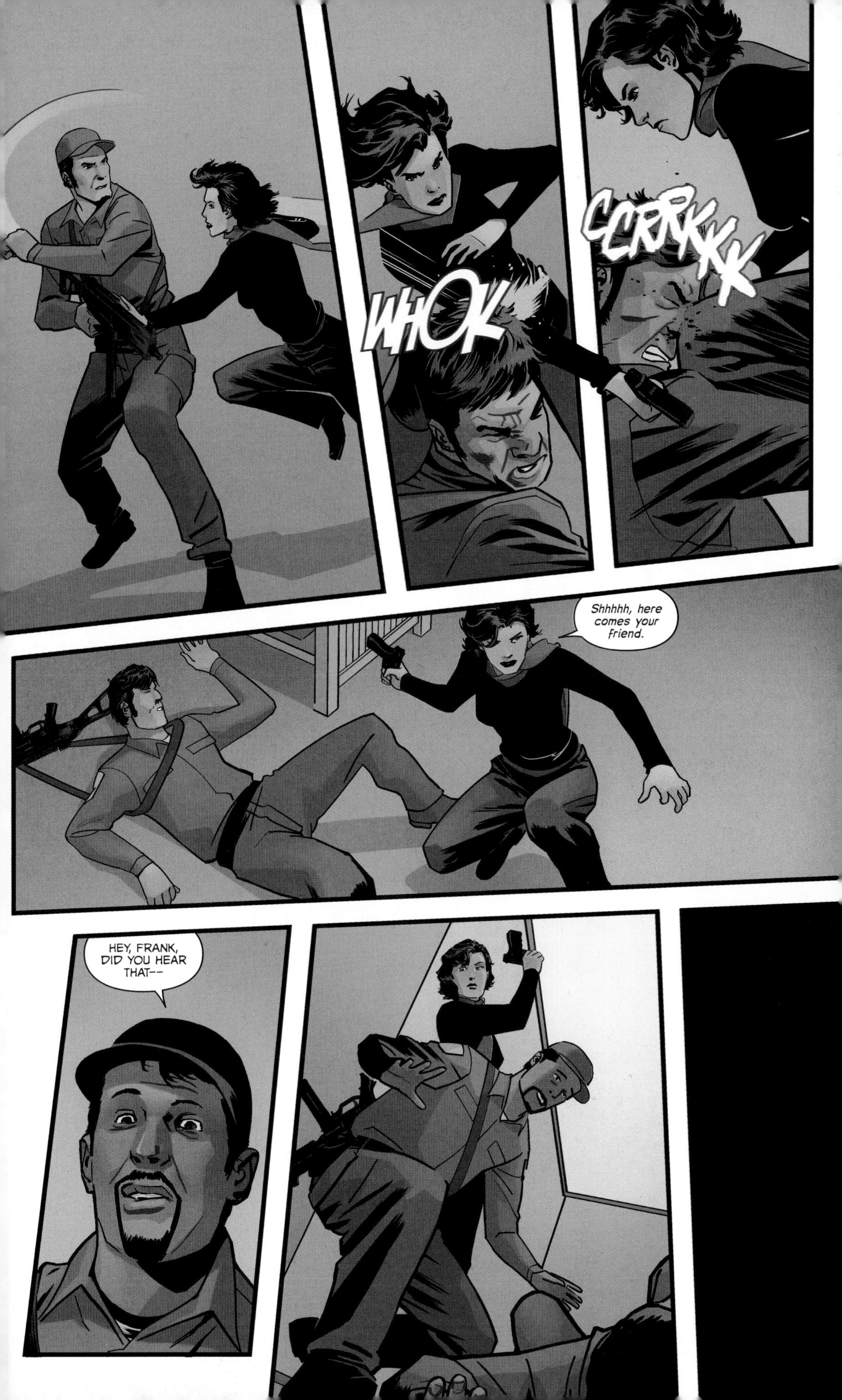
WHOK
CCRRKKK
Shhhhh, here comes your friend.
HEY, FRANK, DID YOU HEAR THAT--

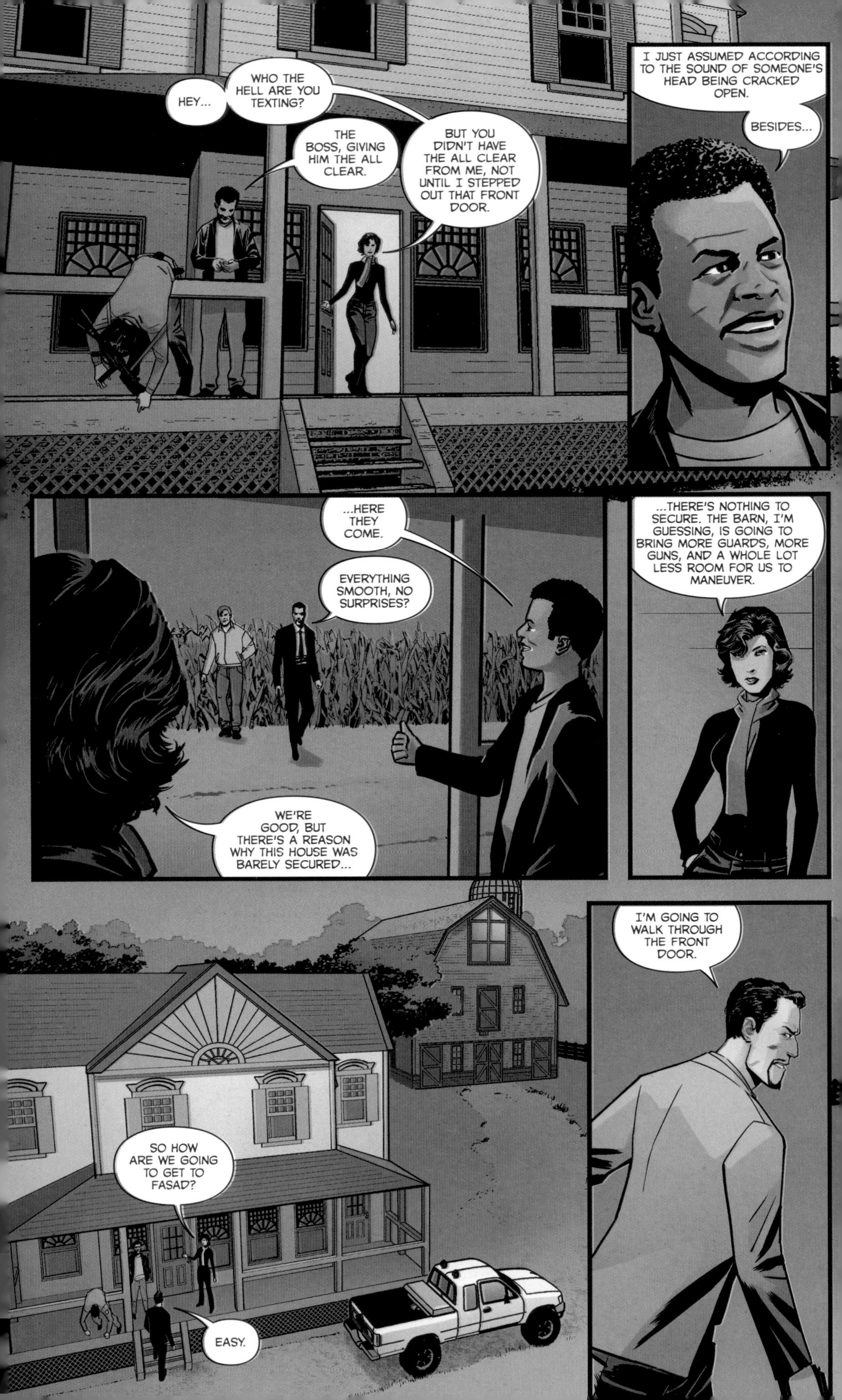
HEY...
WHO THE HELL ARE YOU TEXTING?
THE BOSS, GIVING HIM THE ALL CLEAR.
BUT YOU DIDN'T HAVE THE ALL CLEAR FROM ME, NOT UNTIL I STEPPED OUT THAT FRONT DOOR.
I JUST ASSUMED ACCORDING TO THE SOUND OF SOMEONE'S HEAD BEING CRACKED OPEN.
BESIDES...
...HERE THEY COME.
EVERYTHING SMOOTH, NO SURPRISES?
WE'RE GOOD, BUT THERE'S A REASON WHY THIS HOUSE WAS BARELY SECURED...
...THERE'S NOTHING TO SECURE. THE BARN, I'M GUESSING, IS GOING TO BRING MORE GUARDS, MORE GUNS, AND A WHOLE LOT LESS ROOM FOR US TO MANEUVER.
SO HOW ARE WE GOING TO GET TO FASAD?
EASY.
I'M GOING TO WALK THROUGH THE FRONT DOOR.

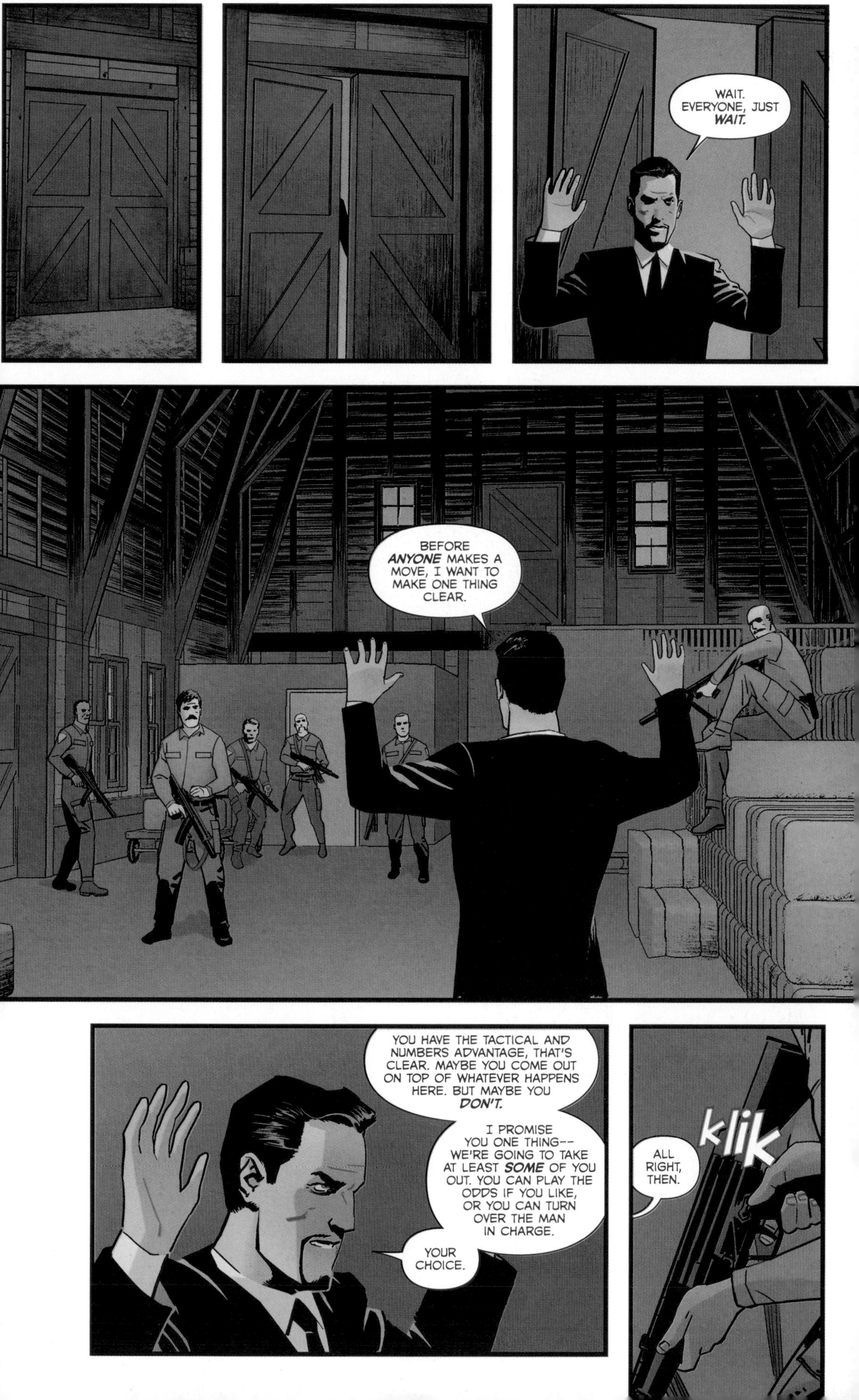
WAIT. EVERYONE, JUST *WAIT.*
BEFORE *ANYONE* MAKES A MOVE, I WANT TO MAKE ONE THING CLEAR.
YOU HAVE THE TACTICAL AND NUMBERS ADVANTAGE, THAT'S CLEAR. MAYBE YOU COME OUT ON TOP OF WHATEVER HAPPENS HERE. BUT MAYBE YOU *DON'T.*
I PROMISE YOU ONE THING-- WE'RE GOING TO TAKE AT LEAST *SOME* OF YOU OUT. YOU CAN PLAY THE ODDS IF YOU LIKE, OR YOU CAN TURN OVER THE MAN IN CHARGE.
YOUR CHOICE.
klik
ALL RIGHT, THEN.

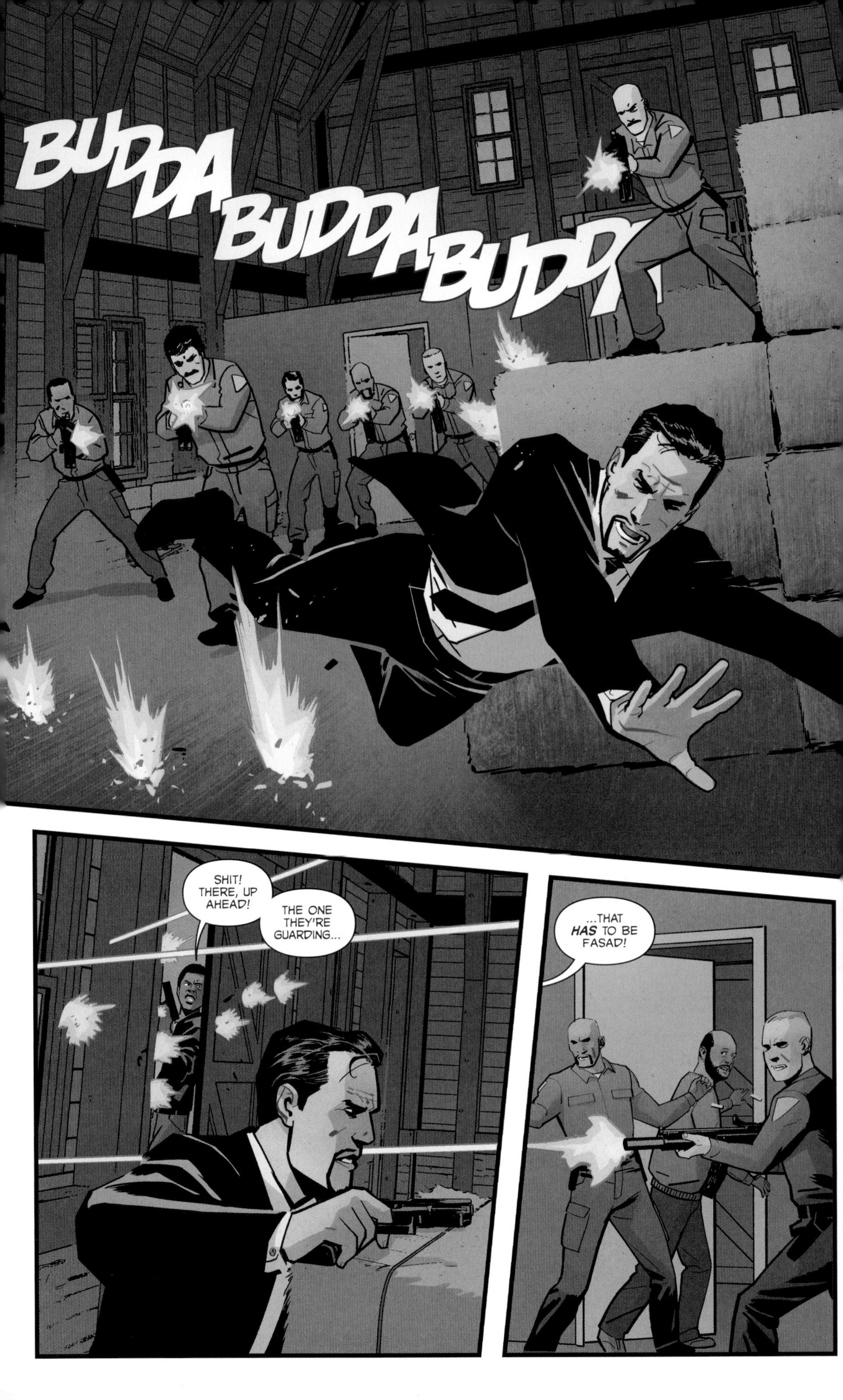
BUDDA BUDDA BUDD
SHIT! THERE, UP AHEAD!
THE ONE THEY'RE GUARDING...
...THAT HAS TO BE FASAD!

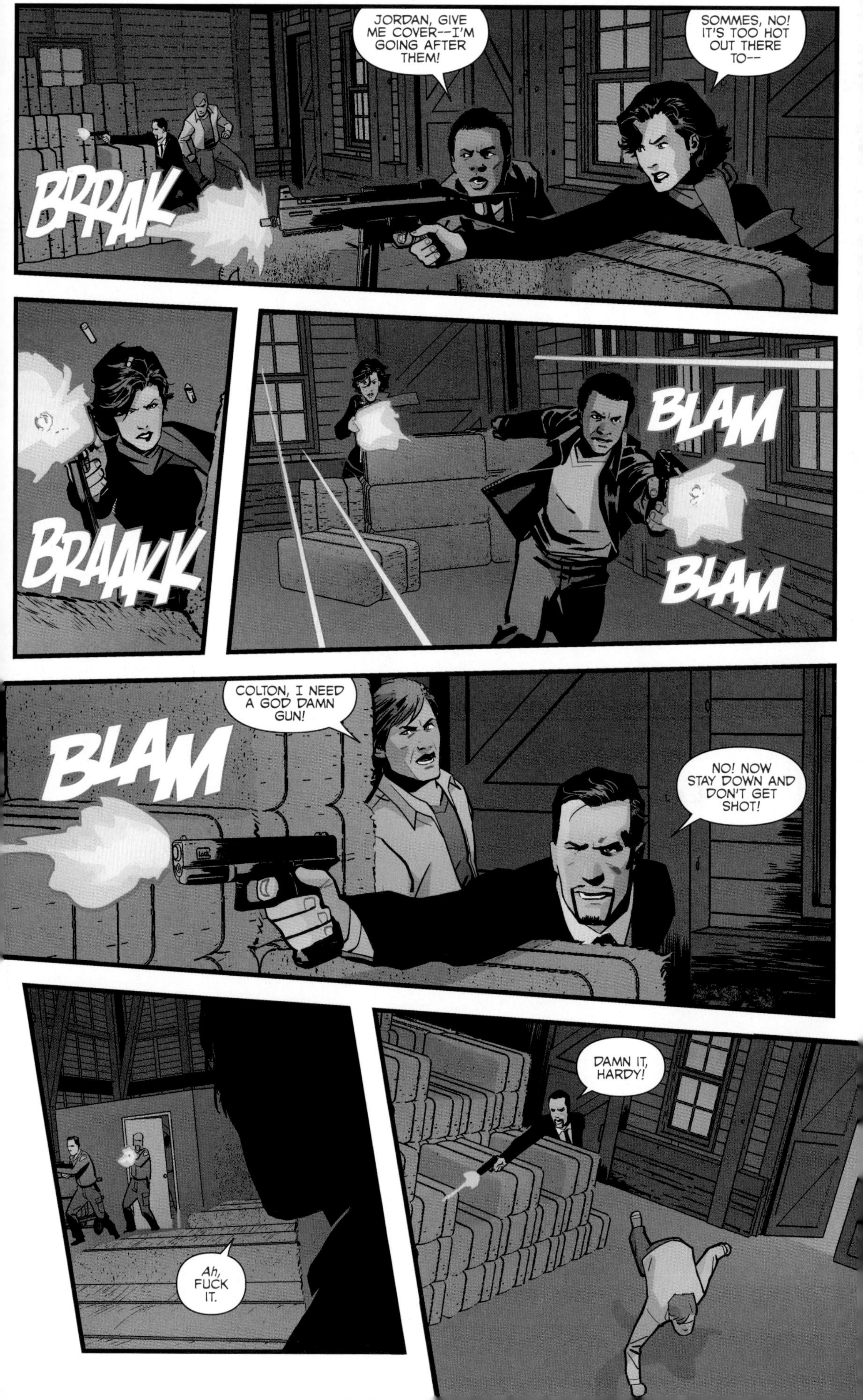
JORDAN, GIVE ME COVER--I'M GOING AFTER THEM!
SOMMES, NO! IT'S TOO HOT OUT THERE TO--
BRRAK
BRAAKK
BLAM
BLAM
BLAM
COLTON, I NEED A GOD DAMN GUN!
NO! NOW STAY DOWN AND DON'T GET SHOT!
Ah, FUCK IT.
DAMN IT, HARDY!

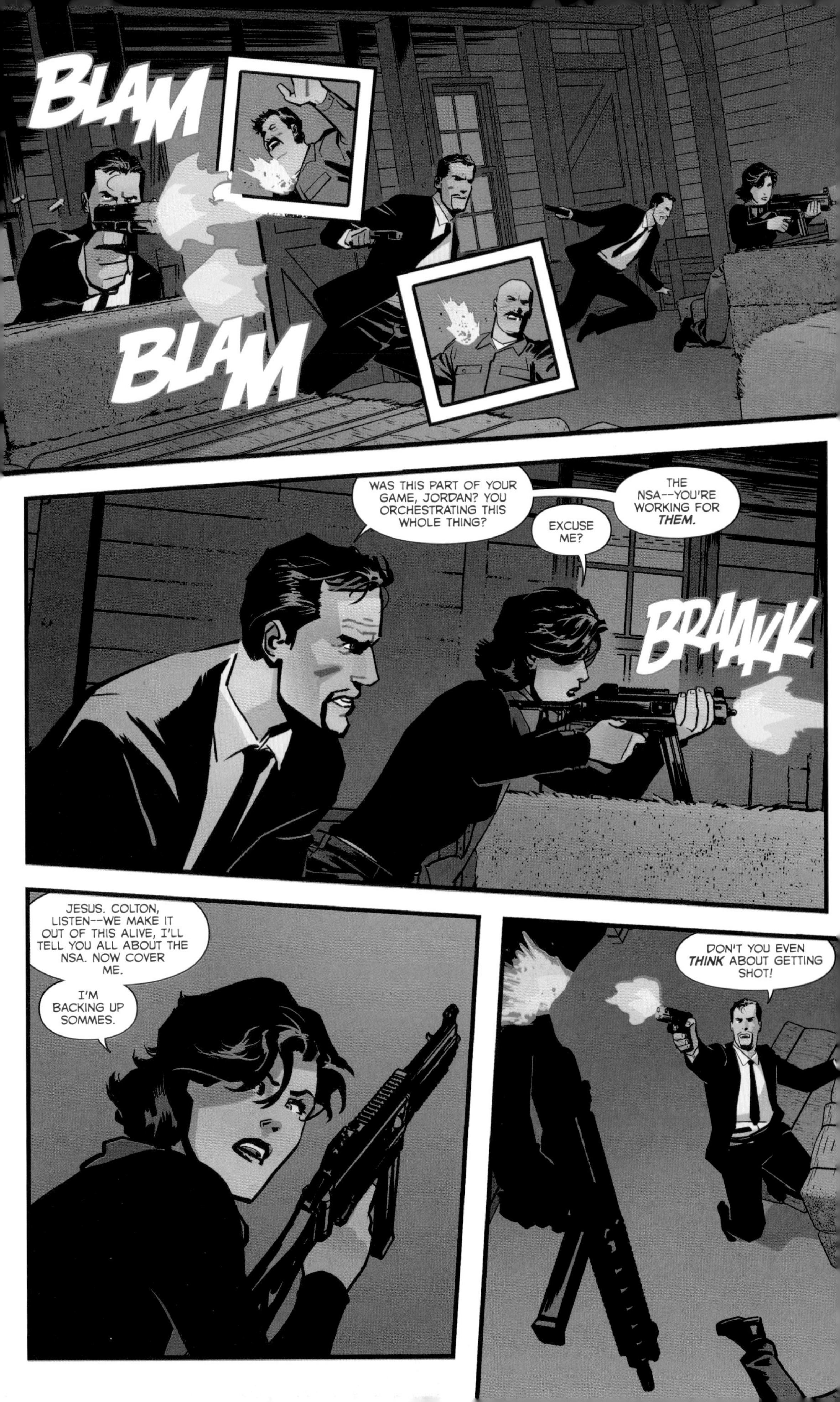
BLAM
BLAM
WAS THIS PART OF YOUR GAME, JORDAN? YOU ORCHESTRATING THIS WHOLE THING?
EXCUSE ME?
THE NSA--YOU'RE WORKING FOR *THEM.*
BRAAKK
JESUS. COLTON, LISTEN--WE MAKE IT OUT OF THIS ALIVE, I'LL TELL YOU ALL ABOUT THE NSA. NOW COVER ME.
I'M BACKING UP SOMMES.
DON'T YOU EVEN *THINK* ABOUT GETTING SHOT!

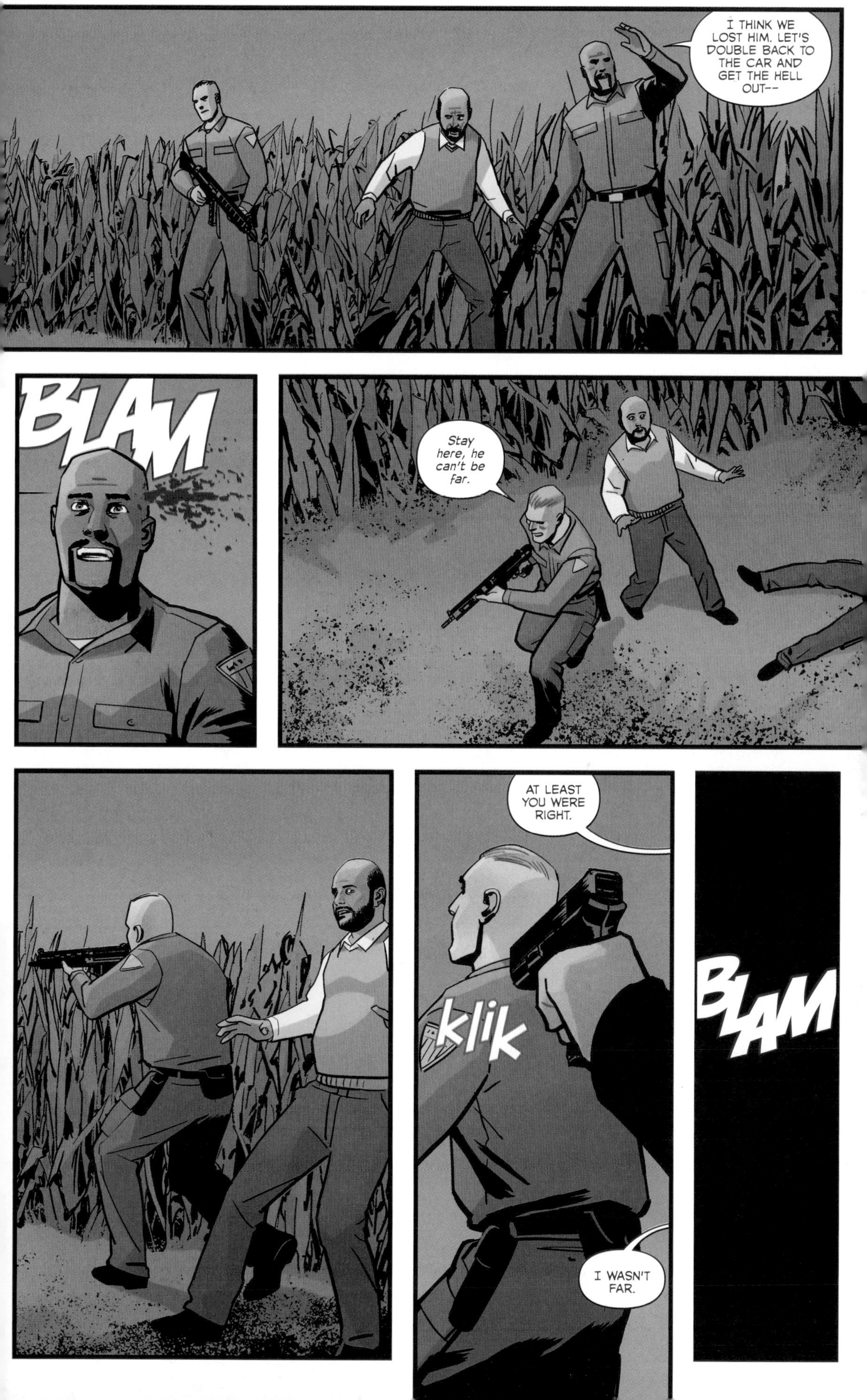

I THINK WE LOST HIM. LET'S DOUBLE BACK TO THE CAR AND GET THE HELL OUT--
BLAM
Stay here, he can't be far.
AT LEAST YOU WERE RIGHT.
klik
I WASN'T FAR.
BLAM

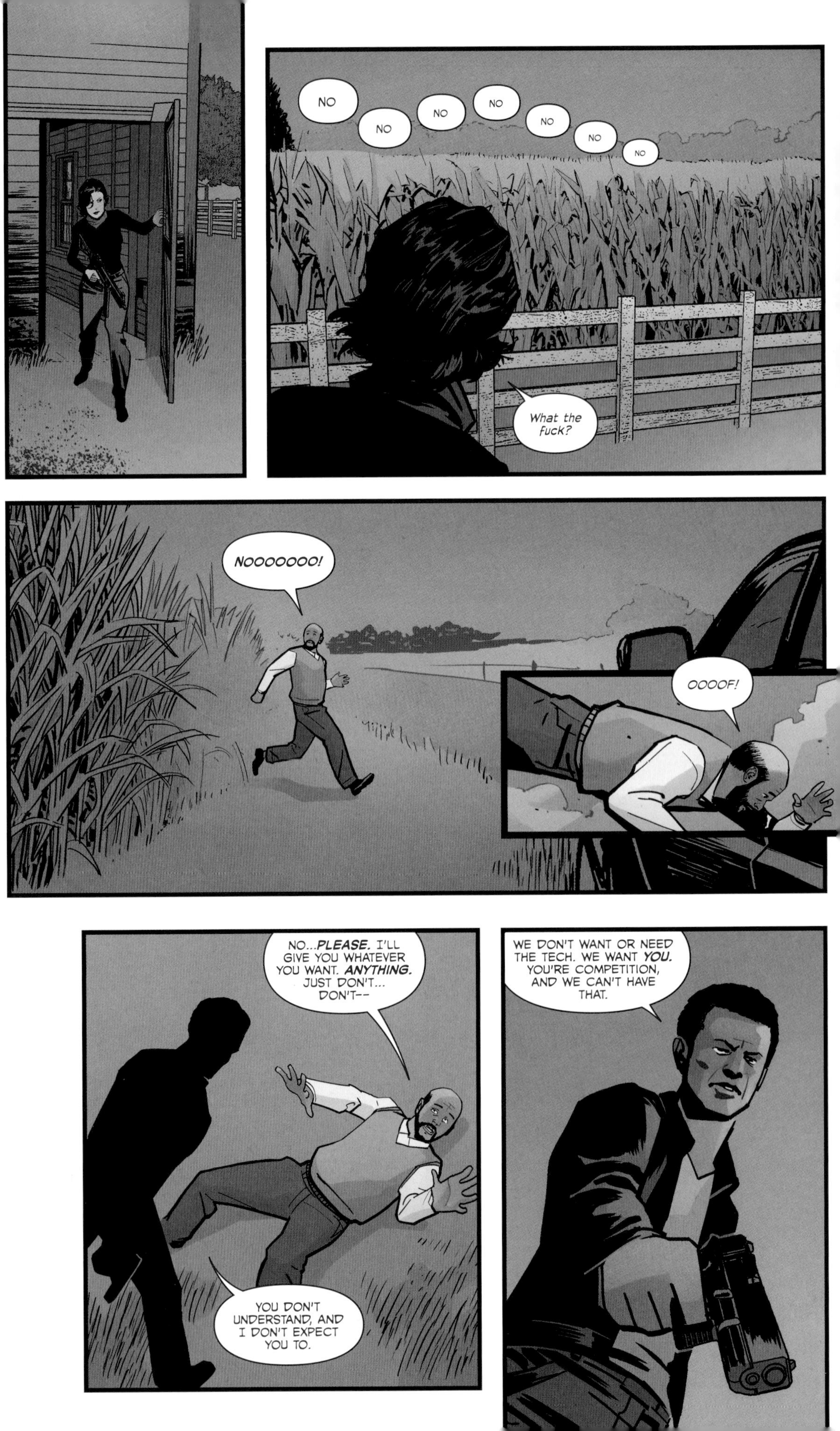
NO
NO
NO
NO
NO
NO
NO
What the fuck?
NOOOOOOO!
OOOOF!
NO...PLEASE. I'LL GIVE YOU WHATEVER YOU WANT. ANYTHING. JUST DON'T... DON'T--
YOU DON'T UNDERSTAND, AND I DON'T EXPECT YOU TO.
WE DON'T WANT OR NEED THE TECH. WE WANT YOU. YOU'RE COMPETITION, AND WE CAN'T HAVE THAT.

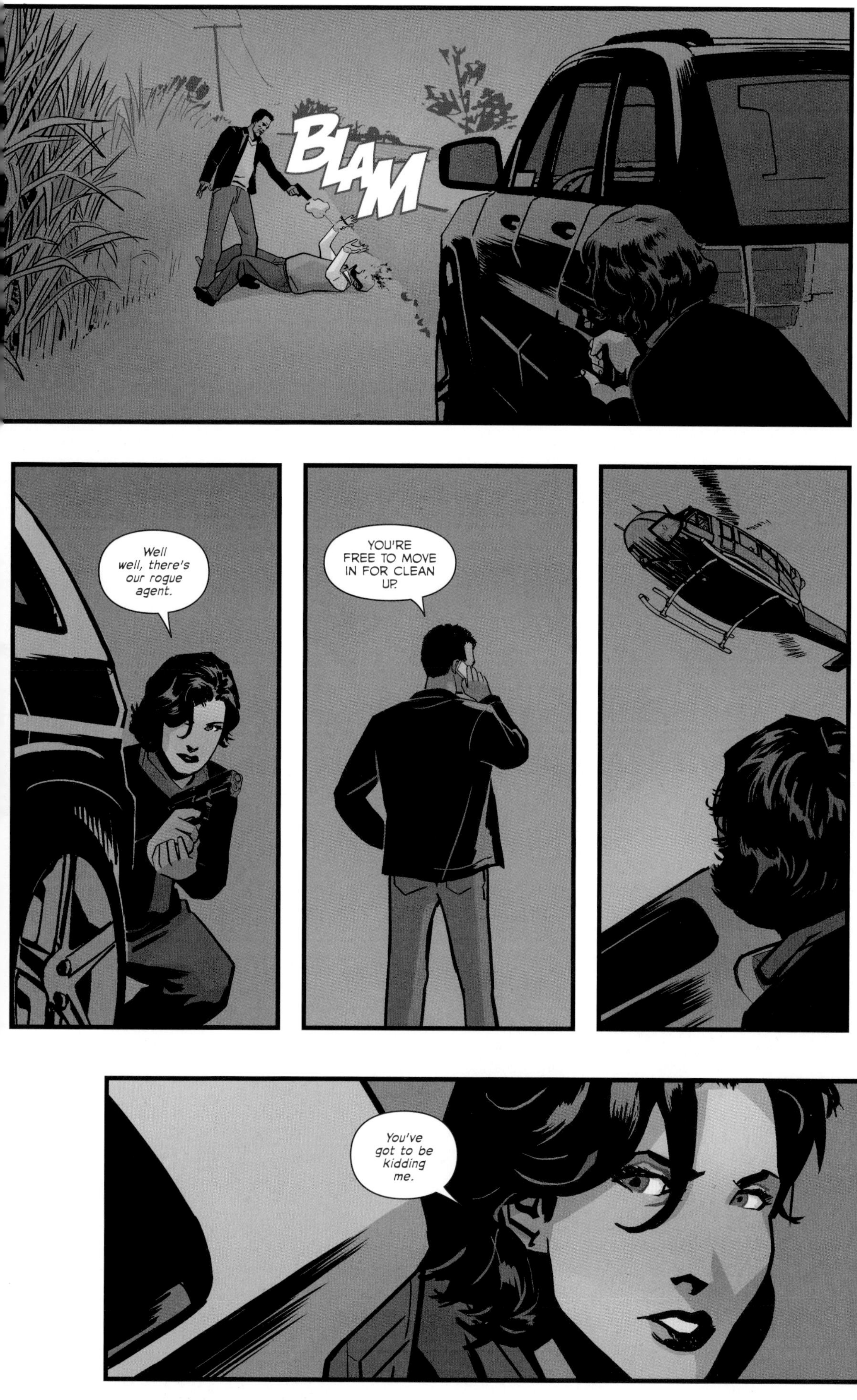
BLAM
Well well, there's our rogue agent.
YOU'RE FREE TO MOVE IN FOR CLEAN UP.
You've got to be kidding me.

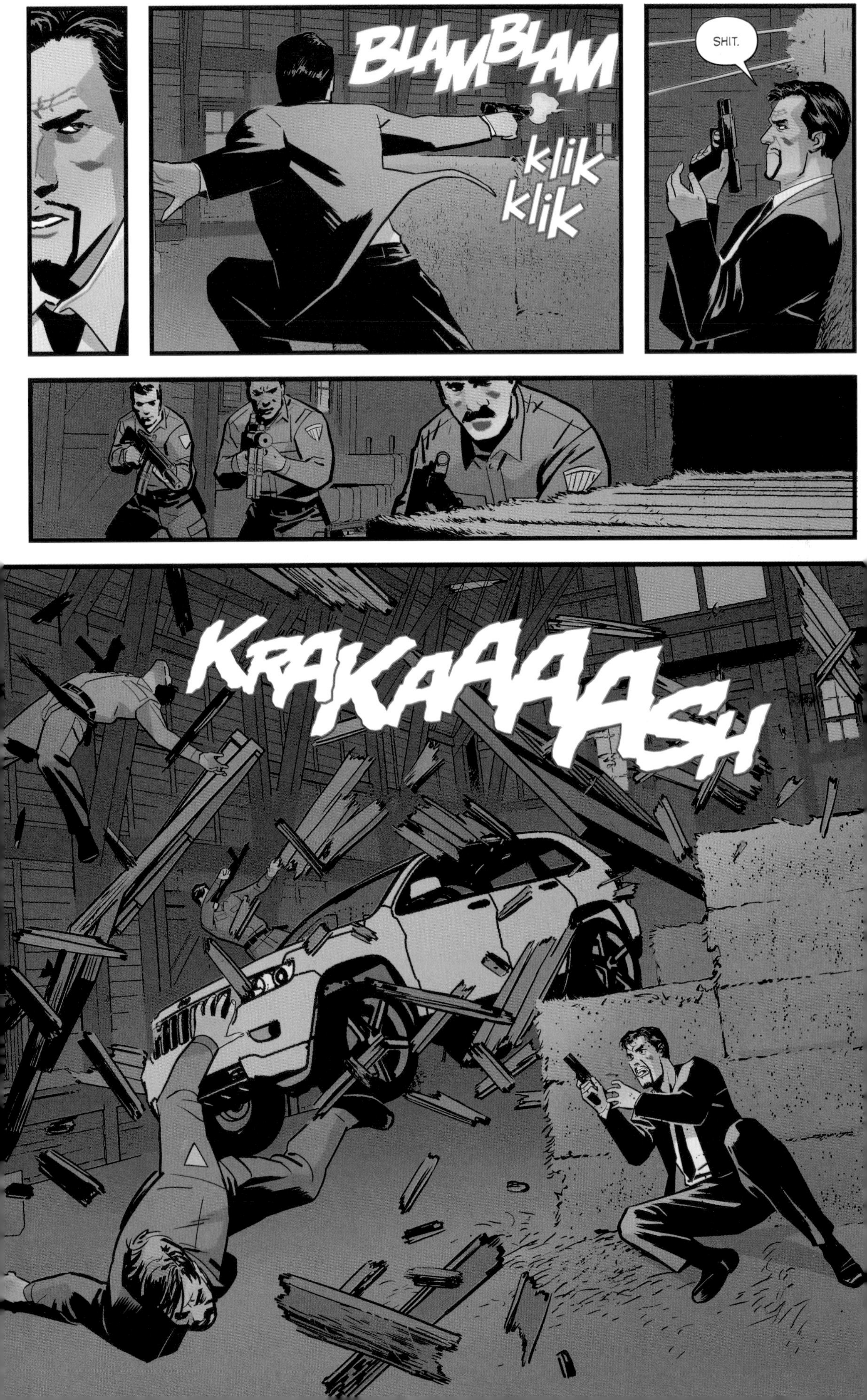
BLAMBLAM
klik
klik
SHIT.
KRAKAAAAASH

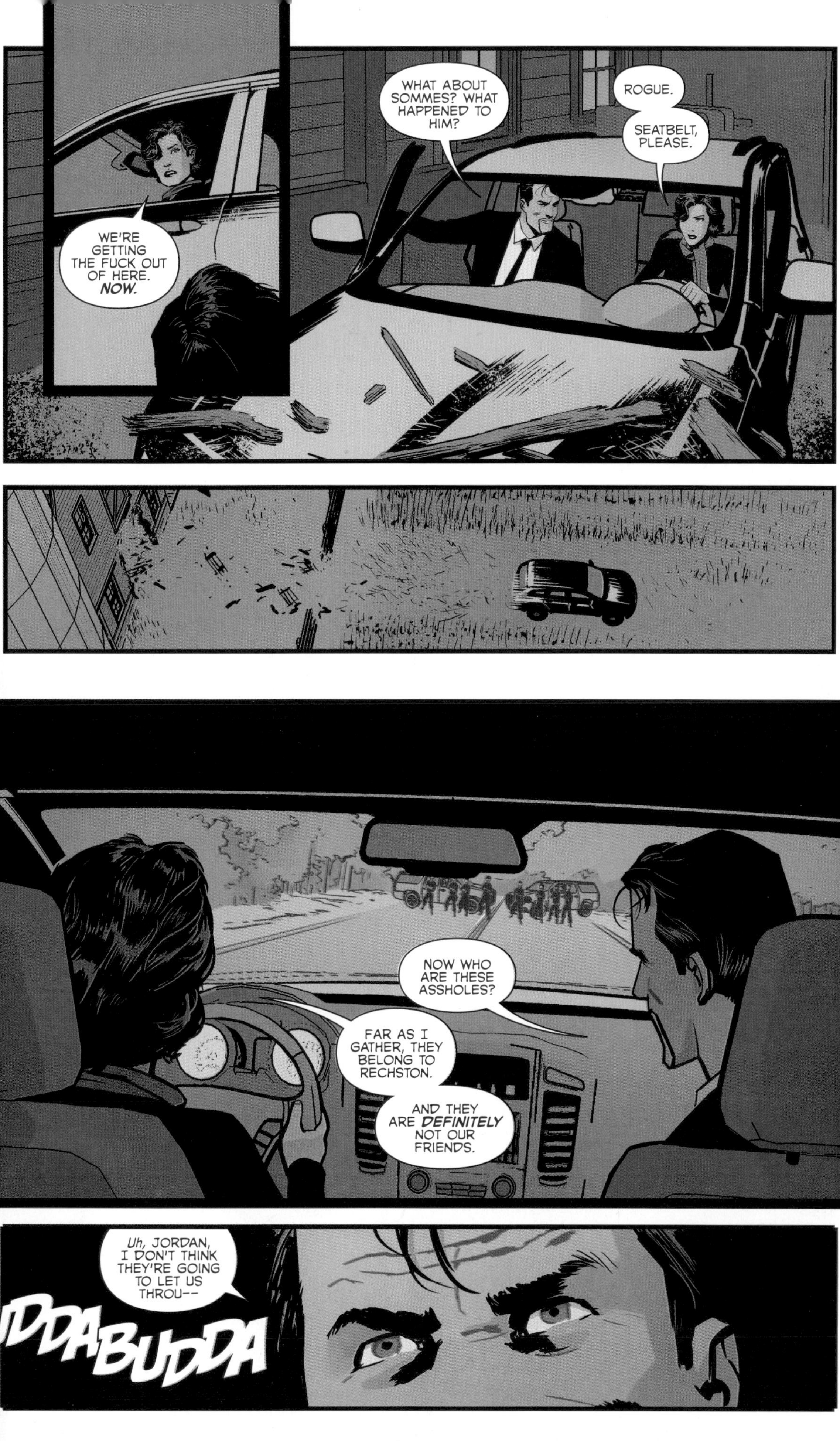
WE'RE GETTING THE FUCK OUT OF HERE. *NOW.*
WHAT ABOUT SOMMES? WHAT HAPPENED TO HIM?
ROGUE.
SEATBELT, PLEASE.
NOW WHO ARE THESE ASSHOLES?
FAR AS I GATHER, THEY BELONG TO RECHSTON.
AND THEY ARE *DEFINITELY* NOT OUR FRIENDS.
Uh, JORDAN, I DON'T THINK THEY'RE GOING TO LET US THROU--
UDDABUDDA

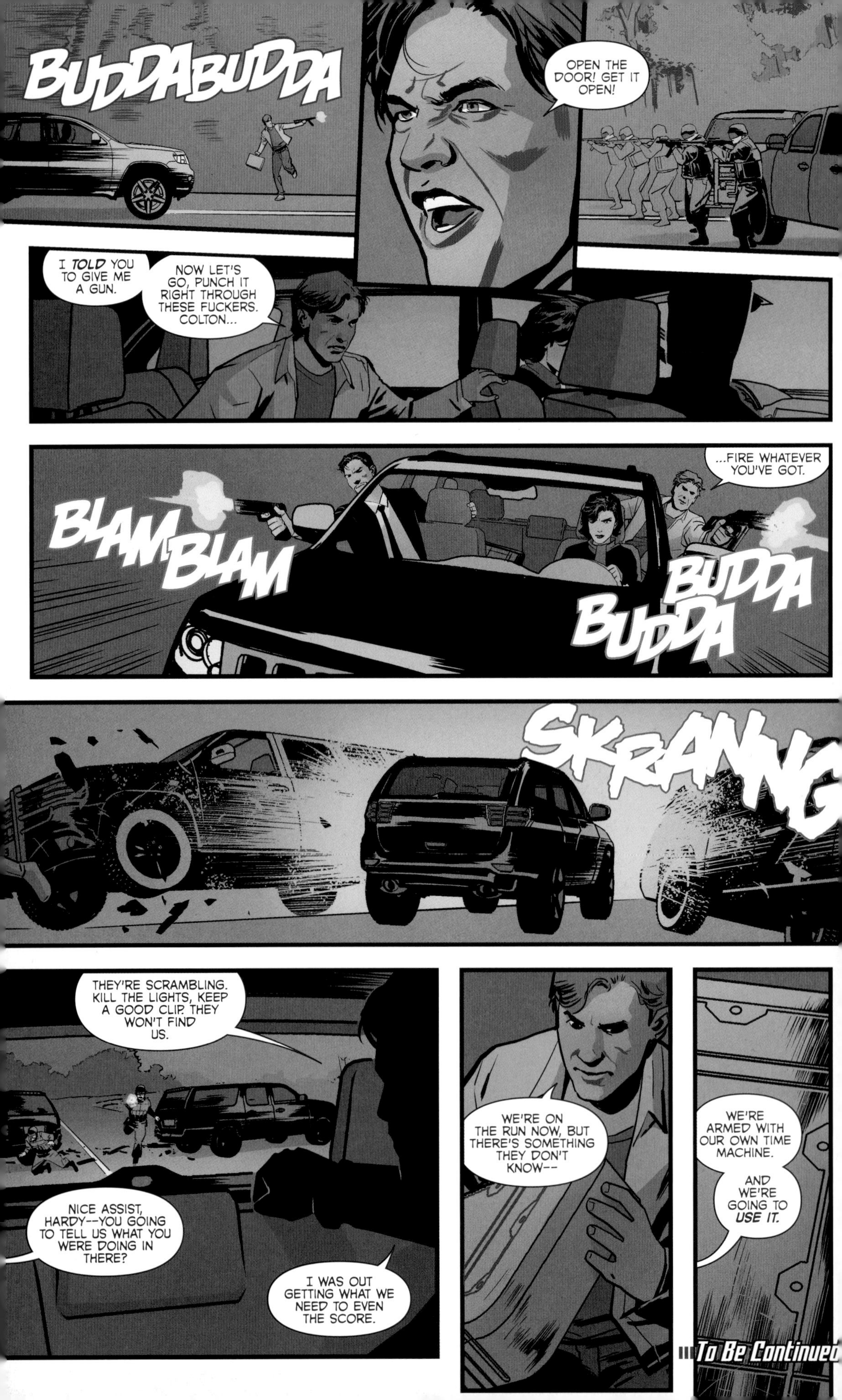
BUDDABUDDA
OPEN THE DOOR! GET IT OPEN!
I TOLD YOU TO GIVE ME A GUN.
NOW LET'S GO, PUNCH IT RIGHT THROUGH THESE FUCKERS. COLTON...
...FIRE WHATEVER YOU'VE GOT.
BLAM BLAM
BUDDA BUDDA
SKRANNG
THEY'RE SCRAMBLING. KILL THE LIGHTS, KEEP A GOOD CLIP. THEY WON'T FIND US.
NICE ASSIST, HARDY--YOU GOING TO TELL US WHAT YOU WERE DOING IN THERE?
I WAS OUT GETTING WHAT WE NEED TO EVEN THE SCORE.
WE'RE ON THE RUN NOW, BUT THERE'S SOMETHING THEY DON'T KNOW--
WE'RE ARMED WITH OUR OWN TIME MACHINE.
AND WE'RE GOING TO USE IT.
To Be Continued

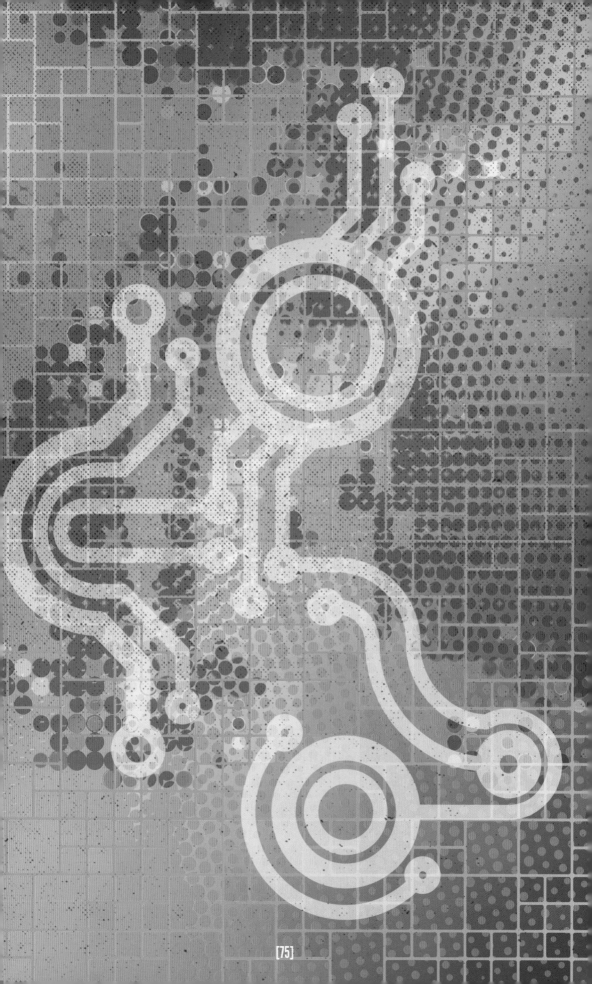

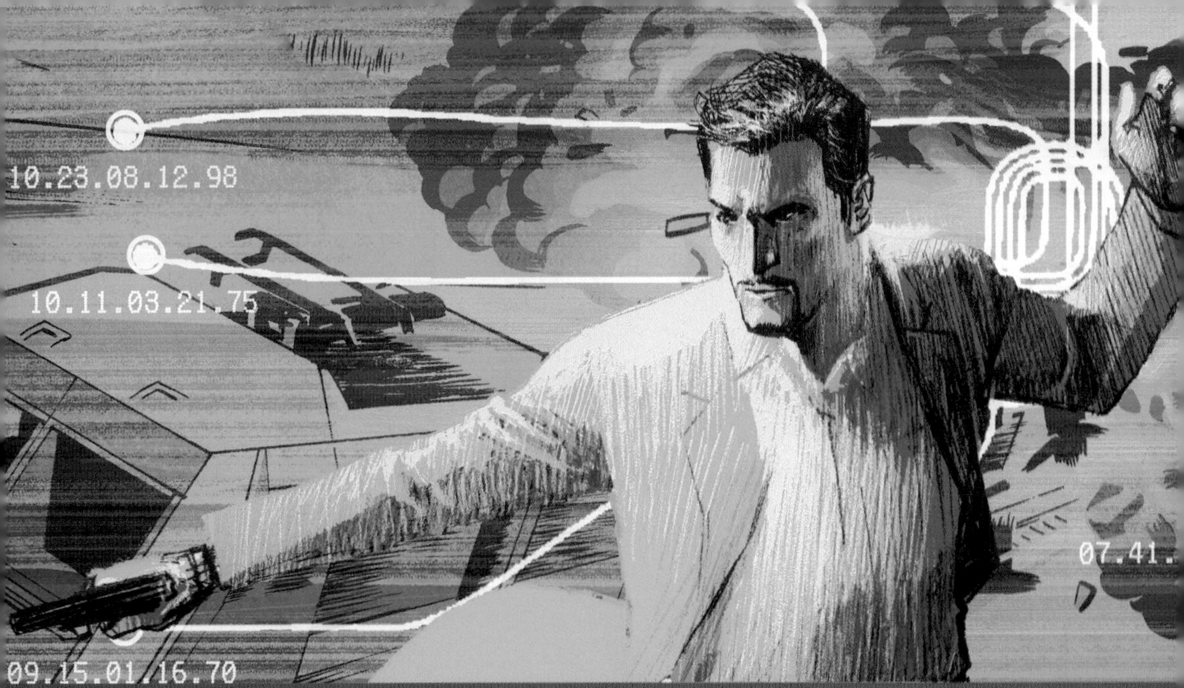
10.23.08.12.98
10.11.03.21.75
07.41.
09.15.01.16.70

ISSUE 4

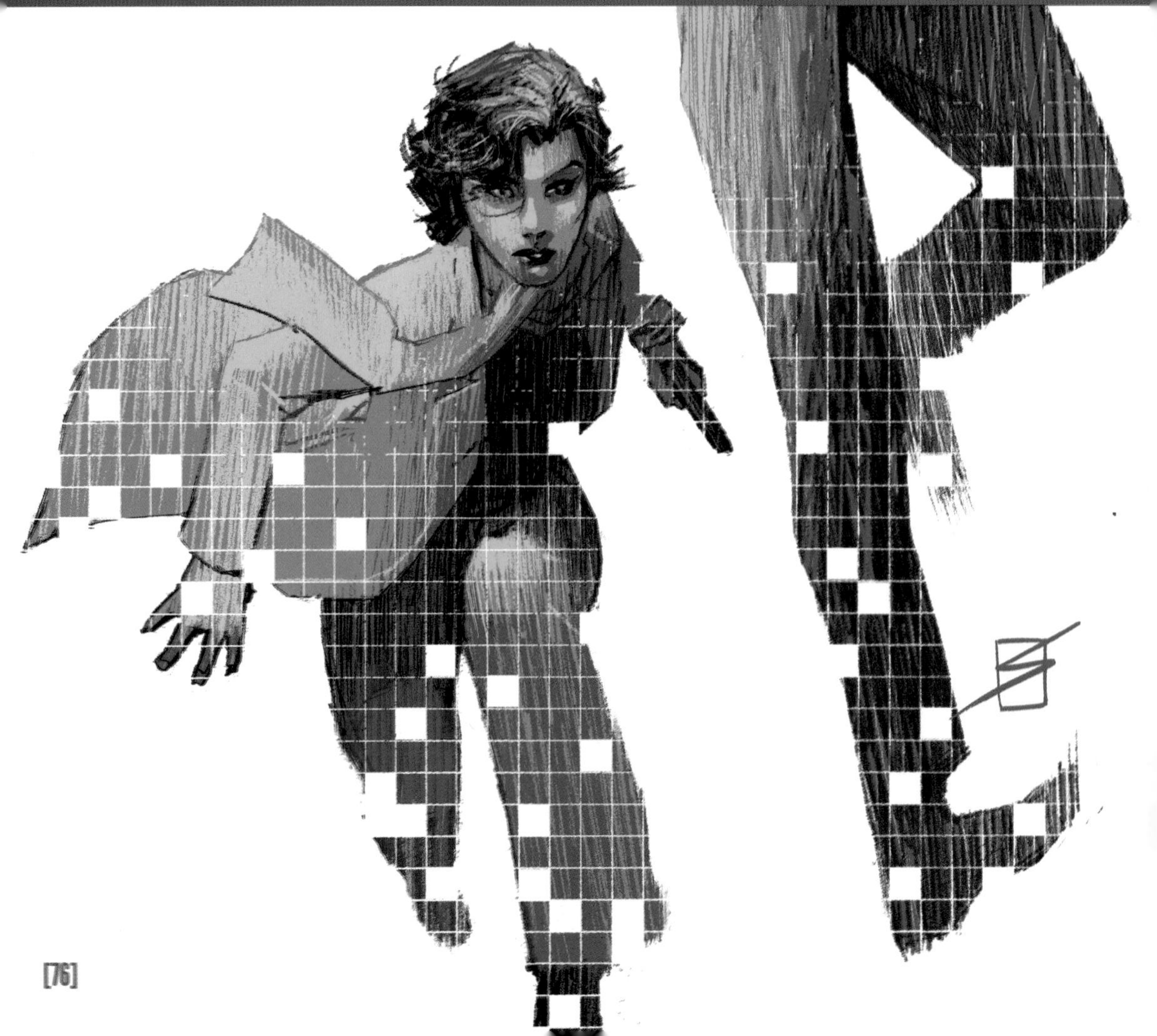

YOU SURE THIS IS NECESSARY? I'M JUST A TECHNICIAN, I DON'T THINK--

YOU HAVE SENSITIVE INFORMATION THAT WE CAN'T AFFORD TO FALL INTO THE WRONG HANDS. PROTECTING YOU IS *ABSOLUTELY* NECESSARY.

NOW--

NOK NOK!

KANAN, GET DOWN ON THE FLOOR, NEXT TO THE BED. AND *STAY* DOWN.

WHO IS IT?

CONCIERGE, SIR. I HAVE A DELIVERY FOR A MR. SAM KANAN.

DELIVERY OF *WHAT?*

I'D HAVE TO OPEN THE BOX TO CONFIRM ITS CONTENTS, AND I'M AFRAID I'M NOT ALLOWED TO--

WHO DELIVERED IT? AND WHEN?

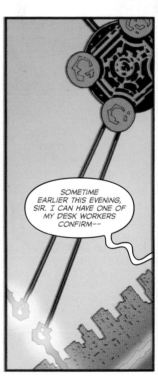

SOMETIME EARLIER THIS EVENING, SIR. I CAN HAVE ONE OF MY DESK WORKERS CONFIRM--

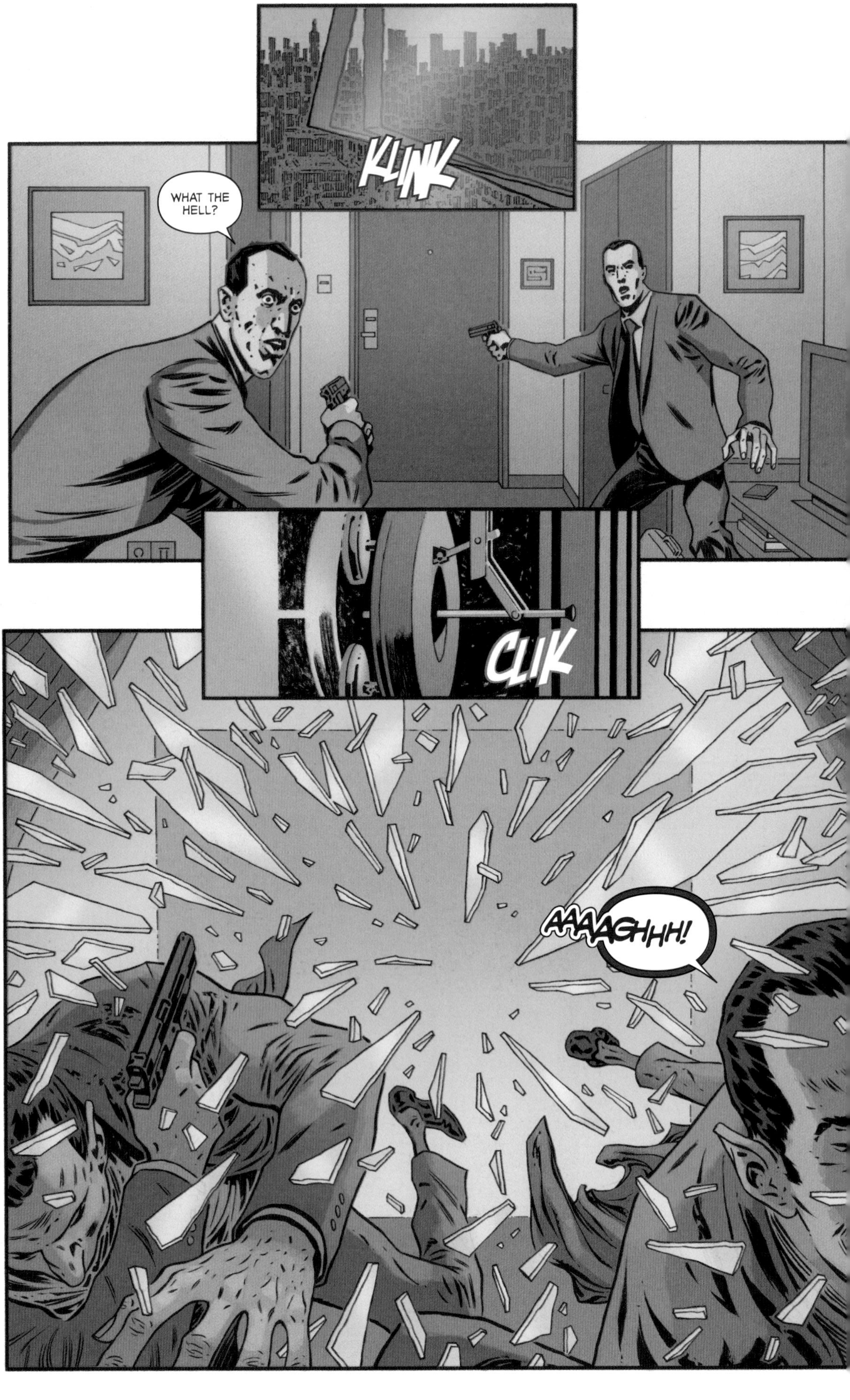
KLINK
WHAT THE HELL?
CLIK
AAAAGHHH!

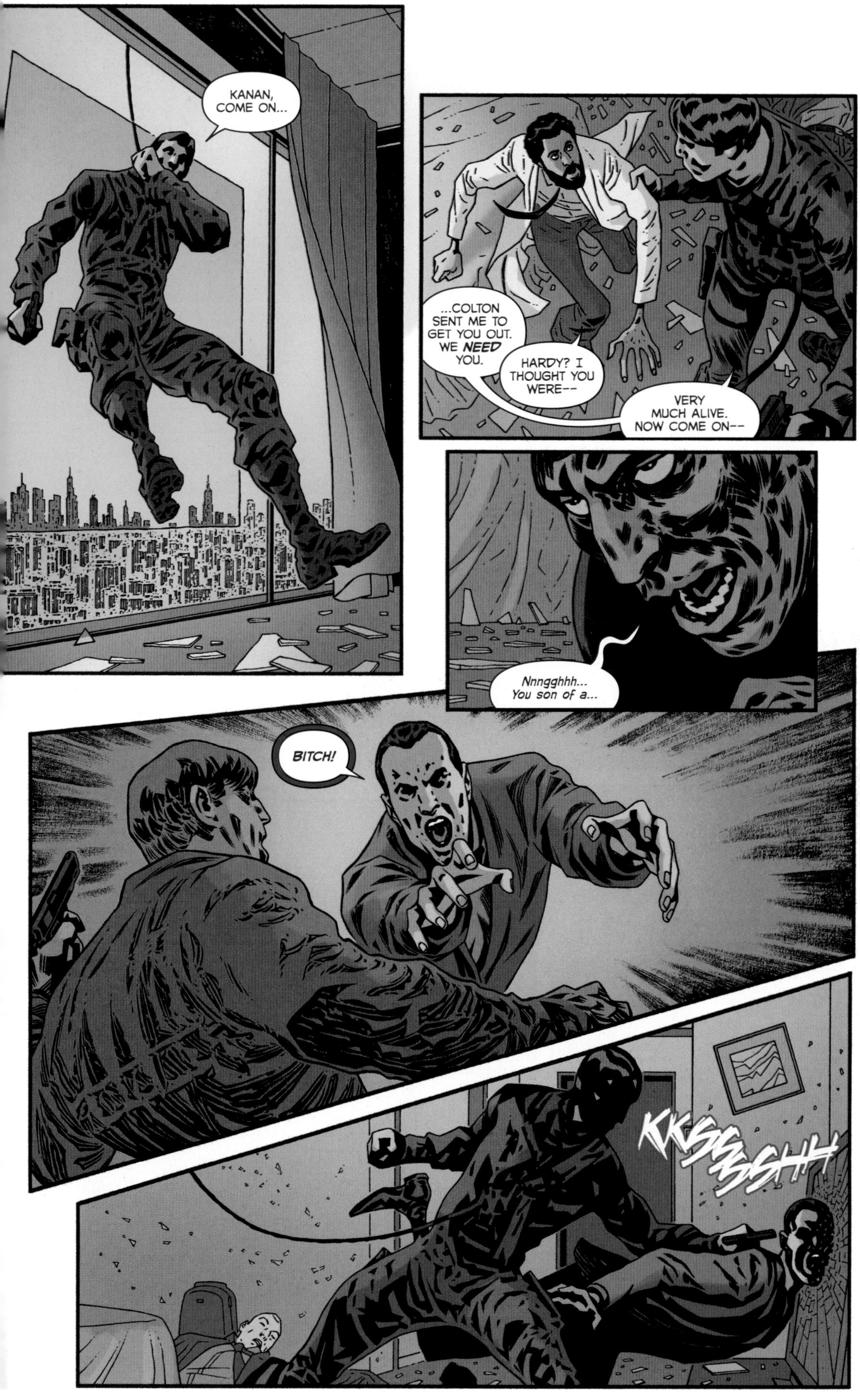
KANAN, COME ON...
...COLTON SENT ME TO GET YOU OUT. WE NEED YOU.
HARDY? I THOUGHT YOU WERE--
VERY MUCH ALIVE. NOW COME ON--
Nnngghhh... You son of a...
BITCH!
KKSSSSHH

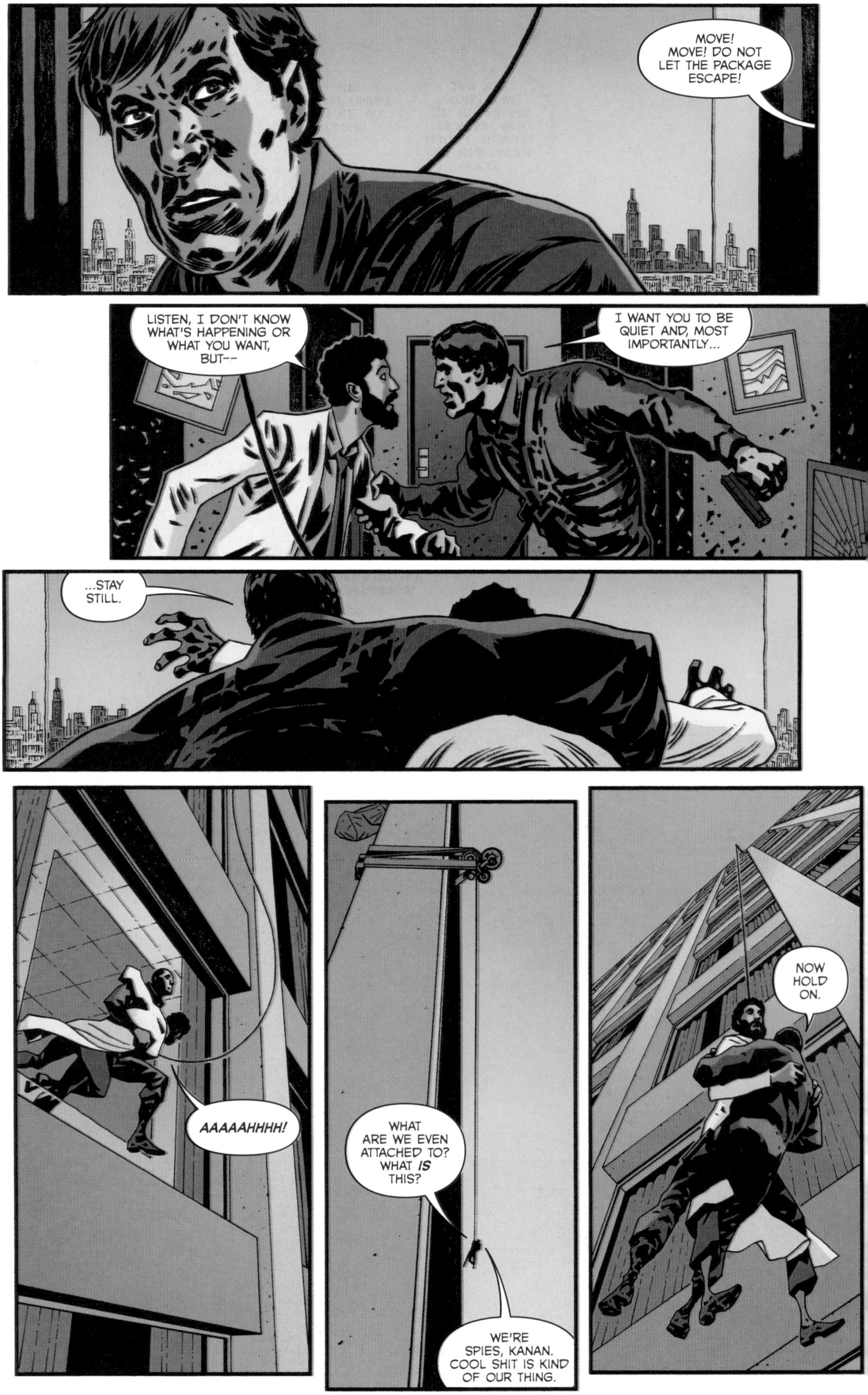
MOVE! MOVE! DO NOT LET THE PACKAGE ESCAPE!
LISTEN, I DON'T KNOW WHAT'S HAPPENING OR WHAT YOU WANT, BUT--
I WANT YOU TO BE QUIET AND, MOST IMPORTANTLY...
...STAY STILL.
AAAAAHHHH!
WHAT ARE WE EVEN ATTACHED TO? WHAT *IS* THIS?
WE'RE SPIES, KANAN. COOL SHIT IS KIND OF OUR THING.
NOW HOLD ON.

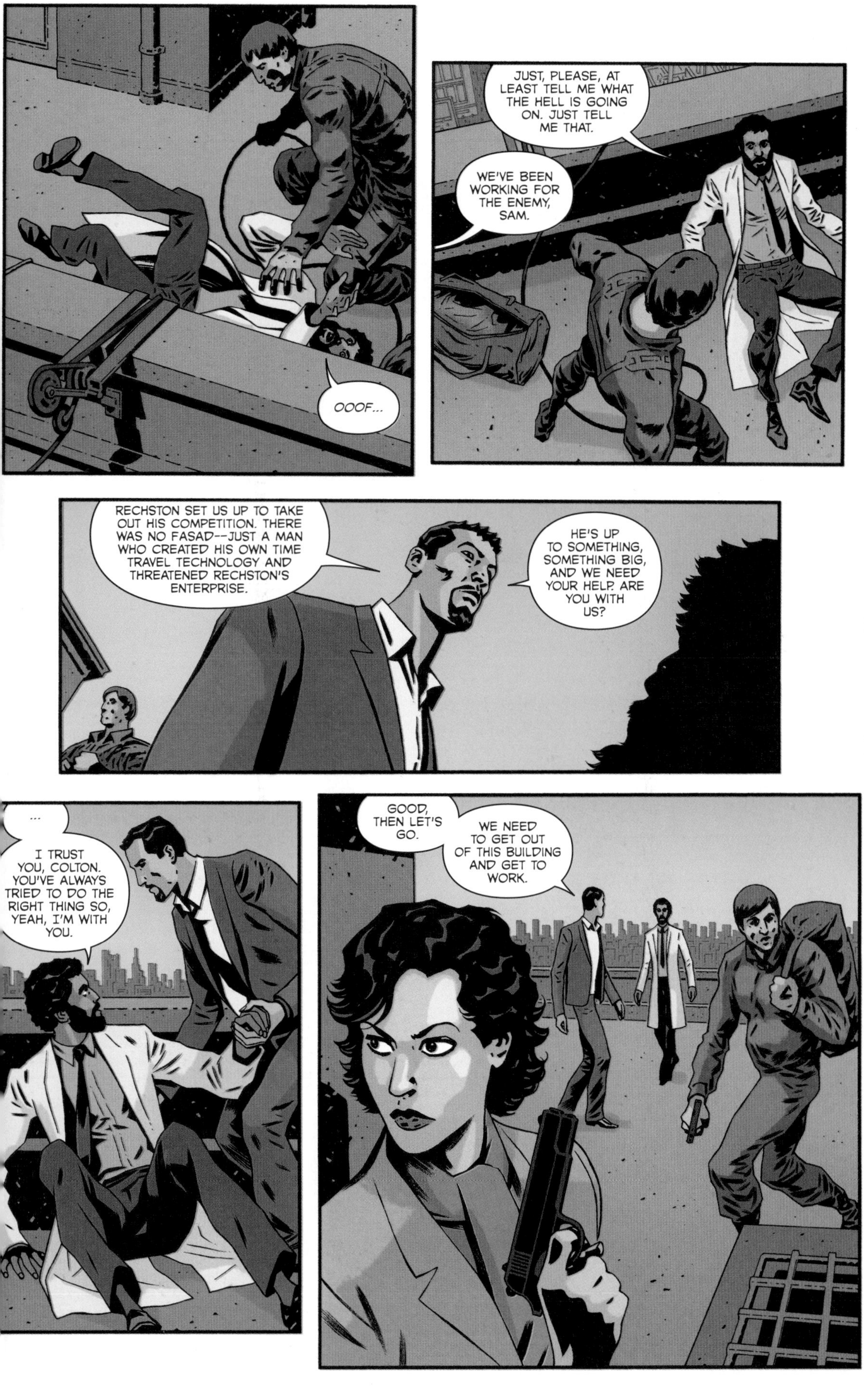
OOOF...
JUST, PLEASE, AT LEAST TELL ME WHAT THE HELL IS GOING ON. JUST TELL ME THAT.
WE'VE BEEN WORKING FOR THE ENEMY, SAM.
RECHSTON SET US UP TO TAKE OUT HIS COMPETITION. THERE WAS NO FASAD--JUST A MAN WHO CREATED HIS OWN TIME TRAVEL TECHNOLOGY AND THREATENED RECHSTON'S ENTERPRISE.
HE'S UP TO SOMETHING, SOMETHING BIG, AND WE NEED YOUR HELP. ARE YOU WITH US?
...
I TRUST YOU, COLTON. YOU'VE ALWAYS TRIED TO DO THE RIGHT THING SO, YEAH, I'M WITH YOU.
GOOD, THEN LET'S GO.
WE NEED TO GET OUT OF THIS BUILDING AND GET TO WORK.

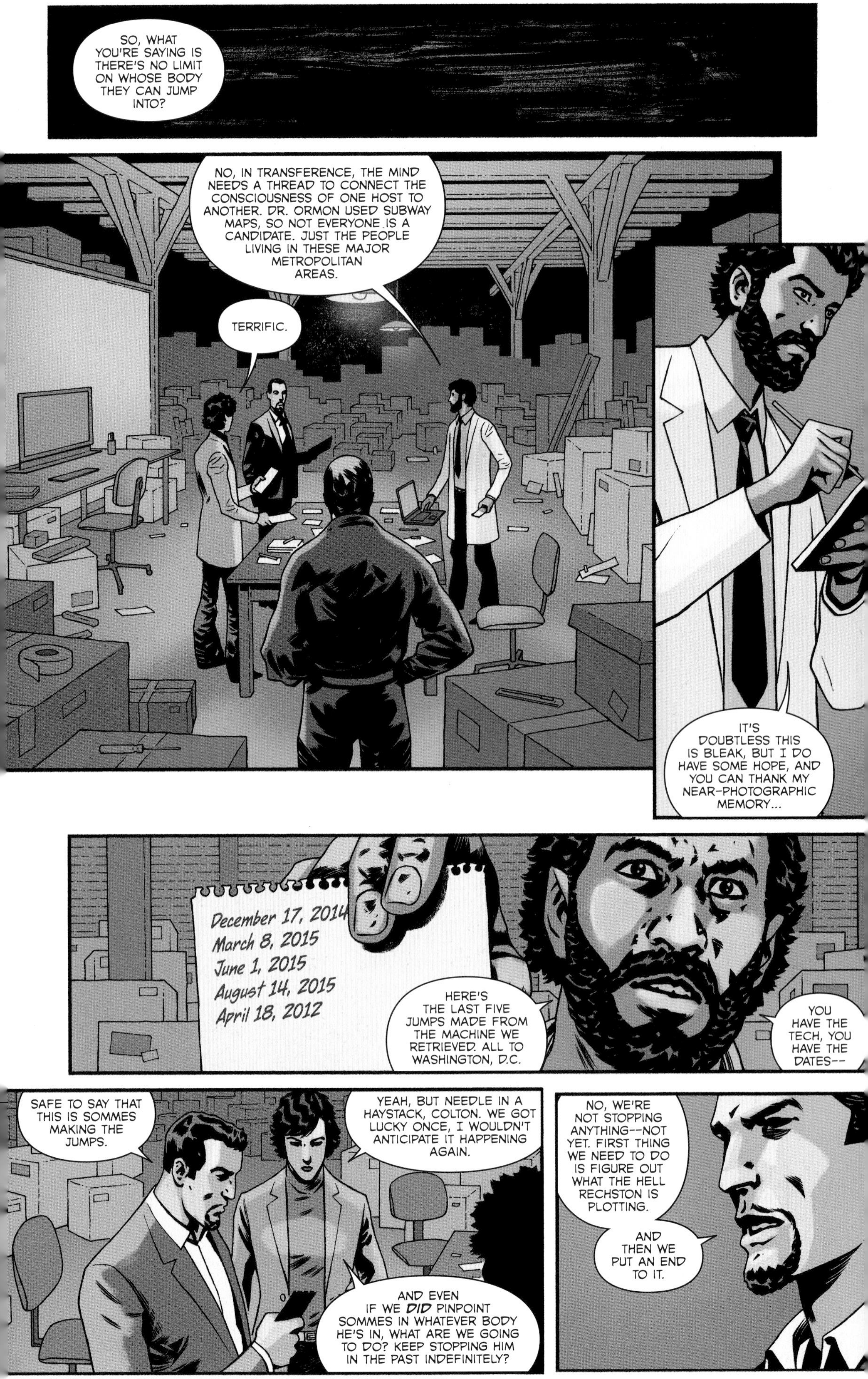

SO, WHAT YOU'RE SAYING IS THERE'S NO LIMIT ON WHOSE BODY THEY CAN JUMP INTO?
NO, IN TRANSFERENCE, THE MIND NEEDS A THREAD TO CONNECT THE CONSCIOUSNESS OF ONE HOST TO ANOTHER. DR. ORMON USED SUBWAY MAPS, SO NOT EVERYONE IS A CANDIDATE. JUST THE PEOPLE LIVING IN THESE MAJOR METROPOLITAN AREAS.
TERRIFIC.
IT'S DOUBTLESS THIS IS BLEAK, BUT I DO HAVE SOME HOPE, AND YOU CAN THANK MY NEAR-PHOTOGRAPHIC MEMORY...
December 17, 2014
March 8, 2015
June 1, 2015
August 14, 2015
April 18, 2012
HERE'S THE LAST FIVE JUMPS MADE FROM THE MACHINE WE RETRIEVED. ALL TO WASHINGTON, D.C.
YOU HAVE THE TECH, YOU HAVE THE DATES--
SAFE TO SAY THAT THIS IS SOMMES MAKING THE JUMPS.
YEAH, BUT NEEDLE IN A HAYSTACK, COLTON. WE GOT LUCKY ONCE, I WOULDN'T ANTICIPATE IT HAPPENING AGAIN.
AND EVEN IF WE *DID* PINPOINT SOMMES IN WHATEVER BODY HE'S IN, WHAT ARE WE GOING TO DO? KEEP STOPPING HIM IN THE PAST INDEFINITELY?
NO, WE'RE NOT STOPPING ANYTHING--NOT YET. FIRST THING WE NEED TO DO IS FIGURE OUT WHAT THE HELL RECHSTON IS PLOTTING.
AND THEN WE PUT AN END TO IT.

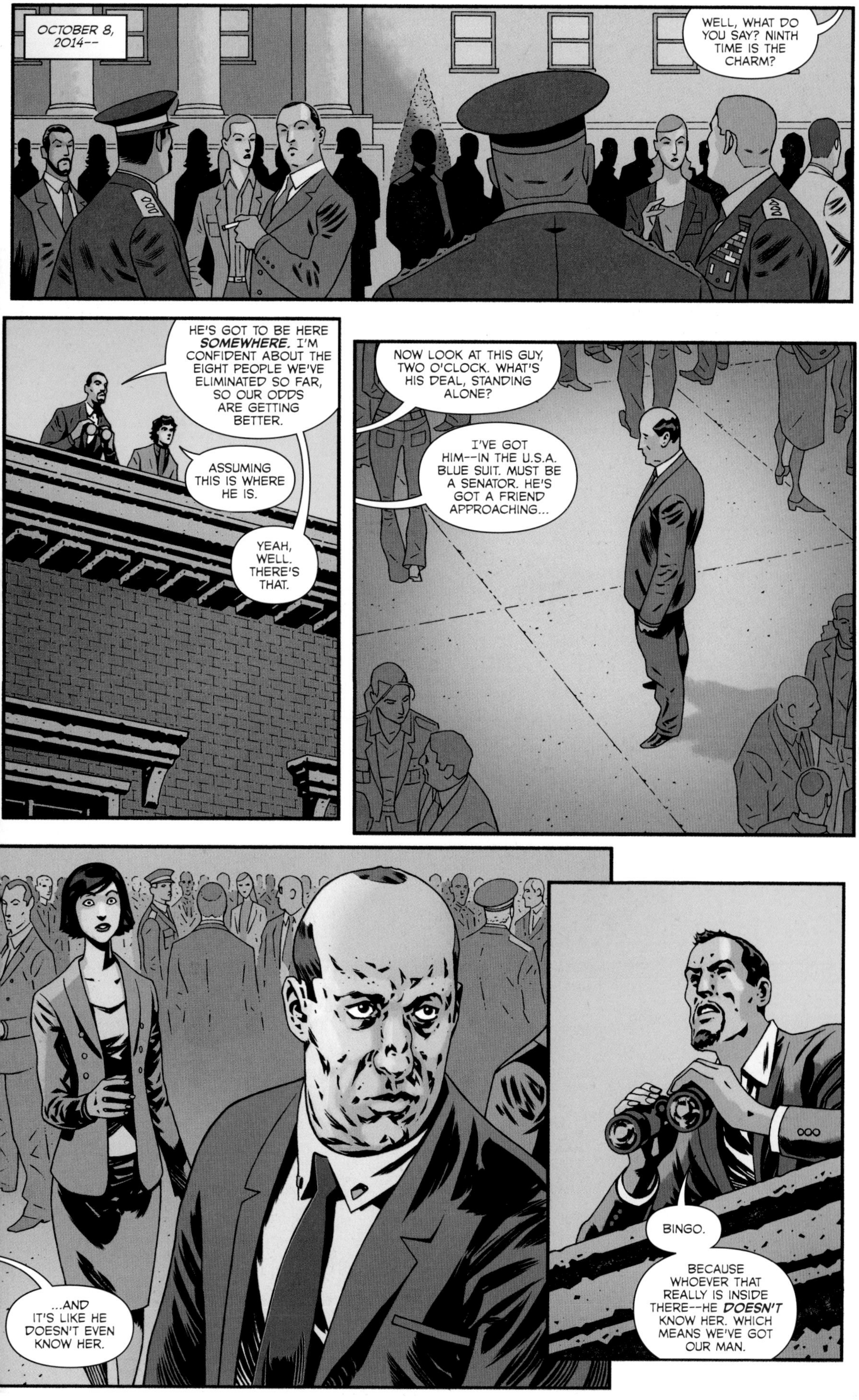
OCTOBER 8, 2014--
WELL, WHAT DO YOU SAY? NINTH TIME IS THE CHARM?
HE'S GOT TO BE HERE SOMEWHERE. I'M CONFIDENT ABOUT THE EIGHT PEOPLE WE'VE ELIMINATED SO FAR, SO OUR ODDS ARE GETTING BETTER.
ASSUMING THIS IS WHERE HE IS.
YEAH, WELL. THERE'S THAT.
NOW LOOK AT THIS GUY, TWO O'CLOCK. WHAT'S HIS DEAL, STANDING ALONE?
I'VE GOT HIM--IN THE U.S.A. BLUE SUIT. MUST BE A SENATOR. HE'S GOT A FRIEND APPROACHING...
...AND IT'S LIKE HE DOESN'T EVEN KNOW HER.
BINGO.
BECAUSE WHOEVER THAT REALLY IS INSIDE THERE--HE DOESN'T KNOW HER. WHICH MEANS WE'VE GOT OUR MAN.

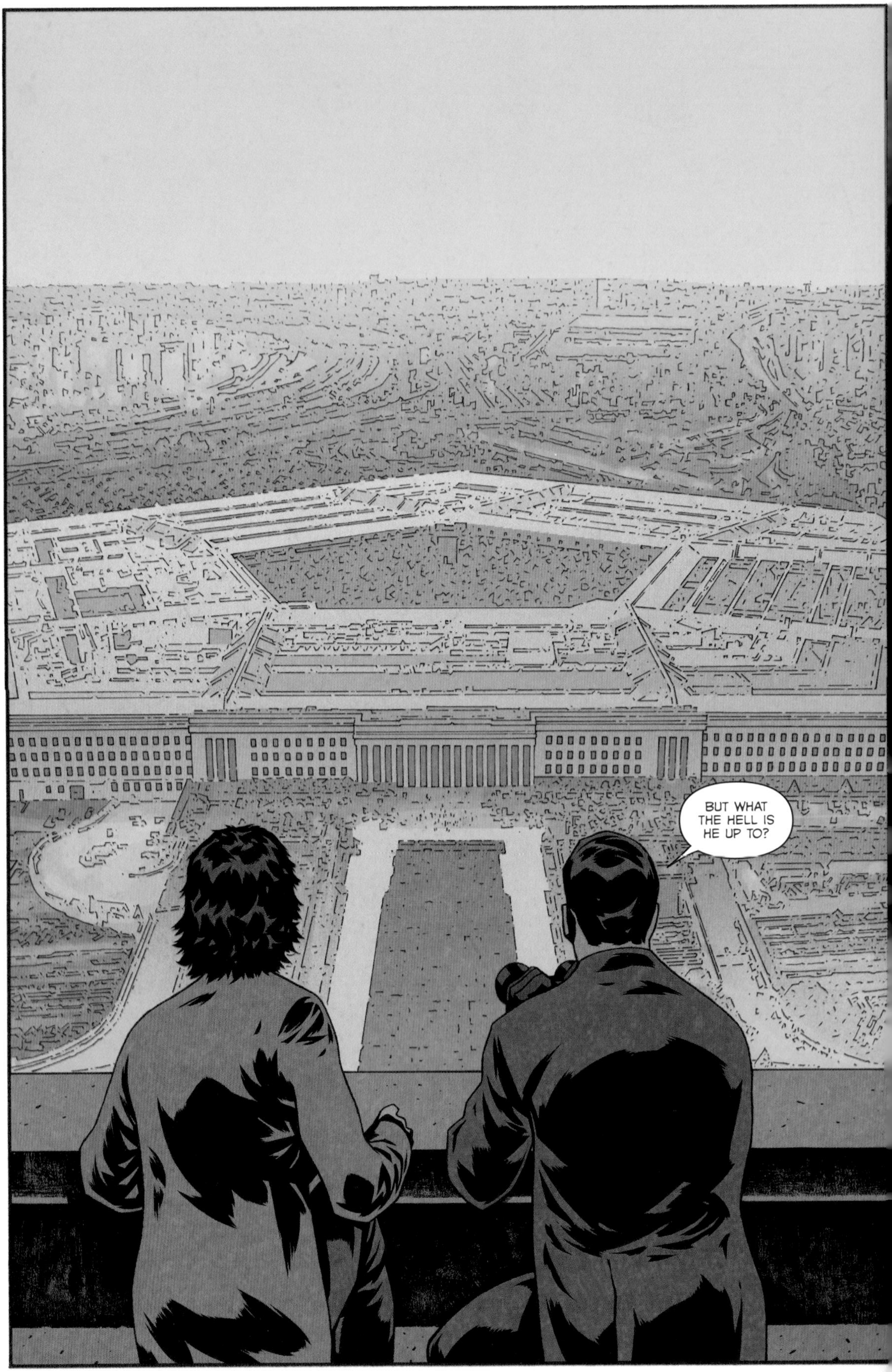
BUT WHAT THE HELL IS HE UP TO?

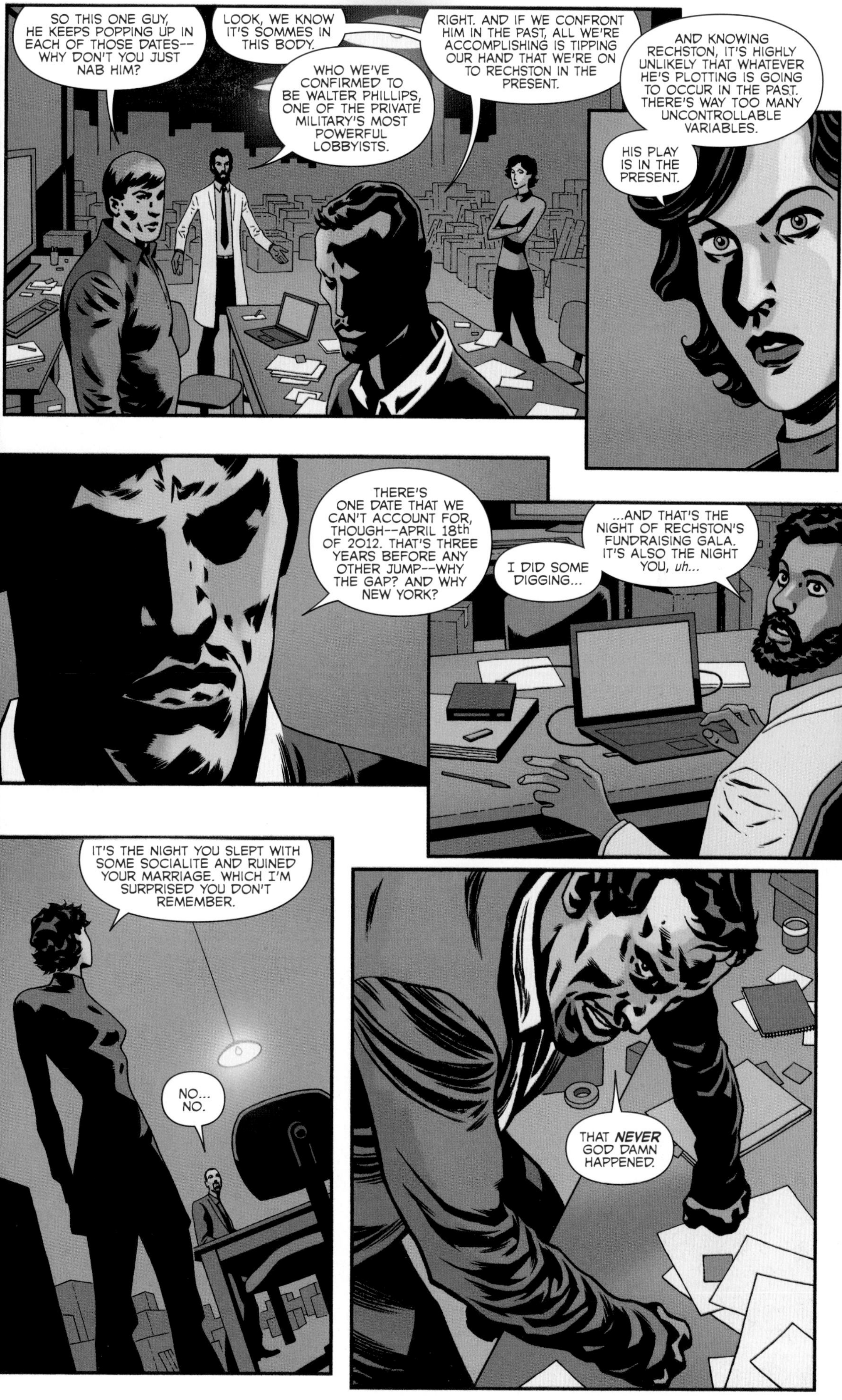

SO THIS ONE GUY, HE KEEPS POPPING UP IN EACH OF THOSE DATES-- WHY DON'T YOU JUST NAB HIM?
LOOK, WE KNOW IT'S SOMMES IN THIS BODY.
WHO WE'VE CONFIRMED TO BE WALTER PHILLIPS, ONE OF THE PRIVATE MILITARY'S MOST POWERFUL LOBBYISTS.
RIGHT. AND IF WE CONFRONT HIM IN THE PAST, ALL WE'RE ACCOMPLISHING IS TIPPING OUR HAND THAT WE'RE ON TO RECHSTON IN THE PRESENT.
AND KNOWING RECHSTON, IT'S HIGHLY UNLIKELY THAT WHATEVER HE'S PLOTTING IS GOING TO OCCUR IN THE PAST. THERE'S WAY TOO MANY UNCONTROLLABLE VARIABLES.
HIS PLAY IS IN THE PRESENT.
THERE'S ONE DATE THAT WE CAN'T ACCOUNT FOR, THOUGH--APRIL 18th OF 2012. THAT'S THREE YEARS BEFORE ANY OTHER JUMP--WHY THE GAP? AND WHY NEW YORK?
I DID SOME DIGGING...
...AND THAT'S THE NIGHT OF RECHSTON'S FUNDRAISING GALA. IT'S ALSO THE NIGHT YOU, *uh...*
IT'S THE NIGHT YOU SLEPT WITH SOME SOCIALITE AND RUINED YOUR MARRIAGE. WHICH I'M SURPRISED YOU DON'T REMEMBER.
NO... NO.
THAT ***NEVER*** GOD DAMN HAPPENED.

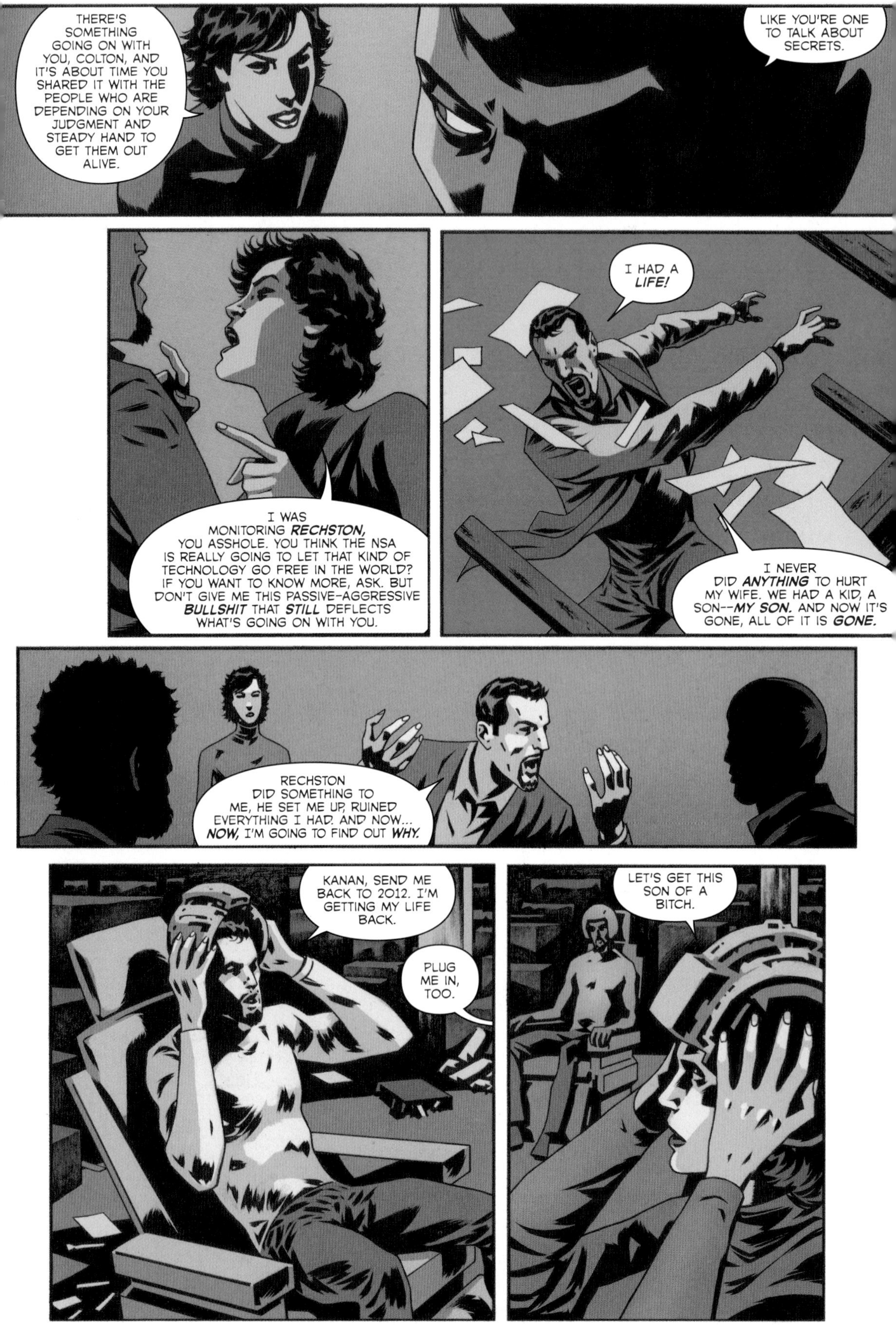
THERE'S SOMETHING GOING ON WITH YOU, COLTON, AND IT'S ABOUT TIME YOU SHARED IT WITH THE PEOPLE WHO ARE DEPENDING ON YOUR JUDGMENT AND STEADY HAND TO GET THEM OUT ALIVE.
LIKE YOU'RE ONE TO TALK ABOUT SECRETS.
I WAS MONITORING RECHSTON, YOU ASSHOLE. YOU THINK THE NSA IS REALLY GOING TO LET THAT KIND OF TECHNOLOGY GO FREE IN THE WORLD? IF YOU WANT TO KNOW MORE, ASK. BUT DON'T GIVE ME THIS PASSIVE-AGGRESSIVE BULLSHIT THAT STILL DEFLECTS WHAT'S GOING ON WITH YOU.
I HAD A LIFE!
I NEVER DID ANYTHING TO HURT MY WIFE. WE HAD A KID, A SON--MY SON. AND NOW IT'S GONE, ALL OF IT IS GONE.
RECHSTON DID SOMETHING TO ME, HE SET ME UP, RUINED EVERYTHING I HAD. AND NOW... NOW, I'M GOING TO FIND OUT WHY.
KANAN, SEND ME BACK TO 2012. I'M GETTING MY LIFE BACK.
PLUG ME IN, TOO.
LET'S GET THIS SON OF A BITCH.

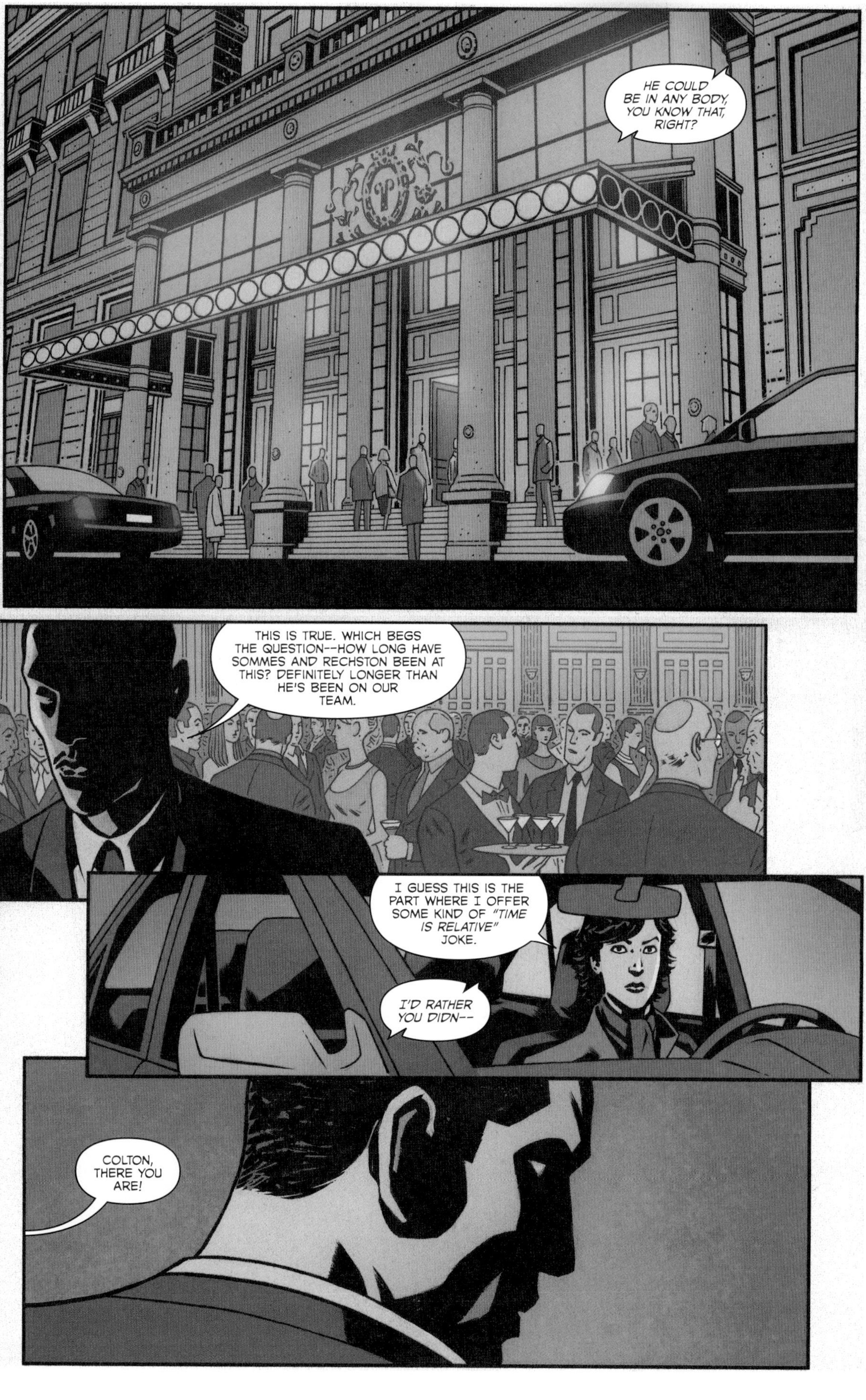
HE COULD BE IN ANY BODY, YOU KNOW THAT, RIGHT?
THIS IS TRUE. WHICH BEGS THE QUESTION--HOW LONG HAVE SOMMES AND RECHSTON BEEN AT THIS? DEFINITELY LONGER THAN HE'S BEEN ON OUR TEAM.
I GUESS THIS IS THE PART WHERE I OFFER SOME KIND OF "TIME IS RELATIVE" JOKE.
I'D RATHER YOU DIDN--
COLTON, THERE YOU ARE!

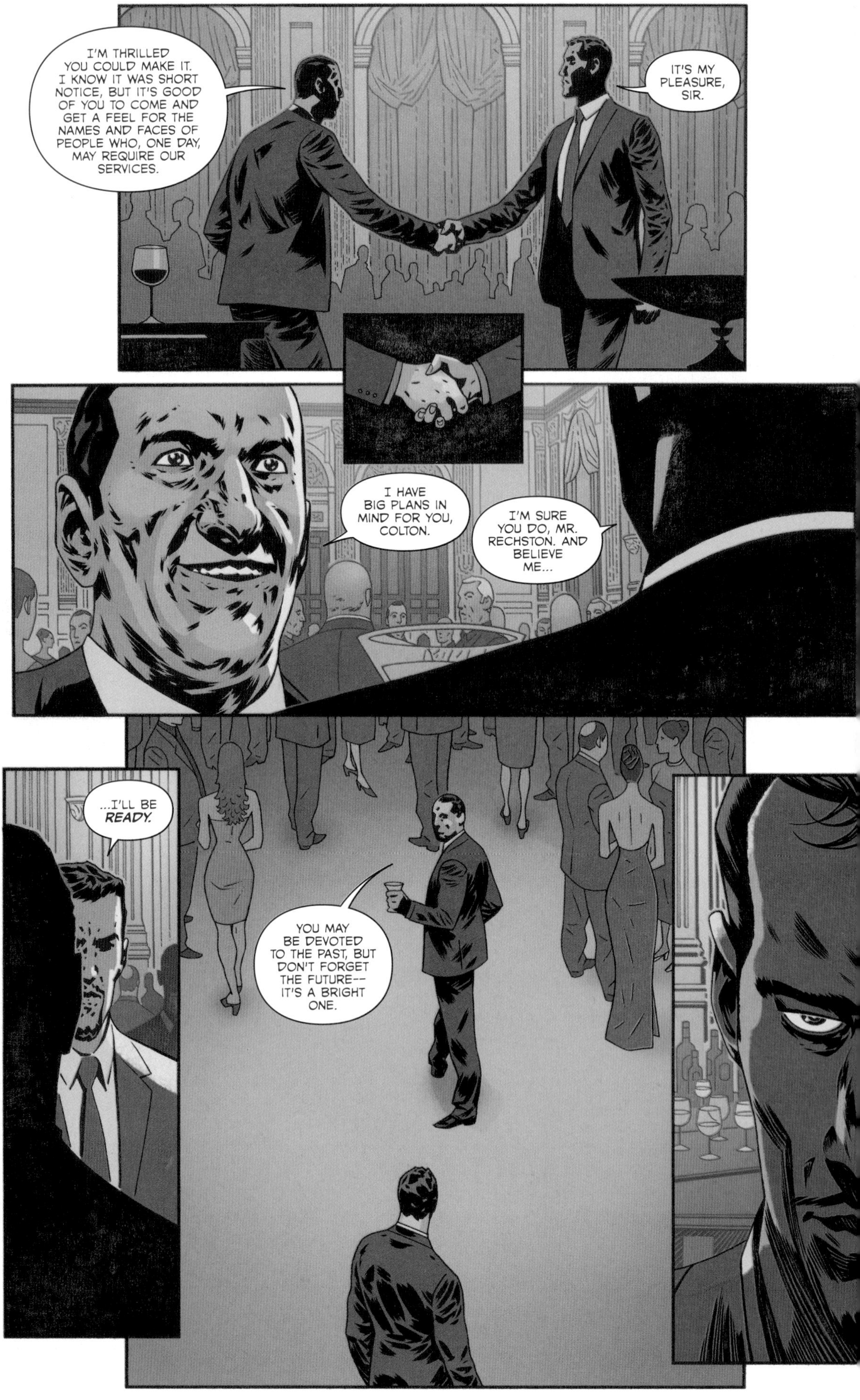
I'M THRILLED YOU COULD MAKE IT. I KNOW IT WAS SHORT NOTICE, BUT IT'S GOOD OF YOU TO COME AND GET A FEEL FOR THE NAMES AND FACES OF PEOPLE WHO, ONE DAY, MAY REQUIRE OUR SERVICES.
IT'S MY PLEASURE, SIR.
I HAVE BIG PLANS IN MIND FOR YOU, COLTON.
I'M SURE YOU DO, MR. RECHSTON. AND BELIEVE ME...
...I'LL BE *READY.*
YOU MAY BE DEVOTED TO THE PAST, BUT DON'T FORGET THE FUTURE-- IT'S A BRIGHT ONE.

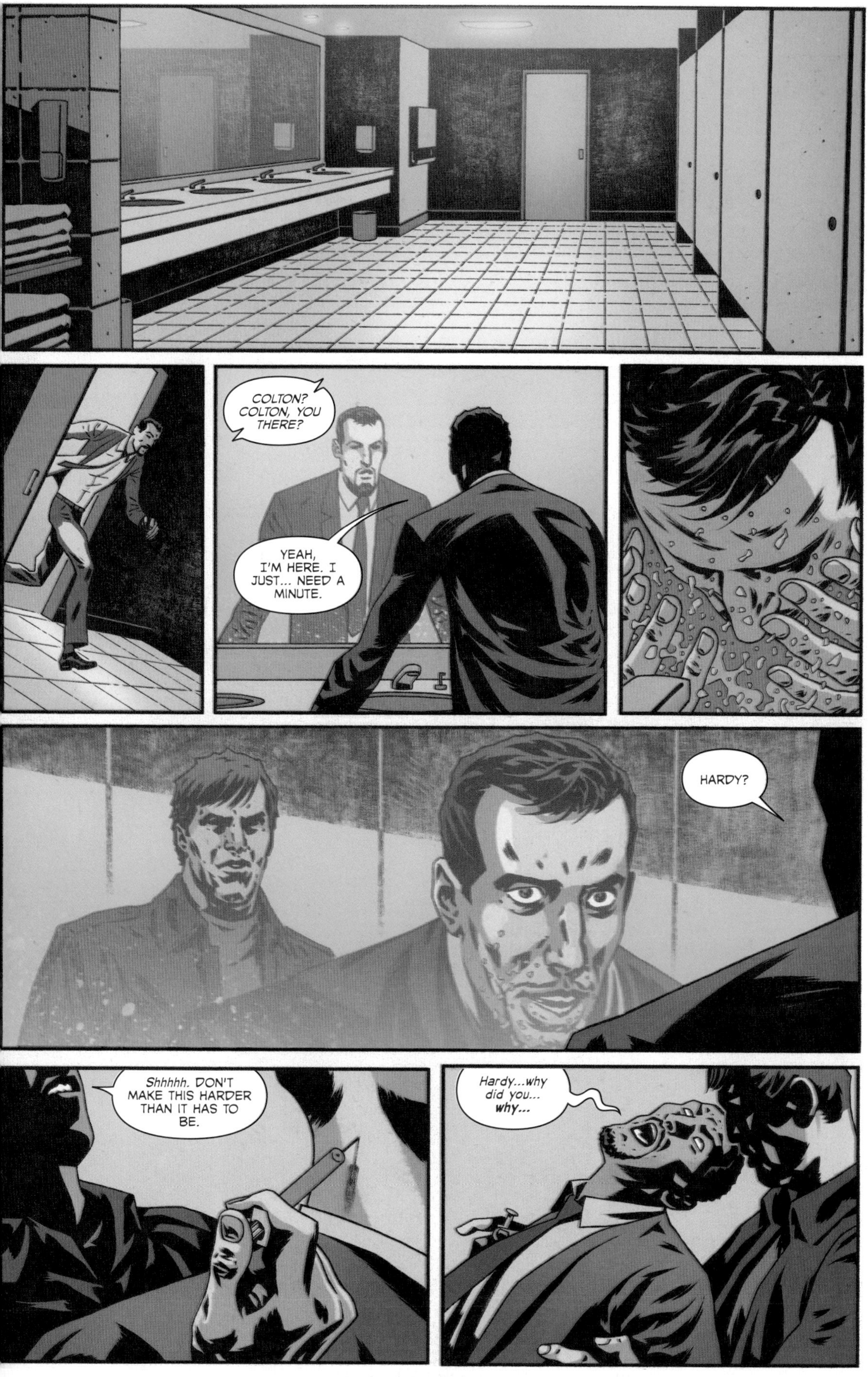
COLTON? COLTON, YOU THERE?
YEAH, I'M HERE. I JUST... NEED A MINUTE.
HARDY?
Shhhhh. DON'T MAKE THIS HARDER THAN IT HAS TO BE.
Hardy...why did you... ***why...***

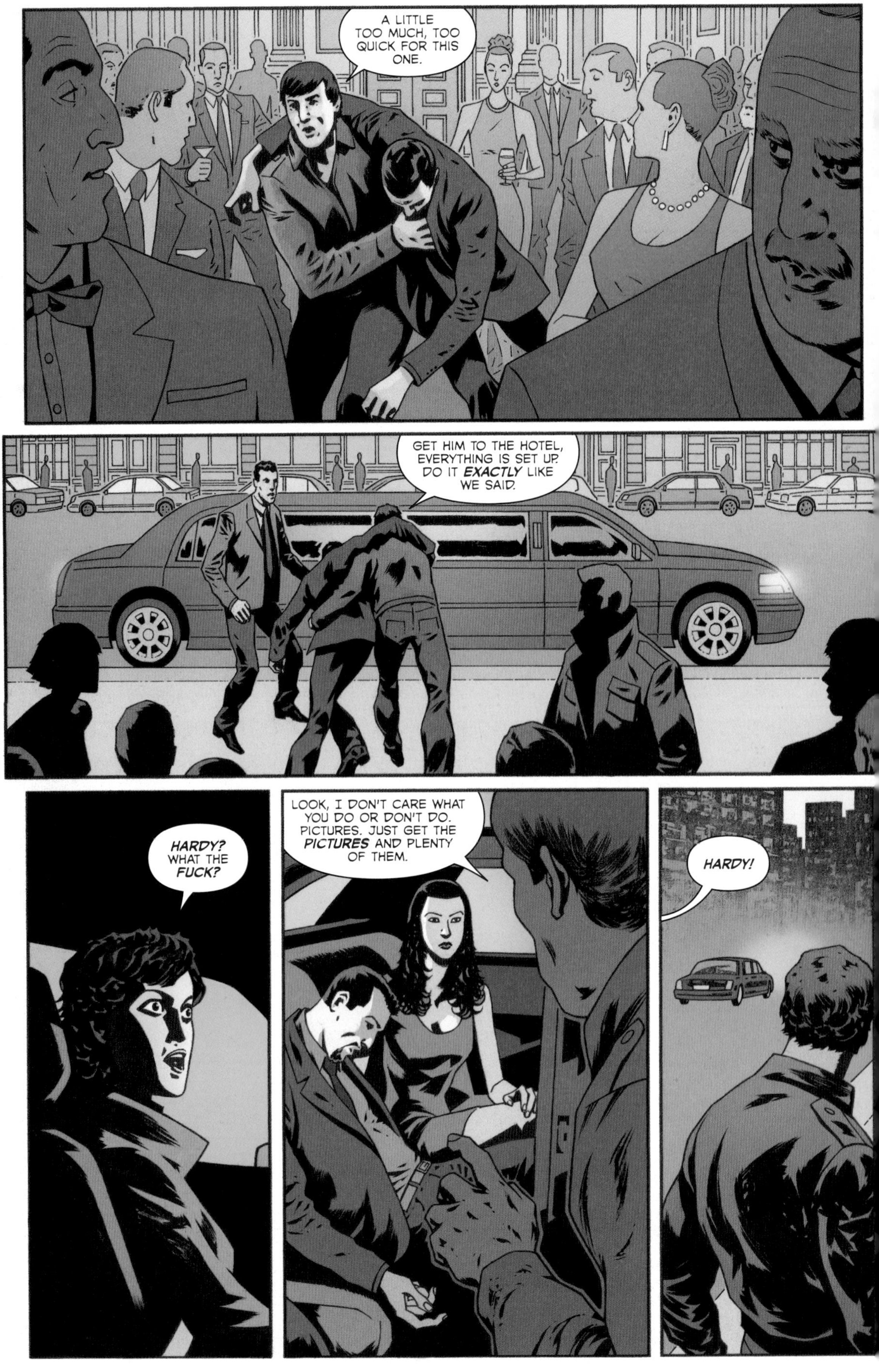

A LITTLE TOO MUCH, TOO QUICK FOR THIS ONE.
GET HIM TO THE HOTEL, EVERYTHING IS SET UP. DO IT *EXACTLY* LIKE WE SAID.
HARDY? WHAT THE *FUCK?*
LOOK, I DON'T CARE WHAT YOU DO OR DON'T DO. PICTURES. JUST GET THE *PICTURES* AND PLENTY OF THEM.
HARDY!

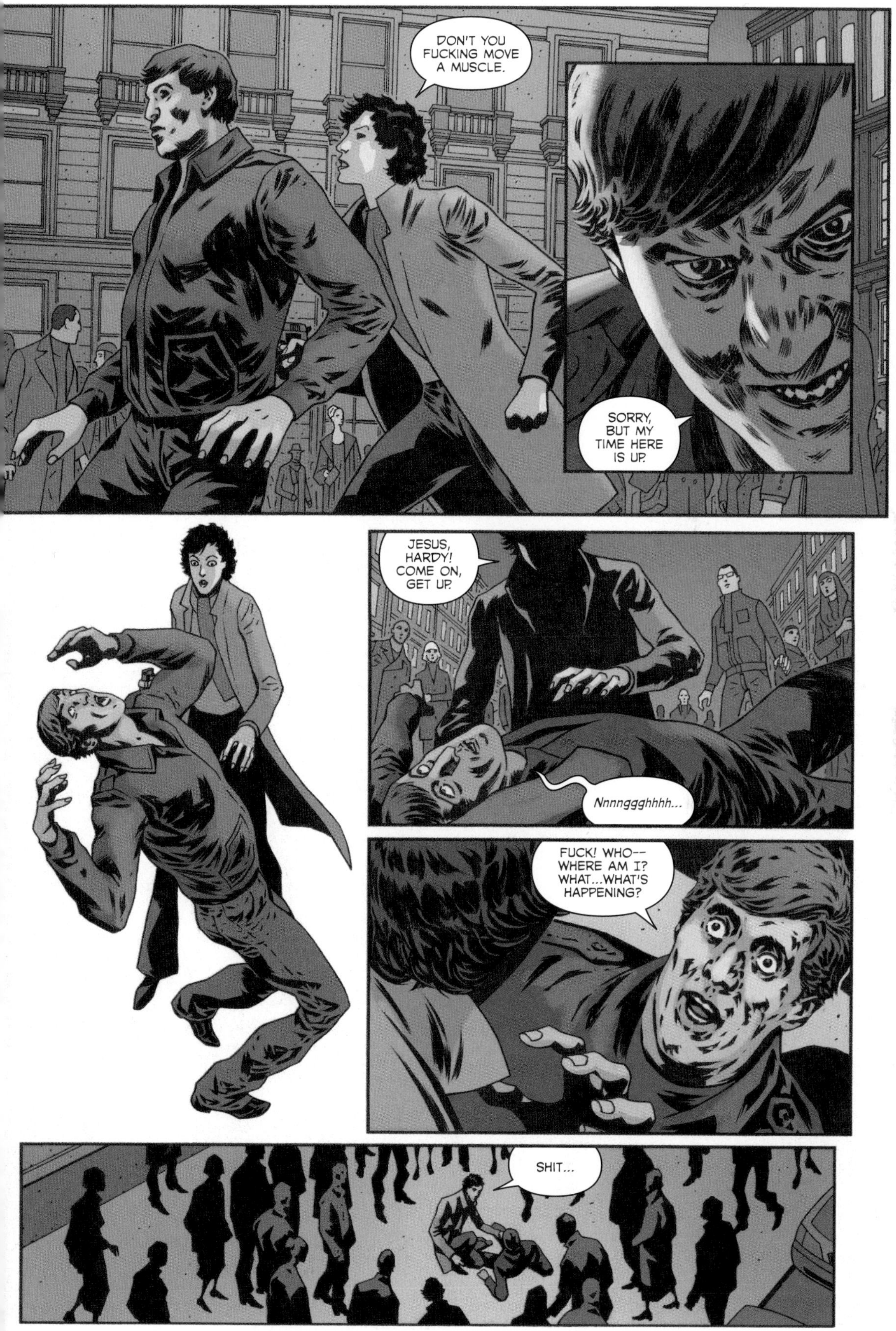
DON'T YOU FUCKING MOVE A MUSCLE.
SORRY, BUT MY TIME HERE IS UP.
JESUS, HARDY! COME ON, GET UP.
Nnnngggghhhh...
FUCK! WHO-- WHERE AM I? WHAT...WHAT'S HAPPENING?
SHIT...

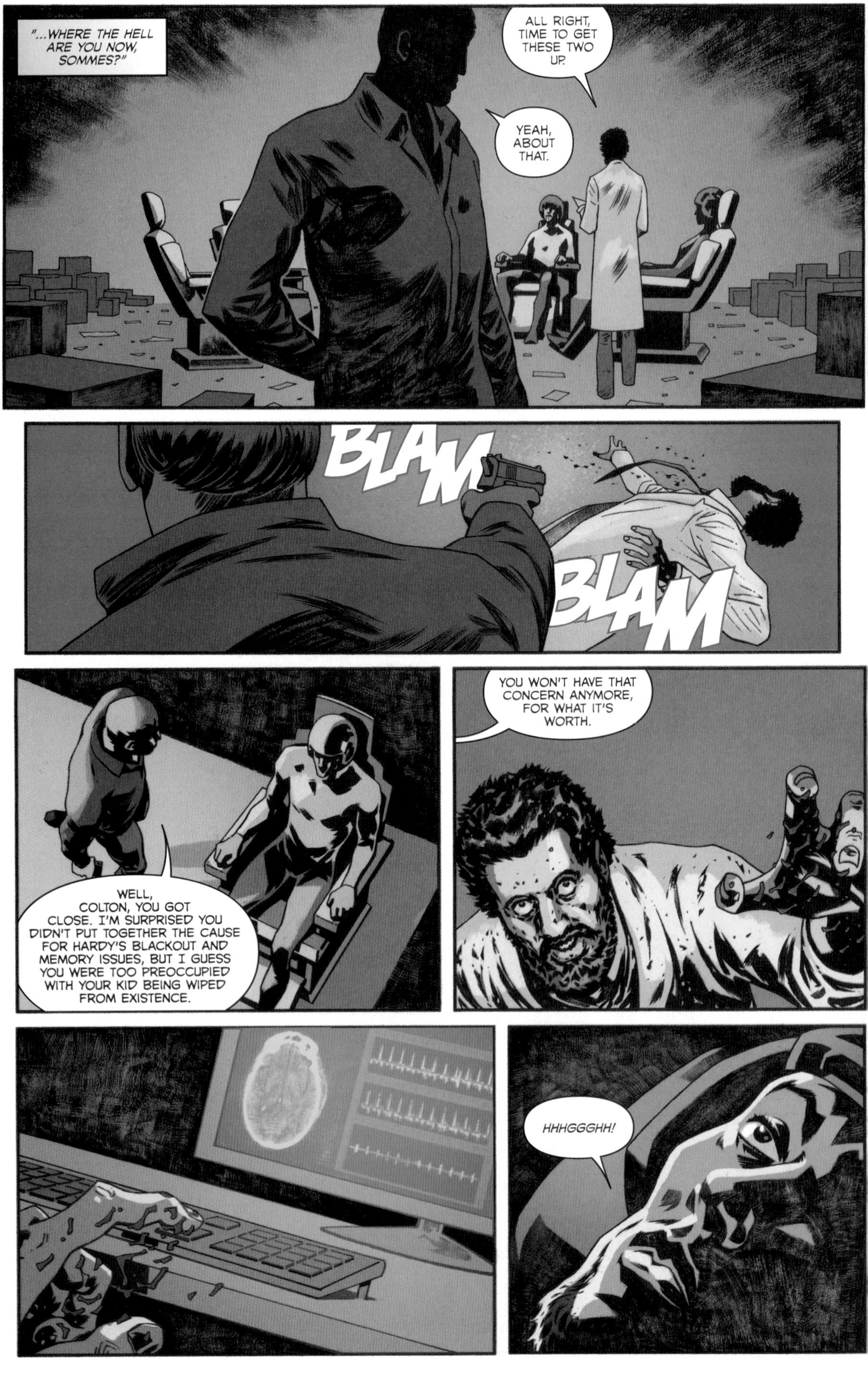
"...WHERE THE HELL ARE YOU NOW, SOMMES?"
ALL RIGHT, TIME TO GET THESE TWO UP.
YEAH, ABOUT THAT.
BLAM
BLAM
WELL, COLTON, YOU GOT CLOSE. I'M SURPRISED YOU DIDN'T PUT TOGETHER THE CAUSE FOR HARDY'S BLACKOUT AND MEMORY ISSUES, BUT I GUESS YOU WERE TOO PREOCCUPIED WITH YOUR KID BEING WIPED FROM EXISTENCE.
YOU WON'T HAVE THAT CONCERN ANYMORE, FOR WHAT IT'S WORTH.
HHHGGGHH!

OOOOF!

BLAM

BLAM

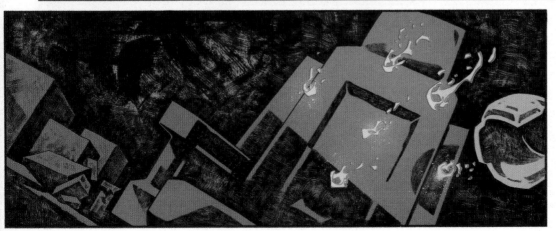

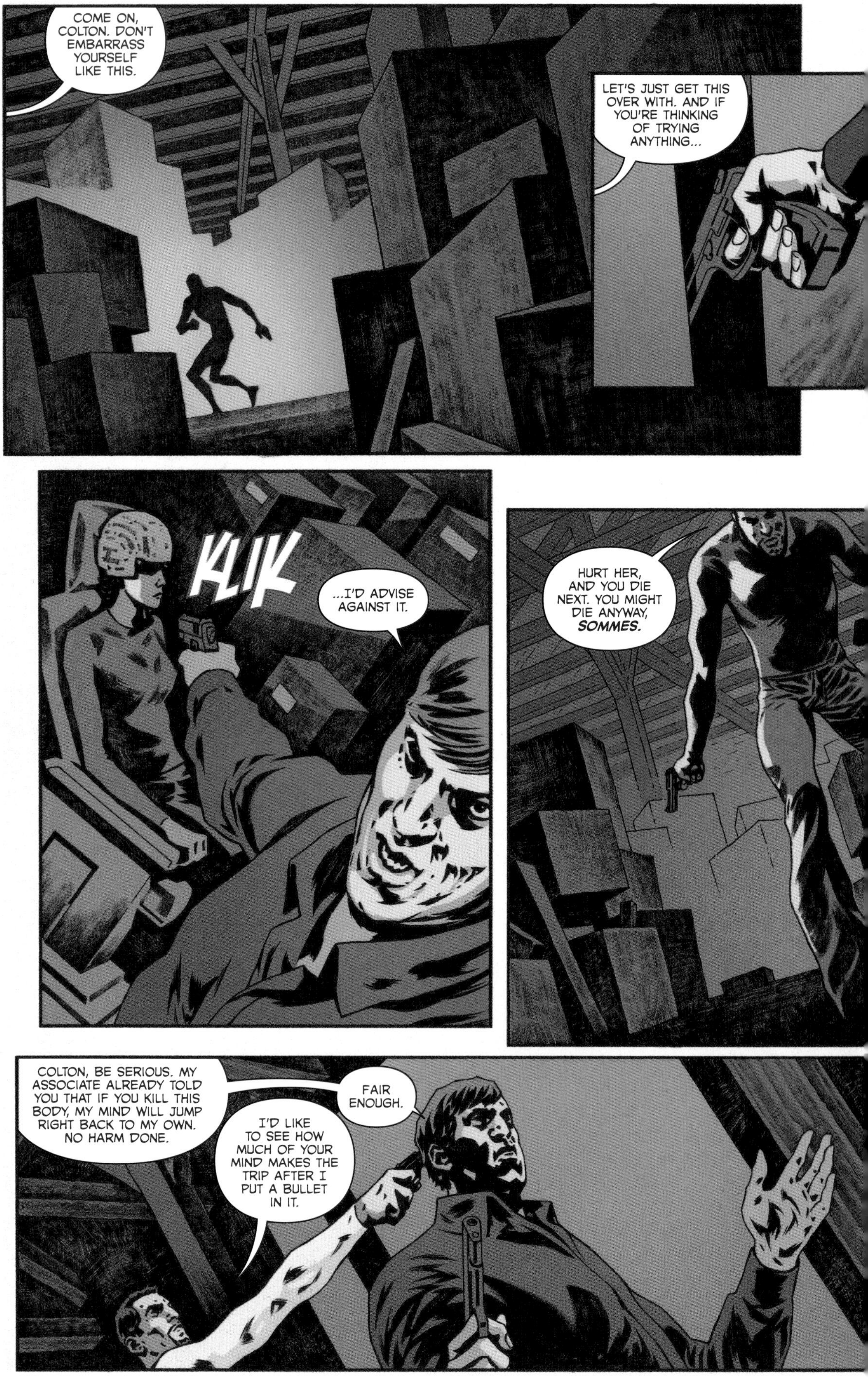
COME ON, COLTON. DON'T EMBARRASS YOURSELF LIKE THIS.
LET'S JUST GET THIS OVER WITH. AND IF YOU'RE THINKING OF TRYING ANYTHING...
KLIK
...I'D ADVISE AGAINST IT.
HURT HER, AND YOU DIE NEXT. YOU MIGHT DIE ANYWAY, SOMMES.
COLTON, BE SERIOUS. MY ASSOCIATE ALREADY TOLD YOU THAT IF YOU KILL THIS BODY, MY MIND WILL JUMP RIGHT BACK TO MY OWN. NO HARM DONE.
FAIR ENOUGH.
I'D LIKE TO SEE HOW MUCH OF YOUR MIND MAKES THE TRIP AFTER I PUT A BULLET IN IT.

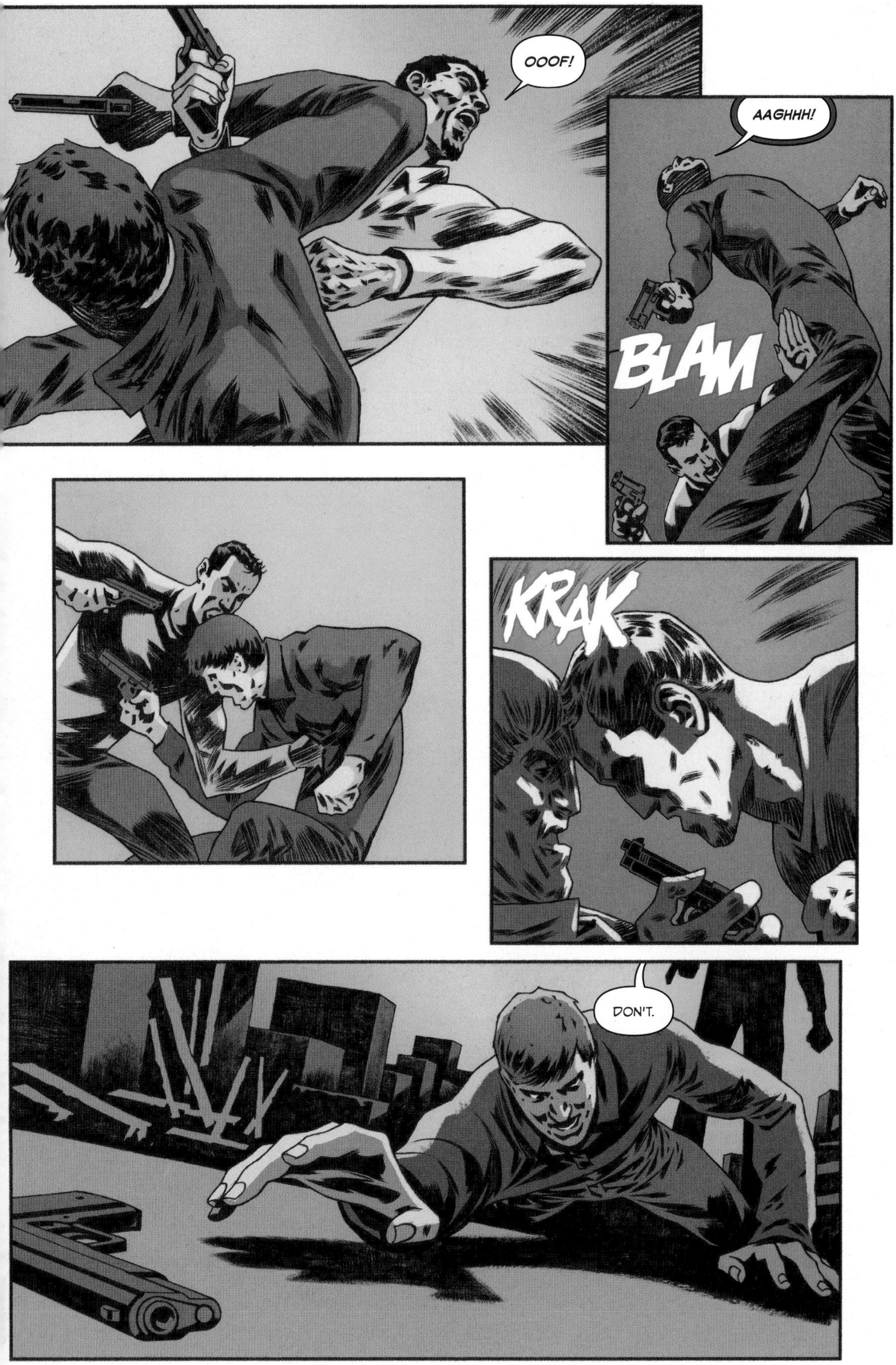
OOOF!
AAGHHH!
BLAM
KRAK
DON'T.

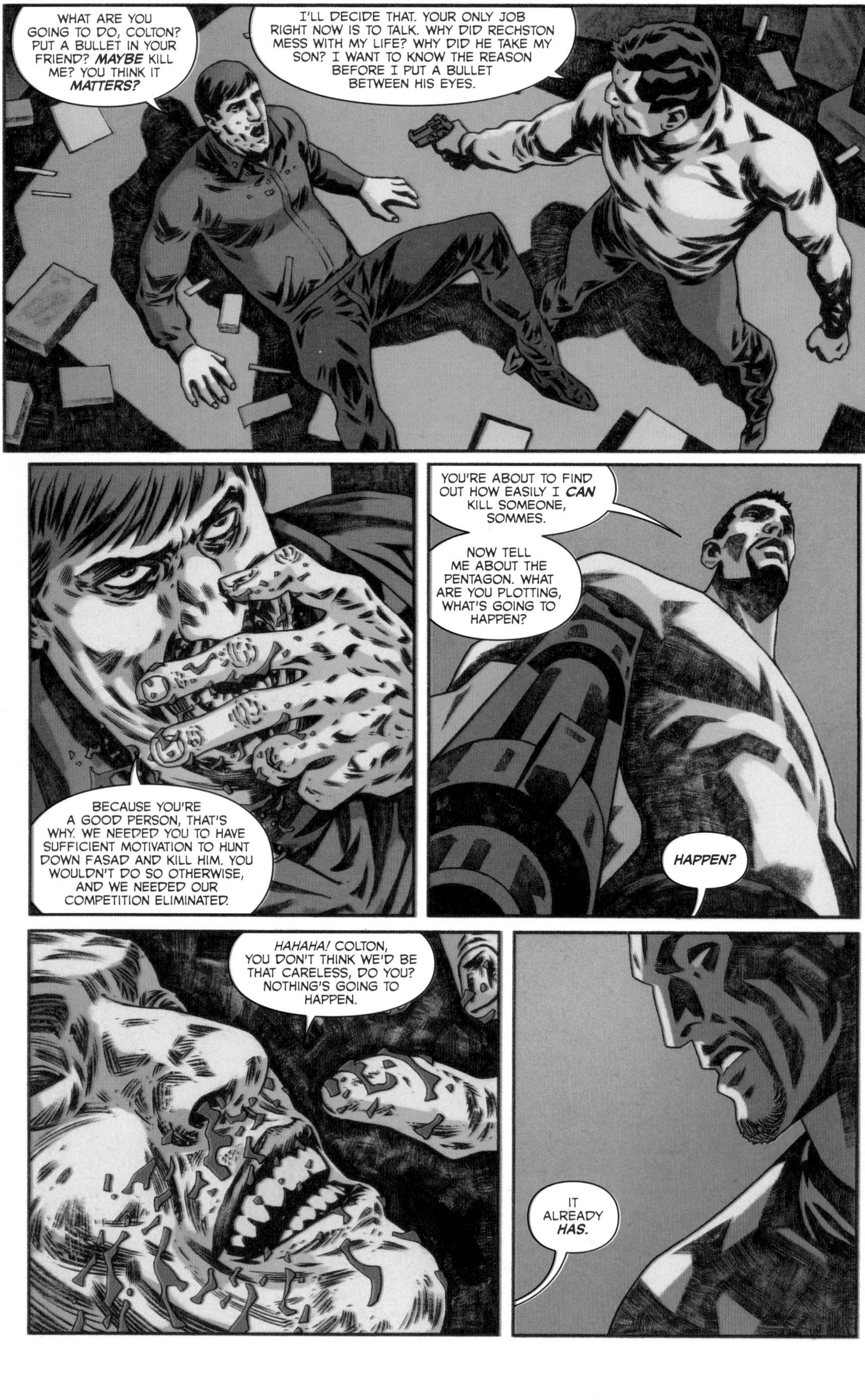
WHAT ARE YOU GOING TO DO, COLTON? PUT A BULLET IN YOUR FRIEND? MAYBE KILL ME? YOU THINK IT MATTERS?
I'LL DECIDE THAT. YOUR ONLY JOB RIGHT NOW IS TO TALK. WHY DID RECHSTON MESS WITH MY LIFE? WHY DID HE TAKE MY SON? I WANT TO KNOW THE REASON BEFORE I PUT A BULLET BETWEEN HIS EYES.
BECAUSE YOU'RE A GOOD PERSON, THAT'S WHY. WE NEEDED YOU TO HAVE SUFFICIENT MOTIVATION TO HUNT DOWN FASAD AND KILL HIM. YOU WOULDN'T DO SO OTHERWISE, AND WE NEEDED OUR COMPETITION ELIMINATED.
YOU'RE ABOUT TO FIND OUT HOW EASILY I CAN KILL SOMEONE, SOMMES.
NOW TELL ME ABOUT THE PENTAGON. WHAT ARE YOU PLOTTING, WHAT'S GOING TO HAPPEN?
HAPPEN?
HAHAHA! COLTON, YOU DON'T THINK WE'D BE THAT CARELESS, DO YOU? NOTHING'S GOING TO HAPPEN.
IT ALREADY HAS.

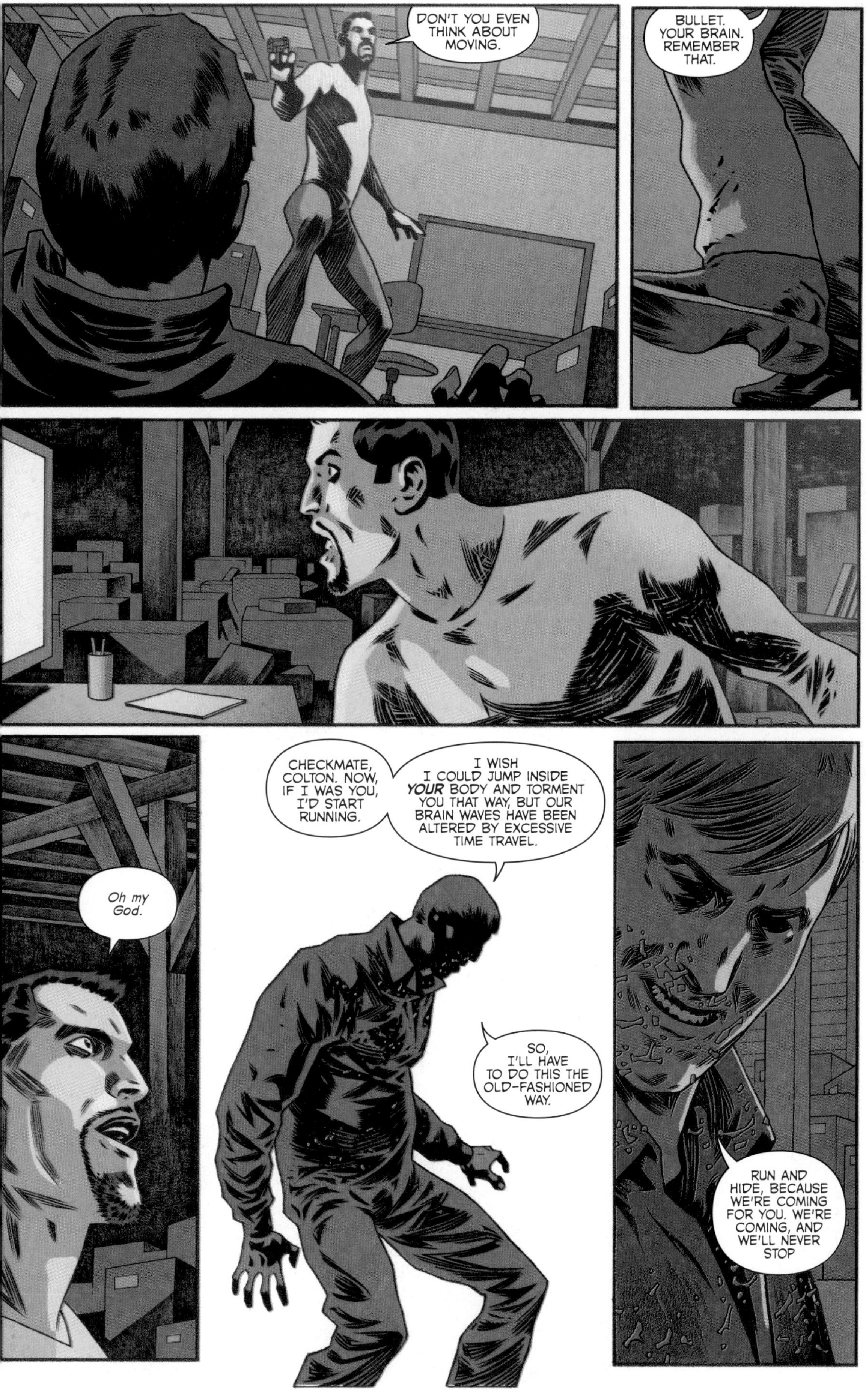
DON'T YOU EVEN THINK ABOUT MOVING.
BULLET. YOUR BRAIN. REMEMBER THAT.
CHECKMATE, COLTON. NOW, IF I WAS YOU, I'D START RUNNING.
I WISH I COULD JUMP INSIDE *YOUR* BODY AND TORMENT YOU THAT WAY, BUT OUR BRAIN WAVES HAVE BEEN ALTERED BY EXCESSIVE TIME TRAVEL.
Oh my God.
SO, I'LL HAVE TO DO THIS THE OLD-FASHIONED WAY.
RUN AND HIDE, BECAUSE WE'RE COMING FOR YOU. WE'RE COMING, AND WE'LL NEVER STOP

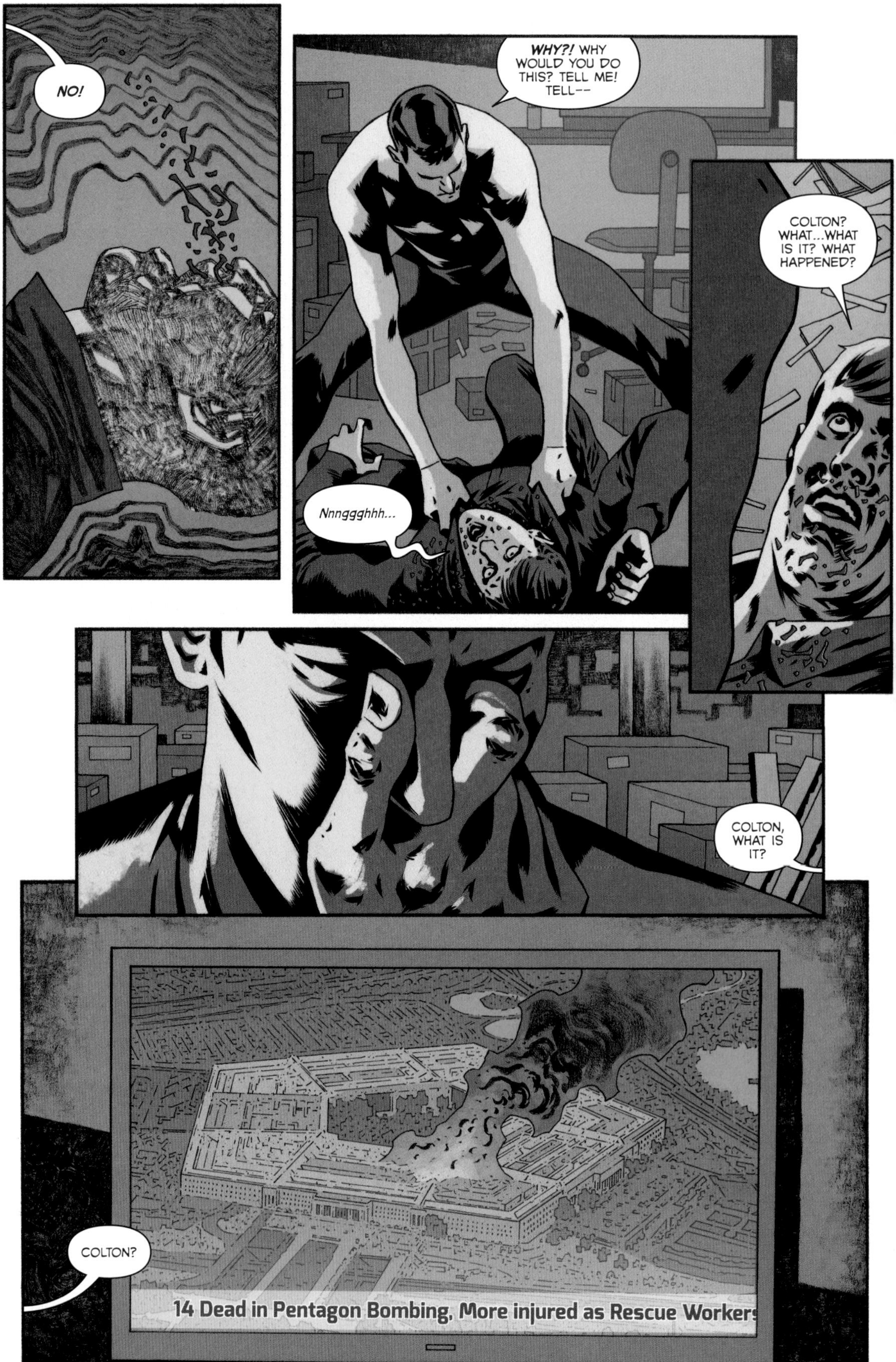
NO!
WHY?! WHY WOULD YOU DO THIS? TELL ME! TELL--
Nnnggghhh...
COLTON? WHAT...WHAT IS IT? WHAT HAPPENED?
COLTON, WHAT IS IT?
COLTON?
14 Dead in Pentagon Bombing, More injured as Rescue Workers
To Be Concluded

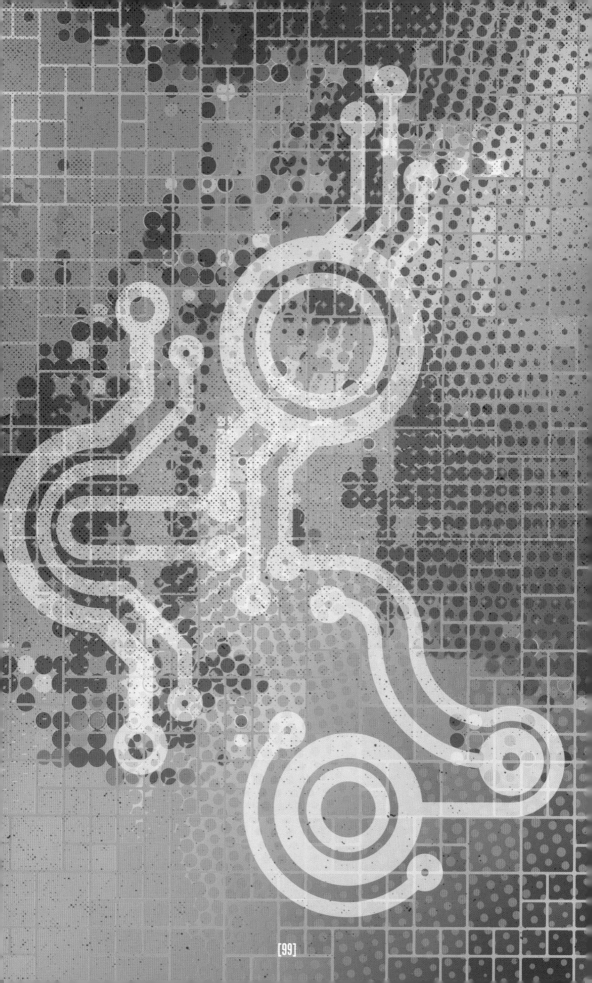

ISSUE 5

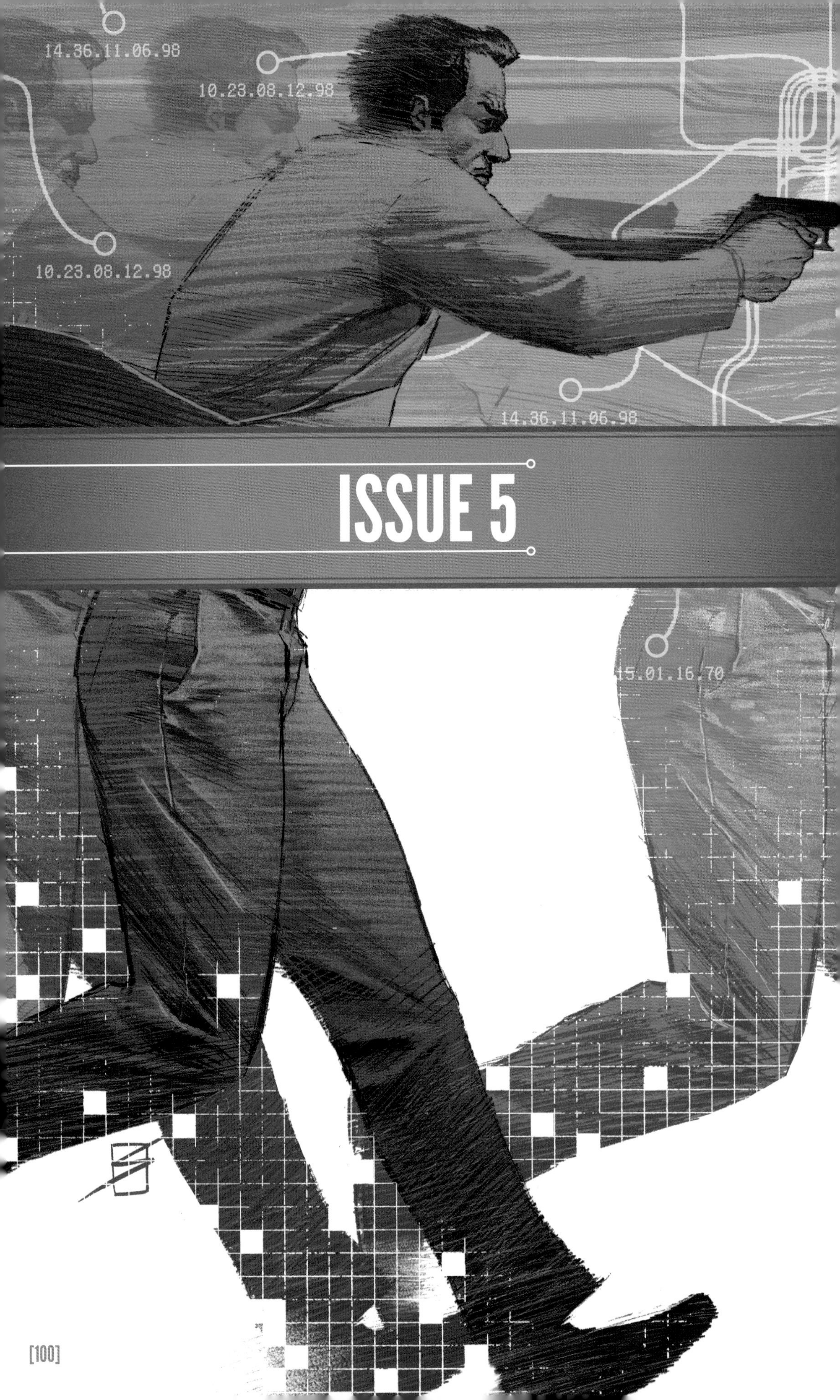
14.36.11.06.98
10.23.08.12.98
10.23.08.12.98
14.36.11.06.98
15.01.16.70

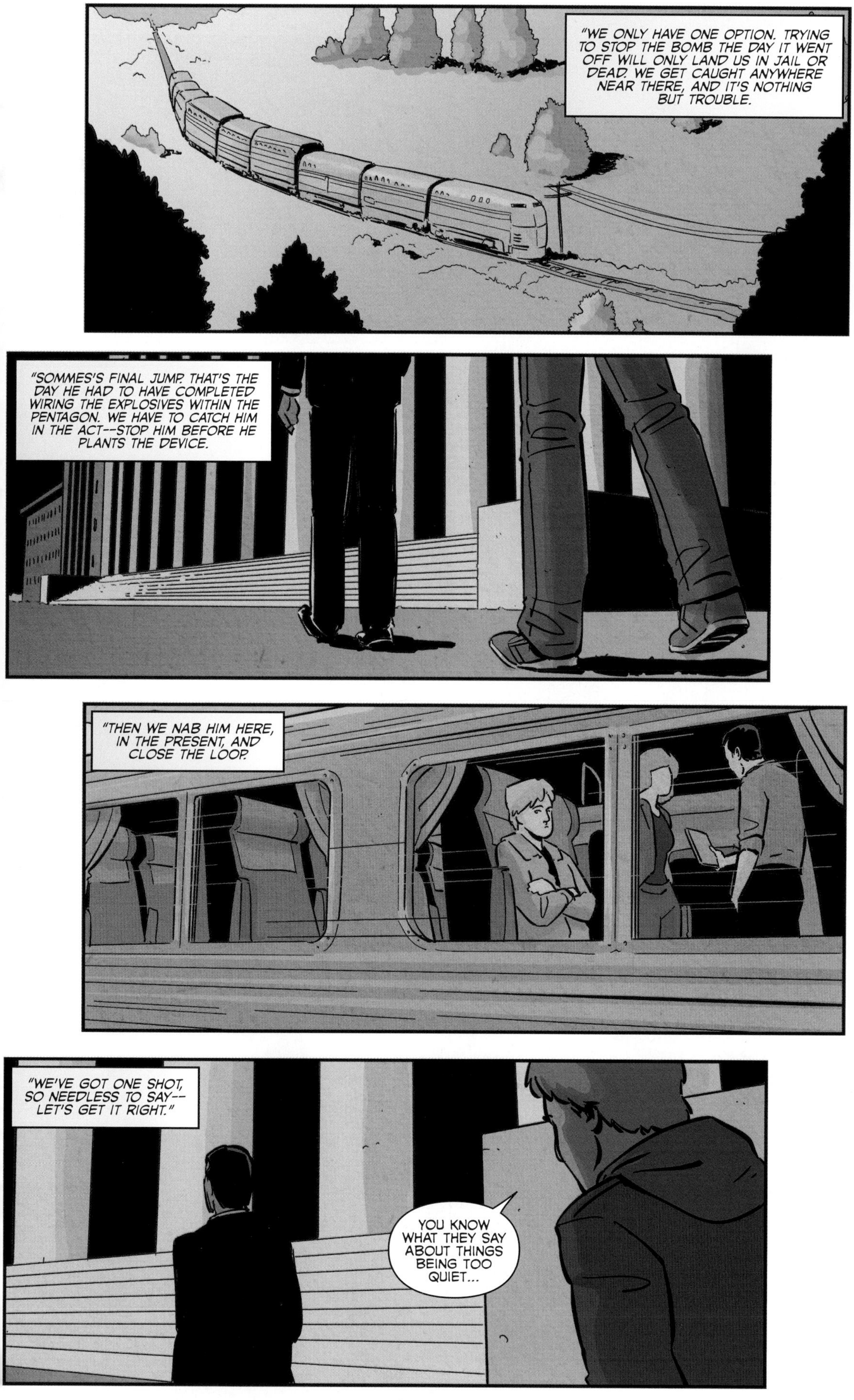
"WE ONLY HAVE ONE OPTION. TRYING TO STOP THE BOMB THE DAY IT WENT OFF WILL ONLY LAND US IN JAIL OR DEAD. WE GET CAUGHT ANYWHERE NEAR THERE, AND IT'S NOTHING BUT TROUBLE.
"SOMMES'S FINAL JUMP. THAT'S THE DAY HE HAD TO HAVE COMPLETED WIRING THE EXPLOSIVES WITHIN THE PENTAGON. WE HAVE TO CATCH HIM IN THE ACT--STOP HIM BEFORE HE PLANTS THE DEVICE.
"THEN WE NAB HIM HERE, IN THE PRESENT, AND CLOSE THE LOOP.
"WE'VE GOT ONE SHOT, SO NEEDLESS TO SAY-- LET'S GET IT RIGHT."
YOU KNOW WHAT THEY SAY ABOUT THINGS BEING TOO QUIET...

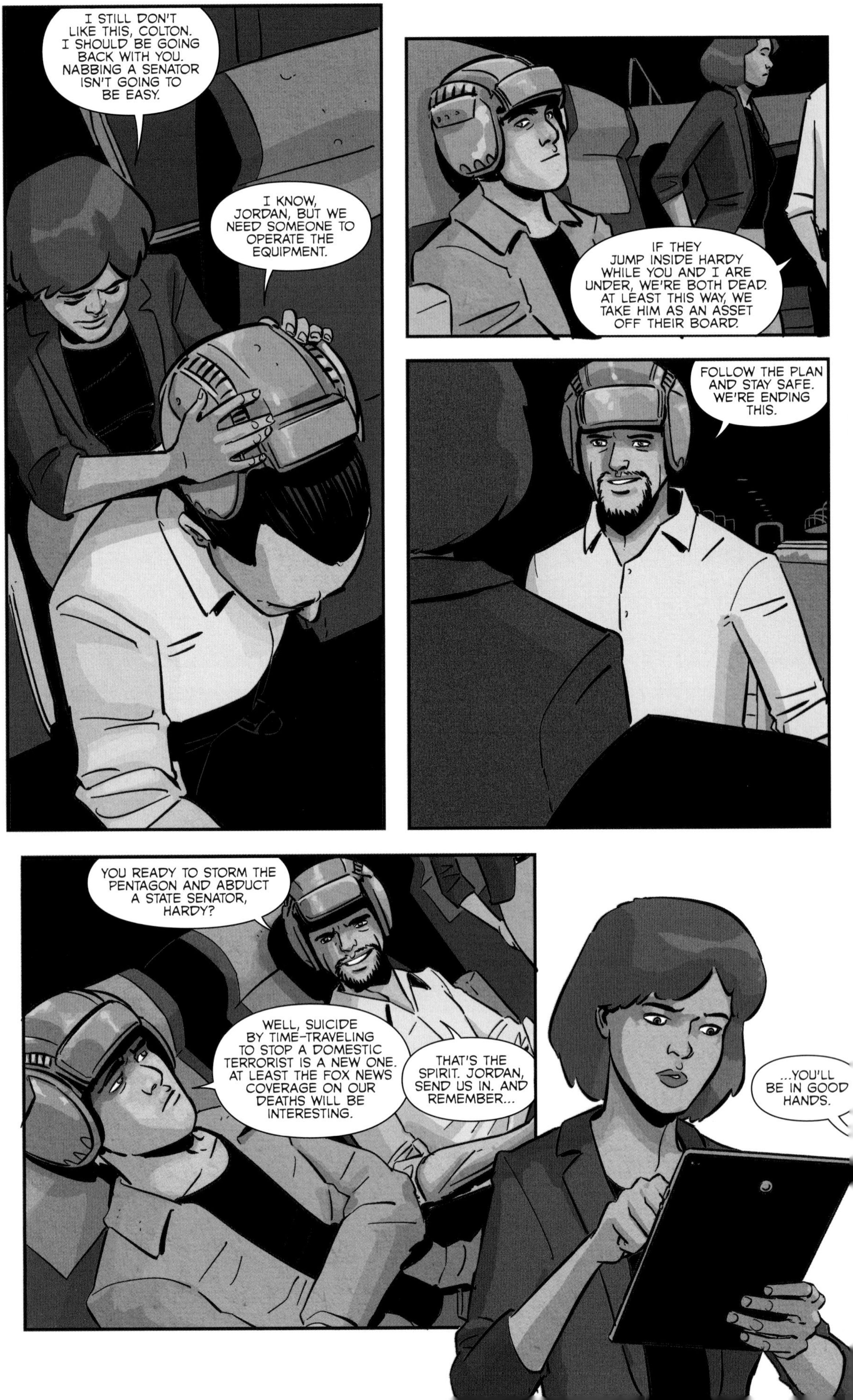
I STILL DON'T LIKE THIS, COLTON. I SHOULD BE GOING BACK WITH YOU. NABBING A SENATOR ISN'T GOING TO BE EASY.
I KNOW, JORDAN, BUT WE NEED SOMEONE TO OPERATE THE EQUIPMENT.
IF THEY JUMP INSIDE HARDY WHILE YOU AND I ARE UNDER, WE'RE BOTH DEAD. AT LEAST THIS WAY, WE TAKE HIM AS AN ASSET OFF THEIR BOARD.
FOLLOW THE PLAN AND STAY SAFE. WE'RE ENDING THIS.
YOU READY TO STORM THE PENTAGON AND ABDUCT A STATE SENATOR, HARDY?
WELL, SUICIDE BY TIME-TRAVELING TO STOP A DOMESTIC TERRORIST IS A NEW ONE. AT LEAST THE FOX NEWS COVERAGE ON OUR DEATHS WILL BE INTERESTING.
THAT'S THE SPIRIT. JORDAN, SEND US IN. AND REMEMBER...
...YOU'LL BE IN GOOD HANDS.

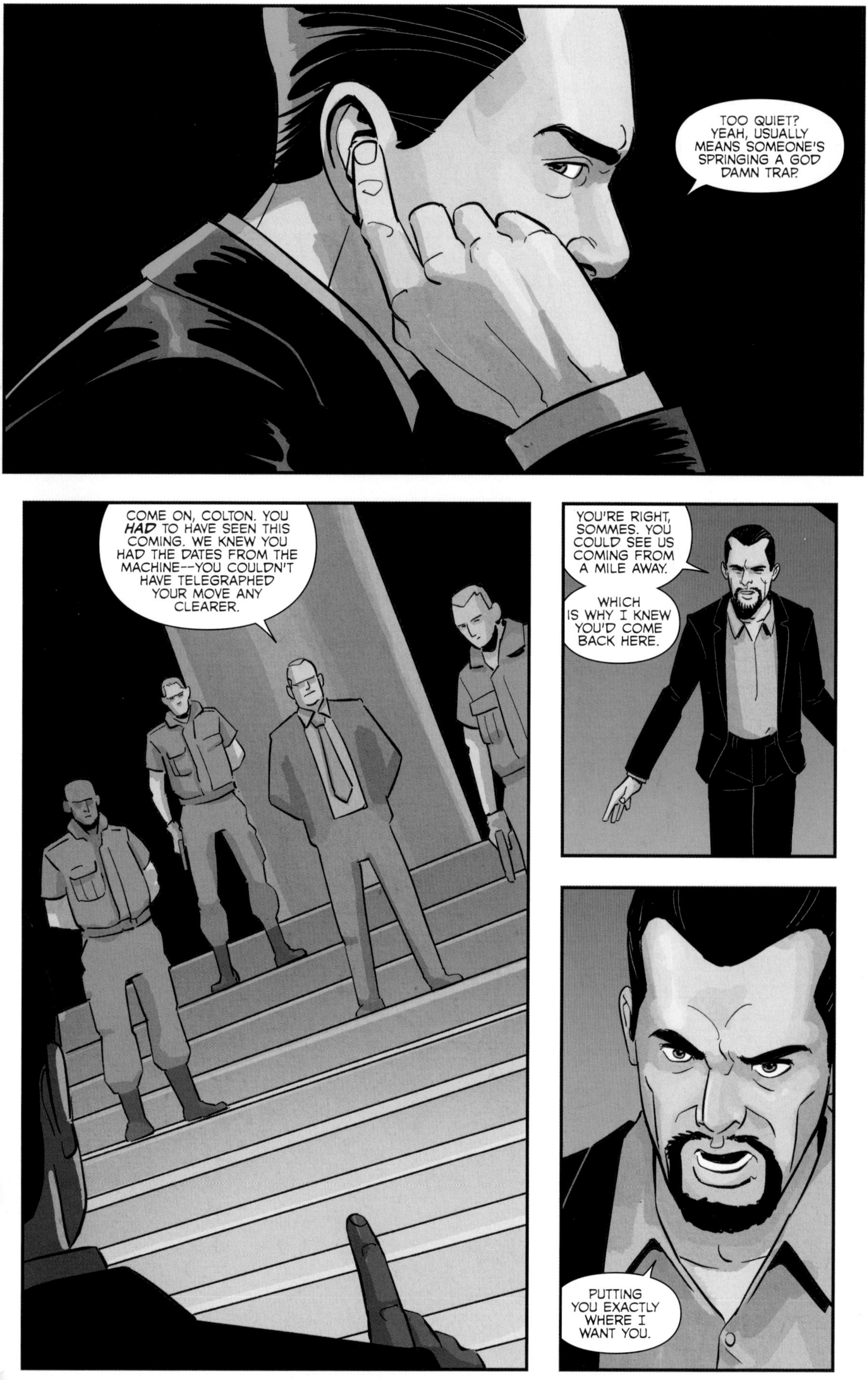

TOO QUIET? YEAH, USUALLY MEANS SOMEONE'S SPRINGING A GOD DAMN TRAP.
COME ON, COLTON. YOU *HAD* TO HAVE SEEN THIS COMING. WE KNEW YOU HAD THE DATES FROM THE MACHINE--YOU COULDN'T HAVE TELEGRAPHED YOUR MOVE ANY CLEARER.
YOU'RE RIGHT, SOMMES. YOU COULD SEE US COMING FROM A MILE AWAY.
WHICH IS WHY I KNEW YOU'D COME BACK HERE.
PUTTING YOU EXACTLY WHERE I WANT YOU.

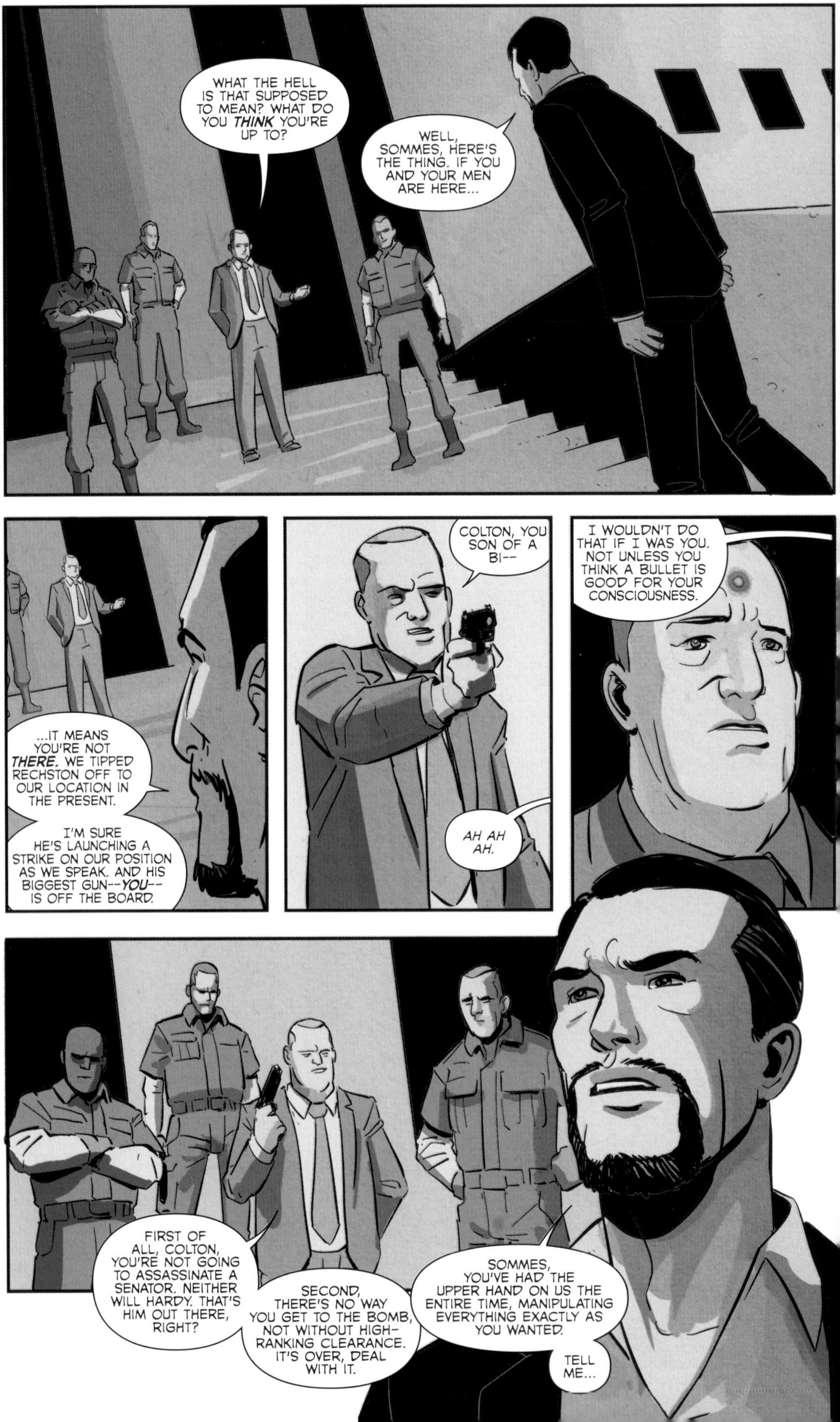

WHAT THE HELL IS THAT SUPPOSED TO MEAN? WHAT DO YOU THINK YOU'RE UP TO?
WELL, SOMMES, HERE'S THE THING. IF YOU AND YOUR MEN ARE HERE...
...IT MEANS YOU'RE NOT THERE. WE TIPPED RECHSTON OFF TO OUR LOCATION IN THE PRESENT.
I'M SURE HE'S LAUNCHING A STRIKE ON OUR POSITION AS WE SPEAK. AND HIS BIGGEST GUN--YOU--IS OFF THE BOARD.
COLTON, YOU SON OF A BI--
AH AH AH.
I WOULDN'T DO THAT IF I WAS YOU. NOT UNLESS YOU THINK A BULLET IS GOOD FOR YOUR CONSCIOUSNESS.
FIRST OF ALL, COLTON, YOU'RE NOT GOING TO ASSASSINATE A SENATOR. NEITHER WILL HARDY. THAT'S HIM OUT THERE, RIGHT?
SECOND, THERE'S NO WAY YOU GET TO THE BOMB, NOT WITHOUT HIGH-RANKING CLEARANCE. IT'S OVER, DEAL WITH IT.
SOMMES, YOU'VE HAD THE UPPER HAND ON US THE ENTIRE TIME, MANIPULATING EVERYTHING EXACTLY AS YOU WANTED.
TELL ME...

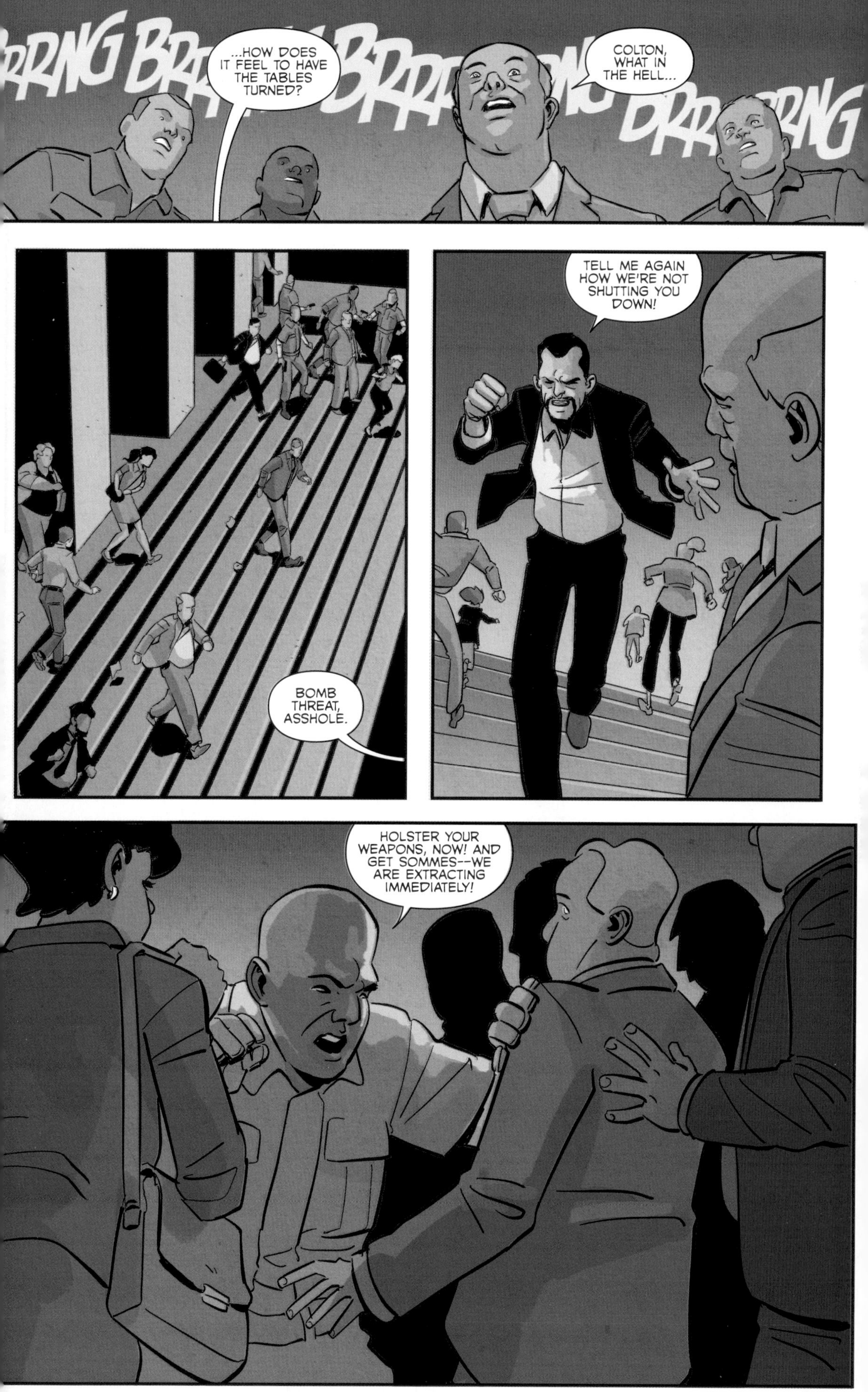
BRRRNG BRRRRNG BRRRRNG BRRRRNG
...HOW DOES IT FEEL TO HAVE THE TABLES TURNED?
COLTON, WHAT IN THE HELL...
BOMB THREAT, ASSHOLE.
TELL ME AGAIN HOW WE'RE NOT SHUTTING YOU DOWN!
HOLSTER YOUR WEAPONS, NOW! AND GET SOMMES--WE ARE EXTRACTING IMMEDIATELY!

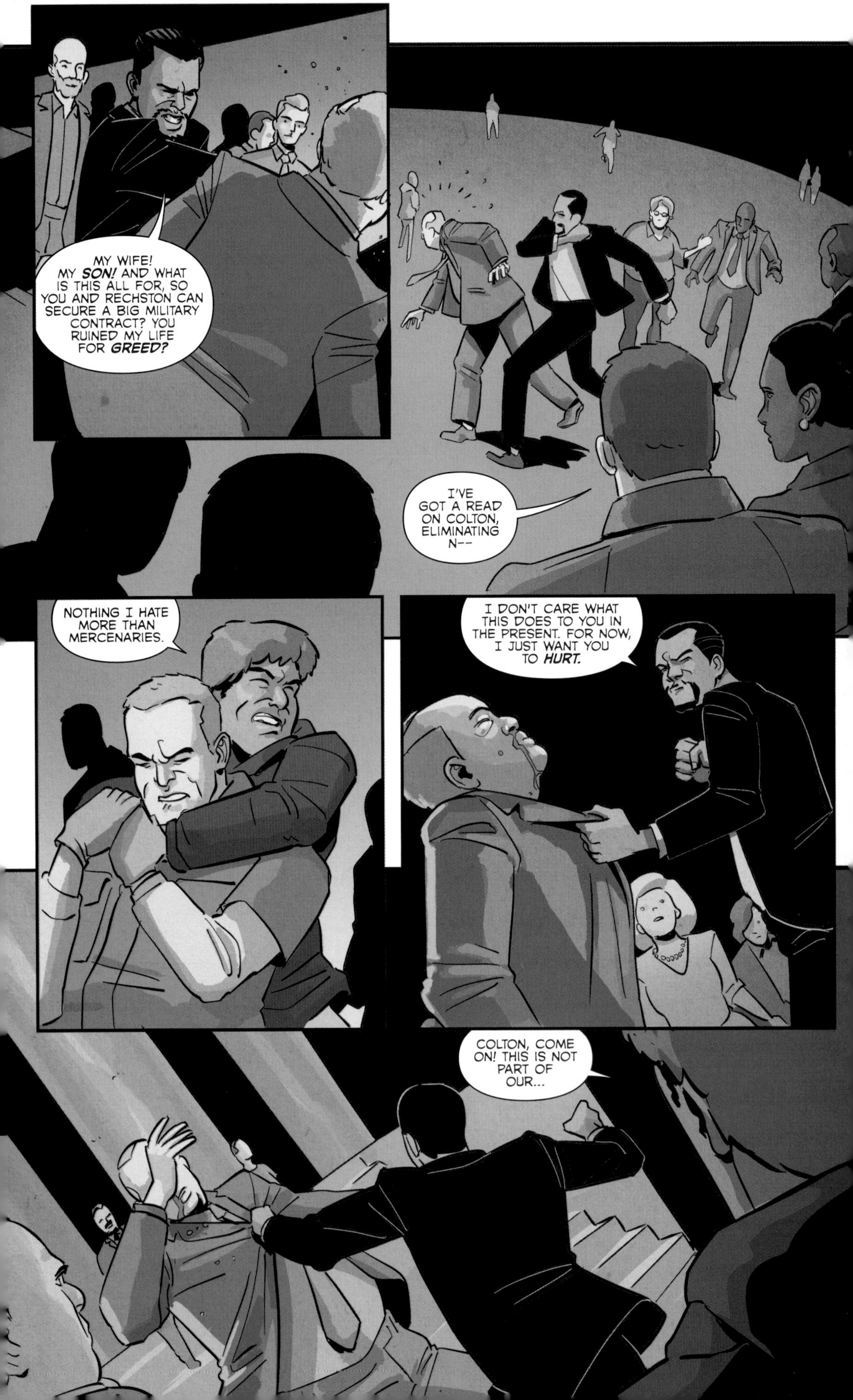

MY WIFE! MY SON! AND WHAT IS THIS ALL FOR, SO YOU AND RECHSTON CAN SECURE A BIG MILITARY CONTRACT? YOU RUINED MY LIFE FOR GREED?
I'VE GOT A READ ON COLTON, ELIMINATING N--
NOTHING I HATE MORE THAN MERCENARIES.
I DON'T CARE WHAT THIS DOES TO YOU IN THE PRESENT. FOR NOW, I JUST WANT YOU TO HURT.
COLTON, COME ON! THIS IS NOT PART OF OUR...

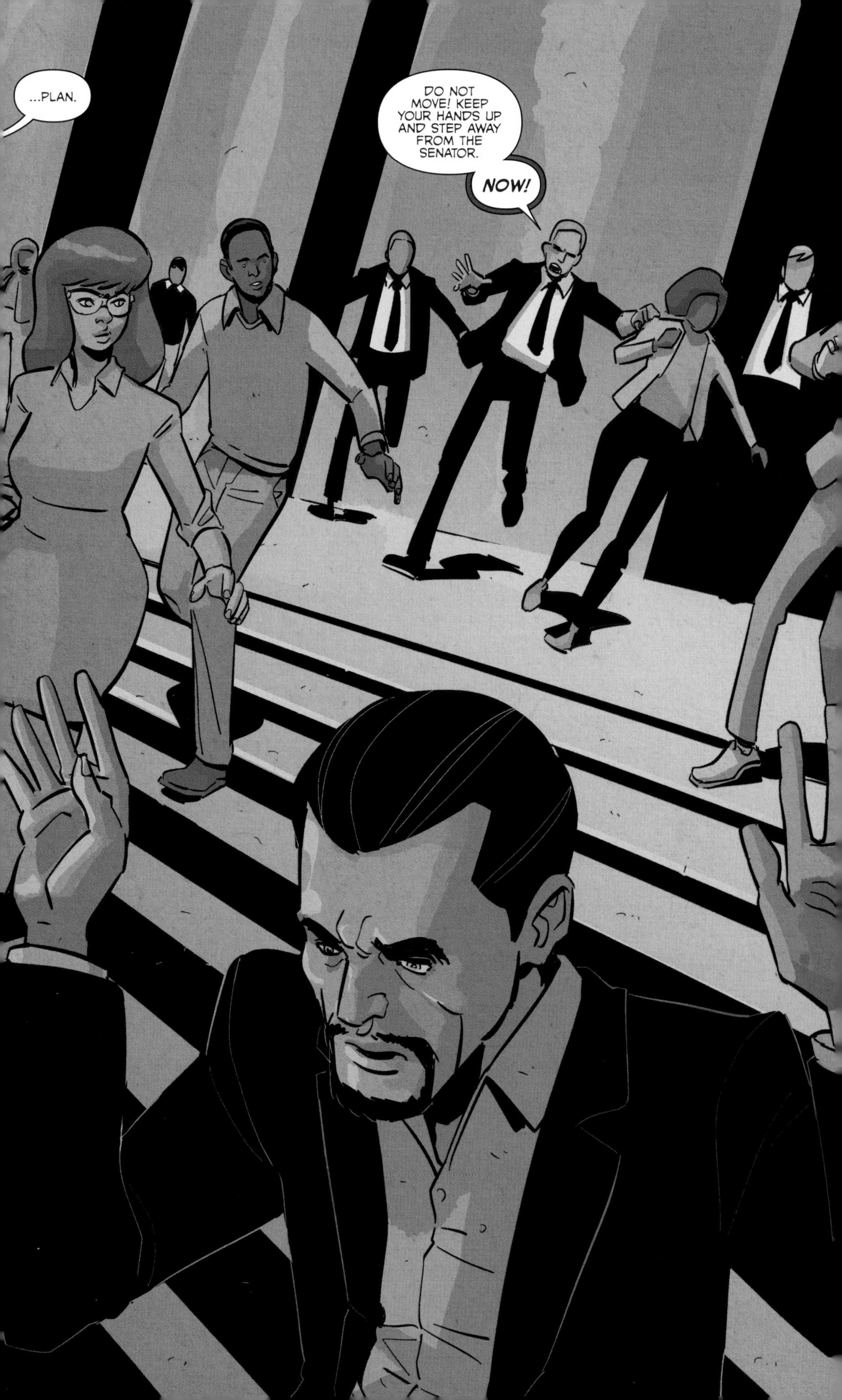
...PLAN.
DO NOT MOVE! KEEP YOUR HANDS UP AND STEP AWAY FROM THE SENATOR.
NOW!

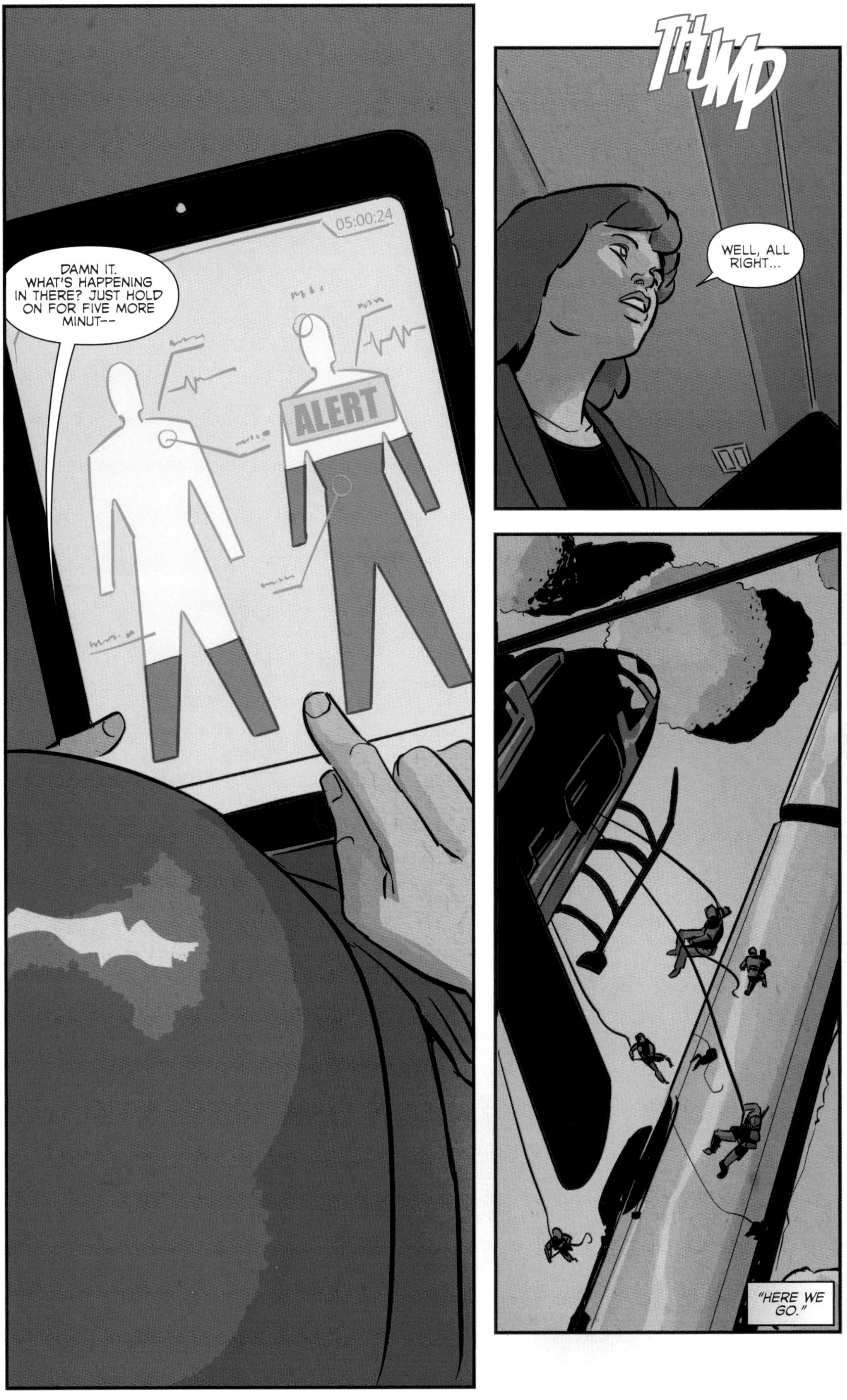
05:00:24
ALERT
DAMN IT. WHAT'S HAPPENING IN THERE? JUST HOLD ON FOR FIVE MORE MINUT--
THUMP
WELL, ALL RIGHT...
"HERE WE GO."

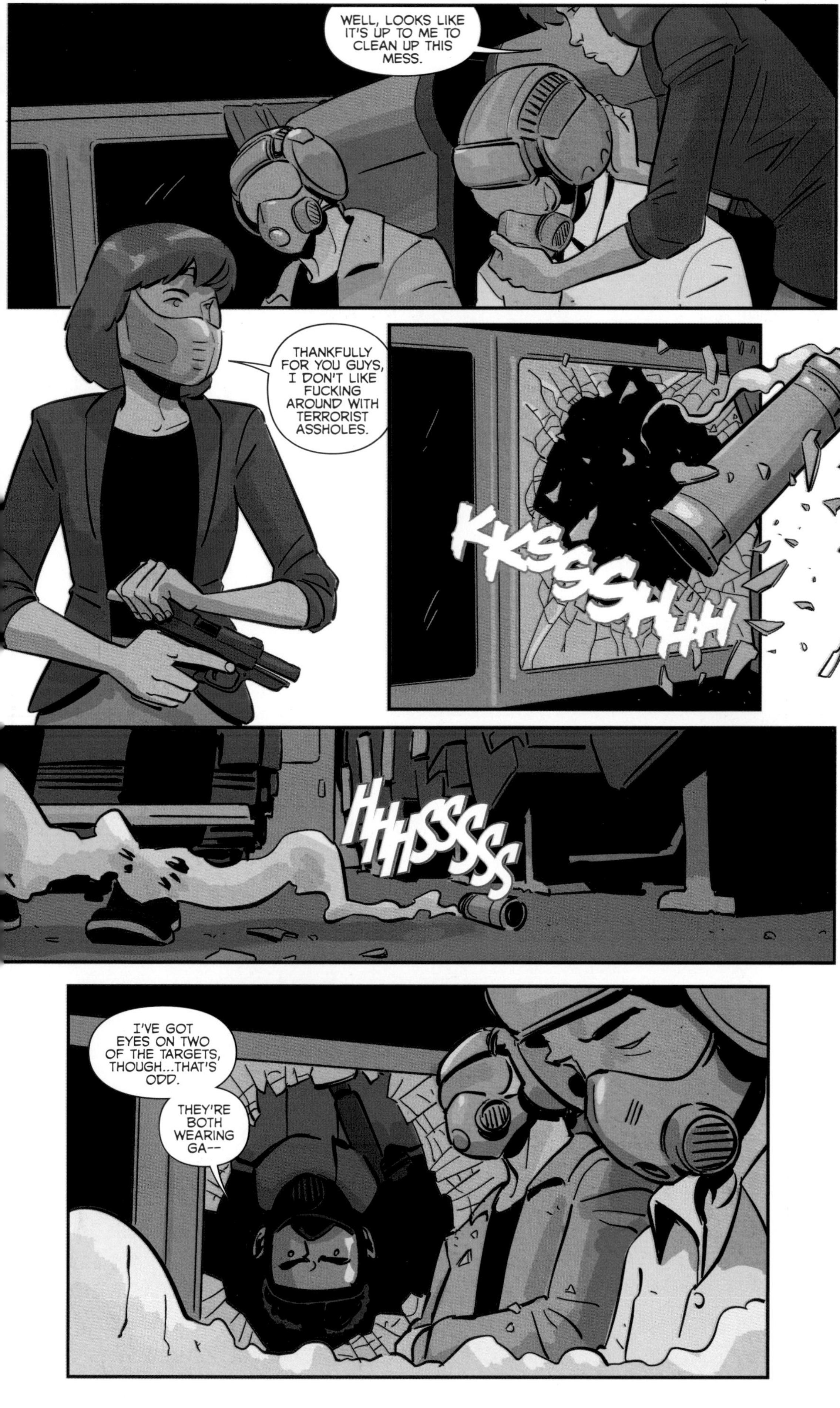
WELL, LOOKS LIKE IT'S UP TO ME TO CLEAN UP THIS MESS.
THANKFULLY FOR YOU GUYS, I DON'T LIKE FUCKING AROUND WITH TERRORIST ASSHOLES.
KKSSSHHH
HHHSSSSS
I'VE GOT EYES ON TWO OF THE TARGETS, THOUGH...THAT'S ODD.
THEY'RE BOTH WEARING GA--

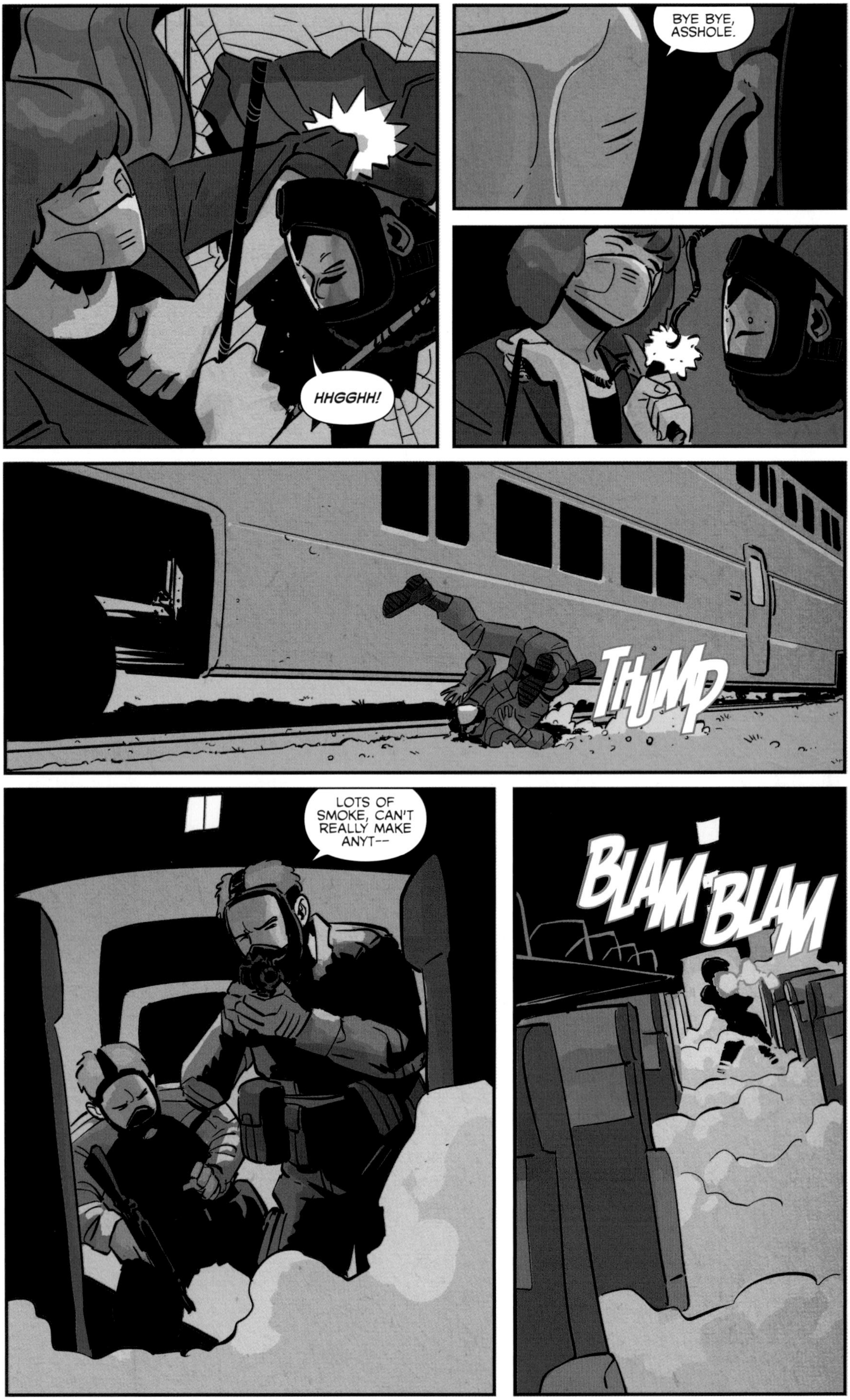
HHGGHH!
BYE BYE, ASSHOLE.
THUMP
LOTS OF SMOKE, CAN'T REALLY MAKE ANYT--
BLAM-BLAM

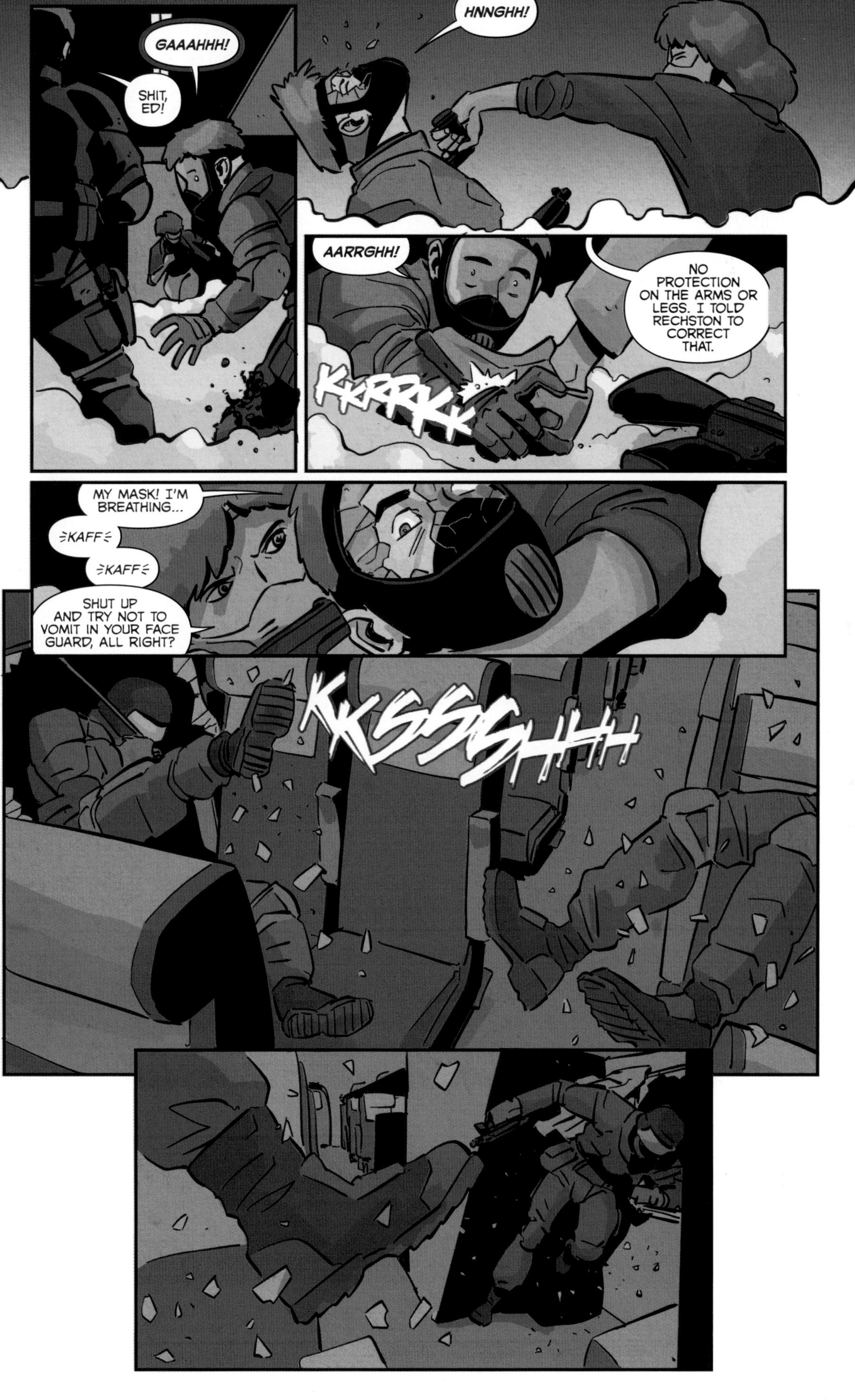

GAAAHHH!
SHIT, ED!
HNNGHH!
AARRGHH!
NO PROTECTION ON THE ARMS OR LEGS. I TOLD RECHSTON TO CORRECT THAT.
KKRRAKK
MY MASK! I'M BREATHING...
KAFF
KAFF
SHUT UP AND TRY NOT TO VOMIT IN YOUR FACE GUARD, ALL RIGHT?
KKSSSSHHH

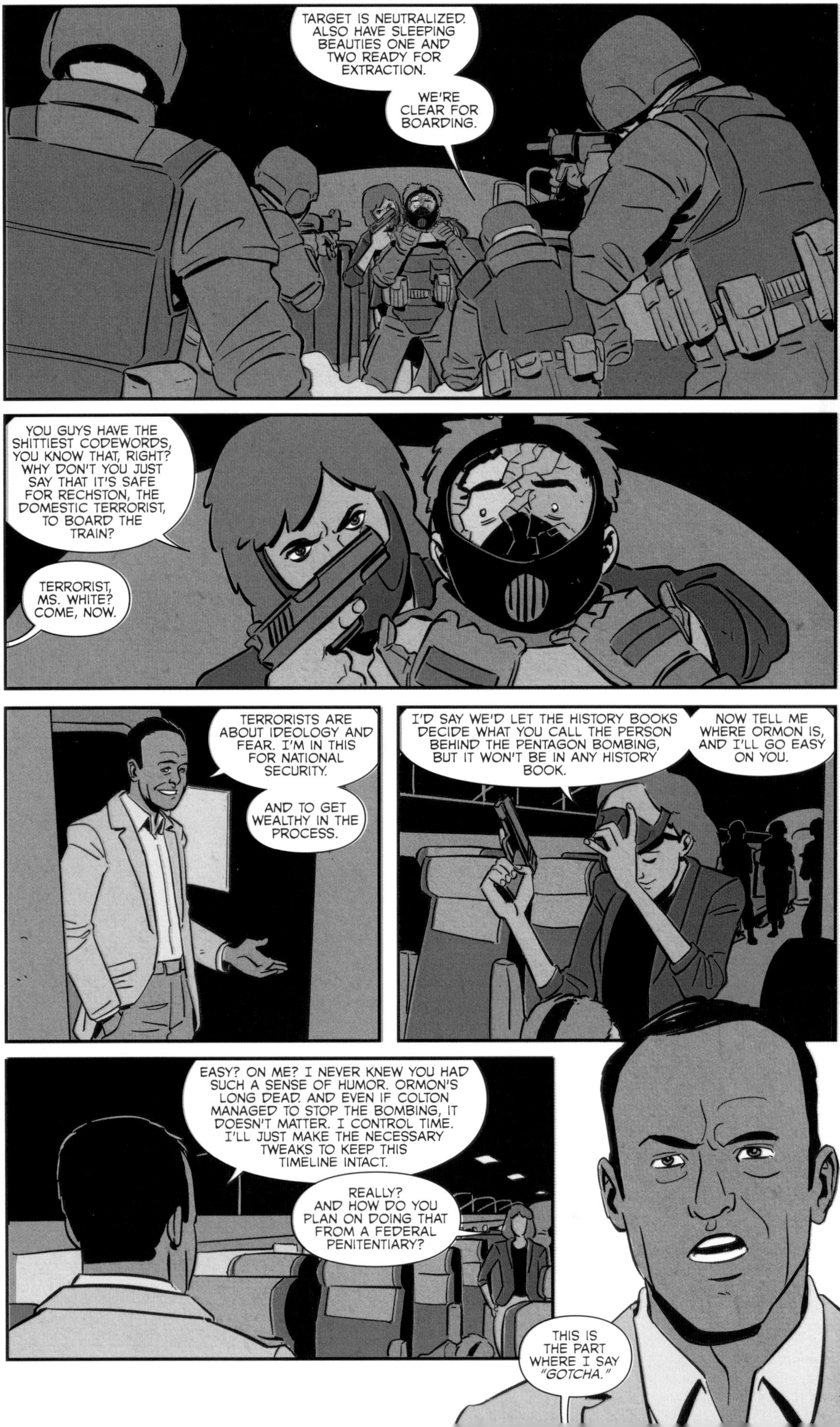
TARGET IS NEUTRALIZED. ALSO HAVE SLEEPING BEAUTIES ONE AND TWO READY FOR EXTRACTION.
WE'RE CLEAR FOR BOARDING.
YOU GUYS HAVE THE SHITTIEST CODEWORDS, YOU KNOW THAT, RIGHT? WHY DON'T YOU JUST SAY THAT IT'S SAFE FOR RECHSTON, THE DOMESTIC TERRORIST, TO BOARD THE TRAIN?
TERRORIST, MS. WHITE? COME, NOW.
TERRORISTS ARE ABOUT IDEOLOGY AND FEAR. I'M IN THIS FOR NATIONAL SECURITY.
AND TO GET WEALTHY IN THE PROCESS.
I'D SAY WE'D LET THE HISTORY BOOKS DECIDE WHAT YOU CALL THE PERSON BEHIND THE PENTAGON BOMBING, BUT IT WON'T BE IN ANY HISTORY BOOK.
NOW TELL ME WHERE ORMON IS, AND I'LL GO EASY ON YOU.
EASY? ON ME? I NEVER KNEW YOU HAD SUCH A SENSE OF HUMOR. ORMON'S LONG DEAD. AND EVEN IF COLTON MANAGED TO STOP THE BOMBING, IT DOESN'T MATTER. I CONTROL TIME. I'LL JUST MAKE THE NECESSARY TWEAKS TO KEEP THIS TIMELINE INTACT.
REALLY? AND HOW DO YOU PLAN ON DOING THAT FROM A FEDERAL PENITENTIARY?
THIS IS THE PART WHERE I SAY *"GOTCHA."*

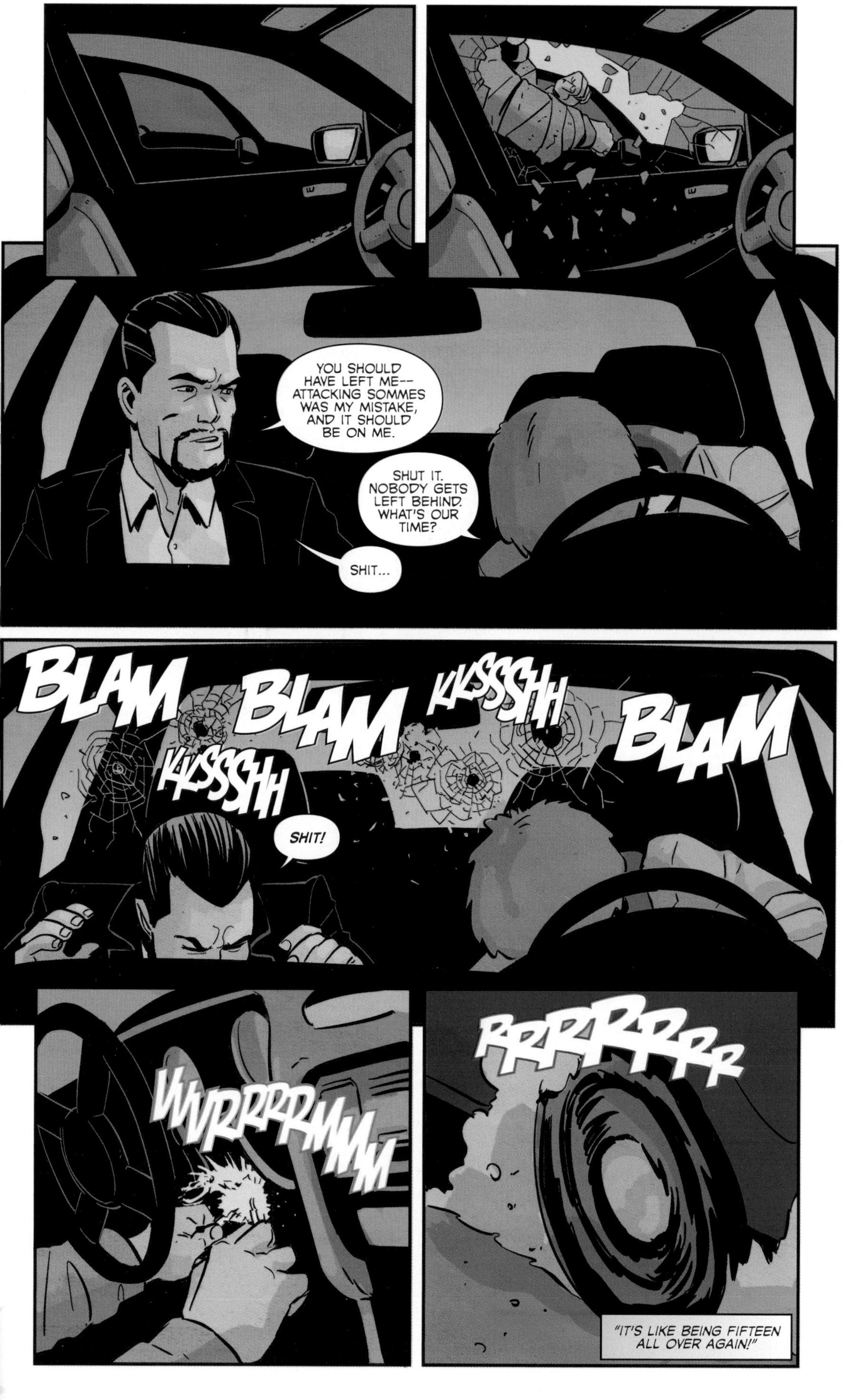
YOU SHOULD HAVE LEFT ME-- ATTACKING SOMMES WAS MY MISTAKE, AND IT SHOULD BE ON ME.
SHUT IT. NOBODY GETS LEFT BEHIND. WHAT'S OUR TIME?
SHIT...
BLAM
BLAM
KKSSSHH
BLAM
KKSSSHH
SHIT!
VVVRRRRRMMMM
RRRRRRRR
"IT'S LIKE BEING FIFTEEN ALL OVER AGAIN!"

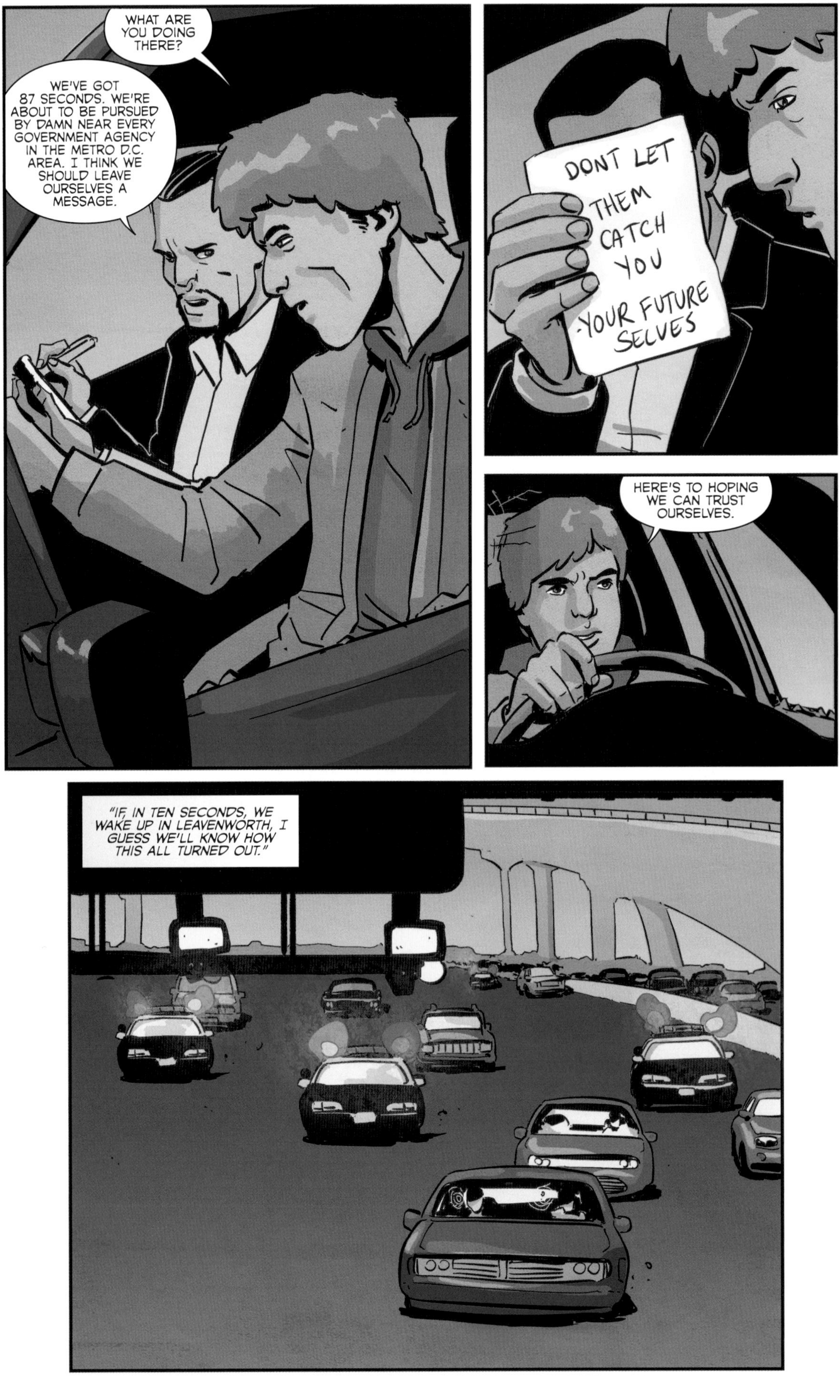
WHAT ARE YOU DOING THERE?
WE'VE GOT 87 SECONDS. WE'RE ABOUT TO BE PURSUED BY DAMN NEAR EVERY GOVERNMENT AGENCY IN THE METRO D.C. AREA. I THINK WE SHOULD LEAVE OURSELVES A MESSAGE.
DONT LET THEM CATCH YOU -YOUR FUTURE SELVES
HERE'S TO HOPING WE CAN TRUST OURSELVES.
"IF, IN TEN SECONDS, WE WAKE UP IN LEAVENWORTH, I GUESS WE'LL KNOW HOW THIS ALL TURNED OUT."

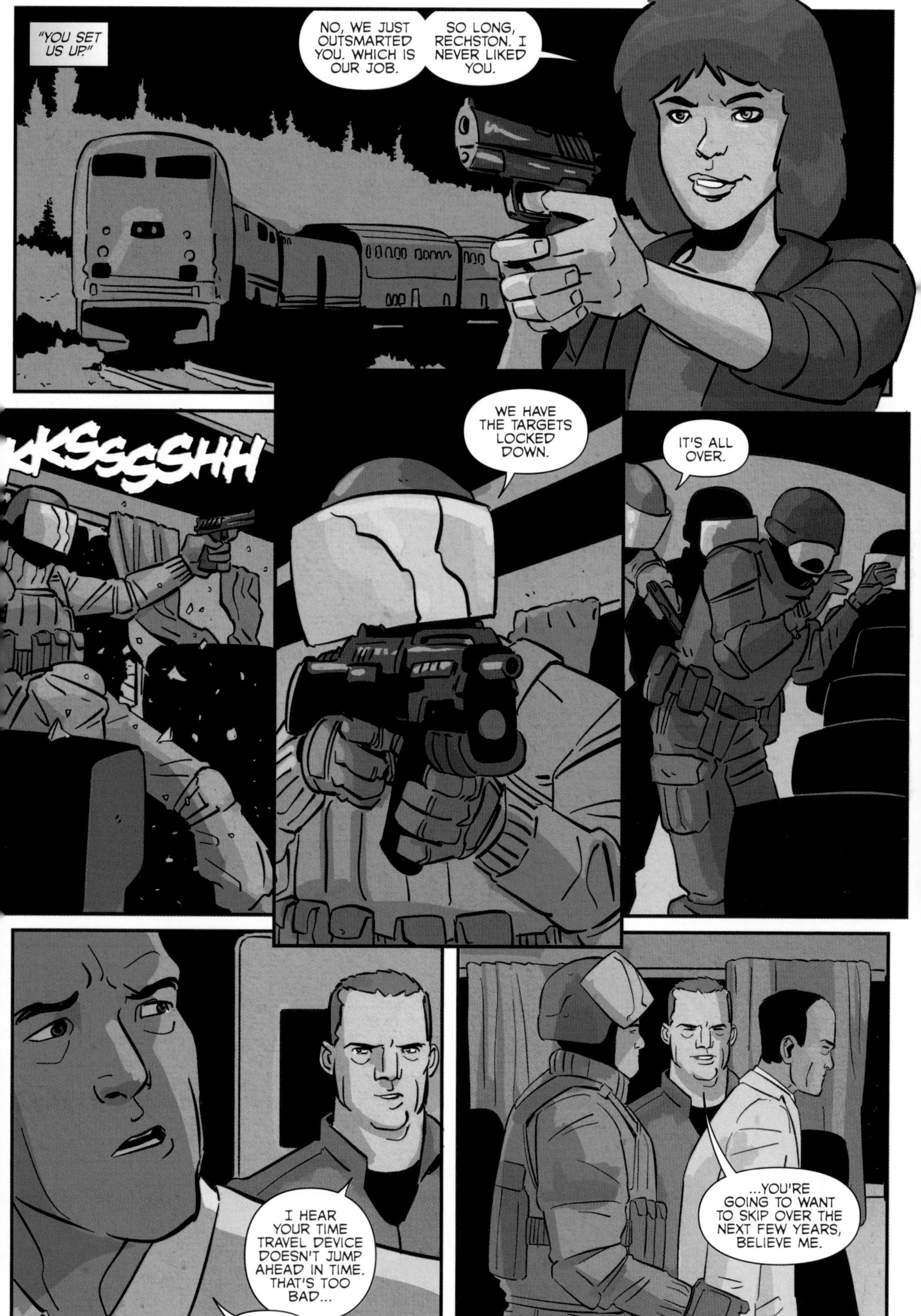
"YOU SET US UP."
NO, WE JUST OUTSMARTED YOU. WHICH IS OUR JOB.
SO LONG, RECHSTON. I NEVER LIKED YOU.
KSSSSHH
WE HAVE THE TARGETS LOCKED DOWN.
IT'S ALL OVER.
I HEAR YOUR TIME TRAVEL DEVICE DOESN'T JUMP AHEAD IN TIME. THAT'S TOO BAD...
NOLAN?
...YOU'RE GOING TO WANT TO SKIP OVER THE NEXT FEW YEARS, BELIEVE ME.

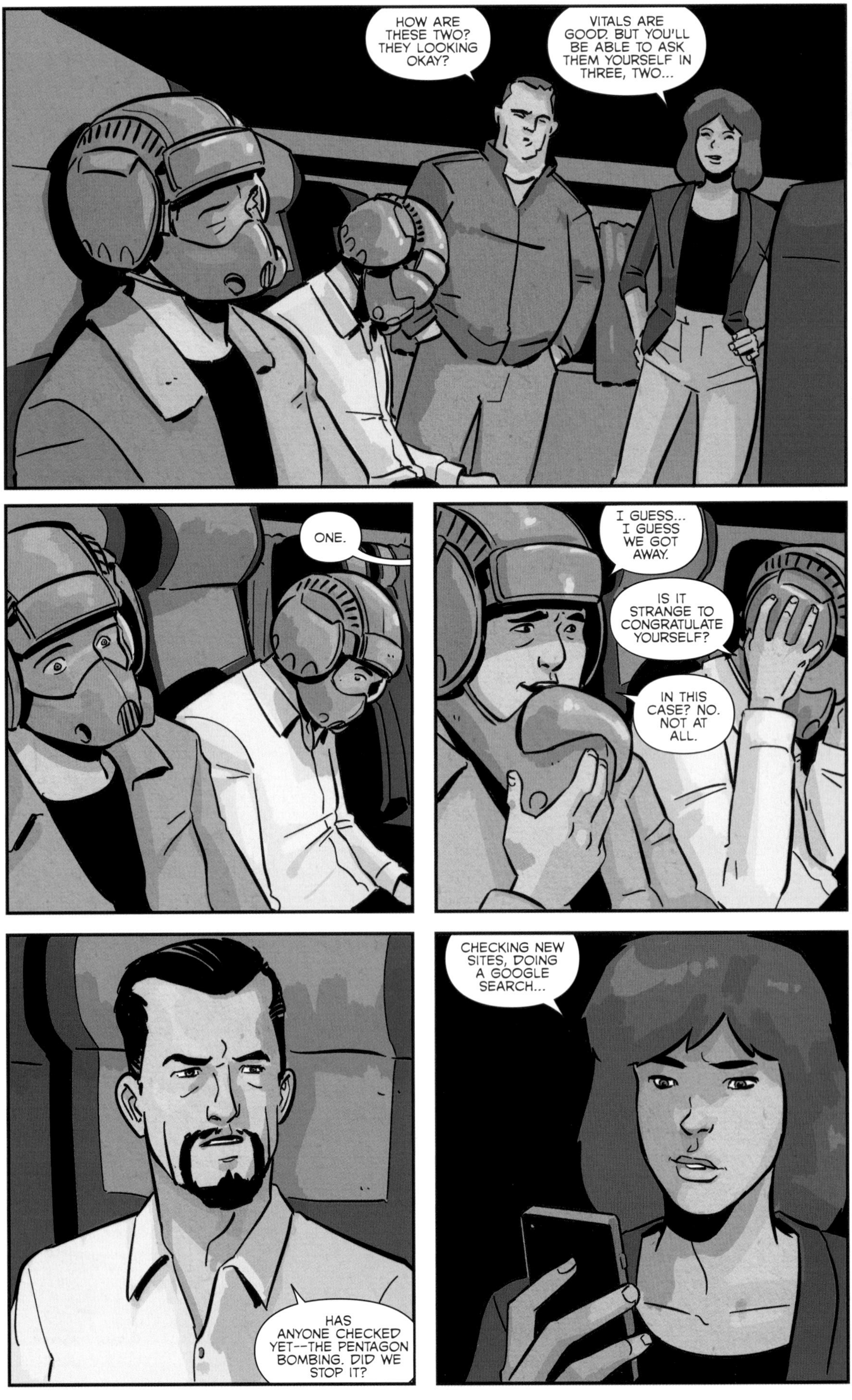
HOW ARE THESE TWO? THEY LOOKING OKAY?
VITALS ARE GOOD. BUT YOU'LL BE ABLE TO ASK THEM YOURSELF IN THREE, TWO...
ONE.
I GUESS... I GUESS WE GOT AWAY.
IS IT STRANGE TO CONGRATULATE YOURSELF?
IN THIS CASE? NO. NOT AT ALL.
HAS ANYONE CHECKED YET--THE PENTAGON BOMBING. DID WE STOP IT?
CHECKING NEW SITES, DOING A GOOGLE SEARCH...

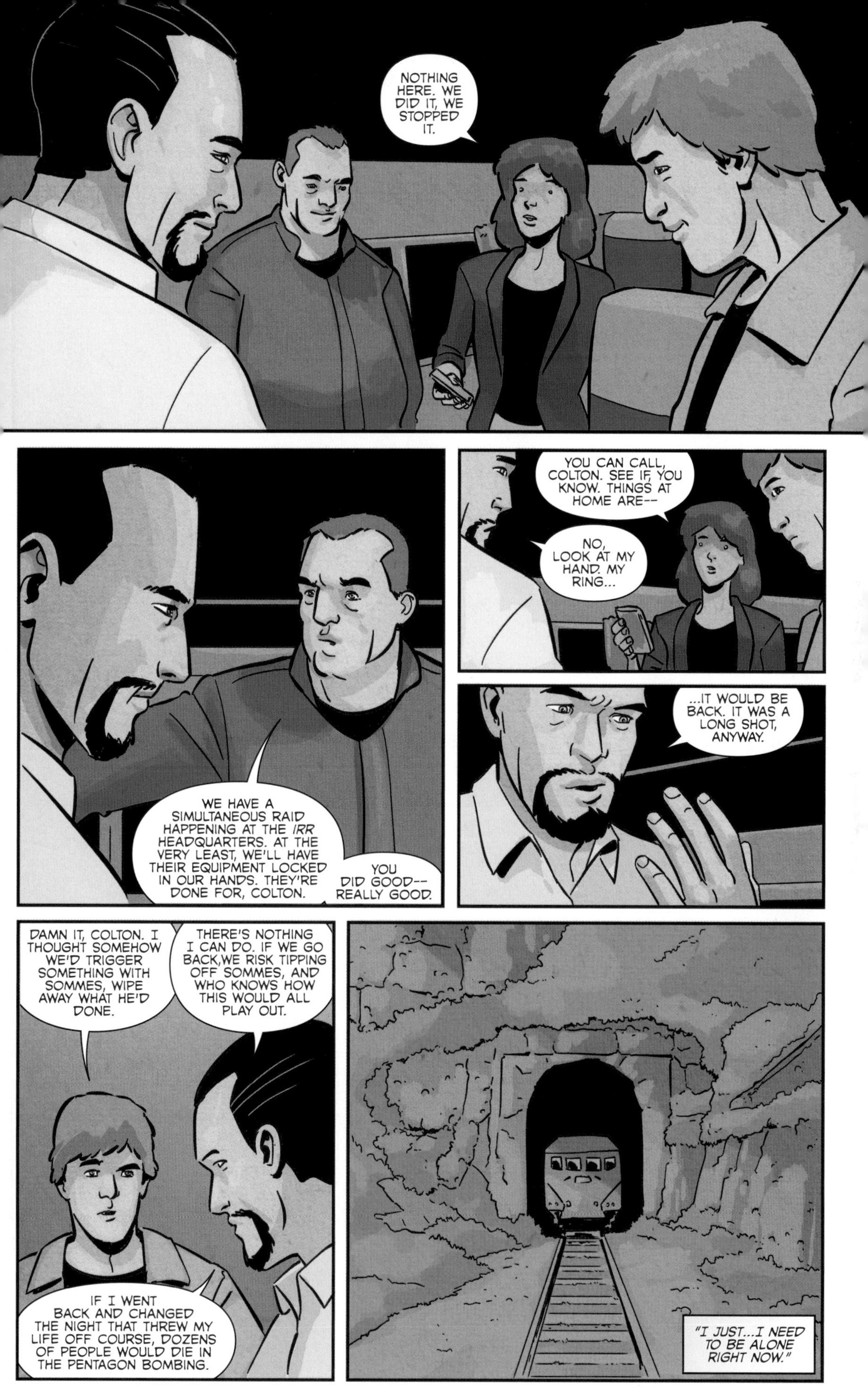
NOTHING HERE. WE DID IT, WE STOPPED IT.
WE HAVE A SIMULTANEOUS RAID HAPPENING AT THE *IRR* HEADQUARTERS. AT THE VERY LEAST, WE'LL HAVE THEIR EQUIPMENT LOCKED IN OUR HANDS. THEY'RE DONE FOR, COLTON.
YOU DID GOOD-- REALLY GOOD.
YOU CAN CALL, COLTON. SEE IF, YOU KNOW. THINGS AT HOME ARE--
NO, LOOK AT MY HAND. MY RING...
...IT WOULD BE BACK. IT WAS A LONG SHOT, ANYWAY.
DAMN IT, COLTON. I THOUGHT SOMEHOW WE'D TRIGGER SOMETHING WITH SOMMES, WIPE AWAY WHAT HE'D DONE.
THERE'S NOTHING I CAN DO. IF WE GO BACK,WE RISK TIPPING OFF SOMMES, AND WHO KNOWS HOW THIS WOULD ALL PLAY OUT.
IF I WENT BACK AND CHANGED THE NIGHT THAT THREW MY LIFE OFF COURSE, DOZENS OF PEOPLE WOULD DIE IN THE PENTAGON BOMBING.
"I JUST...I NEED TO BE ALONE RIGHT NOW."

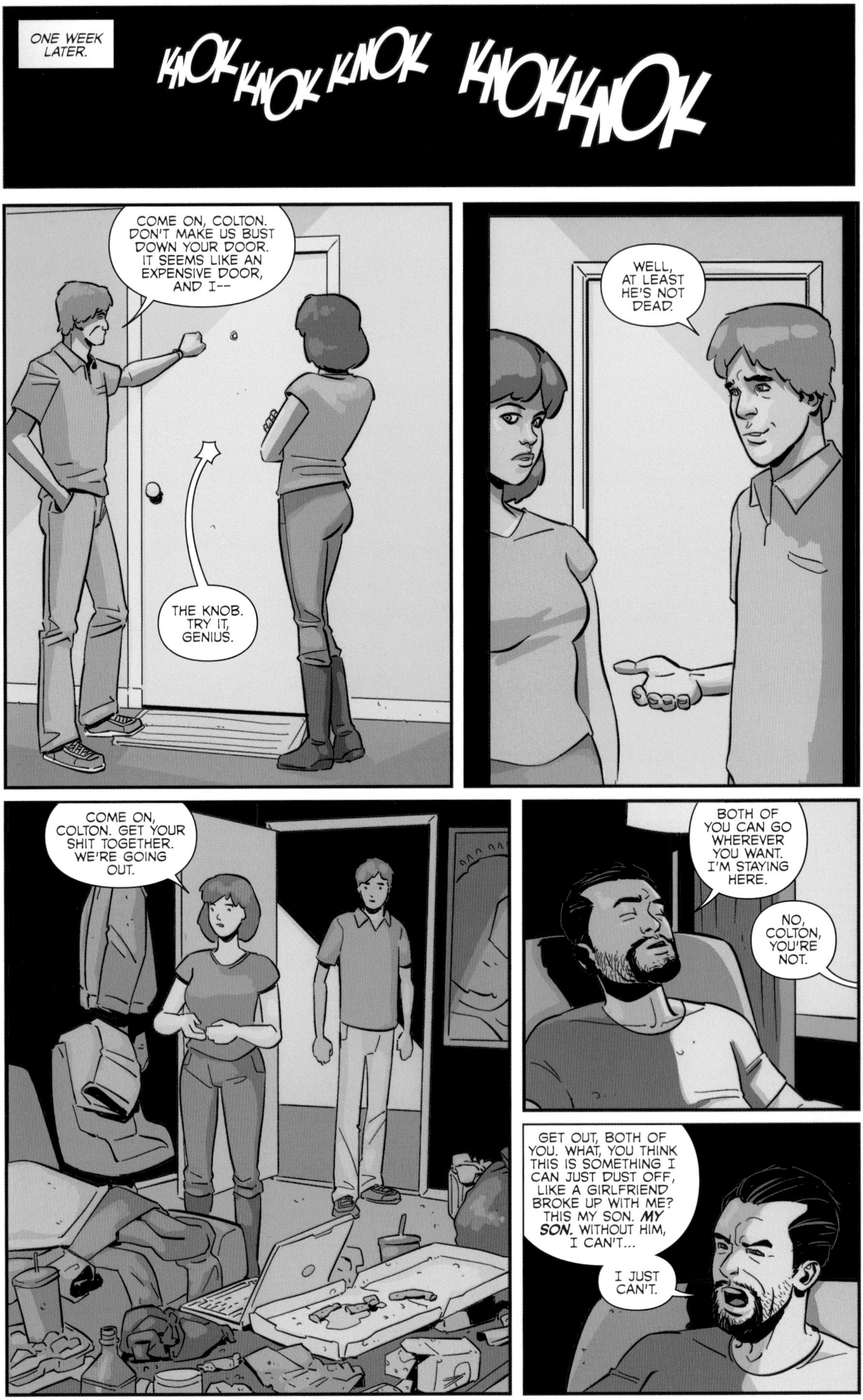
ONE WEEK LATER.
KNOK KNOK KNOK KNOK KNOK
COME ON, COLTON. DON'T MAKE US BUST DOWN YOUR DOOR. IT SEEMS LIKE AN EXPENSIVE DOOR, AND I--
THE KNOB. TRY IT, GENIUS.
WELL, AT LEAST HE'S NOT DEAD.
COME ON, COLTON. GET YOUR SHIT TOGETHER. WE'RE GOING OUT.
BOTH OF YOU CAN GO WHEREVER YOU WANT. I'M STAYING HERE.
NO, COLTON, YOU'RE NOT.
GET OUT, BOTH OF YOU. WHAT, YOU THINK THIS IS SOMETHING I CAN JUST DUST OFF, LIKE A GIRLFRIEND BROKE UP WITH ME? THIS MY SON. ***MY SON.*** WITHOUT HIM, I CAN'T...
I JUST CAN'T.

YOU WERE RIGHT ABOUT SOMETHING, COLTON. IF WE ALTERED THE HISTORY OF THE NIGHT OF THE GALA, WE'D TIP OFF SOMMES.

THERE'S NO TELLING WHAT ADJUSTMENTS HE'D MAKE AND HOW THAT WOULD AFFECT THE TIMELINE. BUT THEN WE GOT TO THINKING...

WE DID THE MATH, AND YOU MUST HAVE KNOCKED TARA UP ABOUT A WEEK AFTER THE GALA. NOW, RECHSTON'S GOAL WAS TO BREAK UP YOUR FAMILY AND GIVE YOU REASON TO KILL FASAD.

WE FIGURED OUT A SOLUTION, AND IT WAS TO KEEP RECHSTON'S GOAL IN PLACE.

BUT WE DELAYED IT. WE KEPT YOU OUT OF THE GALA AND AWAY FROM RECHSTON LONG ENOUGH FOR YOU AND TARA TO... YOU KNOW.

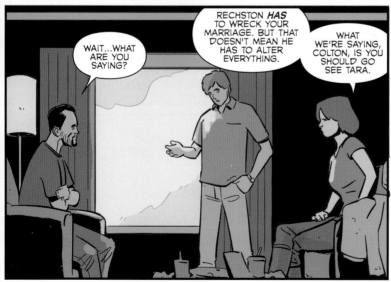

WAIT...WHAT ARE YOU SAYING?

RECHSTON *HAS* TO WRECK YOUR MARRIAGE. BUT THAT DOESN'T MEAN HE HAS TO ALTER EVERYTHING.

WHAT WE'RE SAYING, COLTON, IS YOU SHOULD GO SEE TARA.

HE'S WAITING FOR YOU.

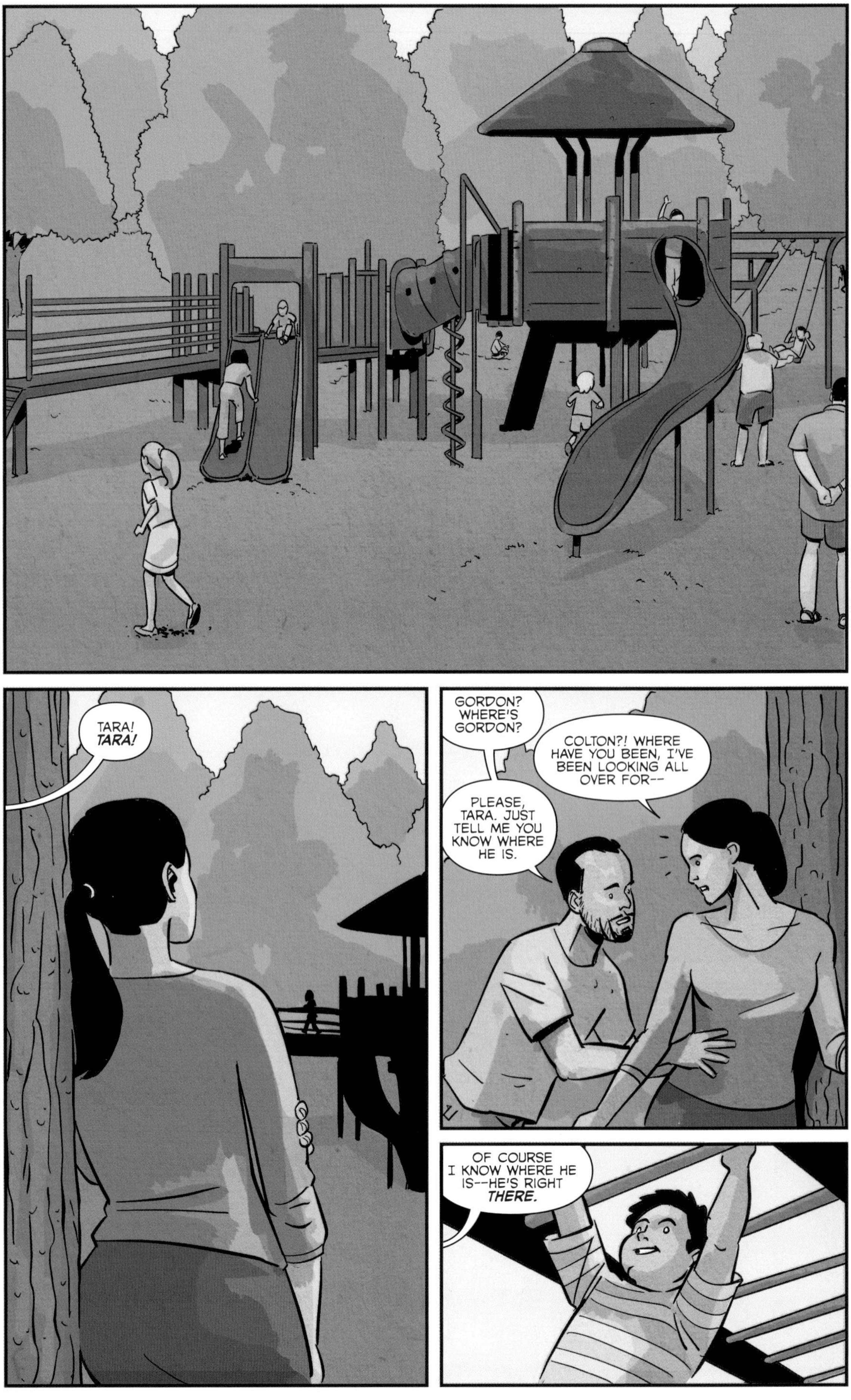
TARA! *TARA!*
GORDON? WHERE'S GORDON?
COLTON?! WHERE HAVE YOU BEEN, I'VE BEEN LOOKING ALL OVER FOR--
PLEASE, TARA. JUST TELL ME YOU KNOW WHERE HE IS.
OF COURSE I KNOW WHERE HE IS--HE'S RIGHT *THERE.*

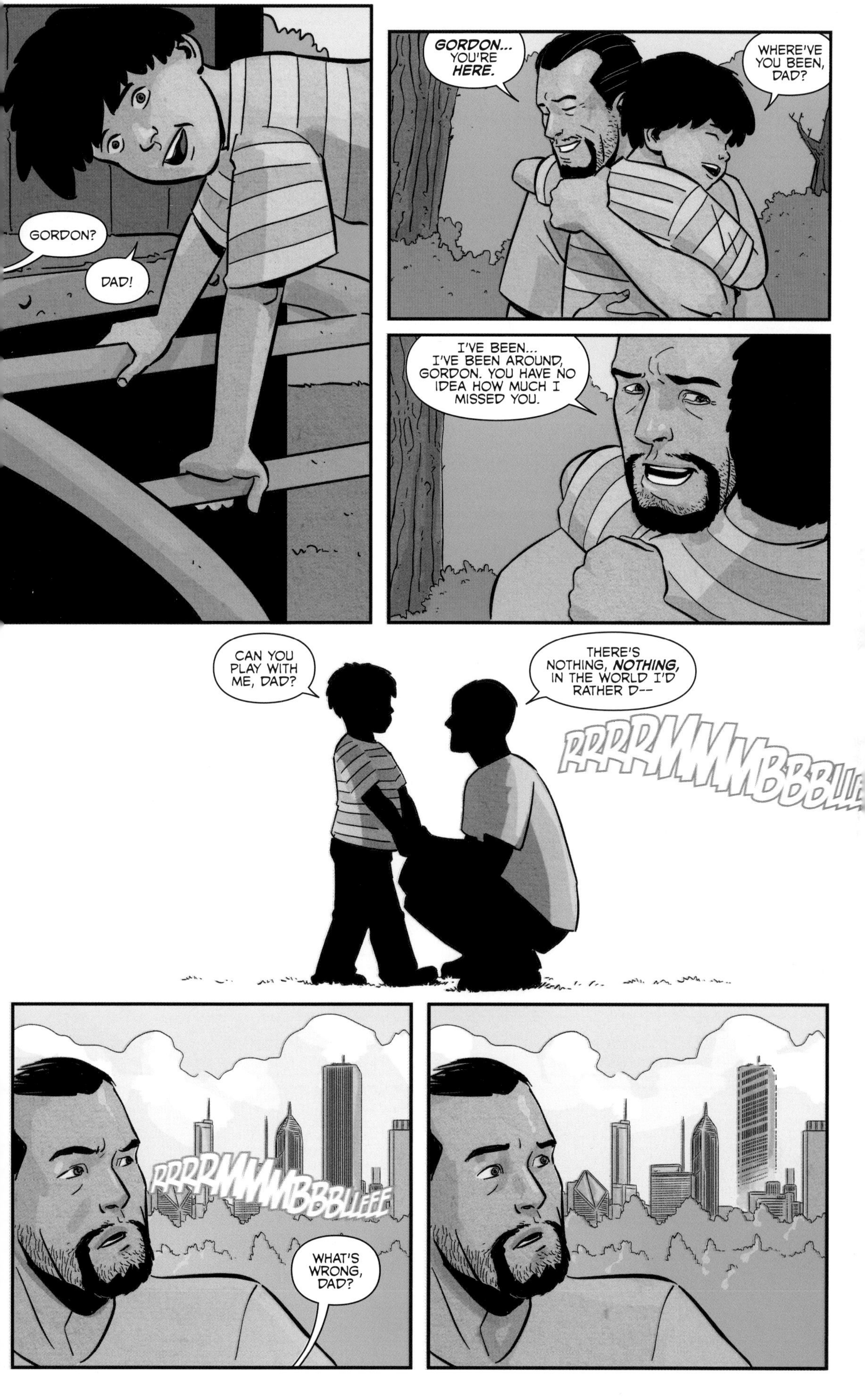
GORDON?
DAD!
GORDON... YOU'RE HERE.
WHERE'VE YOU BEEN, DAD?
I'VE BEEN... I'VE BEEN AROUND, GORDON. YOU HAVE NO IDEA HOW MUCH I MISSED YOU.
CAN YOU PLAY WITH ME, DAD?
THERE'S NOTHING, NOTHING, IN THE WORLD I'D RATHER D--
RRRRMMMBBBLLEE
RRRRMMMBBBLLEEE
WHAT'S WRONG, DAD?

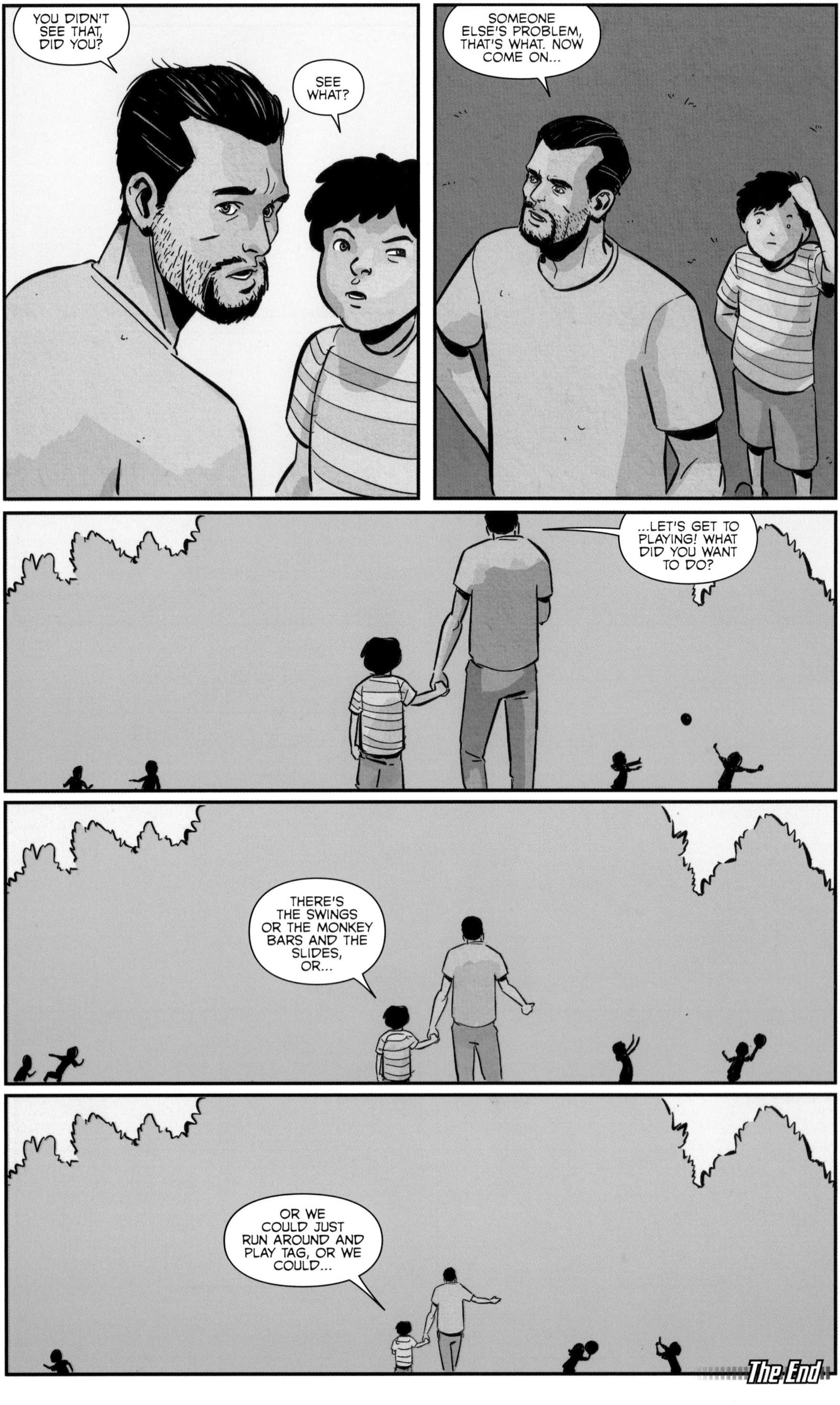
YOU DIDN'T SEE THAT, DID YOU?
SEE WHAT?
SOMEONE ELSE'S PROBLEM, THAT'S WHAT. NOW COME ON...
...LET'S GET TO PLAYING! WHAT DID YOU WANT TO DO?
THERE'S THE SWINGS OR THE MONKEY BARS AND THE SLIDES, OR...
OR WE COULD JUST RUN AROUND AND PLAY TAG, OR WE COULD...
The End

VARIANTS

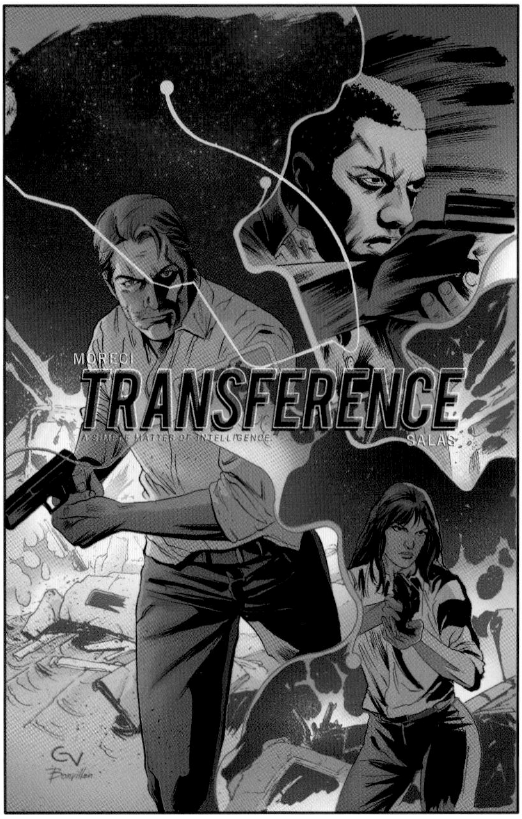
MORECI
TRANSFERENCE
A SIMPLE MATTER OF INTELLIGENCE
SALAS

Issue #1, Art by GIO VALLETTA

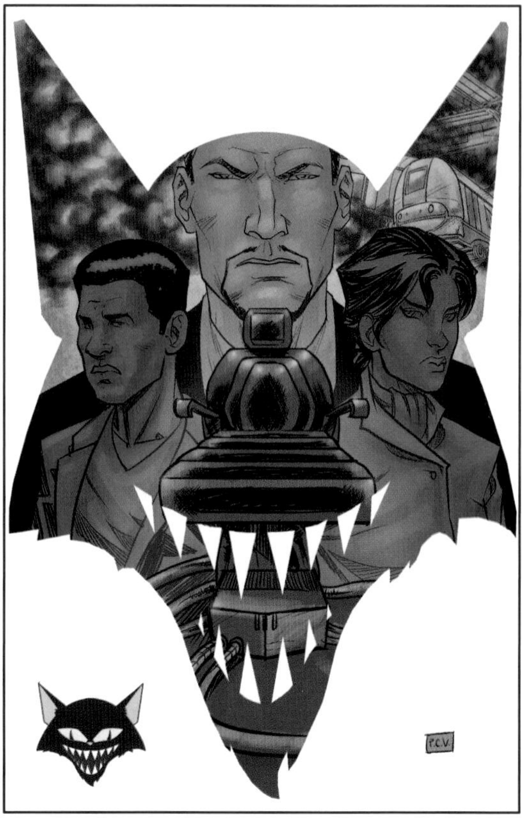

Issue #1 Black Cat Comics Exclusive, Art by PHILLIP SEVY

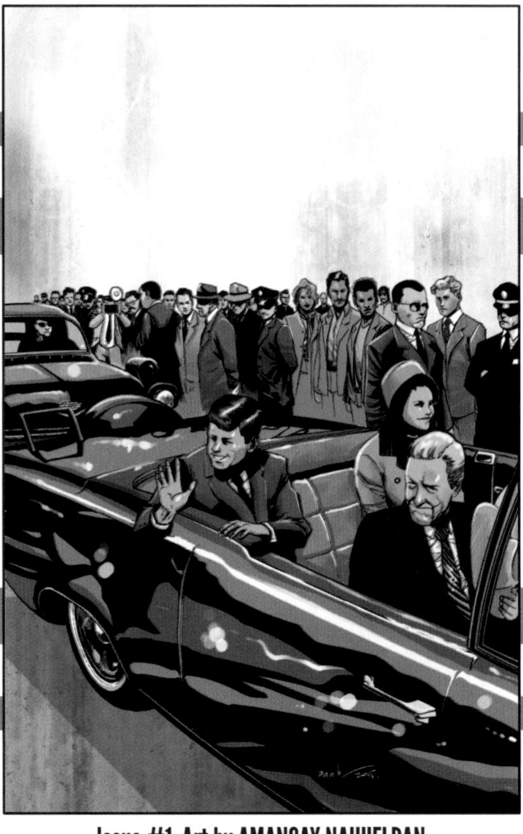

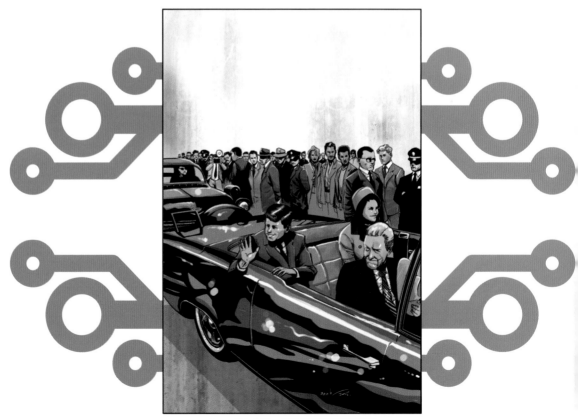

Issue #1, Art by AMANCAY NAHUELPAN

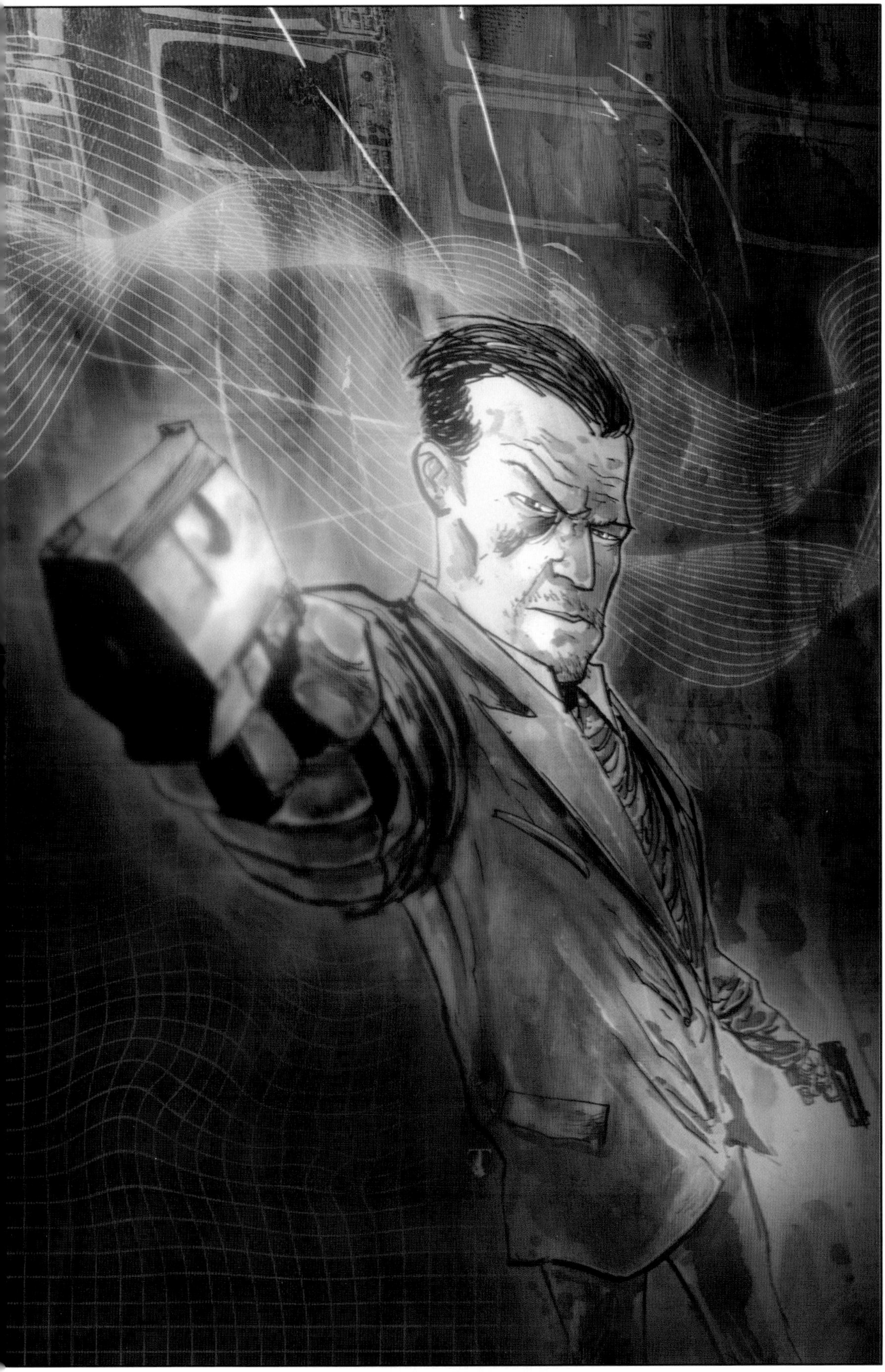

Issue #1, Art by BEN TEMPLESMITH

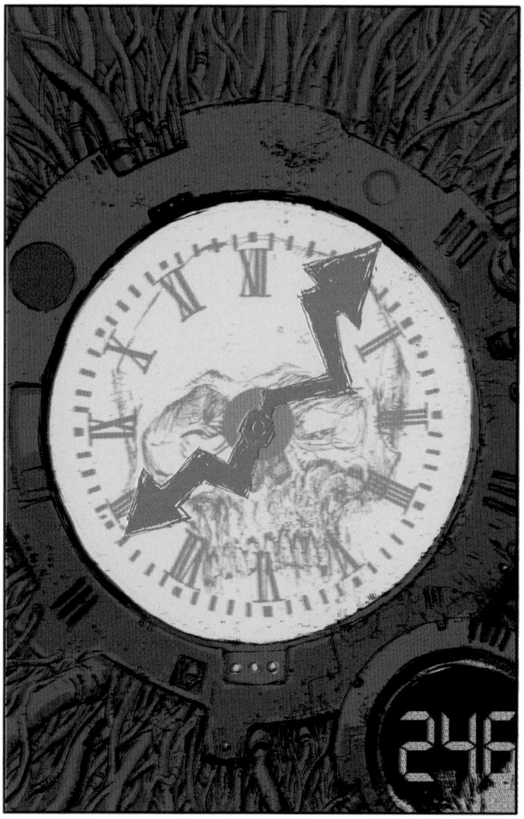
246

Issue #1, 2nd print, Art by NAT JONES

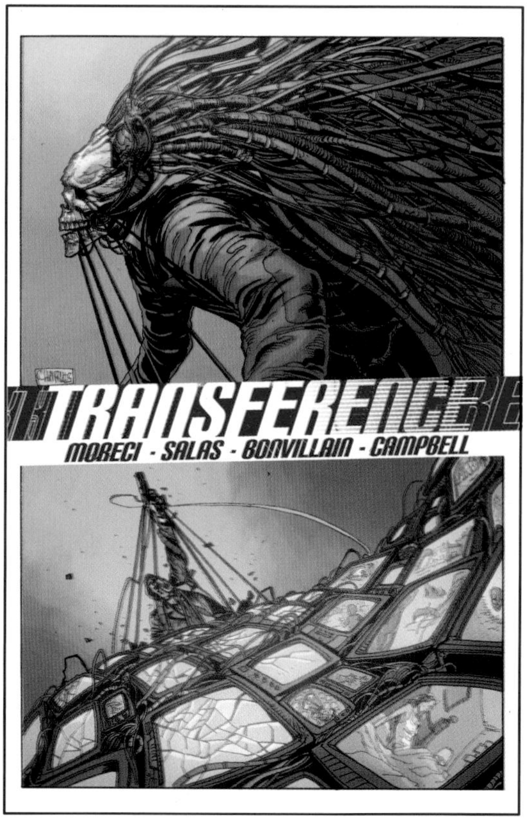
TRANSFERENCE
MORECI - SALAS - BONVILLAIN - CAMPBELL

Issue #2, Art by KYLE CHARLES

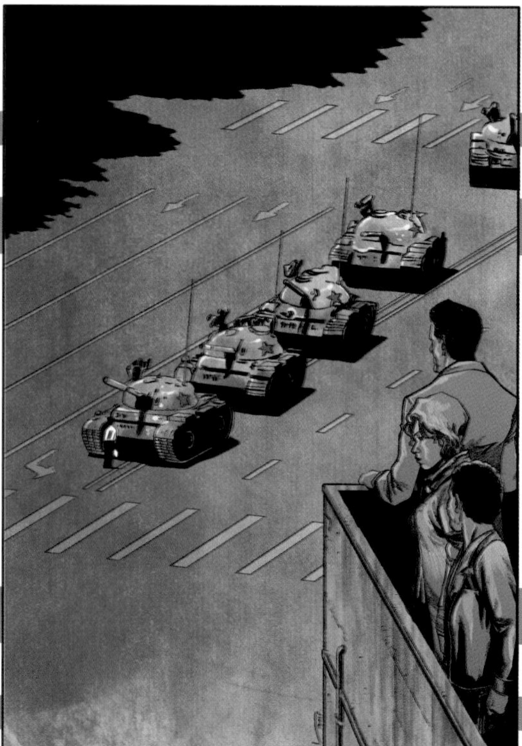

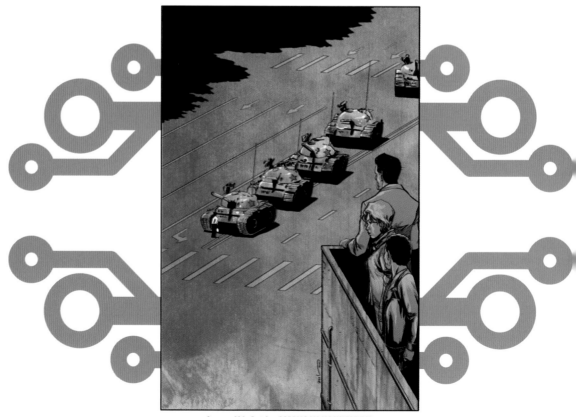

Issue #1, Art by AMANCAY NAHUELPAN

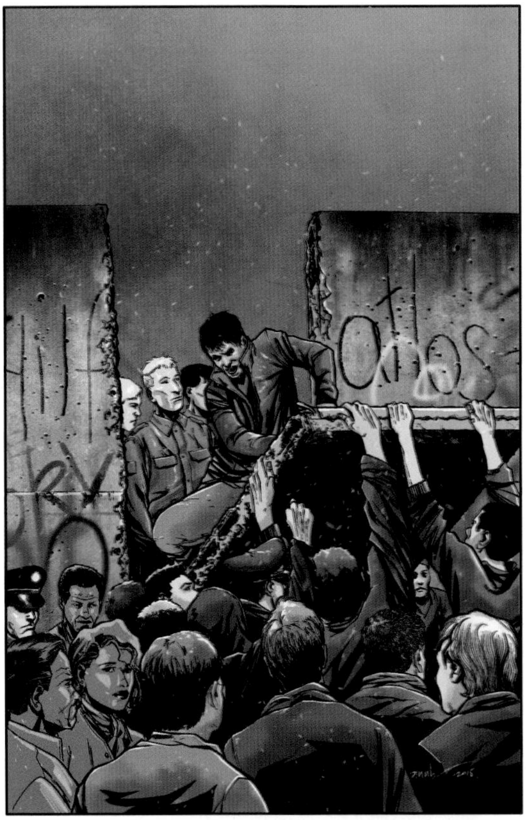

Issue #3, Art by AMANCAY NAHUELPAN

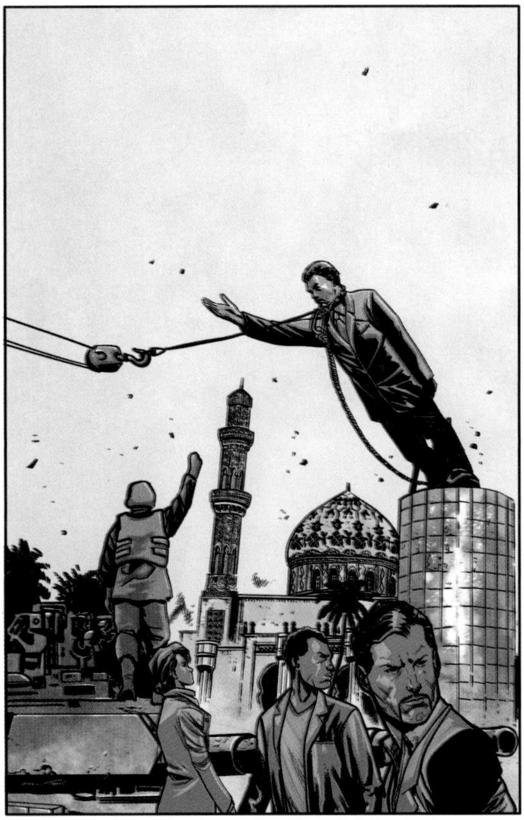

Issue #4, Art by AMANCAY NAHUELPAN

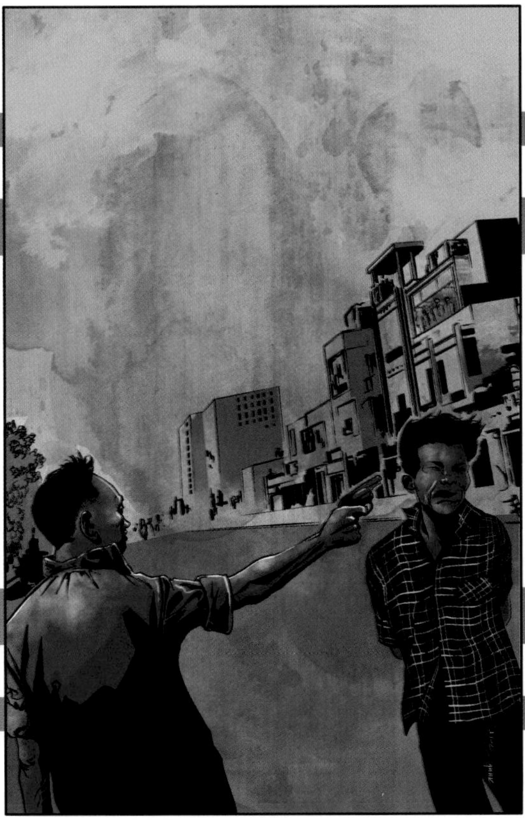

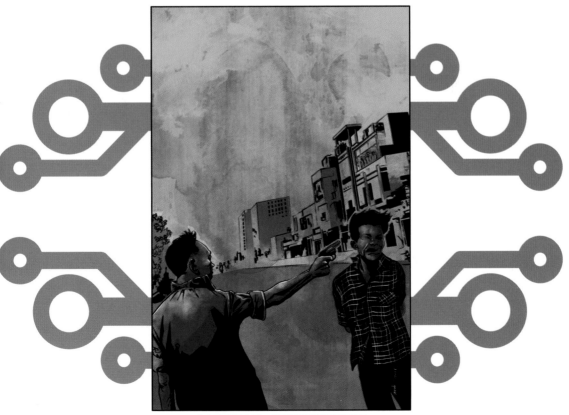

Issue #5, Art by AMANCAY NAHUELPAN